In a BADGER WAY

Also by SHELLY LAURENSTON

In a BADGER WAY

The Honey Badgers Chronicles

SHELLY LAURENSTON

KENSINGTON PUBLISHING CORP.

www.kensingtonbooks.com

KENSINGTON BOOKS are published by

Kensington Publishing Corp.
119 West 40th Street
New York, NY 10018

All Kensington titles, imprints, and distributed lines are available at special quantity discounts for bulk purchases for sales promotions, premiums, fund-raising, educational, or institutional use.

Special book excerpts or customized printings can also be created to fit specific needs. For details, write or phone the office of the Kensington sales manager: Kensington Publishing Corp., 119 West 40th Street, New York, NY 10018, attn: Sales Department; phone 1-800-221-2647.

ISBN-13: 978-1-4967-1437-4
ISBN-10: 1-4967-1437-7

First Trade Paperback Printing: April 2019

10 9 8 7 6 5 4 3 2 1

Printed in the United States of America

Electronic Edition: April 2019

ISBN-13: 978-1-4967-1439-8 (e-book)
ISBN-10: 1-4967-1439-3 (e-book)

PROLOGUE

"*I want my sisters!*"

The general stared down at the eleven-year-old child screaming at him and his soldiers.

He didn't know what had happened. She'd started off as such an amiable asset. Quiet. Unassuming. She hadn't put up a fight when they'd come for her. Her sisters had. The weird pack of people living in a small group of houses in the middle of Wisconsin had barely managed to hold the two older girls back.

Of course, they hadn't really looked like sisters. One was black and tall, the other Asian and petite with massive shoulders—he'd assumed she was a gymnast. His sister's daughter had the same kind of shoulders and she was going to the Summer Olympics.

In all honesty, he'd wanted to give those two girls the number of a recruiter. Anyone who fought that hard should consider life in the military.

But their little sister hadn't put up a fight. She'd just put her head down, grabbed a backpack filled with notebooks, and followed his men out to the car. And she'd kept quiet for the first two weeks.

Then, something had changed. *She* had changed. Drastically. One of the psychiatrists they hired to monitor the child's emotions said she was suffering from a "bout of depression" and that she needed medication.

At first, the general had not wanted to hear about medication. Medicating an eleven-year-old girl seemed the height of inappropriateness in his estimation, and no one wanted to affect the way the prodigy's brain worked. He'd assumed she just needed discipline. She needed to see him as the father figure she'd never had. So he'd gone to see her, trying to engage her in dialogue.

That hadn't helped. She had simply stared at him with a sour expression until, after about a week of visits, she'd suddenly launched a heavy metal lab instrument at him. Nearly got him in the head, too, but he'd ducked in time. Then she'd started screaming, "I want my sisters!" and she hadn't really stopped since.

No matter what they said to her, or tried to bribe her with, she didn't want to hear it. She wanted her sisters and she wanted them *now* apparently.

Despite his best intentions, he'd finally given in to the psychiatrist and he'd gotten approval from his superiors to medicate the girl.

At this moment, medical personnel were waiting outside the lab with a needle filled with whatever drug they'd chosen because Little Miss kept spitting her pills back out when they forced them on her.

The general tried again, "Now, Miss Stasiuk—"

She slammed her hand against the granite countertop. "It's MacKilligan. I'm a MacKilligan!" she screamed. "*And I want my sisters!*"

"I tried," he told her before stepping back. "Nurse?"

The psychiatrist's personal nurse walked in with a stainless steel tray, a filled syringe on top.

As soon as the child saw it, she actually became frightened. Her eyes widened and she scrambled back until she hit the lab table behind her.

"Stay away from me," she begged. "Stay away from me."

"It's all right, Miss Sta . . . uh . . . MacKilligan," he soothed. "We just want to make you feel better. Isn't that right, Nurse?"

The nurse nodded as she moved forward. "That's it."

The child stared at the nurse for a long moment before she suddenly accused, "You're trying to kill me."

That statement was said so calmly but so definitively that everyone in the room froze and stared at her.

"What?" the general asked.

"You're trying to kill me," she accused again.

The general blinked, shocked. "Of course we're not. Miss MacKilligan—"

"*You want me dead!* You're working for the other side!"

"What other side? What are you talking about? No one is trying to kill you. We're trying to help you!"

Her face red, fingers curled into tight little fists, her entire body one taut line of tense muscles, the little viper screeched, "*You're trying to kill meeeeee!*"

Her voice was so loud, the general actually felt she'd made the lab windows shake, but he was sure that was simply his imagination run amok under such strange circumstances.

"No one is trying to kill you!" he yelled over the child's screams. "We built this entire base for *you*. So calm down and take your medicine!"

The nurse stood beside him now and, with a sigh, she called for two orderlies. The men came in and went to the girl, attempting to grab her arms and hold her still. But the fight the general hadn't seen when they'd first brought her in—he saw it now.

Like a whirling dervish of panic, the child swung her arms and legs, spinning away from the men, screaming wildly before she took off running.

"Grab her!" the nurse ordered while the orderlies chased the child around the large lab. But every time they got close to her, she'd duck under their legs, jump over their grasping hands, or throw something at them so she could make her mad escape.

Rolling his eyes, the general nodded at one of his men. That soldier closed the door, cutting off the child's exit route. The general motioned to two others.

With precise movements, those soldiers went for the girl, one sweeping the child up into his arms and holding her with her back against his chest.

"If you will," the general said to the nurse.

She placed the tray down on a lab table and uncapped the syringe. She moved toward the child.

Struggling and screaming, the girl tried her best to fight off the man holding her body while another soldier held her arm out, but these trained men held her easily without harming her.

Grateful this disaster was almost over, the general exhaled and let his gaze roam the room. That's when a metal grate in the ceiling was kicked away by a sneakered foot, slamming into an orderly's head and dropping him to the ground with a serious head wound.

The Asian half-sister of the prodigy jumped from the duct and down to the floor; the older sister followed. When her feet hit the ground, she grabbed the second orderly and tossed him across the room with amazing ease while the other girl charged the soldier holding her sister. As she moved toward him, she suddenly brought up one foot, placing it against the lab drawers. She pushed off toward the other lab station, slammed her other foot against the granite, and launched herself toward the soldier.

She wrapped her entire body around his head, but the soldier continued to hold on to his captive. The second soldier went for the oldest sister, but she grabbed his outstretched arm and swung him into the lab table. Then she grabbed him by the back of his neck, pinning him facedown to the table. She raised her leg and slammed it down on the back of the soldier's calf, breaking his knee. His scream echoed out across the room.

The general sighed in aggravation. He would deserve a medal after this assignment was over. Because this was goddamn ridiculous!

The soldier at the front of the room yanked the door open and yelled out, "I need help in here!" to the ones who stood guard in the hallway. They rushed in. They had their firearms pulled, but they stopped as soon as they entered and immediately lowered their weapons.

The general didn't know why until he felt the cold barrel of a gun pressed against his temple.

"Let my sister go," the eldest calmly stated, loud enough for them to hear but without the panic of her baby sister, "or I'll blow the motherfucker's brains out."

It was a sad day when trained military couldn't handle three little girls, the eldest not even eighteen yet.

With the middle sister still wrapped around his head, the soldier released the little girl. Stevie MacKilligan stepped away from him, brushing blond hair off her face and out of her eyes.

When she was done, she focused on the nurse, who was still holding the syringe.

"You were so ready to give that to me," she said.

"It's just something to help you," the nurse asserted softly, rationally. "To keep you calm."

"Really?" The child snatched the syringe away from the nurse. "Then you try it."

The psychotic little bitch went up on her toes and slammed the syringe into the nurse's neck, pressing the plunger once the needle had entered flesh.

Screeching, the nurse fell back against the lab table. The general understood, though. That had to hurt.

But then the nurse kept screeching, falling to the floor, rolling to her back, and suddenly foaming at the mouth, her entire body spasming wildly.

Until she stopped. Everything.

Moving, breathing . . . living.

The general slowly looked from the nurse's corpse back to the girl.

Her expression smug, she said, "Told you she was trying to kill me."

Charles Taylor ignored the complaints from the She-wolves in his Pack. They wanted him to call the cops. The FBI. Call the White House. Call anybody! "Do something!" they'd demanded in order to get little Stevie back.

But Charles knew better.

Some things you just had to let play out in their own time. And this was one of those times.

His granddaughter and her half-sister had disappeared exactly two-and-a-half weeks after the US government had shown up on Pack territory.

And Charles knew where they'd gone. To get their baby sister back.

His granddaughter and her half-sisters were not like the other kids. They weren't even like the Pack pups. And so instead of intervening, he'd let them handle it themselves.

While the Pack females were busy on the phone, making calls, trying to get information, his granddaughter and half-sister had been holed up in their rooms. Quiet. They'd gone real quiet.

Something so disturbing that Charles had ordered his Pack to stand down. To stop whatever they were doing. They'd thought he'd given up on the little one because she wasn't his granddaughter by blood, but that was far from the truth. He'd simply learned that sometimes a wolf had to stay hidden in the trees until everything blew over.

That was how one survived.

A limo with two military vehicles in front and two behind pulled onto his street.

He sat on the porch whittling a small unicorn from a hunk of wood he'd found in the backyard and didn't move until the limo stopped in front of his house.

He stood, dusting the wood shavings off his jeans and Jimi Hendrix T-shirt.

The limo door opened and his granddaughter came out. She looked so much like her mother it made his heart hurt, but he didn't tell her that. She had enough to worry about.

The middle girl followed. She had a bloody nose and a black eye. She might have gotten it scrapping with some military types, but something told Charles that it had come from her older sister. That little honey badger was nothing but trouble and very hard to control.

And, finally, the youngest. She had her big backpack strapped to her shoulders, and she ran awkwardly to keep up with her bigger sisters.

"Pop," his granddaughter said as she walked by.

"Pop-Pop," said the little Asian one.

"Hello, Grandfather," said the youngest.

"Welcome back."

She stopped to smile up at him and he smiled back. She'd cried once when he hadn't returned her smile, so he always smiled back. Always.

He placed the unicorn in her hand and she grinned. "Lovely artistry," she murmured, studying it before disappearing into the house.

Before he turned around again, he knew that there was a wolf standing within ten feet of him.

Taking his time, Charles looked over his shoulder until he locked eyes with what had to be a Van Holtz. An old Van Holtz, but still, at any age, Charles's Pack had always avoided Van Holtz wolves.

"What?" Charles asked.

"Edgar Van Holtz."

"I don't care."

He smirked. "You should. I'm the reason your granddaughter and her sisters are back with your Pack and not in maximum detention at some army base. They did do some damage. There are many who think that at least the oldest should be charged."

Now Charles smirked. "Please. Like you could hold onto any of them."

Van Holtz nodded, grinned. "Good point." He looked at the door the three girls had disappeared behind. "My suggestion—"

"Which I didn't ask for."

"But you'll get it anyway. Put the little one out there. Like when she was into music. But now do it for science." He handed Charles a folder. "Give this to the oldest. Get Stevie signed up for these science competitions and special grants. It will get her name out there."

"And do what? Make her a bigger target?"

"Our government won't be able to just take her without every news source in the universe going after them, wondering what happened to Stevie MacKilligan. And other governments will have to deal with the US if they try to take her. Again."

"Again?"

"Some foreign interests, when they found out she was too tightly watched at the base, sent in agents to put her down."

Charles's angry frown was so vicious that Van Holtz raised his hands. "Calm down. It was handled."

"By you? Or my girls?"

That smirk. "Good luck, backwoods wolf," Van Holtz said, returning to his limo. "You'll need it with those three."

Charles sneered at what he was sure was a tailored suit hanging off that man. Nothing he hated more than snobby wolves.

His eldest granddaughter came out of the house and stood beside him, watching all the vehicles head off.

"Everyone okay?" he asked.

"Yep."

He handed her the file of information the wolf had given her.

"What's this?" she asked.

"Competitions, grants, all that stuff. You need to get your sister involved."

"For the money?"

"For safety. Get her name out there. Get her known. We don't want anyone doing this to her again."

His granddaughter nodded. "I'll take care of it."

He knew that. She took care of everything. Weight of the world sat on those shoulders.

"Look," he said, turning toward her so they faced each other. "Do whatever you've gotta do to protect your sisters. I've got your back."

"I know you do. I just—"

The screams of sibling hostility exploded from inside the house, and his eldest granddaughter closed her eyes, letting out a huge sigh. She hated when her sisters fought, but Charles didn't mind it so much. It was the only normal thing about the three of them.

She turned to go into the house but stopped long enough to go up on her toes and kiss his cheek.

Without a word, she moved away from him and he faced the

yard again, staring straight ahead. He heard the front screen door open, and his eldest granddaughter barked, "Max! Untwist Stevie's tongue right this second! I don't care what she said to—hey! That does not mean grab her throat! Release Stevie's throat right this second. This very second *or I swear by all that is holy*—"

Charles smiled. Although he knew he shouldn't. He shouldn't condone their behavior, but how could he not find that just so cute?

chapter ONE

Thirteen years later . . .

Doreen thought she was dreaming. Thought it was all imaginary. Something sad and twisted in her subconscious. But when she turned over . . .

The small but powerfully built woman was straddling her elderly husband, her knees pinning his arms to the bed, a pillow over his face. Her husband, Peter MacKilligan, was struggling with all his might to dislodge the woman who was on top of him. But nothing he did worked.

Her husband was old. Nearly eighty-five. But his body didn't show his true age. He looked like he was still in his fifties. He was strong. Still boxed, lifted weights, swam every day in their indoor pool. He'd always told her it was genetic. "The men in my family are all like that," he'd say.

And yet . . . he couldn't get this woman off him.

Doreen turned and reached for her cell phone, but that's when the woman spoke.

"I wouldn't if I were you," she said. She had an accent. Sounded like her husband's half-siblings from Scotland.

Doreen looked at the woman over her shoulder. She was still on top of Pete. Still pinning him to the bed. Still smothering him with a pillow.

"Here's the thing, luv," the woman calmly explained in the midst of killing a man. She even had a smile. A large, bright smile. "You can call for help. Use your phone. Or just scream

for one of Pete's boys. And help will come. I'll run, of course.
They won't catch me. I'm fast, ya see. I'll be gone and you'll
have stopped this. How proud you'll be. But then . . . one
night . . . when everyone's forgotten about you, I'll be back."

Pete's struggles slowed and, after a little longer, stopped.

Leaning back, the woman pulled away the pillow and pressed
two fingers to Pete's throat. Satisfied, she slipped off him and
came around their bed, sitting down next to Doreen.

Brushing her hands against each other, as if she was dusting
off flour after making bread, she continued, "And when I come
back, I'll peel that pretty face right from your skull. Wouldn't
like that, now would ya?

"Of course not," she said, patting Doreen's knee through the
bed sheet. "I'm sure you wouldn't like that at all. My Great-
Uncle Pete always had an eye for the beautiful ladies. What are
you? Wife number six?" She shook her head. "I never get it.
You marry once, I understand. You marry twice . . . sure. First
one could have easily been a mistake. But after that . . . you're
just an idiot."

She crossed her legs, picked some lint off her jeans.

"Now," she went on, "like I said, you could scream and
cry and call for help. Or, you can wisely keep your mouth
shut. Wait until I'm long gone and call for one of Pete's boys.
They'll think he died natural. Let them. They won't want an
autopsy. MacKilligans don't like that sort of thing." She sighed,
sounding disappointed. "That's why I had to do it this way,
you see. I would have much preferred to put a leather strap
around his throat and wring the life from him. It would have
taken ages, too, but there's honor in that—for both of us. Because for our kind . . . it takes a lot to kill us. But I guess you
don't know much about that, huh?" She sniffed the air. "Yeah,
full-human . . . so you don't know about any of that. But you
can count yourself lucky. You'll get a nice bit of cash from the
estate and can go on and live your life as long as the Almighty
allows. Won't that be nice? Rather than waking up again . . .
and finding me standing over *you*?"

Doreen forced herself to nod.

"That's a good lass." Again, she patted her knee and Doreen fought the urge to recoil. To run screaming from the room, the building . . . the state.

The woman stood, stretched her back. The sound of bones cracking had Doreen cringing.

She watched the woman walk across the room to the open window she'd probably come through.

"Now don't forget," she added before slipping back out as soundlessly as she'd slipped in. "Lots of tears for his sons, and lots of 'He can't be dead. He can't be dead.' That'll impress the family. And they deserve that, don't you think?"

Then with that disturbing grin still on her face, she was out the window and out of Doreen's life.

Shaking with a fear she'd never known, Doreen slipped deep into the covers next to her dead husband and waited until the alarm clock went off. Then she got up, went to one of her stepson's rooms, and, while the family gathered, rushing around to call the doctor they had on payroll and the lawyer who kept them all out of prison, she sobbed and sobbed and kept repeating, "He can't be dead. He can't be dead."

When he went to bed late that night, he thought she'd be there to complain about his long hours working, but then he remembered . . . he didn't have a wife like everyone else. He had Irene Conridge. The genius.

Niles Van Holtz—"Van" to his friends and Pack but "Holtz" to his mate—found his full-human wife still doing her own work in her very messy office. Her gaze fixed on her computer screen, her fingers flying over the keyboard, desperately trying to keep up with her even faster brain.

He didn't wait for her to notice him. She never would. Instead, he leaned down and kissed her neck.

"I'll be right with you," she said, still working. "Go have lunch and I'll meet you downstairs."

"It's three in the morning."

Her hands froze on the keyboard. "Oh. All right."

Van sat down on the floor, his back resting against her desk. "Did you eat at all today?"

"I had breakfast." When he continued to stare at her, she added, "A very large breakfast. Is there a reason you're here?"

Van rested his arms on his raised knees. "They found three more."

Irene dropped back into her seat, her lips slightly parted. It took a lot to stun her, but here they were.

"Burned?"

"Yes."

"The same other issues?"

"Yes. Hybrids in the process of shifting into or out of their human forms when killed, but, for whatever reason, none turned completely back to human, which they should have when they died. We all shift back to human after we die."

Irene shook her head. "Fascinating. He's really advanced his work."

"You know, we don't know it's him."

"It's him," she snapped. "Trust me, it's him."

"Because you don't like him?"

"I don't like most people, but he's the only one with the science to come up with this."

"That's because he's been working on ways to change DNA to get rid of the most deadly diseases. Like cancer and diabetes."

"I wish you would just admit that you don't believe it's him because he's one of you. A fellow shifter."

"You're right, I have a very hard time believing any shifter would do this to another."

"Because you refuse to believe some shifters are more human than others. He's also a scientist and I know *my* own kind. We can rationalize almost anything as long as it doesn't touch our work. We can give you very logical reasons why we're doing it—even when we know it's wrong. Trust me when I say, he is no different. At the very least," she added, "we need to investigate him thoroughly."

"My people have already started but it would be great if we could get someone on the inside."

"I already told you that I'm out . . . he loathes me."

"Do you have any idea how many times you've made that statement to me about *so* many people?"

"I could calculate it, but I'm sure the final tally would be quite large." She raised one finger. "There is one option that—"

"No," he said firmly. "We're not going to discuss this again. Those three are too unstable."

"First, it amuses me that you think you can force edicts on me like 'We're not discussing this again.' Of *course* we're discussing this again, and we'll discuss it as often as *I* like."

And that's why he adored his wife. She never took any of his shit.

"Second, I'm not talking about all three of them. She has connections to him that we can use to our benefit."

"But doesn't she loathe you too?"

"Oh, yes. Absolutely. I doubt she'll ever forgive me for what I did. But the difference is I have an *in* with this one."

"Is that what you call a seventeen-year-old boy?"

Irene smiled. "He's better than nothing."

chapter TWO

Three days later . . .

Shen Li opened the cabinet door over the refrigerator, and that's where he found her. Panting and sweating, her legs pulled tight into her chest, her eyes wide and bright gold.

Her eyes were normally blue, so he sensed that gold wasn't a good thing at the moment.

She was also naked. Very, very naked. Why the hell was she naked?

"I'm fine," she said before he could speak. "I'm fine, I'm fine, I'm fine."

"You want me to close the door?" he asked.

She shut her eyes, turned her head toward the corner, and nodded. Desperately.

Shen closed the door and faced the room. He knew immediately what the problem was.

It was the bears.

A roomful of them.

That would scare most normal people, but Stevie MacKilligan was not a normal person. Not even by his standards. And his standards were pretty liberal, being that he wasn't really normal either.

How could he be when he could shift into a giant panda? An ability built into his DNA, like his mother's brown eyes and his father's weird knuckles.

But even by shifter standards, Stevie was not normal.

Cute. Interesting. But definitely not normal.

Which was why Shen knew she'd stay trapped in that cupboard until the end of time if he didn't help.

"All right," he said to the bears. "You guys need to go."

They glanced at him . . . then went right back to eating the baked goods that Stevie's eldest sister Charlie had put out before she'd left the house. He'd heard her heading downstairs before the sun was up just so she could bake, meaning only one thing—she was stressed out.

And when Charlie baked, the bears showed up to feed. A situation that didn't bother Charlie but freaked out poor Stevie.

The bears continued to ignore Shen, but he wasn't surprised by that. He was dealing with a room filled with grizzlies, polars, and black bears. Bear breeds that didn't really consider pandas one of their own. Pandas just weren't terrifying enough because pandas didn't let the little things bother them. They didn't explode in a violent rage when someone startled them. And panda mothers never ripped off someone's head because he was too close to their children. Nor did panda fathers go on hunger-fueled rampages because a meal or two had been missed.

They were pandas. They just rolled along through life. Happy to be happy.

And, like his brethren, it took a lot to push Shen to actually unleash his anger. He'd always had a very high tolerance for bullshit.

Still, he knew that Stevie didn't have that tolerance. High or otherwise. Although he'd never actually seen it in action, Stevie's two sisters seemed to have a deep-seated fear of their baby sister "snapping her bolt" as it was called. Apparently it went beyond mere wild-animal rage and into something else altogether.

Not in the mood to deal with whatever cleanup that sort of thing entailed, Shen decided to end this before it became nasty.

He walked out of the kitchen, through the dining room, and straight into the living room. He grabbed the duffel bag he kept behind the chaise lounge, returned to the kitchen, dropped the bag on the floor, and pulled out his favorite weapon. He leaned against the refrigerator and began his assault.

First, he unleashed his fangs and used one to strip off the leaves, which he'd eat later. He then used his back teeth to crack down on the green bamboo shoot, breaking off a piece that he could then chew. Then he did it all over again. And again. And again.

The sound radiated across the room until he saw that every eye in the place was locked on him. Bears—especially grizzlies—hated what they called "weird sounds." And they found the constant chewing of bamboo by giant pandas among the most irritating. Mostly because it rarely stopped.

It took three minutes, but when they saw him go in for another bamboo stalk, they all picked up what was left of their treats, their cups of coffee, and walked out the back door.

Grinning, Shen tossed the bamboo back in his duffel bag and reached up to knock on the cabinet door.

"You can come out now. They're all gone."

He opened the refrigerator door and pulled out a bottle of water. But just as he started to take a drink, he realized that Stevie still hadn't come out.

Frowning, he used his free hand and opened the cabinet door again. Stevie was still curled tight into the corner, her hands dug into her hair, her thin naked body tense and shivering.

"Stevie? You o—"

She came at him then. Exploding from the cabinet, the top half of her body leaning out, extremely large fangs coming toward his face.

Shen jerked back and felt the enamel of her fangs brush against his lips before snapping closed on nothing but air.

Then she roared. Loudly. The windows in the house rattled before she disappeared back into the cabinet, slamming the door after her.

"Well . . . that wasn't normal," Shen said to no one.

Charlie MacKilligan began to rub her temples and glanced up at the gorgeous man who stood beside her. A migraine was starting to settle behind her eyes and that was never a good thing. It made her tense and she tended to say things she couldn't take back when she was tense.

But she knew what was going on here. They were building up to something. Attempting to lull her into a false sense of security with mindless chatter before they made their move.

Her father often did the same thing so she was used to it. Of course the fact that her worthless father often tried this same technique on her made Charlie angry and distrustful of the people who'd pledged to protect her and her sisters.

Apparently, the shifter world had decided that hybrids were worth their time to protect. This was the first Charlie had ever heard that. Most purebreds didn't know what to do with her and Stevie. Not only were they the combined DNA of two different species, they were the fucked-up offspring of Freddy MacKilligan, which everyone found way more offensive than the intermingling of different species.

It wasn't fair, really. That they'd been hit twice like that. By their mothers' poor choices in men and their father's . . . uselessness.

Big fingers gently stroked Charlie's cheek and she smiled up at Berg Dunn. Her big grizzly bear. Literally. He could shift into a grizzly bear. The morning after her cousin's wedding a few weeks ago, she'd woken up to find herself sleeping on top of his back, bear fur tickling her nose. He'd shifted in the night and it was shockingly weird to realize that her head was resting on his grizzly hump like it was a hard pillow. Then, as she was sitting up, trying to shake herself awake, she'd watched a big bear butt walk past the open bedroom door; followed a few seconds later by another bear. Those were Berg's triplet brother and sister lumbering by. They'd also shifted that morning and were wandering around their house in their bear forms. Apparently something they did whenever the mood struck them. Something Charlie couldn't do because, unlike her sisters, she couldn't shift. Something else she blamed on her father.

"Headache?" Berg softly asked.

She didn't bother to lie to him. She'd never believed in suffering in silence if she didn't have to. "Yeah, but it'll be fine."

The *once they get out of here* was implied.

Charlie glanced over at her younger sister to see how she was holding up. As usual, Max was on her phone. She lived on that thing, making Charlie wonder if her sister had an entire other life that she was unaware of. Then again . . . she probably didn't want to know one way or another.

Max stopped texting long enough to scratch the right side of her face, where she had those fresh scratches going from her eye down her cheek.

"What happened to your face?" she softly asked because she was too bored not to.

"Nothin'," Max lied.

"You messing with that cat again? Leave the cat alone."

Max lowered her phone. "I want her off our property. She's spraying everything. It's driving me nuts. Besides . . ." she suddenly added, "I can take her."

"*Dude.* She's a cat that brazenly lives in a neighborhood filled with *bears*. That's not brave. That's crazy. She's a crazy cat and she'll tear your eyes out. So stop it!"

Max started to reply—because she could just never let things go—but the sound of someone clearing his throat distracted her.

Charlie looked across the giant desk she and her sister were sitting in front of. The wolf male on the other side raised one eyebrow. "Do you mind?" he asked.

"Well—" Max began, but Charlie put her hand on her sister's forearm to stop her.

"Of course," Charlie said nicely. "Please. Go on."

"Thank you."

This was Niles Van Holtz. Head pooch of the Van Holtz Pack. Or alpha dude or . . . whatever they called themselves.

Charlie had the feeling that Van Holtz thought because she was half wolf, she'd respond to him like the rest of the wolves in the world seemed to. But she didn't. Because she was also half honey badger and because her wolf grandfather hated the Van Holtz Pack. "Rich pricks," was how he described them.

And Van Holtz was rich. His family had a chain of very expensive restaurants around the world and he had private offices in almost all the major cities in the States and Europe, complete with a full staff. All those offices weren't for the restaurant business, though. Van Holtz was also in charge of an organization called The Group. They took care of shifter problems and, to The Group, those shifter problems included hybrids. During the time he'd been in charge, Van Holtz had somehow managed to also team up with Katzenhaus, which protected the cat nation and the Bear Protection Council (BPC). Those two organizations protected their own species worldwide and, until recently, didn't really bother with hybrids unless they had to.

But, according to a very smug Van Holtz, "That's all changed. We protect everyone now, don't we, ladies?"

And, at the time, he'd put those wolf eyes on Mary-Ellen Kozlowski of Katzenhaus and Bayla Ben-Zeev of BPC, and what he got back was a less than enthusiastic, "Yeah. Sure."

Of course, the protection of the MacKilligan sisters wasn't what really had Charlie dealing with any of these people from shifter worlds she knew very little about. It was the problem that was surrounding Charlie and her sisters. The same problem that had been making their lives nightmarish ever since they'd been born. Her father. Always her father. But this time he'd brought company with him. The Guerra twins out of Italy. Caterina and Celestina. Two very vindictive, angry wenches who were not only Freddy MacKilligan's half-sisters—which had been unknown to Freddy and the rest of the family for most of the twins' lives—but who had also just found out they were honey badger shifters.

Angry, vengeful, spiteful honey badger shifters.

Short of a war involving nuclear powers, there was no other worse combination in the universe.

Add in that they were very wealthy women with no real boundaries, and everyone in this room knew that the Guerra twins had to be dealt with. Quickly.

Since they'd last been seen at the wedding of Charlie's cousin, however, the twins had gone deep into hiding and had been very quiet, which did not fool Charlie or her sisters at all.

Those bitches weren't gone; they were plotting.

"There is something else we need to discuss with you," Van Holtz said, his folded hands resting on his giant desk.

Ahhh, here it comes.

"About your Uncle Pete . . ."

Charlie gazed at Van Holtz; then she looked over at Max.

"Do we have an Uncle Pete?" Charlie asked her sister.

"We have several Petes. A few Peters. Most are out of Glasgow."

"This is your Uncle Pete in New Jersey."

Charlie stared at Van Holtz again before asking her sister, "We have an Uncle Pete in New Jersey?"

"Maybe. MacKilligans have a lot of Petes."

"He is your father's uncle, actually," Van Holtz clarified.

"So he's our Great-Uncle Pete," Charlie said. "Yeah. We don't know him."

"Well, sadly, he has died."

"Uh-huh."

"And we believe that he was murdered."

"Shot in the head somewhere in Brooklyn?" Charlie guessed. "Because we've lost a few MacKilligan men that way over the years."

"No. He died in his bed."

"A MacKilligan dies in his bed and you think he was murdered? MacKilligan men don't usually end that way."

"What makes you think it was murder?" Max asked. "If he's our great-uncle, isn't he, like, a thousand years old?"

"Not quite."

"MacKilligan men, when they're not shot in the head," Charlie explained, "they tend to live a very long time. Sadly," she added, thinking of her father. The man who would not die.

"There is evidence he was suffocated. Maybe with a pillow . . ."

Charlie frowned. "Are you sure he's a MacKilligan? Because that doesn't sound right."

"My sister's correct," Max said. "Most MacKilligan siblings start trying to kill each other with pillows by the time they can crawl."

"It's true," Charlie insisted when she saw the look of growing horror on Van Holtz's very handsome face. "My sisters and I didn't do that, of course. But, then again, we weren't babies together. So we missed the whole infanticide period of the honey badger childhood. Anyway, what all that means is most of our family has developed a tolerance for that sort of thing. I'm not saying a badger couldn't be killed that way, but it would take *ages* to put one down with a pillow. And a lot of strength to keep them pinned to the bed."

"It's really just faster to shoot them in the back of the head," Max said. "We specify back of the head because shooting them in the front causes damage but doesn't always kill. We have very hard heads. So, depending on the bullet, it may not actually rip through the skull and get to the brain."

"And we have quite a few cousins that, if a bullet did hit them in the brain, we're still not sure it would actually do any damage because they are that stupid." Charlie glanced at Max. "Right?"

"Absolutely. I hit one of my cousins with a bat once . . . it did nothing. It was wood. It broke . . . on his *head*."

"And Max took a really strong swing—"

"Okay!" Van Holtz barked, holding up his hand. "Please stop. I can't listen to this anymore. What I'm telling you is that we are certain your great-uncle was murdered. That's all you need to know."

"And we need to know that . . . why? Exactly."

"Because. There's going to be a funeral. A large one. We've heard your relatives from Scotland will be coming."

Charlie leaned back in her chair and stated flatly, "We're not killing our cousins for you."

Van Holtz's eyes grew ridiculously wide. "That is *not* what we're talking about!"

"It's not?" Max asked. "Because it makes sense. They'll all be in one place and we can pretty much just mow them all down. Women and children first!"

"*No!*" Van Holtz yelped before he looked away and took several deep breaths. "That is *not* what we're asking."

"Ohhhh," Charlie said. "So you just want us to go to the funeral so we can *spy* on our family. Right?"

Van Holtz glanced over at his younger cousin Ulrich Van Holtz, who everyone called Ric.

"I see." Charlie brushed nonexistent lint off her jeans. "Because a honey badger family is not nearly as important as a pack or pride or a teddy bear picnic."

"I don't think bears call themselves . . . that."

"Look," Ric said, "we're not trying to have you do anything you don't want to do. And we are not interested in family business information. But we were hoping that you could provide us with information about—"

"Our Uncle Will," Charlie finished for the also good-looking younger Van Holtz. Did all their males look that good?

"Your uncle is a very dangerous man," Ric went on. "We're not even sure how he's being allowed in the States, but he is and we want to know why he's coming here."

"I know why he's coming here," Charlie replied, glancing at her sister; Max smiled back because it was hitting her too. "If Will is coming here, he's coming here for *one* reason. And that's to make my dreams come true. He's coming here to kill my father." She clapped her hands together. "Isn't that awesome?"

Van Holtz stared at them for several seconds before he admitted, "Sometimes I have *no* idea how to respond to you."

Shen continued to stare at the closed cabinet door until he realized someone was standing beside him.

"Did I hear roaring?" the kid next to him asked.

Shen looked over at the teen he was paid very well to protect. It was why Shen was living in this house with three women he wasn't related to or dating. Because even his family needed space from the seventeen-year-old. But Stevie liked the kid and, to Shen's continual surprise, Kyle Jean-Louis Parker liked Stevie. Shen hadn't thought the kid, a child prodigy, liked anyone.

"Yeah," Shen replied, "you heard roaring."

The kid then asked, "Stevie?"

"Stevie."

"Huh. What did you do?"

"Nothing. I even cleared out the bears that were sitting in the kitchen eating sticky buns."

"Oh. There were other bears here?" He nodded. "Yeah, that's gonna freak her out. She is only comfortable around you giant pandas and the Dunn triplets."

"That's why I got rid of them. But she still wouldn't get out of the cabinet. And when I went to check on her again, I saw fangs that really shouldn't belong to . . . *anyone* on this planet."

"Fangs?" Kyle frowned. "She flashed her fangs at you?"

"She didn't flash anything. She tried to take my face off."

"That's not good. That's really not good."

"I get that, but I'm not exactly sure what we're supposed to do if she won't come out." He shrugged. "I guess we can wait until her sisters get back."

"I don't think we should do that."

"Why not?"

Kyle took hold of Shen's arm and pulled him into the living room. "We have a slight issue."

"Kyle, when you say, 'We have a slight issue,' I know that you mean we have a big fucking problem. What big fucking problem do we have, Kyle?"

"Um . . . well . . . Stevie has mentioned to me that she's concerned her meds have not been working lately, which happens sometimes with certain medications. And especially when you're dealing with a honey badger metabolism."

"Wait . . . what? What are you talking about?"

"Stevie has a panic disorder. Her meds help her control it. Usually. But she's a shifter and a hybrid who's part honey badger . . . so fixing that issue is not as easy as finding an overpriced Manhattan psychiatrist and getting a new prescription. She's been in contact with her doctor but he's in Germany and the meds are on their way, but there's no guarantee they'll work and—"

"You know," Shen finally cut in, "this sounds like not my problem. Or my business. So I think I'm just going to go—"

"No, no. We have to do something."

"I really like you better, Kyle, when you don't care about anyone."

"I care about those who are important. And I deemed Stevie important many years ago. What she can do with her brain will make a difference in this world . . . unlike yours."

"Yes, insulting me will definitely make me more eager to help."

"I'll say it again . . . we have to do something. Now."

"Why?"

Kyle again grabbed Shen's arm, this time more urgently, and dragged him *back* into the kitchen. Then he reached up and opened the cabinet door. Shen was ready to jump back in case Stevie tried to bite his face off again. But she didn't. Instead, all he saw was her cute naked ass bumping and grinding because the other half of her was trying to crawl through a hole she'd dug inside the top of the cabinet. He could hear her claws tearing into the wood, brick, and whatever else she was coming in contact with during her desperate escape out of the now-safe kitchen. He was sure that if she'd hit titanium, she'd tear that out too. She wouldn't let anything get in her way.

"You see?" the kid pointed out. "She's *burrowing.*" He closed the cabinet door. "If we don't deal with this now, she'll destroy the entire house within the hour."

"Where are her sisters?"

"They went out with Berg. So it's just you and me."

"And what do you suggest we do?"

The kid was silent for a moment before he asked Shen, "My sister's paying for long-term disability insurance for you, right?"

There are bears. There are bears. There are bears. Run away! Run away! Run away!

She heard her rational voice attempt to reason with her irrational brain. *You're fine. The bears are gone. You're safe. Just calm down!*

But she couldn't calm down. She couldn't listen to her rational voice. She couldn't stop herself from tearing into a home that did not belong to her.

All she knew was that she was in great danger and she had to get away. By any means necessary! Oh. Wait. That was from Malcolm X. Was that appropriation? That felt like appropriation. Good God, what was happening to her?

You are spiraling, her rational voice warned her.

And she knew her rational side was right. She *was* spiraling. But she couldn't help it. Her system was in overload, her meds had stopped working, and if she didn't get away, she would shift right inside the house, destroying it and possibly half the neighborhood in the process.

So she kept digging. Nothing would stop her from digging!

"This is not my problem," Shen argued. "This is a MacKilligan problem."

"Stevie is one of my best—"

"Only."

The kid glared at him. "I have friends."

Shen squinted at him. "Do you?"

"She is one of my *best* friends and I will do what is necessary to care for her."

"Then call her sisters and let them deal with it."

"I told you they're out with Berg in the city. It'll take them time to get back here. The house will be gone and Stevie will be underground by then. *Burrowing* her way through the neighborhood and destroying a lot of house foundations in the process. I'm assuming the bear neighbors won't take that well."

No. They wouldn't. But still . . . "I will not accept responsibility for her. I barely want to do that for you."

Lips pursed, the kid pulled open the cabinet door again, and now Shen could only see Stevie's bare feet. They hung out the hole she'd dug, twisting and twirling as she continued to work her way through the inside of the building to get out.

"Dammit," Shen muttered. The kid was right. At this rate, she'd dig a tunnel that went straight from the kitchen to the roof.

Sighing, Shen reached up and grabbed Stevie's feet.

"You should be doing this," he growled at the kid when Stevie screamed and started to kick at him to get away.

"I'm an artist. I can't risk my hands. You know that."

Smirking little prick. Honestly, the things Shen did for money.

Going up on his toes and taking a good grip on her ankles, Shen pulled down and out, yanking Stevie from the safety of her burrow and slamming her to the floor.

He cringed. He hadn't meant to pull so hard, but that slam to the floor didn't stop her either. Nope. Stevie just kept screaming, swinging giant claws, and kicking out her feet while letting everyone know, *"You'll never take me alive! You won't eat me alive!"*

Deciding that no female was pretty enough to deal with this level of bullshit, Shen flipped her over, grabbed her around the waist, and lifted her off the floor. He tucked her under his arm like a big sack of rice, making sure her arms and legs were pointing away from him, and started toward the front of the house.

"Get her something to wear," he barked at the kid.

"Where are we taking her?" Kyle asked, grabbing what looked like a bright yellow dress off a chair in the dining room.

"I have no idea," Shen admitted. "But we can't keep her here."

"You're right." Kyle raced toward the front of the house so he could open the door for him. "But I think I know exactly who can help us. She's in town right now. So it's perfect."

"Who are you talking about?"

Kyle glanced at the still fighting Stevie. "Just trust me."

"I don't trust you."

"We're taking her to someone who can help. I promise."

Shen hoped so. Because Stevie had abruptly gone from screaming and swinging to completely rigid and hissing. It reminded him of a stray cat his parents kept finding behind their house. It kept pissing back there and the smell reached into his mother's kitchen. Every time their father tried to remove the cat, it acted just like this.

They reached the SUV parked in front of the house and Shen jerked his head toward his back. "Get the keys. Open the doors."

Kyle pulled the keys from the back pocket of Shen's jeans. He remotely unlocked the vehicle and reached around Shen to open the back door.

"Once we're on the road," Shen continued as he moved forward to place Stevie inside the vehicle, "we'll call her sisters. Tell them to meet us at your family's . . . family's . . ."

Shen stopped to assess the situation.

Stevie had spread her legs and arms wide so that she could clamp her feet and hands against the SUV's metal carriage, stopping Shen from pushing her inside.

Honestly, he had not expected that. Why would he expect that? Why would he expect a grown woman with tiger and honey badger DNA in her system to act like a common house cat?

Taking a breath, Shen again tried to push her inside, using his chest against her back. After the second failed attempt, he barked, "*Seriously?*"

That got him another hiss.

"You know what we need," Kyle ruminated. "A cat carrier. We probably don't even need a big one either. Stevie can make herself into a small ball without much effort."

"What?" Shen asked. Then he barked, "Shut up."

Man, he wished Stevie's sisters were here. This was what they were really good at. At least Charlie was. She knew how to calm her baby sister down, coax her out of cabinets without violence, and keep her from tearing Max's eyes from her head. Shen didn't know how Charlie did it and, to be honest, he didn't have time to learn. It was early. He was hungry. And all he really wanted to do was sit down and eat a few pounds of the bamboo that he had stowed in his room. Not play nursemaid to a former prodigy with panic issues because a few grizzlies and polar bears were in her house.

When the pushing continued not to work, Shen became desperate and said to Stevie, "Okay, listen up. I know you are under

a lot of stress and need new meds or whatever. And I really want
to help you. But that means I need you to get in this car *right
now.*" When she didn't move, he suddenly had a brilliant idea
and added, "So stop being a *princess* and get in the goddamn car."

It was as if a light went on in her head, and the cat in his
arms suddenly turned into a pissed-off woman.

"Princess?" Stevie snarled. An insult he'd noticed Max had
tossed at Stevie more than once, which had always led to a violent confrontation of some kind between the sisters. "*Princess?*"
she now yelled.

"Yes, you're being a princess right now."

Her head turned and kept turning until her nose lined up
with her spine.

"*I'm* being a princess? *Me?*"

"Ahhh!" Shen yelped in surprise. "Is what your head doing
normal? *At all?*"

"Don't try to distract me from your insult!"

"Turn back around! *You are freaking me out!*"

"Oh, calm down," she taunted as she turned her head forward. "You big baby."

Annoyed by the insult and noticing that her arms and legs
were no longer gripping the outside of the SUV, Shen shoved
her inside.

"*Hey!*" she complained as he closed the door in her face.

"Like a house cat," he muttered, snatching the keys out of
the kid's hand.

"This is so entertaining!" Kyle crowed.

"Get in the fucking car, psychopath."

"I'm just a narcissist," Kyle calmly explained. "My older
sister, Delilah, though . . . now *she's* a psychopath," he added
with a big grin. "Clinically diagnosed and everything!"

A princess? He'd called her a *princess.* Her? Stevie Stasiuk-
MacKilligan?

She was as far from a princess as anyone could be. And Stevie
knew that because she'd actually *met* royals. She'd performed
for them when she was a child and then had given them tours

around the labs she'd worked at when she was a teenager. And the one thing Stevie was absolutely sure of was that she was no princess.

How could she be? She was constantly aware of others' needs and feelings. That's why she was invited places and Kyle Jean-Louis Parker was thrown out of places. Because, like a true prince, he could not care less about anyone's feelings but his own.

So that giant panda actually calling Stevie a princess did nothing but upset her. Because it wasn't true.

She was not a princess!

"What are you yelling about back there?" Shen barked at her from the driver's seat.

Stevie blinked. Uh-oh. She'd said that out loud, hadn't she? She hated when she did that.

"Then stop doing it," Shen ordered. "You're distracting me."

Her eyes narrowed on his fat panda head. She was tempted to slap him right in the back of it.

Kyle unbuckled his seat belt and turned so he could reach back and grab her hands, holding them in place.

"Let's play our 'We're better than you' game," he said with false cheer.

Stevie cringed, realizing she'd spoken her thoughts out loud again.

"I threatened his big, fat panda head, didn't I?" she asked Kyle.

"You did," Shen told her. "And my head is not fat."

"It's not small!" she barked back.

"Stevie," Kyle said, voice strong, "look at me. Focus on me. Because I'm fascinating."

"I'm not a princess," she felt the need to point out again.

"Of course you're not. I wouldn't be friends with a princess unless she was a *lot* richer than you are."

Stevie nodded. "Thanks, Kyle. That makes me feel so much better."

The panda pulled up to a light, stopped, and let out a long sigh before looking back at her and asking, "*Seriously?*"

★   ★   ★

Berg Dunn was always amazed at how Charlie managed people, depending on who they were and how they fit into her life.

When she spoke to the head of Katzenhaus, Charlie was friendly and polite and often told Mary-Ellen Kozlowski exactly what she wanted to hear while doing exactly what Charlie actually wanted to do. And when confronted by the cat, Charlie didn't slap her down or shoot her in the head, as she'd been known to do with those who put her sisters at risk.

But Charlie was always direct and honest when she dealt with Bayla Ben-Zeev of BPC. Berg had originally thought that was due to his relationship with Bayla and BPC, but no. It had nothing to do with him; Charlie just respected Bayla and she was always direct and honest with those she respected. They often didn't agree, but both ladies were too smart to ever challenge each other. They were aware neither would come out of that particular confrontation alive.

Then there were the Van Holtz wolves. Charlie never smiled at them. Was never honest with them. And more than once, Berg was terrified she was going to throw Max at them. Literally. Just pick her sister up and chuck her at Niles Van Holtz because throwing honey badgers at a person is an excellent way to get someone's face ripped off.

She just didn't like them. And they were as nice and polite as they could possibly be. Berg didn't know wolves could be so polite. Yet no matter how polite they were or the fact that Charlie was half wolf, it didn't seem to change her lack of desire to make the leaders of the very powerful Pack her allies.

And he thought he knew why. Because Charlie didn't trust them. Not yet anyway. And if Charlie didn't trust you, she had no use for you.

Sadly, the Van Holtzes hadn't realized any of that yet, so they didn't see the problem with asking Charlie to spy on her own family. She might have little patience or respect for the MacKilligans, but they were still her family.

"Again," Van Holtz cut in, his voice curt, "and for the sixty-thousandth time . . . we are *not* asking you to destroy your family."

"Just kill them," Max casually tossed in, forcing Berg to sit in a nearby chair and look out the big windows of the office so that he didn't laugh in anyone's face.

"No!" the wolf barked. "We do not want you to kill *anyone*. Especially women and children."

"Hhhmmm" the sisters said in unison, shaking their heads.

"Yeah," Max said. "That is not a good idea. To kill the men first and leave the women and children alive . . . because they will retaliate. Especially the . . . uh . . . cubs?"

"I thought it was pups," Charlie said.

"Maybe it's badgerlings . . . like ducklings?"

"Awwww. That's cute."

Van Holtz placed his elbows on his desk and buried his head in his hands.

"So, yeah. The badger*lings* . . . yeah," she said to her sister, "I like that too. The badgerlings are definitely something you want to wipe out real early in the process."

Max's phone vibrated and she looked down at it. "Excuse me a minute," she said before standing and moving to the far side of the room.

Charlie stared at Van Holtz. "So does that work for you?"

"*No!*"

"No need to snap, White Fang."

Van Holtz's younger cousin quickly stood and moved in front of the desk, blocking his uncle's now-gold wolf eyes from Charlie's view.

"How about we just let this go?" he suggested. "We'll deal with the Will MacKilligan thing on our own. How about that?"

Charlie shrugged. "That's fine with me."

"Great! I think that's it then."

"Okay."

"Wait, there is one thing," Van Holtz said, slapping his cousin's hip until he moved off his desk. "I was wondering next time when you come, if you could bring your sister."

Charlie pointed behind her. "She's right there."

"Your youngest sister."

"Oh . . . uh-huh."

Max suddenly appeared in front of Berg. She leaned in and whispered against his ear—and he was working really hard not to cringe away from her; she was just so close to a major artery that it was uncomfortable—"We need to go."

"Okay. Why?"

"Just trust me. But if I say it to Charlie, she'll panic. So can you do it?"

"Yeah. Sure."

"Great." She moved away from him—*Thank God!*—and toward the office door.

Berg could see Charlie again and she was nodding at whatever Van Holtz was saying, a halfway pleasant smile on her face.

With a shrug, Berg stood and went to her side, crouching down.

"I just think," Van Holtz was saying, "that it would be great to meet her. I've heard so much about her."

At a pause in the conversation, Berg leaned in and said, "It's time to go."

"Oh." She looked at him. "Everything okay?"

"Yeah. But we have another appointment."

"Okay." Charlie stood; the Van Holtz men stood with her.

She held out her hand and Van Holtz took it, giving a firm shake. He then tried to pull his hand back, but Charlie held it and tugged him forward a bit.

Gazing into his eyes, she said, "You stay the fuck away from my baby sister or I'll find out where you live. Sneak into your house. And, while your wife is sleeping next to you, I'll peel the skin off your body. And if you don't believe me, ask the Peruvian drug lord who once kidnapped my sister. His wife never even knew I was there . . . and your wife won't either. So . . . stay away from my baby sister, so I don't have to make your wife weep." She smiled. "Okay? Do we understand each other?"

Van Holtz didn't answer, he just kept staring at her. So did his younger cousin.

"Great!" she said to his non-answer. "Speak to you guys soon."

Charlie turned and followed Max out the door. Berg paused long enough to say, "Uh . . . ummmm . . . okay, bye."

Head down, he followed Charlie and Max to the elevator at the end of the hall.

Once the doors closed, Berg observed, "That seemed a little . . . strong."

Charlie's smile was faint. "I like clarity."

Berg expected more on the subject, but nope.

Turning to Max, Charlie asked, "Is there a problem?"

"Got a call from Shen. Stevie's meds stopped working."

Charlie cringed. "I was afraid that was going to happen."

"Don't worry, though. Kyle went to his mom's town house downtown. He said she could help." Max shrugged. "Let's face it, with those kids of hers, I'm sure she's got some great psychiatrists on speed dial."

"That could have gone better," Ric said, dropping into the chair near his cousin's desk.

"They're crazy." Van was still standing there, staring off, his expression blank and confused. "They're absolutely crazy."

"I thought we'd already figured that out." Ric shook his head. "So now what?"

"Plan B, I guess."

"Plan B? You want me to call Dee-Ann and—"

"Dear *God,* I'd never ask your wife to involve herself in this in any way."

Ric smirked. The fear in his cousin's voice was, to say the least, entertaining.

"No offense, of course," Van eventually added.

"Of course."

"No. I've got a better plan. My wife—"

The snort-laugh was out before Ric could stop it.

Ric cleared his throat. "Sorry. You were saying?"

"*My* wife is in town—"

"Great. We should have dinner togeth—" The glare was so harsh, Ric stopped speaking.

"—and she, I'm sure, can handle this."

When Van didn't add a wink to that statement, letting Ric know he was joking, Ric nodded and said, "Of course. I'm sure . . . that Irene Conridge, PhD, internationally known for making a *Pope* cry, can deal with three women—one of which just threatened to skin you alive while the other happily offered to mow down the women and children of her own family— without *any* problems."

Van rubbed his nose. "Your sarcasm is noted, cousin."

"To paraphrase my wife, just sayin'."

chapter THREE

Kyle unlocked the front door to his parents' rental home and walked inside. He turned back and watched his friend step in behind him. Stevie had her arms wrapped around her middle, hands clasped around her elbows, and her eyes darted around the hallway. It was like she was expecting some kind of random attack that could come from anywhere.

Over the years of knowing her, Kyle had seen Stevie under stress. He'd seen her become stressed over what many would consider little things. He'd seen her lash out when she heard noises she didn't like or scream hysterically when someone touched her shoulder. He was used to that.

He was not used to *this*.

This quiet, tense, softly growling Stevie. This Stevie was freaking him out. It wasn't what she was or wasn't doing, though. It was her energy. An intense, dangerous energy that had the jackal in him ready to head for the hills. And his jackal side was something Kyle didn't really deal with. It was there, it was a part of him, but as an artist, he felt he didn't need it. He barely acknowledged it.

But for the first time, he felt it scratching inside him. Panicked and ready to bolt.

"Why don't you wait in here?" Kyle softly suggested, gesturing to the grand ballroom with a wave of his hand because he was afraid to touch her.

Stevie nodded and walked in. Kyle turned and started down

the hallway, but his overly familiar bodyguard yanked him back by his shoulder.

"Where the fuck are you going?" the giant panda demanded.

"To get someone who can help her."

"You're leaving me alone with her?"

"Aren't you the trained professional?" Kyle demanded, turning to face the security guard his sister insisted he have with him anytime he was away from the family. "Can't you manage one tiny woman until I get back?"

"That's not my job. I'm supposed to be managing one tiny boy."

As Kyle was at least two inches taller than the six-foot panda, he didn't take the bait. He wasn't so easily taunted into giving someone what they wanted.

"I'll be back. Keep her away from everyone."

Kyle headed deep into the house, ignoring the bear's "Wait . . . what do you mean? *What does that mean?*"

He knew where his family would be if they weren't in the grand ballroom practicing or working. The kitchen. It was where the Jean-Louis Parker clan gathered. But as he neared that room, he heard strange sounds for the middle of the day. He heard children laughing and running. Giggling and screaming.

For most houses with lots of children, these might be considered normal sounds, but not for the Jean-Louis Parkers. If they were home at all this early in the day, each of them would want quiet so that they could do their work. Usually, the only sound they tolerated was the music that came from Coop, Cherise, or their mother, Jaqueline. His older sister Oriana was a dancer, but she wore earbuds to listen to her music. So the only sounds that came from her was of her toe shoes against the floor and the occasional snarl when she couldn't get a move exactly right. His other, younger siblings leaned toward math, science, and art. All of them demanded silence and hours to work alone. Especially in the summer when they weren't forced by ridiculous government laws to attend regular schools with regular, useless children.

So what were these annoying noises Kyle was hearing?

He finally reached the kitchen and pushed the swinging door open. He immediately froze, a faint sense of panic inching up his spine.

"Shit," he said out loud.

"You cursed," a child he'd never seen before told him, pointing her finger. "You cursed. You cursed. You cursed."

Thirteen-year-old Freddy—although he preferred to be called Frederick now—pushed the child toward the back door. "Go away."

Still chanting, the kid walked off and Freddy turned toward Kyle, grabbing his T-shirt and raising himself on his toes so he could more easily look his brother in the chin.

"*Help me*," he growled.

"What is going on?" Kyle demanded, looking around the room. There was evidence of children *everywhere*. Stickiness, half-eaten sugary things, electronic handheld games . . . that were covered in more stickiness. It was disgusting!

"Mom decided we needed a playdate with the wild dog pups across the street. She and Dad felt we weren't getting enough—"

"Of a real childhood," Kyle finished for his brother. He rolled his eyes. "Don't blame Mom. This has Dad written all over it. Dad and Toni."

The only two normal people in their family, Kyle's eldest sister Toni and his father, Paul, were lovely human beings, but they sometimes managed to get in the way of "the work." And "the work" was all the rest of them cared about despite the fact that each of them focused on different things. Kyle was a sculptor. Freddy was all about physics. Family members were divided between the artists and the scientists/mathematicians, but each of them was a prodigy. All except poor Toni, his oldest sibling, and their father. They were nothing but average people with average lives.

Kyle shuddered at the thought.

"Where's Dad now?" Kyle asked.

"Out back with most of the children and a few wild dog adults."

Kyle glanced back down the hall; remembered why he was here. "You know what would be great?"

"For me to make a run for it while you distract everyone?"

"No. For you to take everyone back over to the wild dog house. For a little while."

"I don't want to do that. I want to get back to work. I thought you, of all people, would help me get back to work."

"Later. Just get everybody out."

"Why?"

"Would you trust me?"

"But I don't trust you." Freddy's eyes narrowed. "You just want the house to yourself."

"I don't, but believe what you want. Just do what I'm telling you and get everybody over to the wild dog house. *Now.*"

"Fine. But I'm not happy."

"I am aware." Kyle moved away from his younger brother and headed toward his eldest, Cooper. He was standing by the refrigerator, a bottle of soda in his hand; chatting with one of the adult wild dogs.

"Excuse me," Kyle interrupted. "Can I speak to my brother for a moment?"

"Sure!" the wild dog cheered. Then he stood there. Smiling.

Kyle took a breath. "So go away."

"Okay!"

Coop chuckled as the wild dog went outside. "Why can't you be nice?"

"I don't even understand what that means. Now, have you seen Aunt Irene today? She texted me earlier. Is she still here?"

"I think she's upstairs with Mom. Why?"

"I need her—"

The rest of Kyle's words became lodged in his throat when he glanced out one of the windows that overlooked the yard. While Freddy did his best to shepherd the annoying wild dog pups and the adults back to their own home, Kyle saw who stood by one of the tables, his eldest daughter leaning beside him, wearing a hockey jersey six sizes too big for the girl. Although Kyle had no doubt that one day, that "little girl" would grow up to be a very large and dangerous female. Just like her father.

Her father. Bo Novikov. Homicidal hockey player and great organizer.

And if Bo Novikov was here with his kids that meant . . .

"Where is she?" Kyle demanded of his stunned brother, grabbing him by his T-shirt and yanking him close. "*Where is she, Coop?*"

Wow! That had to be the best soda in the world! The Jean-Louis Parker twins had told her it was when they handed her the bottle. Even though the soda was caffeine and sugar free, it tasted so great! She couldn't believe how great it tasted!

Blayne continued to backflip her way down the hallway. She didn't know why she felt the need to backflip down the hallway of the Jean-Louis Parker home, but she did! And it felt awesome! Look how in shape she was. Even after giving birth to several *giant* children, but her shit was still tight, as they say! She should have gone into gymnastics. She would be a great Olympian! A totally positive representative of the United States of America! Why? Because Blayne loved everyone!

She loved animals! She loved shoes! She loved tiny furniture that people put into fancy dollhouses! She loved everybody! She loved the world! The world!

Blayne's legs slammed into something and she wouldn't have thought much of it except that she heard an "Oooof!" that surprised her. She landed on her feet and turned to see Shen Li holding his head.

She knew Shen! She loved Shen! He was a giant panda! How cool must it be to be a giant panda? Pretty cool, Blayne bet.

"What are you doing?" Shen asked, rubbing the entire left side of his face and glaring at her.

"Backflips!" Blayne told him. "I love backflips!"

With his hand still pressed against his face, the panda stared at her, eyes narrow. "Are you okay, Blayne?" he asked.

"I'm *great!*" Blayne turned and spotted someone standing alone in the massive ballroom entrance. She immediately felt bad for that person. They were so small and alone. But they weren't really alone! Because Blayne was here!

Grinning, Blayne charged over to the stranger and threw her arms around the woman's shoulders, squeezing her tight from behind.

"Hi! I'm—*aaaaaaaaaaaaaaaaaaaaaaaaaaaaaaaaaaaaaaaahhhhhhhhhh-hhhhhhhhhh!*"

Shen's head was still throbbing from where Blayne's feet had hit him, but in the haze of his pain he knew something was wrong with the always pleasant wolfdog. Her energy level was off the charts, which was saying a lot because Blayne always had a high energy drive.

Still, he wasn't exactly surprised when she suddenly caught sight of a very quiet Stevie, gazing forlornly into the ballroom. He—sadly—also wasn't surprised when Blayne ran up behind her and threw her arms around Stevie to give her a big hug. Blayne had become known for her attack hugs. And Shen definitely wasn't surprised when Stevie's response to that hug was to scream hysterically.

The girl panicked at squirrels. *Squirrels.* Non-attacking squirrels too.

So getting grabbed by some random stranger would make her panic, but Shen never, in a million years, ever expected what happened right after Stevie began screaming.

With Blayne on her back—and still screaming—Stevie abruptly turned, her eyes wild and panicked . . . and she began to shift.

But she shifted into something Shen had never seen before. Not ever.

The fangs came first, bursting out of her gums. He'd thought the ones he'd seen in the cabinet were terrifying. But these were worse. So much worse. Because these fangs weren't just long, they were also wide. Rows on top and bottom. To accommodate those fangs, Stevie's head shifted next. Her nose growing into a snout; her ears turning into just holes against her head; her neck expanding, muscles rippling.

Orange, black, and white fur exploded over every bit of skin. Giant, lengthy claws burst from her fingertips and her toes. Powerful muscles covered her legs and arms.

When she landed on all fours, Shen thought she was done. She wasn't.

Stevie's entire body began to grow.

And grow.

And grow.

In length and width.

In horror, Shen watched as little Stevie MacKilligan grew into . . . something absolutely *enormous*.

She was the color of a Siberian tiger, but she was still a honey badger. A giant twenty-foot-long and ten- to fifteen-foot-wide orange, black, and white honey badger with humongous paws.

Blayne had fallen off Stevie's back when she'd shifted, and, in full panic mode, the wolfdog jumped to her feet and turned to run. But Stevie brought her head down and grabbed Blayne by the back of her T-shirt, lifting her off the ground. The wolfdog screamed hysterically as Stevie tossed her into the air, then caught her by the back of her T-shirt again, letting Blayne hang from one of her giant fangs.

Unable to move, Shen watched Kyle slide to a stop in front of the open door.

"Oh, my *God*," he gasped.

Blayne, struggling to get loose, yelled out, *"Get me out of here!"*

Kyle looked at Shen. "What are we going to do?"

Shen glanced around, wondering who the kid was talking to. When he didn't see anyone and understood the kid was talking to him, he asked, "What do you expect me to say?"

"We have to do something!"

Coop ran down the hall until he reached them, freezing when he spotted what took up most of his family's ballroom.

And, unfortunately, right behind him was Bo "The Marauder" Novikov. Hockey pro, former child prodigy—of hockey—and well-known rude bastard.

He was also Blayne's husband.

"*Blayne!*" he barked when he saw his mate hanging from Stevie's fang. "What did you do?"

Blayne glared. "*You're blaming me for this?*"

"Get down from there right now!" Novikov ordered.

Poor Blayne, still hanging from that fang, threw up her hands. "Are you fucking kidding—"

Stevie suddenly shook her head and Blayne's T-shirt ripped, sending her flying into the far wall. But when she landed on the floor, she managed to get to her feet and attempted another run.

A giant paw slammed down in front of Blayne. She turned and tried to run the other way, but another paw ended that. Then the first front paw suddenly swiped the air and Blayne went flying again, only to be slapped the opposite way by the other paw.

That's when Shen understood that Stevie was playing with Blayne like a house cat playing with a toy mouse. Or a live one.

Novikov growled and gold-brown hair suddenly dropped from under his white hair, passing his shoulders. A minor lion's mane, because Novikov was another hybrid. A polar bear–lion.

The hockey pro shifted, forcing Shen to grab Kyle and Coop to yank them out of the way so the pair didn't get crushed under the big hybrid's bulk.

Roaring, gnashing his . . . tusks—yes, Novikov had what could only be called tusks coming from his maw—he charged into the ballroom, destroying the closed second door in the process.

"Stevie!" Shen yelled, pushing the Jean-Louis Parker brothers back before running forward. He didn't know what he was going to do, but he wasn't about to let Novikov kill—

Shen slid to a stop, then quickly reversed course, turning and charging back seconds before Bo Novikov's shifted body exploded through the wall.

Tossed out of the room by little Stevie MacKilligan.

"We are so fucked," Coop said softly.

★   ★   ★

Max had stopped on the sidewalk to tie her bright pink Converse sneaker. The color matched her current hair color perfectly and she liked that.

But just as she began to stand, the roar that rattled the windows of the entire block had her head snapping up and she looked at Charlie. Eyes wide, her sister stared back and together they took off down the street to reach the house they knew Kyle's family was staying at for the summer.

They went up the stairs and started banging on the door to get someone to open it, but then Charlie's grizzly came up behind them and with one kick, the door flew open.

Max followed Charlie into the house. The first thing she saw was Kyle and his brother Coop. The eldest jackal had his younger brother pushed against the wall and stood in front of him, ready to sacrifice himself for Kyle, should that become necessary.

Standing in front of the damaged entryway to some massive room stood Shen, Kyle's hired protection. The giant panda was always calm in the face of trouble, but he was definitely out of his depth now. And it showed. His eyes wide, his entire body tense. All those muscles straining and rigid. He was ready to react to anything that might happen.

And a few feet away from Shen was . . . something. Something white and gold with tusks. And out cold.

She pointed. "What the fuck is that thing?"

"*Seriously?*" Shen barked, abruptly snapping out of his shell-shocked state. "*That* freaks you out?"

"No need to get terse," she complained, moving past him. "And at least my sister doesn't have *tusks*."

Having made her point, Max headed to the entryway, Berg by her side. But she stopped him, grabbing his forearm. "Not you."

"Why not?"

"You'll just freak her out more."

"But—"

"Go to the wild dog house across the street," Kyle told Berg. "Don't let any of them come over here."

"Come with me," Berg suggested to Kyle as he headed to the front door.

"I won't leave my friend," Kyle stated dramatically, making Max roll her eyes.

"*Now* you decide to care about others?" Coop demanded.

Berg headed out alone and Max went to the entryway to stand by Charlie, where they watched their baby sister.

What could they say as they watched her curled in a ball on the floor, a human being caught between her front paws, that she kept . . . gnawing on before she occasionally flipped her prey into the air, caught her, and then rolled to her side again so she could gnaw and toy with her captive.

It seemed the woman was still alive and . . . and . . .

Max narrowed her eyes and stepped farther into the room. She knew that woman. She knew her!

Charlie was desperately trying to figure out how she could keep her baby sister out of prison for murder when Max suddenly stepped farther into the room and pointed in Stevie's direction. She thought she was going to order Stevie to put the woman down this instant but instead Max accused, "You hugged her, didn't you? *Didn't you?*"

Not dead—*thank God!*—the woman yelped, "*I was just saying hi! Now get her off me!*"

"I should let you burn! *You deserve it!*"

Shaking her head—because Charlie really didn't know what the fuck was going on—she stepped close to Max and *Charlie* ordered Stevie to put the woman down.

"Stevie Stasiuk-MacKilligan! You put that idiot woman down right this instant!"

"Hey!" the idiot woman complained while she pressed her legs against Stevie's front fangs so that they didn't go into her mouth, "that's not fair!"

"Shut up!" Charlie and Max said in unison.

Charlie stepped closer and clapped her hands together several times. "Stevie! Put her down! Right now!"

Stevie stared at Charlie for several seconds, but a roar from outside the room had their sister scrambling to her paws and rearing up on her hind legs, that idiot woman still in her mouth.

"Stevie! No!" Charlie cried out seconds before Stevie began burrowing up into the floor above.

If she got into the walls of the house, they might never find her. The fact that she was twenty or so feet long didn't mean anything. She was still mostly honey badger and she could burrow like a champ. And if she was freaked out enough, they might not find her for days. Weeks. She could end up living in the subway tunnels!

Charlie's grandfather's house was never quite the same after Stevie had her first real breakdown and burrowed into the walls. It took many days before they could get her out, but they could hear her scratching away inside the walls, and food kept disappearing from inside the cabinets.

It wasn't until Charlie had hidden some Xanax in balls of soft French cheese that Stevie finally calmed down enough to come back out and face her fears with her sisters by her side.

Charlie, however, was in no mood to go through that again. But before she could say anything, Max charged across the room and leaped up, grabbing hold of Stevie's right hind leg. Of course, Max was only about a hundred and twenty pounds while Stevie, in her shifted form, was nearly two tons.

Just as Charlie started to follow after Max, a shifter with tusks—*Tusks? Really?*—came charging into the room and over to Stevie. He leaped up and wrapped his front legs around the lower half of Stevie—all that Charlie could see at this point since the other half had already made its way into the second floor—and yanked.

Charlie turned her body away as part of the ceiling came down with the two hybrids and poor Max.

"Max!" she yelled, making her way through the debris. "Max!"

By now, a raging Stevie had gotten to her paws and was squaring off with the tusk guy. The real problem, though, was the screaming human she had caught between her jaws and didn't seem in the mood to give up anytime soon.

But Charlie would have to worry about that *after* she found out whether Max was dead from having part of a building fall on her.

Pushing aside the ceiling that was now on the floor, Charlie desperately dug. She was so focused on her task, it took her several seconds to realize that Shen was right next to her. Helping. Brave panda.

"Got her!" Shen suddenly announced while pulling. He dragged Max out from under a giant chunk of plaster. There was blood on her face and she was covered in dust and debris, but with a sudden headshake, her eyes opened and she smiled.

"That was *awesome*," she laughed, still being held up by Shen.

Charlie started to laugh with her until something hit her in the side and she went *flying*—

Shen pulled Max into his arms and scrambled back. He wanted to get to Charlie but first he had to get out of the way of the two raging hybrids.

Charlie almost hit the far wall when Novikov's big ass slammed into her, but her baby sister's very long tail reached out and caught Charlie before she could. Then she tossed her toward Shen, and he had to tuck Max under one arm so he could use the other to catch Charlie.

With both women in his arms, he jumped to the left, trying to get out of the way of the ongoing battle. He wished he could get to poor Blayne, but he didn't see how he could without being crushed in the melee. Even if he shifted, he still would be no match for these two.

At least three tons of raging hybrid fighting over a wolfdog that just wanted to get out and away.

Honestly, he'd laugh if the whole thing wasn't so terrifying.

Max pulled his arm off her waist and dropped to the ground. Then she lifted her big sister's head by the chin. Charlie was unconscious, so Max slapped her. Charlie responded by slapping her back, and Shen let out a relieved sigh, knowing that at least these two weren't dead.

Charlie tapped his arm and motioned for him to let her

go. When she touched the ground, she rubbed the side that Novikov had hit and winced from the pain. Shen was guessing that something had been broken, but he knew that wouldn't keep Charlie from stopping her baby sister's rampage.

"What are we going to do?" he asked, raising his voice to a shout in order to be heard over all the roaring.

"Any chance you have a tranq gun?" Max asked.

"I don't work for a zoo so . . . no."

"We need to get Stevie to drop her prey," Charlie reasoned. "Once we get that woman back to that thing with the tusks—"

"Really?" Shen couldn't help but ask. "*Both* of you are judging my man's tusks?"

"—we'll be able to calm her down," Charlie went on.

"Or we could startle her out of this," Max suddenly interjected.

"Startling her was what got us into this," Shen felt the need to point out.

"And startling her again might just get her out." Max gestured to the ruined entryway. "And that woman is the one who can do it."

Charlie turned and her frown was deep. "My God, what is *she* doing here?"

Shen looked to see what had the sisters so concerned and was surprised to see Kyle's mother standing in the entryway. She appeared horrified, which seemed the proper response considering what was going on. So he couldn't understand what the two women were talking about until Kyle's mother took a step back, revealing her best friend, Dr. Irene Conridge.

The famed full-human scientist walked farther into the room. She surveyed the damage and then the two battling hybrids with cold blue eyes.

Crossing her arms over her chest, she waited. For what, Shen didn't know.

Charlie grabbed his arm and started to pull him. He knew she was dragging him toward the hybrids, but he didn't know why. What, exactly, was she expecting him to do?

Novikov threw himself at Stevie, but she turned and her tail caught him around the throat. She wrenched the pro hockey player one way, then the other. Then she began banging him against the floor. Over and over.

Shen grimaced, wondering if there was any way to stop Stevie when she suddenly glanced in Conridge's direction and froze, mid-slam; poor Novikov hanging from her prehensile tail.

There was nothing but silence in the room, everyone sort of waiting. Waiting for Stevie to do something. And she suddenly did.

She flicked her tail, sending Novikov sailing across the room to crash into the wall at the far end, leaving a healthy dent before sliding to the floor and landing on his face.

Blayne, who'd been caught in Stevie's maw all this time, was spat toward the other end of the room. Then Stevie turned her big body and opened her maw.

Shen girded himself for another one of her destructive roars, but before she could do anything, Irene Conridge spoke.

"Well, well, well." Cold as ice. That was Dr. Conridge. Cold as ice. "If it isn't the little prodigy that *couldn't.*"

Shifted Stevie jerked back as if Conridge had punched her. And, in that second, she shifted back to human.

Naked and pointing her finger at Conridge, Stevie marched forward. "You . . . *you!*"

Conridge laughed. "Eloquent as always, I see."

Stevie started running toward Conridge, and Shen pushed past Stevie's sisters and caught up to her before she reached the unmoving full-human, grabbing Stevie around the waist and lifting her up. He prayed she didn't shift again. Her weight alone would crush his sturdy panda bones to dust.

"You evil cow!" Stevie spit out, her wiggling naked body over Shen's shoulder. The only way he could hold on to her was by gripping her bare thighs and, sometimes, her ass. "Did you really think you'd stop *me?* Did you really think you'd block me from getting into CERN?"

"That was a pity hire," Conridge mocked.

"*Pity?*" Stevie screeched, sounding not like the emotionally wrecked female Shen had seen the last hour or so, but more like a crazy person he'd avoid on the Manhattan streets. "*You arrogant cun—*"

"Time to go!" Shen yelled over Stevie's next insult, carrying her out of the ballroom. He stepped into the hallway, and Kyle—still being held back by his older brother—pointed at the stairs a few feet away.

Shen carried the still-screeching Stevie up the stairs. Although now her screeching was indecipherable. It was just angry yelling. There might be words in there somewhere, but he couldn't make them out.

He carried her into the first empty room he found and kicked the door closed. Then he placed her on the floor and pushed her away from the door, afraid she'd try to charge it. She didn't. Instead, she yelled, "*Pity? I was a pity hire?*"

Shen thought a moment before replying, "Soooo, we're just not going to discuss the fact that you can turn into a one-ton, tiger-striped honey badger?"

"That's right!" she immediately barked back. "We're *not* going to discuss that! And it's closer to *two* tons."

Shen nodded. "Okay then."

chapter FOUR

Charlie helped Stevie's cat toy to her feet. "Are you okay?" she asked, wincing a little when dark brown eyes lashed over to her.

"No," the woman snarled. "I am *not* okay."

"You're still alive," Charlie said, trying to sound helpful. "That's good, isn't it?"

The woman started to speak, stopped herself with a grunt, and turned away from Charlie. She went over to help the dude with the tusks, and Charlie faced her sister.

"Ooops," Max muttered. "This has turned awkward."

"Ya think?"

"What are we going to do?"

Charlie looked around at the damage to the ballroom. Half the ceiling was on the floor. Parts of the wall had big holes in it, and one section was just outright destroyed. Several windows had been blown out. The floor was scored with claw marks.

Charlie blew out a breath. "I don't know how we're going to keep a lid on this."

"Kill everybody? Burn the house to the ground?"

Charlie knew her sister was just kidding, but still. She shoved the smaller woman before facing the cat toy and tusk dude. Max skidded across the floor about fifty feet and, when she stopped, she laughed, "I was joking!"

Ignoring her sister, Charlie looked at the pair, the woman helping the now-human male up. "I am so sorry about all this."

"She's dangerous," the woman warned. She got the male to

his feet and then faced Charlie again. That's when the woman's shoulder suddenly jerked forward, a loud *snap!* ricocheted throughout the room.

"What, exactly, is going on with your bones?" Charlie had to ask.

"Really?" the woman barked, moving toward Charlie, finger out and pointing. "You are going to stand there and judge *me*?"

"Well, you have to admit it is strange."

"Strange?"

The male put his arm around the woman's waist and pulled her back, which Charlie appreciated for many reasons, but mostly because he used the woman's body to block any further sight of his dick. Something Charlie didn't really need to see at the moment.

"All I'm saying," Charlie attempted to reason, "is that as hybrids . . . we're all a little strange. So there's no reason to point fingers. Or say anything to anyone about this little incident."

"Incident?"

"Well—"

"Your sister is a menace!"

"You hugged her," Max reminded the woman when she again stood beside Charlie. "Which is the same thing you did to me at the Sports Center."

"Shut up!"

"I'm just suggesting," Charlie went on, "that we keep this among ourselves. No reason to bring in anyone else. Not when we're all a little . . . different."

"Different?"

The male suddenly sighed and told the woman, "You really need to stop screaming-slash-repeating everything she says, Blayne. It's getting annoying."

The woman spun on the male, now pointing a finger at him. *"Annoying?"*

Stevie pulled on the T-shirt that the giant panda handed her before continuing with her rant. *"That woman is such a bitch!"*

"Dr. Conridge isn't that—"

"Do you know," she cut in, not in the mood to hear him speak, "she actually wrote an article for *Science America,* in which she disputed not only my theories but my actual belief system?"

Shen frowned. "Your belief system in God?"

Stevie stared at the bear. "What God?"

"Okay," he said. "So it wasn't about that. Good to know."

Max watched the couple bicker over who was more annoying. She didn't understand people. They argued over the weirdest shit. Wasn't life hard enough without making yourself miserable over bullshit?

Kyle and his brother stepped behind Max and Charlie.

"Are you two okay?" Coop asked.

Max shrugged. "We're fine." Of course, they were used to all this. They'd been there when Stevie began shifting around the age of eleven, when she hit an early puberty. Back then, she'd shift into a honey badger the size of a full-grown tiger with, of course, those stripes.

Charlie had immediately been freaked out by Stevie's size. Afraid that the other breeds wouldn't accept her as she was. Charlie always felt the need to protect Stevie, and for good reason. But after the first time they saw their baby sister shift while she was studying for the SATs at their grandfather's dining table, Charlie's concern grew exponentially. Because Stevie clearly didn't have control over her issues. She panicked easy. She cried easy. She exploded into rage *real* easy. And when she did all three at the same time . . .

Max, however, was less worried because the one thing that Stevie had over both her and Charlie was her ability to self-analyze. She understood how dangerous she could be. How unstable. She was the first to insist on seeing a therapist, on retiring from music because of the pressure it put on her, on learning calming techniques, on getting medications to manage her depression and panic. Anything to help her deal with her issues.

Max respected that more than anything else her sister did. It wasn't easy to be that self-aware, but Stevie was. And she was good at it. What she didn't understand, she learned. She read books. She talked to specialists. She didn't shy away from her problems. She embraced them and learned how to deal with them, taking care not to lose what made Stevie the prodigy, the genius, but also ensuring that she wouldn't harm anyone.

So what had just happened, Max knew, would eat away at her baby sister. Would torture her in a way it would never torture others.

Unless . . . of course . . . she found something else to distract her first.

And while Max was trying to come up with something that would be a worthy distraction, Stevie stormed into the ruined ballroom—thankfully in her human form and in a long T-shirt—and stomped her barefooted way over to a smirking Irene Conridge.

"And let me tell you something else!" Stevie snarled at Conridge. "If you think that I—"

Shen ran into the room, placed his hands on either side of Stevie's hips, lifted her up, and quickly left. Apologizing the entire way.

"Sorry, sorry. I've got her. I've got her. No need to panic. Everything is just fine."

Even though Max couldn't see either of them, she knew that Shen carried Stevie back up the stairs because she could still hear Stevie bitching about it, complaining that he wouldn't let her go and how wrong Irene was as a scientist and a human being.

This went on until a door slammed closed somewhere in the house.

Max smiled at Charlie. "I'm starting to like that bear."

"Put me down this instant!"

Shen did as he was ordered, now that they were safe in a bedroom.

Stevie faced him, her face beet red from anger. "I am not done with her."

"I know. But I'm not sure this is the time to start raging at important people."

"Important? Irene Conridge? *Really?*"

"Look, I won't even pretend to understand what you two are bickering about—"

"Bickering?"

"—but you nearly tore this house down around a very nice family of jackals. Maybe you should take a break."

Her eyes widened and Shen prepared himself for the explosion to follow.

"I . . . you . . . if . . ." Stevie suddenly screamed. Not loudly or wildly. But in frustration. And then she sat down on the edge of the bed. "Dammit, you're right."

Shen frowned. "I am?"

"Yes. You are." She looked up at him. "Why do you find that so surprising?"

"I've been working around this family for a while now. I have yet to meet a current or former child prodigy who has ever told me that I was right about anything. You're the first."

She let out a long sigh before replying, sounding a little tired, "Because I'm even weird among the prodigies." She finger-combed her hair behind her ear. "And if I hurt you—"

"I'm fine. Not even a scratch."

"But that woman . . . is she alive?"

"Blayne?" Shen couldn't help but smile. "Trust me. If you didn't kill Blayne outright . . . she's fine."

"She scared me," Stevie admitted. "I wasn't expecting—"

"I know."

She shook her head. "Who goes around hugging strangers from behind?"

Now Shen sighed. "Blayne does."

"This is *not* my fault," Blayne Thorpe insisted to her husband.

The mammoth man had a very large indent in his forehead and was bleeding from lacerations on different parts of his body while Blayne's bones were busy snapping back into place. But neither seemed the worse for wear. Thankfully. Irene could

only deal with twenty or thirty issues at one time. A few more
and she might get frustrated.

"Look at this!" Jackie said, gesturing to the walls. "Those
wild dogs are going to make such a big deal about this."

"You do know that *you* are also a wild dog? Jackals, dingoes,
the bush dog, the coyote, and, as much as it annoys them, the
gray wolf are also included on that list. So talking about the
owners of this house like they are some lower form seems non-
sensical to me."

Jackie slowly faced Irene, her lips pursed, one foot tapping.
Eyes narrowed.

"Too soon?" Irene asked, before she snorted a little laugh
and walked out of the room.

She'd just started up the stairs when she heard Kyle.

"Aunt Irene?"

"Stay, Kyle," she ordered, chuckling when he did exactly as
she'd said.

Since no one in the family was on the second floor of
the house after the drama in the ballroom, she found Stevie
Stasiuk-MacKilligan easily, chatting with the large protector
that Kyle often used. Shen Li was one of the few people who
could tolerate her best friend's son although Irene had been
surprised to find out that he was a great panda shifter. Such an
odd breed for humans to choose to shift into . . . then again . . .
she'd just seen a giant honey badger tear apart her friend's rental
home, soooo . . .

Without knocking, Irene pushed the door open and stepped
in.

The young scientist jumped to her feet and there was a sudden and disconcerting appearance of fangs.

"You're not going to ruin this part of their home, too, are
you?" Irene asked. "Where will the children sleep?"

"Dr. Conridge—" Shen began, but Irene waved his concern
away and closed the bedroom door.

"It's all right, Shen. Miss MacKilligan and I are old friends."

The fangs receded while MacKilligan's shock grew, large
blue eyes blinking wide. "We are *not* friends."

"Is it because I often forget who you are?"

"No, you don't. And it's *Doctor* MacKilligan. Or Ms."

"Oooh," Irene couldn't help but mock. "A tiny feminist, are we? My generation breaks all the boundaries and your group comes in and pretends to be above it all?"

MacKilligan started toward her but Shen was there to catch her, pulling her back.

"Perhaps we can all meet later," he suggested. "For a tasty lunch? Or coffee!"

"Yes, that's what we want," Irene teased. "For your little friend to shift into King Kong in the middle of a Starbucks on Fifth Avenue."

"*King Kong?*" MacKilligan screeched, coming for Irene again. But the bear caught her around the waist, held her back with big, strong arms.

"How dare you—"

"I'm just joking," Irene said, not letting the girl finish. "Can't your generation of trailblazers take a joke?"

Irene moved across the room and sat in a large club chair, crossing her legs and staring at the seething MacKilligan and uncertain Li. "Now, we must figure out what we're going to do about you, little miss."

"Do about me?" MacKilligan snapped. "You mean put me down like a stray dog?"

"Trust me. If any government gets its hands on you, they'll treat you *much* worse than any stray dog. In fact, you'll be lucky if all they do is put you down."

Stevie stopped struggling in Shen's arms and stared at the woman she'd hated since she was fourteen. She'd been working on her dissertation for her first PhD. It had been suggested by one of her benefactors that she take her work to Irene Conridge in Washington State for a "frank overview." As someone who had read all of Irene Conridge's books before she was six, she was thrilled by the very idea.

Until she'd actually met Conridge. Without even looking at

her, Conridge had tossed Stevie's manuscript onto her desk and sneered, "Is that really the best you can do?"

Shocked, Stevie had taken her paper and gone home. She'd worked for a few more months before going back to Conridge.

And had gotten nearly the same response, "Really? Is this the *best* you can do?"

Another few months of work. Her sisters began to worry. Her stress level went up. But she wasn't about to be defeated. Her idol wanted a perfect dissertation, so she'd get one.

The third time she'd sent her dissertation ahead and followed a week later. With her long legs up on her desk and her black and gray curly hair in a very messy bun, Conridge had asked, "Honestly, child, is this really the *best* that you can do?"

That's when Stevie's rage had welled up. She could feel her fangs itching to break free. Her claws nearly clearing past her nails. She knew there was only one way to hold back the tiger-striped badger yearning to break free and tear a chunk out of Conridge's very human throat . . .

"As a matter of fact," Stevie had snarled, "it *is* the best I can do, you old cunt!" Then Stevie had swiped her dissertation off the desk, making sure to knock down the pictures of Conridge's smug husband and their smug-looking children, and stormed out.

The fact that the third iteration of her dissertation ended up winning nearly every award known to science for that year short of the Nobel—and she'd only lost that to an entire group from Norway who'd invented a functioning mechanical heart that worked in pigs—meant nothing. All those awards and citations and newspaper articles spouting about how she was the future of science were boxed up somewhere in her grandfather's house in Wisconsin. She couldn't even bear to look at them. Because all she'd wanted was Conridge's approval, and she'd never gotten it. Something she'd hated the old bitch for ever since.

At the time, Charlie had been terrified that Stevie would walk away from science, and Stevie had definitely entertained the thought. But, to quote Max, "She's too stubborn to give up shit."

And Max had been right. Although Stevie felt the disappointment every day, she'd refused to give up something else she loved after she'd already walked away from music.

Stevie pushed Shen's arms off her waist and walked around the bed until she could sit on it while facing Conridge.

"So what do you want?"

"To help you."

Stevie couldn't stop a harsh snort. "You? Help me? Why?"

Conridge leaned forward and said, sounding deeply earnest, "Because I love you."

Shocked, Stevie blinked and jerked back a bit. *"What?"*

Conridge laughed. "Just kidding. I barely love my children and I actually ejected them from my own body. If that's how I feel about them, why the hell would I love you?"

Shen let out another long sigh. "I don't see how this is helping anyone."

"Just be quiet," Conridge told him. "You are a very sweet freak of nature, but you don't have nearly enough active brain cells to interject yourself into *our* conversation."

Shen nodded his head. "I see why you're Kyle's favorite."

Conridge locked her gaze with Stevie's. "The boy has always had good taste *and* good sense. He brought you to me for a reason, *Doctor* Stasiuk-MacKilligan. Because I'm the one person who can and will help you without feeling the need to lock you up or put you down. Of course"—Conridge suddenly smiled and Stevie had the urgent need to make a run for it—"that situation could change at any minute."

"I don't hear anything," Kyle whispered to Max and Charlie. They were still downstairs, the kid refusing to go up after his aunt or to let them go up after their sister.

"That's because we're downstairs and they're upstairs."

Kyle, with an exasperated expression, glanced at Max over his shoulder. "That's so we can keep living. I swear, I think all you honey badgers have a death wish."

Max smirked. "Not our own deaths."

The kid's back tensed. "Stop trying to terrorize, Max!"

How could she, though? When she was just so damn good at it.

Dr. Conridge had walked out of the room but returned a moment later with a pair of jeans.

"These should fit you," she said, handing them over. "They belong to Kyle's sister. The dancer. You seem thin enough."

While Stevie slipped them on, Dr. Conridge jotted down some information on a pad from the bedside table and handed it to Shen.

"Take her here. They'll be waiting for you."

"Manhattan Behavioral Center," Shen read out loud.

Zipping the jeans, Stevie informed Dr. Conridge, "I can choose my own mental hospitals, thank you very much."

"I know you can. You and your strange obsession with checking yourself in every few months is something that fascinates the science community. But the Behavioral Center isn't a mental hospital. You'll find people there who can actually help you."

Stevie folded her arms over her chest, her gaze narrowing on Dr. Conridge.

"Why are you doing this?" she finally demanded. "We both know you're not a good person. You're not helpful. What do you want from me?"

"Do you remember Dr. Matt Wells?"

"I dated the asshole for six months. Of course I remember him."

"Bad breakup?"

"Bad enough. Max put him through a wall and Charlie ran him down with her pickup truck." She glanced at Shen, probably saw the look on his face. "He's lion."

"And?"

"That means he was asking for it."

Dr. Conridge leaned against the chest of drawers. "Would you be averse to getting in touch with him again?"

"Setting aside the fact that he's a lousy lay, an arrogant prick, and is one of those insecure men who feel women shouldn't be scientists because we're 'distracting,'" she said with finger quotes, "why the hell would I want to willingly get near him again?"

Dr. Conridge looked off, took in a breath. After a few seconds, she said to Stevie, "I think he's experimenting on hybrids."

Stevie's expression didn't change, but she suddenly shifted her weight from one leg to the other. "What makes you think that?"

"Because we keep finding the bodies."

Stevie's arms fell to her sides.

"All hybrids?" Shen asked.

"All hybrids. The Group, my husband's organization, is on it but Wells is very careful, very protected, and very smart."

"But I heard he was doing good work," Stevie said.

"In biogenetics." Dr. Conridge brushed stray hairs off her forehead. "I could be wrong about him. But we can't get close enough to find out."

"But you think I can."

"Men are men. No offense," she added, glancing at Shen.

"I'm a panda."

"Sometimes," Dr. Conridge continued, "they can't help but brag to old girlfriends. To prove that they didn't need them to be successful." She shrugged. "It's at least worth a try."

"What exactly do you expect him to tell me? 'And on the weekends, I'm Dr. Mengele'?"

"I think he has a second lab. Not in the city. We need to know where that lab is."

"All right," Stevie replied, no hesitation. "I'll see what I can do."

"There is one thing, though."

"Which is?"

"My husband has expressed concern about your sisters."

"If my sisters find out you've involved me with this," Stevie said matter-of-factly, "they'll kill you and your husband, and the cries of your devastated offspring won't interrupt their REM sleep one bit. So if I were you, I'd keep my mouth shut."

"Fair enough." Dr. Conridge pointed at the piece of paper Shen still held. "When you go to the Behavioral Center, bring your sisters. My contact will want to meet them too. Her name is Dr. Becca Morgan. A trained and highly respected psychiatrist and, I believe, some kind of cat . . . or dog . . . or something. Something furry that can do tricks if I promise her enough treats."

"How does your husband tolerate you?" Stevie sneered.

"The same way I'm sure this one tolerates you. He ignores the bullshit and focuses on the ass. At least that's how Holtz has always explained it to me."

Shen shook his head. "We're not . . . together."

"I make him uncomfortable," Stevie admitted. "He told my sister Max that his penis becomes erect every time I hug him."

"I said no such—"

But before he could finish, Stevie reached over and grabbed his cheeks. "But look at this adorable panda face! Just so cute!"

Shen gently pushed her away. "I *really* need you to stop doing that."

Dr. Conridge suddenly laughed. "Oh, look. His penis *does* become erect!"

chapter FIVE

Shen had tried to get away. From both Dr. Conridge and
Stevie MacKilligan, but he and his company had been hired
by the Jean-Louis Parker family. That meant they could assign
him to a different child or, in this case, friend, any time they
wanted.

Which was exactly what happened.

Kyle graciously offered to stay with his family while Shen
"escorted" the ladies to the Manhattan Behavioral Center.

"Why can't Berg do it?" Shen had asked, not really in the
mood to chaperone anyone at the moment. Even the MacKilligan sisters.

"Yeah," Berg asked, "why can't I take them?"

In response, Kyle simply pointed . . . up.

And he did that because Stevie was hanging from the hallway ceiling by her claws.

"Oh, come on, Stevie," Berg had sort of whined. "I thought
we'd gotten past this."

"You're an apex predator," Kyle had reminded Berg.

"You're kidding, right?" Shen had to ask. "Am I the only
one who *saw her*?"

Kyle started to reply but Stevie had unhooked herself from
the ceiling and dropped to the ground, startling all three males.
Then she was on Shen in seconds, her hand over his mouth, her
eyes wide, head shaking.

Not sure what the problem was, Shen had gently pulled her
hand off his mouth and asked, "What?"

Up on her toes, she'd glanced over his shoulder and whispered, "Just don't talk about it. Don't talk about what you saw. Trust me on this."

She'd pulled her hand away after that and moved around him, smiling as her sisters had come down the hall.

Now they were driving in silence on their way to the Behavioral Center.

The building had underground parking and the whole complex seemed to be owned and operated by the Behavioral Center. As Dr. Conridge had promised, they were expected. The bear security guard gave a grunt as he lifted the gate. His way of telling Shen to drive on.

Shen parked the SUV and followed the sisters to the bank of elevators. They stepped into the first one and took it to the twelfth floor. A pretty receptionist smiled at them as soon as they walked in.

Shen was fascinated by the reactions of each sister to such an innocent and important—for the company—business move.

Charlie smiled in return, but while she smiled her intense gaze bounced from one side of the room to the other. A predator on the lookout for any danger that might put her weaker Packmates at risk.

Max grinned, but it was the grin of a predator catching sight of prey that had no idea how much danger she was in. The honey badger wanted to "play," but Shen wasn't going to let that happen.

And Stevie? She stopped in her tracks, eyes narrowing on the receptionist, expecting the absolute worst from that smile. Seeing all sorts of danger where there was none. That was Stevie's major problem in Shen's opinion. She saw no danger where there was danger—like taking Bo Novikov's wife for her own personal cat toy—and believed there was major danger where there was none. Like with the poor receptionist.

"Dr. MacKilligan?" the female asked Stevie before the sisters could say a word.

Now glaring at the woman—and Shen knew it was because she was trying to figure out how the woman knew her name . . . so smart and yet so honey badger—Stevie started to bare a fang, but Shen leaned past her and said, "Yes. This is Dr. MacKilligan."

"Excellent. Dr. Morgan is waiting for you, Dr. Mac—"

"We're all coming," Charlie abruptly cut in.

Max, who was in mid-sit on one of the couches, a recent copy of *Rolling Stone* in her hand, sighed loudly before straightening and tossing the magazine aside.

"That's not necessary, Charlie," Stevie stated quietly.

"Together or we *all* leave," Charlie insisted.

"Don't argue with her," Max said, heading off down the hall. "Let's just get this over with."

"Wrong way," the receptionist called out, smirking when Max spun around and came back, crossing by the desk and heading down the other hallway.

"Get that look off your face," Max warned, "before I rip it off your head."

Charlie and Stevie followed Max, and Shen went to a couch and dropped on it.

The receptionist, still smirking, asked, "Would you like some bamboo tea, sir?"

He grinned at the fox. "That would be awesome."

Dr. Becca Morgan sat across from the three females who'd come to her office.

Conridge, an old associate she'd never have called a friend, but whom she understood well because prodigies and geniuses were one of her specialties, had warned her that the two women would invite themselves into the appointment.

"They are very protective of their sister."

She understood. Child prodigies—former and current—often had protective families. Usually the parents but sometimes siblings or a spouse. Even when the prodigy was grown up, almost an elderly adult, they often had some relative fluttering around them, attempting to protect the genius from themselves. Totally understandable.

But as the eldest—who seemed to speak for the group—

gave the backstory of her youngest sister while the middle sister sat there, studying Becca's office with curious, plotting eyes, and the youngest kept her eyes completely shut while she softly chanted something to herself the entire time, Becca realized this was not a simple case of "former prodigy with protective family."

Not even close.

This was something completely different that needed her immediate attention.

As much as she hated to admit it, Conridge had been right when she'd said, "Trust me on this . . . you're going to love this one."

"And that's it," Stevie heard Charlie say to Dr. Rebecca Morgan, a psychiatrist with an impressive reputation and a list of books that she'd written or cowritten that could fill an entire bookstore shelf. She was a much respected practitioner with degrees from Wellesley, Harvard, and Columbia. Plus a Rhodes Scholarship. "And that's it?" Dr. Morgan repeated back.

"Yes."

There was a moment of silence, but Stevie barely noticed it because she was busy reciting the chant she'd been using the last few weeks: "Please don't eat me. Please don't eat me. Please don't eat me."

She was chanting it to herself because she'd found it was the only thing that kept her from screaming and running out of the room anytime she had to be around bears she didn't know. She didn't mean to be scared of fellow shifters. She didn't *want* to be this scared of them, but she couldn't help it.

Grizzlies and polar bears were known *maneaters*. Something Stevie simply couldn't get past. That at any moment, they could shift to their animal form and pop her in their mouths like a Tootsie Roll! Unless she shifted herself and destroyed the entire building.

A situation that also wouldn't end well for her.

"What is she doing?" Dr. Morgan asked.

"She's chanting," Max replied. "She's afraid of you."

"Me?"

"You're a bear. And bears eat people."

"So do tigers."

"That doesn't matter."

"Okay," Dr. Morgan suddenly announced and Stevie heard something hit the floor. It sounded like Dr. Morgan's feet.

Had she been sitting at her desk with her feet up while Charlie had been telling their story? Was that normal for a mental health expert?

"First," Dr. Morgan went on, "open your eyes, Dr. MacKilligan. *Now.*"

Stevie managed one eye.

"*Both* eyes, Dr. MacKilligan," Dr. Morgan insisted.

It took a few seconds, but Stevie did it. Making her kind of proud of herself.

All six feet, three inches of Dr. Morgan still sat behind her desk, her arms on the wood, her fingers interlaced. Brown and gold hair reached below her ears without any real style to it. In fact . . . she might just cut her hair herself. Her glasses didn't look like the latest style either. They were just big, which probably made it easy for her to read lots of books and paperwork. But they made her already big brown eyes look even bigger. She had to be nearing sixty, but she was a very healthy and *strong* nearly-sixty-year-old.

"Let me see if I understand this," the psychiatrist began. "All three of you ladies are half-sisters because your father is, to use your words, Ms. MacKilligan, 'a whore that can't stop fucking anything that moves.' When you were still adolescents, your mother"—she gestured to Charlie—"and the woman who adopted you two"—she gestured to Max and Stevie—"was brutally murdered in front of all of you. Forcing you three ladies to make a desperate run for your lives, by yourselves, across country, to get to the safety of a wolf Pack that really only tolerated you two." Again, she gestured to Max and Stevie. "Because of your father, all three of you have had to protect each other, and sometimes—I'm assuming based on the vagueness of your wording, Ms. MacKilligan—you've killed people."

"I never said *killed*," Charlie replied.

"Uh-huh." Dr. Morgan stared at Charlie for nearly a minute before returning to her point. "And even now, all three of you are again in danger because of your father. And despite everything that has been going on—in the past and present—*she*"—she pointed at Stevie—"is the only one that needs a therapist. Did I get that right?"

"Yes," Charlie and Max said in unison. When the doctor focused on her, Stevie shrugged.

Dr. Morgan let out a sigh and stood. "Okay."

Watching the woman stretch so easily toward the ceiling, Stevie started to chant again, but Dr. Morgan's sharp, "Do *not* shut your eyes," made her stop immediately.

She came around the desk and motioned to Charlie. "Please," she asked nicely, gesturing toward the door.

After reassuringly rubbing Stevie's shoulder, Charlie stood and headed out the door. Dr. Morgan also gestured to Max, but she just shrugged and said, "Nah. I'm fine."

The doctor reached over Stevie—and she couldn't help but cringe away from her—and snatched Max up by the back of her neck. She held the tough extra flesh there that was part of the honey badger's defenses.

"Hey!"

Dr. Morgan ignored Max and carried her out the door. That's when Stevie's chant changed.

"Please don't eat my sisters. Please don't eat my sisters. Please don't eat my sisters."

Dr. Kelly Lewis was in the middle of texting her mate a recent shot of her tits when there was a knock on her office door and her business partner walked in. A young, black woman was with her. She sort of smelled like wolf, but then again . . . she also didn't. It was weird, but Kelly was used to weird. She liked weird.

She was a wolf that liked weird, which was good because the other weird thing was that Becca had a snarling, snapping honey badger dangling from her right hand.

Kelly didn't know why and she wasn't about to ask. She liked things to just unfold.

"This is Dr. Kelly Lewis," Becca said to the young woman she ushered into Kelly's office. "She'll be helping you."

"I don't need help," the woman replied.

"Oh, my sweet girl," Becca laughed. "You so do."

Then Becca and the violent badger were gone.

Kelly gestured to the free chair across her desk. "Please. Sit."

"Look," the woman began without sitting, "I really don't have time for this and I'm really just here for my baby sister since she's the one who really needs help . . . not that I don't need help or whatever . . . I'm sure everyone needs help at some time in life and I'm no different, but I have so much going on and like with my aunt who keeps calling me but I don't want to deal with that right now, because she's probably calling me about poor, dead Great-Uncle Pete . . . or maybe she's calling me for something else, but I can't imagine why after we kept that polar bear from ruining my cousin's wedding . . . of course, couldn't have won that fight without Berg . . . then again we could have but not without killing the polar and his friends, which I'm glad we didn't have to do because that would have really ruined the wedding and I'm sure Berg wouldn't have liked that at all, which I would have hated because I really do love him . . . so much . . . and I like and am learning to love his siblings, but they're triplets and the other two are always around, lurking, and you have no idea how off-putting it is to turn around in your kitchen and find three extremely large grizzlies standing behind you . . . lurking . . . but I guess it could be worse . . . true, the twin aunts no one knew about are trying to kill us, and I'm just waiting to find out how my father has fucked over our lives again with his unbelievable stupidity and someone is always trying to kidnap Stevie . . . plus Berg's dog has this weird hacking thing going on and I want to get him to the vet before that turns into something, and I think there's something wrong with the plumbing with our rental house, which, of course, has me again thinking about saving money so that I can actually purchase a house, plus life is a nightmarish gamble of car accidents and falling air conditioners and plane parts so you really need money for those unplanned scenarios that can occur at any time and, not to be too broad, but what about world politics and our risk as a country of getting into more wars and how long before there is a strike on American soil, which may or may not affect my sisters because we do travel a lot so we could be out of the country, but that doesn't really protect us, now does it . . . but then again—"

"Okay," Kelly finally cut in when she began to become concerned the woman would keep talking until every bit of air left her body and she would end up slumped over dead on Kelly's very expensive rug, which she'd had flown in from Israel less than a month ago. "I'm going to stop you here and suggest that we start with something a little simpler than world politics and your dog's hacking problem."

"Simpler? Such as?"

Kelly gave a little smile before suggesting, "Oh, I don't know. Maybe . . . your name?"

Dr. Deb Ortiz-Paredes was marking corrections on her latest manuscript when her door was kicked open and Becca stomped into her office with a threatening honey badger dangling from her fist.

"I've got one for you." She dropped the badger into a chair and then held the poor woman in place by pressing her hand against the top of her head. It was like she was trying to squash her.

"I have quite a full plate," Deb replied, trying very hard not to laugh.

"Ohhhh, it doesn't matter. This is one you make room for. Trust me."

Deb placed the proofs on her desk aside and studied the growling female under Becca's hand.

As a forensic psychologist who specialized in sociopaths and criminally violent schizophrenics, Deb knew that Becca had wonderful instincts . . . plus Deb had another book due after the one she was currently working on. So maybe her friend and business partner of the last fifteen years had found Deb her next study subject.

"Okay," Deb told Kelly. "I can take it from here."

"Great." Kelly walked out, closing the door behind her.

The badger still sat in the chair, her gaze searching the room.

"So," Deb began, "Ms.—"

"MacKilligan."

"—Ms. MacKilligan."

"Just call me Max."

"Fine. Max. So what brings you here, Max?"

Deb expected a lot of "I don't belong here" type stuff, but that didn't happen. Instead, the woman's gaze slid across the room and over Deb's desk, until those dark, *dark* eyes locked on her, and the badger said nothing. Just stared at her.

Grinning, the jaguar leaned back in her chair and said, "Let's begin . . . shall we?"

Dr. Morgan returned to her office, closed her door, and came over to her desk. She sat down and let out a sigh before grabbing a fresh legal pad from a stack on the table behind her desk. She spun her chair around, took out a pen, and looked at Stevie.

"Okay, Dr. MacKilligan," she said, smiling at her. But, for once, Stevie didn't feel threatened by that grizzly smile. It just seemed . . . friendly. Nice. Just a nice smile . . . from a man-eating grizzly bear. "First, let's talk about what you need from *me*."

chapter SIX

When Shen found the little rip in the wallpaper behind his head and began to pull at it—he thought maybe something was behind it and he wanted to see!—the pretty receptionist who had become a lot less nice the longer Shen sat in her waiting room came over and slapped his hand away.

"Can you not sit still for three minutes?"

"It's been like ten hours."

"Less than an hour. Just sit. And stop playing with everything. You're worse than the grizzlies!"

Still bored, Shen took out his phone again and went to his favorite news sites, then checked his texts. A full-human woman he had been trying to set up a date with had finally gotten back to him but—to his horror—she was suggesting dinner with her parents. Shen couldn't tell if she was trying to get him to run away screaming or was seriously asking him to dinner with her parents. For their first date.

Unsure, he forwarded the text to his two sisters. Kiki responded first with one emoji after another. All of them suggesting she was laughing hysterically at him.

Zhen texted back a simple message: *RUN FOR YOUR LIFE.*

Shen was trying to figure out how to nicely decline the date since he didn't like the idea of being one of those guys who simply didn't respond. He had two sisters who had been forced to deal with assholes like that for years, and he wasn't about to become one himself.

But before he could gently explain that he had to move

back to China for the foreseeable future, the three sisters returned to the waiting room with what seemed to be three different therapists.

So each sister had gotten her own therapist? That actually made sense to Shen. A lot of sense.

The sisters stood silently as Stevie's doctor arranged additional appointments and handed her a prescription slip. "You can get this filled downstairs. You'll need to use our pharmacy, of course."

Stevie nodded, but that was it.

Once done, and without a word, they headed to the elevator and went down to the pharmacy on the first floor. Another twenty minutes there to get the medication and then they were on the road heading back to Queens.

The sisters said nothing the entire way home, each looking out a window.

Shen stopped at the McDonald's near the Queens house and picked up a few burgers and several large orders of fries. Each sister declined to order with a shake of her head and continued silence.

He parked the SUV in front of the house and everyone got out. Shen dropped off his food on the coffee table in the living room. He walked to the first-floor bathroom, washed his hands, then went to the refrigerator in the kitchen and grabbed a bottle of water. On his way through the dining room, he grabbed one of his duffel bags filled with bamboo stalks and returned to the living room.

Putting the food out and turning on the television, Shen only took one bite of his Quarter Pounder before Stevie suddenly walked into the living room, turned, and proceeded to scream back toward the dining room.

Shen tried to understand her, but then Charlie and Max joined in and the three sisters stood right in the archway, just screeching.

Screeching so intensely, the veins on Stevie's neck bulged, appearing ready to explode. Her face was beet red and she was talking with her hands. Well . . . screeching with her hands.

All three gestured wildly but Shen had no idea what anyone was saying because they were not only screeching but screeching fast. Like speed-screeching.

After about three minutes of this, Stevie suddenly leaned her head back, and the roar that exploded from her throat shook the windows and . . . maybe . . . the entire house? Shen wasn't positive but the roar was powerful.

Charlie and Max stopped their own screeching. Stevie lowered her head, and, slicing her hands through the air, announced, "That. Is. It!" There was a long silence, and the MacKilligans stared at each other until Stevie added, "You both know what I'll do. And you both know I'll do it. We're not having this discussion again."

"I need to bake," Charlie announced, heading to the kitchen.

Max just walked away, the back door slamming shut a minute later.

Stevie, her jaw tight, stood in the archway for another two or three minutes until she finally sighed and swung her giant backpack off her shoulder. Digging around for a bit, she eventually pulled out the paper bag she'd gotten from the pharmacy. She took out the bottle of pills and read the label.

"I need to take this with food."

Shen picked up one of the Quarter Pounders and held it out to her, but Stevie's nose crinkled in distaste. "No thanks."

She turned, started toward the kitchen. Stopped when she heard pots banging. Spun around and headed toward the front door, but the local stray cat came charging in from one of the open windows, followed by a shifted Max, who didn't seem to care it was the middle of the day.

"Leave that cat alone, Max!"

A few seconds later, they heard Charlie bark, "*Max!*" and then the back door opened and closed, probably meaning the cat and the badger had been tossed out of the house.

With a long sigh, Stevie faced Shen and he motioned to the pile of burgers he had on the coffee table, again offering what he had.

Stevie came over and picked one up. "Thank you," she said

with a sigh and moved back to the other side of the room, heading toward one of the wing-backed chairs across from Shen. She was turning to sit down when big hands slapped against the window, causing Stevie to scream and drop the burger as one of the MacKilligans' grizzly neighbors put his face close to the glass and yelled, "Is your sister baking? I thought I heard baking noises!"

Shen shook his head, annoyed with his fellow bear. He would think the locals would have stopped doing that sort of thing by now. The MacKilligan sisters were not the kind of women a bear, cat, wolf, or man would want to startle. They made the horror of grizzly-boar rage seem like a toddler's temper tantrum. Not only because Stevie shifted into . . . whatever the hell it was she shifted into, but also because her sisters didn't really bother with shifting when they were startled or confronted. Charlie had a way with firearms that he hadn't seen even from trained military professionals, while Max did love her edge weapons. She could slice and dice like an old-school butcher, but she moved like a dancer or gymnast. And she really enjoyed it. She enjoyed hurting those who hurt or attempted to hurt those she loved.

That made her more than a predator. It made her a killing machine. A shark in a honey badger body.

Shen picked up the SUV keys, his wallet, and sunglasses, and walked over to a panting Stevie, who was trying desperately not to panic. He slung her backpack over his shoulder and took hold of her arm.

"Come on," he said, pulling her along behind him.

"Where are we going?"

"To get you some food and a break from . . . everything." He glanced back at her. "I think after the day you've had, we can both agree that you deserve it."

Coop placed a plate of cookies in front of his twin sisters, Zia and Zoe. He then sat down across from them while his sister Cherise poured milk into two tall glasses.

"We need to discuss this," Coop said. Twin sets of brown eyes stared at him. "You do understand that what you did was wrong, don't you?"

They chewed Oreos, their mouths moving in unison, while they continued to stare and not answer. It was something they did to unnerve people. Even blinking at the same time. And all that did unnerve Coop. But he refused to let nine-year-old brats terrorize him by pretending they were live-action dolls from *The Shining*.

"Are you listening to me?" he demanded.

The expressions on those cold, blank, adolescent faces suggested that no they weren't listening to him. But those expressions changed when an arm came around Coop's shoulder and a hand slammed onto the table, making the twins jump and their eyes go wide.

Toni, Coop's eldest sister, who'd been called home after what they were now calling "the incident," leaned down so she could look right into the twins' faces.

"Do you two know what you did?"

Instead of attempting to intimidate Toni—something that would never work on the She-jackal who ruled this family with an iron paw—they began making excuses . . . and lying. Lots of lying.

"Quiet!" Toni barked after a minute or two of said lying. She threw her messenger bag behind her, uncaring there was a laptop inside. Luckily, her wolf mate, Ricky Lee Reed, was standing behind her and caught the bag before it hit the floor. "I don't want to hear another lie from either one of you."

Zia began to lie in . . . Russian? Coop wasn't positive. And Zoe chose to lie in French. As language prodigies—to the point where they'd created several of their own—that was their go-to move when they knew they were caught. But Toni knew the twins' moves better than she knew her own.

"*That is enough!*" Toni bellowed.

The twins immediately stopped speaking, looking down at the kitchen table.

"I can't believe that you two would do something so stupid and *mean* as poisoning Lame. And she's always been so nice to you two!"

Zia frowned. "It's Blayne."

"And we gave her soda, not cyanide," Zoe stated.

"Knowing what that would do to her! Have you seen the living room? The living room we do not own!"

"That wasn't our fault!" Zoe argued.

"Yeah. That was that giant thing!" Zia pointed in the direction of the damaged living room. "It was trying to kill her!"

"You hopped up Blayne on sugar," Coop reminded his sisters, "and then she startled poor little Stevie."

"Not our fault," Zoe said while Zia shook her head. Neither willing to take blame.

"Bullshit."

A little shocked, they all looked at the end of the table toward Cherise. When no one said anything, she reiterated, "Bullshit. They know it"—she pointed at the twins, then at herself— "and we know it."

"And if you think this is the end of your problems—" Toni began but was cut off by a scream coming from the second floor.

Toni looked around the room. "Mom? Aunt Irene?"

"Went over to the wild dog house," Coop explained. "They haven't come back."

"The boys?"

"Went to the library."

"Alone?"

"Dad took them. They won't be long."

Kyle ran into the room and stood behind Cherise's chair, using her as his human shield.

"Really?" Coop had to ask.

"She has that crazy look in her eyes and I'm willing to sacrifice Cherise to save my beautiful, beautiful hands."

"What about my hands?" Cherise wanted to know.

"Oh, please," Kyle huffed. "You play the cello. The *cello*."

Their twenty-one-year-old sister stomped into the kitchen holding a pair of jeans in each hand.

"Where is it?" Oriana demanded, glaring at everyone.

"Where's what?" asked Toni, the only one among them brave enough to talk to Oriana when she was like this.

Oriana had been a little on edge lately. A ballerina prodigy since she was five, Oriana had finally gotten her chance to dance with the Fuller-James Ballet Company of Manhattan and was well on her way to becoming the company's prima ballerina. However, that position was currently being held by a tough full-human Russian who had been playing this game a lot longer than Oriana had. That was hard for Coop's younger sister. Oriana had always gotten everything she'd wanted in the dance world, and her battle with the lead dancer was—from what Coop had heard—getting pretty nasty.

He knew his younger sister too. Knew she would never give "some bitch" the pleasure of seeing her sweat, which Coop completely understood. There was a twelve-year-old Italian prodigy pianist that Coop called "The Asshole" every time the kid showed up on TV.

So he knew what his sister was going through. Unfortunately, unlike Coop—who took his rage out on his piano or by playing video games on his computer that required him to kill a lot of zombies or World War II Nazis—Oriana tended to pour her rage and panic into being obsessive. And she could be pretty obsessive. Like now.

Shaking her clothes at her family, Oriana barked, "Where are my jeans?"

"You're holding them," Coop kindly pointed out, which nearly got his head bitten off.

"Not these jeans, you idiot! The jeans *between* these jeans. Those are the jeans I want! I had them organized in a certain way, I go to class and rehearsal, and come back . . . and now things are displaced. *Why are they displaced?*"

Cherise muttered, "Wow," and lowered her eyes so as not to challenge her fellow canine.

Toni raised her hand toward Oriana, palm out. "Maybe you should calm down."

"I want my jeans back."

"How about I buy you a new pair of jeans?"

"I don't want a new pair. *I want the pair that belongs between these two!*"

"You need to stop yelling!"

"I'll yell if I want to!" Oriana screeched, her voice so high that the twins began to yelp and howl in response.

"I'm sorry," Kyle interrupted, unable to help himself. "You notice your jeans are 'displaced'"—he said with air quotes—"but not that there's a giant hole in the middle of the grand ballroom?"

"Did my jeans cause the giant hole?" Oriana asked.

"No."

"Then I don't give a fuck! I just want my jeans back!"

Now the three oldest siblings muttered together, *"Wow."*

They walked into the Panda Garden restaurant and all the employees called out, *"Shen!"*

Stevie took a step back, ready to bolt, but a moment later she knew she wasn't in danger. These weren't grizzlies and black bears. These were giant pandas. The cutest of all bears! As far as Stevie was concerned.

But she knew when she said that, it always annoyed Shen, so she kept the words to herself.

Shen greeted everyone in the restaurant with a wave of his hand before walking to a table and pulling out a chair for Stevie. She sat down and he took the seat catty-corner from her.

"Hiya, Shen." Dorie, the waitress's badge said. She had two menus in her hands.

"Hey." He took a menu, but began rattling off a list of food without even looking at it. And all of it involved bamboo. Bamboo lo mien. Bamboo chow fat. Stir-fried bamboo. Steamed bamboo. Sliced chicken and bamboo.

"And you?" Dorie asked Stevie.

"Three orders of chicken with mushrooms and steamed rice. No honey anywhere near my food."

"Three orders?" Shen repeated, smiling.

"I'm hungry," she admitted.

Dorie took the menu back from Shen and walked away, then she returned and asked Stevie, "I know what he wants, but what do you want to drink?"

"Oh. Uh. Water, please. Bottled."

"Sure."

When she was gone, Stevie added, "I really want a beer, but . . . I don't know if that's a good idea."

"With new meds? Probably not."

"Exactly."

The water arrived and, once the waitress had again gone away, Stevie pulled the bottle of new meds out and took two pills. Her doctor wanted her to take two for her first dose. "To do a hard reset of your system," she'd said. After that, it was once in the morning and once in the evening. Always with food and lots of water.

After gazing at the pills for a long moment, Stevie blew out a breath, popped them in her mouth, and drank several gulps of water.

She put the bottle down, carefully placed her hands on the table, and looked up to find Shen watching her closely.

That's when her head hit the table and she went completely limp.

"Holy shit!"

Shen reached across the table to lift Stevie up and get her to the closest shifter-friendly hospital he could find. But as soon as he had hold of her shoulders, she began laughing.

"Are you joking around?" he demanded.

Stevie sat back, still laughing.

"The way you were looking at me," she said around her laughter, "it was like you were waiting for me to die."

Shen sat back down. "Stop fooling around."

His grumbles, though, only made her laugh harder.

Dorie came back to the table, gaze bouncing back and forth between them before she asked, "I forgot, do you guys want soup?"

"Sizzling rice with chicken," Shen said automatically, abruptly realizing Stevie had said the same thing at the same time.

They smiled at each other and Shen felt . . . something he wasn't used to feeling. Like this "zing." Her smile gave him a zing. He didn't get a lot of zings.

Stevie pulled out a folded piece of paper and slowly opened it. She sighed, gazing at it.

"What's that?"

"A list from my doctor," she said, smoothing it out on the table. "Things she wants me to do as well as taking my medication."

"Tough stuff?"

"No, but ridiculous. Like she wants me to meditate."

"I heard meditation is great."

"It's awesome. I make Charlie do it to help with her anxiety. But I already meditate."

"You do?"

"Yeah." She stared at him for thirty seconds. Shen kept waiting for her to say something and she finally did . . . "Bam! Just meditated."

"Right. Of course." Shen cleared his throat. "What else is there?"

"Make friends." She looked up at Shen. "Make friends? I have friends."

"Do you?"

"Yes. They're all forty- and fifty-year-old scientists from China and Russia and South Korea . . . but they're my friends."

"Do you see them when you're *not* working?"

"What does that have to do with anything?"

"Okay. What else?"

"Casual time with my sisters." She gave a hard shake of her head. "Is she kidding? I spend *all* my time with my sisters."

"Yeah, but do you spend *casual* time with your sisters? Like, going out to dinner at a restaurant or binge-watching movies while lounging on the couch? Or do you only spend time with your sisters when they're either protecting you or you guys are running for your lives?"

Again, she stared at him for about thirty seconds. Not to meditate, though. "*Fine!*" Stevie snapped. She again looked down at the sheet of paper. "Okay, what about this? She wants me to start exercising." She threw her hands up. "Exercising? Me?"

"Why not you?"

"First off, I don't need to. I'm a shifter."

"But you have no muscle tone."

"I do too!"

"No. You don't. And you come from two very muscular species. Look at Max. She's honey badger and she is one big muscle, from her head to her toes. Like a pit bull. And Charlie has those wolf shoulders. I've seen smaller linebackers in the NFL. But you . . . like a twig." He tapped the table with his forefinger. "You know, this is a great place to start. Exercise. We can do that."

"We?"

"You need friends and you need exercise. I can provide you with both."

She grinned. "Sex?"

"Why would anyone want to have sex with a stuffed toy?"

Stevie blew out a breath. "You're really not letting that go, are you?"

"That you referred to me as a stuffed toy? No."

"As *cute* as a stuffed toy. It was a compliment!"

"I'm not going to let you make me feel bad because I'm super cute. The survival of my species relies on our super cuteness. Do you think the Chinese government would be fighting to protect us if we weren't so damn cute?"

"Shen's right," Dorie said, carefully placing the big bowl of steaming soup onto the table, followed by two smaller, empty bowls. "The Chinese government adores giant pandas. Both shifters and full-bloods. In fact, there's a port city right outside of Shanghai . . . panda only. No hunting allowed. Or bamboo stealing. Death penalty offense."

Dorie held up a bowl of rice. "Ready?" she asked.

Shen nodded and Dorie poured the rice onto the soup. The sound of sizzling rice filled the air along with the fragrant scent of the soup.

"My absolute favorite," Stevie sighed out.

And there went that smile again. And the zing.

That goddamn zing.

"And that was my morning," Irene finished with a one-shoulder shrug.

Van blew out a breath. "You know, I really thought being threatened with an actual skinning would be the more interesting story. I was wrong."

"I have to agree. And she threatened to flay you. That's the correct terminology."

He placed his elbow on his desk and rested his chin on his raised fist. "Because that's the most important part of this conversation."

"It is." Irene leaned back in the chair and crossed her legs. Van, unable to help himself, growled.

Irene smirked. "Stop that."

"You started it." He lowered his arm. "So did you tell my cousin?"

"Ric?" she clarified, since Van had a lot of cousins. "Of course not. Because I knew he'd tell the psychopath."

"He calls her his wife."

"The biggest mistake we could make would be to eliminate Dr. Stasiuk-MacKilligan simply because she's a giant freak of nature that could destroy half this city in record time."

"But you're essentially trying to turn her into a honeypot. Is that really any better?"

"Than dying at the paws of Dee-Ann Smith? Yes. And I am *not* turning her into a honeypot. I didn't tell her to have intercourse with him."

"Do you really think Wells will tell her anything?"

"You know all about wolves and bears and cats, but I know male scientists. If he thinks for a second he can impress her, he'll tell her anything."

"And if her sisters find out what you've talked her into?"

Irene shrugged. "Then we get Dee-Ann and her Irish cat friend involved. But not until we have to. As a last resort."

She brought her hands to her face, rubbed her forehead. "I'm afraid we will have only one chance at this."

After they gorged themselves on some of the best Chinese food Stevie could ever remember eating, they walked down the street to stop at a local ice cream place.

Stevie had been here before. Bears came here a lot but there were lots of full-humans, too, allowing her to feel much safer.

The place was pretty packed on this summer day, but Stevie managed to find them a table near the back. She ordered one of the delicious banana splits and Shen got something called "the Panda Palace." She didn't ask, but she was sure bamboo was going to be involved.

Once the waitress had gone to get their orders, Stevie asked, "Can I talk to you about something without you telling my sisters?"

"Why would you ask me that?"

"My sisters are concerned about me right now and they'll ask you questions when we get back or later tonight when they think I'm asleep. They'll get you when you least expect it, and before you know it, you'll be telling them everything I said, but I don't want to have this conversation with them for a reason. It's something I need to work out for myself, but I need to talk to somebody about it and Kyle's not here."

"You do know Kyle's seventeen, right?"

"What does that have to do with anything?"

"He's a child. He should be coming to *you* for advice."

"He does come to me. And despite Kyle's age, he's a very thoughtful young man. I, personally, believe that he'll be a philosopher in his later years."

Shen rolled his eyes and his lip curled in disgust before he let out, "Ech." He motioned to her. "So what do you want to talk to me, a grown man, about?"

"Have you ever thought about what your life would be like if you didn't shift?"

"No, because I know what it would be like. It would be miserable."

"You think so?"

"Yeah. Nothing is more awesome to me than"—he leaned in and lowered his voice—"shifting and hanging from a tree limb, in the sunshine . . . or snow and just being me. Oh!" he suddenly added. "Even better, getting a big ball, wrapping myself around it, and just rolling around a yard."

"Seriously?"

"It's the best. What do you like to do when you are . . ." He glanced around, saw the full-humans and vaguely finished, ". . . your other-self?"

Stevie gazed at the panda for several seconds before she admitted, "I like to play with Blayne. Or something Blayne-like." She leaned forward. "Human toys are the best because they kind of fight back. And the screaming weirdly entertains me."

"I get that. But that's a typical predator thing."

She nodded. "I guess."

"I wouldn't worry about it."

"Why?"

"At the end of the day we're all human. When I"—he cleared his throat—"*change*, I'm still me. I still know what I'm doing."

"You mean you have control."

"Right."

"But what if you don't?"

"But I do."

"Yeah, but *I* don't."

"Wait . . . I don't . . ." Shen shook his head. "What are we talking about here?"

Stevie leaned in. "What if, with medication, I could stop shifting . . . forever?"

★　★　★

Max, covered in stolen honey and bee stings—and some of those truly aggressive bees that just wouldn't let go—trotted through a hole in the back fence that she'd created and cut through the yard. When she reached the front fence, she shifted back to human and batted off the bees, pulled out the stingers, and leaned against the fence.

That's when she caught sight of Berg and Dag circling an Escalade that had parked in front of the house.

The bears on this street didn't like strangers in general, but since Max and her sisters had moved in, they'd been extra protective. Something that Max found extremely entertaining.

"I smell cat," Dag announced to his brother.

Berg leaned in and took several sniffs against the window. "That's a big cat . . . and . . ." He sniffed a few more times. ". . . And cheesesteak."

"There's cheesesteak?" Dag pressed his nose against the glass again. "That's definitely cheesesteak."

"We could order cheesesteaks from Jersey Mike's."

"Yeah . . . but I'm hungry *now*. And the window is open a little." Dag forced his hands between the window and the metal of the vehicle. He then pushed hard, forcing the window down with a squealing sound that made even Max cringe a little.

Dag only managed to get it halfway down and couldn't get his massive body inside. Although it was humorous to watch him try.

After the third attempt, Dag stood and stared at his brother over the top of the vehicle. Some unspoken words passed between the two triplets.

Berg went to the back of the vehicle and, again, after looking at each other, they both squatted down and Max watched, her mouth wide open, as the brothers lifted the Escalade up and tipped it toward Dag. Everything that was inside came rolling toward the window.

"Shake it left," Dag ordered.

And they did. They shook the Escalade to the left.

"Right."

Then the right. Then left again. Like someone trying to shake a certain color out of a box of M&M's.

When none of that seemed to work, they dropped the vehicle and Berg went to stand by his brother's side.

"Maybe we should just call Jersey Mike's," Dag suggested.

"Yeah. But we still don't know whose Escalade this is." Berg wrapped his hand around the inside of the open part of the window. "Maybe if it's unlocked we can just—ooops."

Max closed her eyes and lowered her head, giving herself a moment so she didn't laugh out loud. Hysterically. But the vision of that bear standing there . . . holding that door in his hand . . . because he'd pulled it off the Escalade, was something that would be burned into her mind until she died.

"That was an accident," Berg said—and Max believed him.

"I know," Dag replied. "But since it's open anyway . . ."

Dag leaned in and, eventually, ended up crawling inside, followed by Berg once he leaned the door he'd been holding against the SUV's back end.

Together, the pair began to rip apart the inside of the vehicle, still looking for those cheesesteaks. Oh . . . and information. Apparently.

Max heard footsteps and looked to her right. A male was walking toward her, grinning as he eyed her naked body. The bears on Carthage Street had seen Max naked so many times, none of them reacted to it anymore. But this guy . . .

He stopped next to her and leaned against the fence, his elbow resting near her face.

He was good-looking and, Max could now smell, a male lion. A handsome, muscular cat who probably adored his foam green Escalade the way the dogs in their house loved their rubber toys.

"Hey," he said, flashing a handsome grin. "How you doin'?"

Max could have played with him. But she wasn't really in the mood. It had been a long day already and she just didn't have the energy. So she simply nodded her head toward his SUV and watched the cat's gold eyes grow impossibly wide before he took off running.

"Hey!" he screamed. "What the fuck—"

By the time the lion reached the SUV, Berg had already gotten out . . . and stood up. He was at least six-ten and wide. Oh, so very wide.

That didn't seem to bother the proverbial king of the jungle . . . and New Yorker. He started yelling at a shocked—and a little hurt—Berg.

"What are you? Stupid? What the fuck are you doing in my truck? Who the fuck do you think you are?"

Dag got out, holding an empty brown paper bag. Max was guessing that bag had once held the cheesesteaks the bear kept smelling.

"Oh, what?" the lion demanded. "You think you and your boyfriend can scare me? You two think I'm afraid of you?"

But the Dunns really weren't the problem. Nope. It was what surrounded the lion.

Max cleared her throat—she was still naked so she figured he'd notice anything she did at the moment—and he spun to face her, but instead faced an annoyed Britta. Although the bond of the triplets had not been tested quite as much or as doggedly as the MacKilligan sisters' bond, Max had no doubt that Britta would go as far as Charlie should her two brothers ever be at risk.

And the male lion sensed that.

"Well—" he began.

But that's when more bears showed up, slowly surrounding the cat. Britta was clearly angry, but the others were just curious. They didn't like cats on their territory, but they really only chased the pack of wolves that lived several blocks over because the howling annoyed them so much.

Max watched the cat closely from her little spot, noticing how he kept his hands down by his sides. But his fingers twitched. Not a lot, but just enough to tell her what she needed to know.

The front door to the house opened and Charlie came out. She stood on the stoop and called out, "Hey, guys. There's stuff on the table in the backyard if you're interest—"

Most of the bears were gone before she finished her statement, jumping over the fence and tearing across the yard to reach the table in the back.

The Dunns, though, were still standing there. The boys confused, Britta just glaring.

That's when Charlie said, "I've kept some stuff in the kitchen, but they'll find it if you guys don't get it now."

Britta moved first, ramming her shoulder into the cat's before she walked off toward the house. Her brothers soon followed, after Berg handed the SUV door back to the cat.

"Really?" he demanded of the bears' backs.

Now, it was just the cat . . . and Max. While he tried to figure out how to put his door back on—useless, she'd heard the metal hinge bend then break—Max climbed over the fence and crept up behind the lion. She waited until he sensed her, and then she grabbed him by the shoulder and rammed her foot into the back of his leg. He dropped to one knee with a short roar and Max pressed her claws against the cat's neck. Right by the artery.

"Why are you here, kitty?" she asked.

"I'm just visiting—"

"Don't lie to me. I'm not a bear. I'm not a cat. I'm definitely not a dog. And if you don't think I'll tear your throat out and bury you in our backyard beside the tree the bears use to scratch their backs . . . you are woefully wrong. So I'll ask you one more time. Why are you here?"

He didn't answer right away, so Max pressed her middle claw into his neck, just above the artery, making sure she scraped it.

"I'm Katzenhaus," he angrily growled out.

"And what's a Katzenhaus kitty doing in bear-ville?"

"Watching out for you three freaks."

"Really? Well, good job!" she laughed. "Because we both know it's not just you." She used her free hand and pointed. "There's a kitty there. And there." She leaned over him and pressed her finger against his nose. "And there!"

He pulled his head back. "It's for your protection."

"Of course. I'm sure it has nothing to do with my Uncle Will coming to town."

"I don't know what you're talking about."

"Liar, liar, I'll set you on fire." He tried to pull away from her, but she yanked him back. "Look, you can't be here. The bears aren't going to be okay with that, and you should know better than to have empty food bags in your car. That's only going to attract more bears. *But* your friends can stay where they are, if you want. Just keep in mind that if they do anything to upset my sisters"—she grinned—"I'll kill all of you. And, in case your boss didn't tell you, I'm *really* good at that. Now all my sisters are good at it, too, but *I* don't have a moral issue with wiping out the lot of you. Do we understand each other?"

"I understand you're nuts."

Max nodded. "Then we do get each other." She stared at him a moment until she finally had to admit, "Your hair is amazing." She removed her claws from his throat and buried both her hands—claws now retracted—into his gold mane and ran her fingers through it. "Look at this thing. It's so thick and well-conditioned!"

The cat pulled away from her so quickly, he slammed into his own SUV.

He pointed at her. "Stay away from me."

"Do I make you uncomfortable?" she asked.

"Yes!"

"Good. Remember that feeling . . ." She grinned again. "Hopefully it won't be your last."

Max turned her back on him and headed to the house. Fresh clothes were waiting for her on the swing, but the house dog—she could never remember the dog's or the dog's girlfriend's names—had put his big body on top of them.

"If I asked you nicely to move . . . would you?" All that got her was an eye briefly opening before the dog went back to sleep.

Shrugging, Max walked naked into the house to get another set of clothes and see if her sister had saved her anything with honey in it. She had her hand on the banister of the stairs that would take her to her room when Britta walked out of the kitchen, a giant, half-eaten honey muffin in her hand, crumbs around her mouth.

"Katzenhaus?" she asked.

"Katzenhaus," Max replied.

She heard Charlie talking to Berg in the kitchen, so Max added, "Keep it between us, huh?"

"Sure. But if they bother you . . . come to me."

Max nodded. "Will do."

She jogged up the stairs and walked down the hall to her room, smiling as soon as she entered.

The plate sat on her side table, a pile of still-warm honey buns waiting just for her.

"It's stupid. And if you think it's not stupid, you're stupid too."

Stevie was shocked. She'd never seen Shen truly angry at . . . anything, actually. He'd certainly never been really angry at her. Not like this.

"I'm just trying to—"

"I know what you're trying to do and it is *stupid*."

"I didn't mean to upset you," she said softly, eyes downcast on her now-melted banana split.

"Do not try that lost-little-girl thing on me. It won't work."

Annoyed he'd caught her, Stevie shoved her split away with a flick of her finger and dropped her forearms on the table.

"Fine," she snapped, gaze focused directly on him. "What do you want me to say?"

"Say you won't do this. Say you won't talk about it again. It's wrong and you know it."

"What's wrong? What do you think I'm talking about?"

Mirroring her, Shen dropped his forearms on the table and leaned in. "Genetic engineering."

Stevie couldn't hide her surprise. He even had the terminology right.

"Don't look at me like that. I'm not stupid. And I saw *The Boys from Brazil*," he added in a whisper.

Stevie crossed her eyes. "Seriously?" she demanded. "You think I'm trying to clone Hitler?"

"You're trying to change who you are. You talk about using medication, but you're really talking about that ex-boyfriend of yours. Who's killing people, by the way. No wonder you agreed to work with Conridge. I should have known."

"But what if he's figured out something?"

"By testing on unwilling victims?"

"We don't know they're un—"

"Stop. You know, you act like you're something that has to be fixed. There's nothing wrong with you."

"I have anxiety, depression, and panic attacks. And with a thought, I can change into a two-ton thing that no one in this universe has ever seen. I could have destroyed a city block this morning."

"But you didn't. What you need to do is manage that side of yourself like you manage your anxiety and panic attacks. Learn to control it. Like the rest of us do."

"I'm not like the rest of you. In so many ways."

"Right. You're a genius. And if you wanted to, you could *create* something that could demolish an entire city block."

Stevie couldn't help but smirk. That's what got her picked up by the government when she was still a kid. They wanted her science so they could do just that. Destroy city blocks. But she'd burned all her notes and refused to help them.

"Since your brain is so dangerous," Shen went on, "maybe we should fix that. Cut out the part of you that makes you smarter than almost anyone else in the world."

"That's ridiculous."

"Is it? Because that's basically what you're trying to do to yourself. What you are, what you can become, is just as important a part of you as that brain you're so arrogant about. If someone said they wanted to 'fix that' would you want me to stop them?"

Stevie hated Shen at the moment. She hated him because he was right and they both knew it. And she hated him for not letting her do this thing. This thing that would protect everyone. Especially her sisters.

"But Max and Charlie—"

"Would beat the living *shit* out of you if they knew. That's why you didn't want me to tell them in the first place."

"Will you tell them?"

"Not if you promise not to do it."

"But basic research—"

"No. I mean it, Stevie. I won't say anything to your sisters, but if you start down this road ever again . . . I will get a bullhorn and stand in Charlie's kitchen and yell it while she's baking."

Stevie dropped back in her chair. "Fine."

"Good." He reached across the table and picked up the melted banana split, holding it aloft for the waitress.

When she arrived he said, "Could you get us a re-do of our orders. We got so into our conversation, we never had a chance to eat."

"Sure. But you know we'll have to charge you."

"No problem, sweetie." Shen grinned at Stevie and she could see his front fangs peeking out. "It's my treat."

chapter SEVEN

She'd stopped speaking to him and they'd eaten their desserts in silence. Angry silence. But that was okay. He was fine with her being angry. He preferred an angry Stevie to a self-destructive Stevie. And what else could he call what she'd been planning for herself but self-destructive?

He parked the SUV and got out. By the time he stepped onto the curb, she had stormed her way up the house's front steps and now stood on the porch, staring at the swing where Max was sitting.

Shen moved in beside her and turned, quickly taking a step back. "What happened to your face?"

"Don't get so dramatic," Max complained, ignoring the large diagonal skin tear from her forehead, across her nose, to the opposite jaw.

"Max," Stevie said with a shake of her head. "You can't keep getting into street fights with that cat."

"A cat did that to you?" Shen asked.

"That fucking thing is rabid."

"It's not rabid," Stevie replied. "Although if you are so concerned about rabies, you really should stop chasing those squirrels."

Shen pointed at her face. "You really should . . . clean that."

It was like the cat had dug in all the claws from one paw and just ripped downward at an angle. A few more hours and the wound would go septic.

"Don't worry about my face." Max lowered her phone. "Where have you two been?"

Knowing the constant bickering between Stevie and Max, Shen could only imagine the reply Max would get from her baby sister, but he never expected—

"On a date!"

Max raised a brow at Shen but he immediately shook his head. "No, we weren't."

"You took me out to eat," Stevie replied calmly. "That's a date."

"I was being nice."

"That is so cute," Max said, now grinning. The effort made her wounds bleed. "What else did you guys do?"

"Then he took me out for ice cream."

"That's totally a date, dude."

"We did *not* have a date."

Stevie held up her middle and forefinger and said, "Two desserts. He bought me *two* desserts."

"Awwwww. That is so cute!"

"And we're going on a date tomorrow."

"We are not!"

"You promised to take me to the Sports Center tomorrow morning," she said, appearing completely innocent when she was not innocent at all! "Didn't you?"

"Yes. I guess I did."

"The Sports Center, huh?" Max glanced at her sister, then asked, "You think she's kind of fat? She needs to lose a few pounds?"

Shen frowned. "What? No! Of course not."

Stevie put her hand on his shoulder. "He said if I wanted to be his girlfriend, I'd have to be a certain weight. I have to lose at least another twenty."

He started to argue, but quickly realized they were just messing with his head. Which Shen did not appreciate. He already had sisters who used to torture him like this while he was growing up; he didn't need to experience that again.

"I'm going inside."

"No kiss good-bye?"

He growled and started toward the front door, but an SUV pulled up at the curb and one of Kyle's sisters came storming out from the driver's side.

Kyle came running out after her, but she was fast. Not surprising. She was the dancer.

She came up the stairs and went right to Stevie.

"Give me my jeans," she ordered.

"Pardon?"

"You heard me."

"Sorry, sorry, sorry," Kyle chanted, going around his sister and standing by Stevie's side. "Stevie, you remember my sister."

"Oh." Stevie smiled. "Hi. Nice to meet you."

"We've met. Now give me my jeans."

"Your jeans?"

"The ones you took from the house earlier today."

"Ohhhh." She nodded. "Right. I borrowed them."

"Right. Now give them back."

Berg and Dag came from around the side of the house; Berg's gaze on Shen's, the pair cringing at the same moment.

"Well," Stevie glanced down at herself, "I'm still wearing them."

"Take them off."

"You may want me to wash them."

"She's not wearing panties," Max explained, clearly enjoying herself. "She's gettin' pussy juice all up in your jeans!"

"Max!" Stevie barked.

"Ewwwww!" Kyle's sister whined. "Get them off! Get them off! Get them off!"

"Look, my idiot sister is right. I'm going commando here. Let me throw them in the wash first. I'll get them to you tomorrow."

"But I want them now."

Stevie looked at Kyle.

"O-C-D," he replied.

"O-C-D?" she clarified. "Or O-C-D personality disorder? Because those are two different things and—"

"I know what the differences are."

"And? Which is it?"

He shrugged. "Let's put it this way. She's one good trauma away from full-blown O-C-D."

"Oh. I see."

"You two do know I can hear you, right?"

"But do we *care* that you can hear us?" Kyle asked. "That is the true question."

"I hate you."

"Look," Stevie interrupted, "I hate to do this, but you'll get the jeans tomorrow."

"Why tomorrow and not now?"

"Do you want them washed first?"

"Yes."

"Then tomorrow."

"Why?"

"Because I'm about to fall asleep and I'm going to be out for a few hours."

"What are you talking about?"

But Stevie didn't answer Kyle's sister. Instead, she held up one finger and called out, "Shen?"

That's when Shen jumped forward, his arms out, and like a freshly cut tree, Stevie just went down.

When he caught her in his outstretched arms, she was already snoring.

"Is she okay?" Kyle's sister asked, actually showing concern.

"She does this sometimes," Max said, going back to her phone. "After one of her . . ."—she briefly glanced around—". . . episodes. Just drop her in bed, Shen. She'll be fine."

Shen picked her up in his arms, glaring at Max. "She needs to lose a few pounds? What's wrong with you?"

"I was joking! God!"

"No wonder that cat hates you."

"That cat is trying to kill me!"

"I don't blame her!" Shen barked before he went into the house.

As he headed into the dining room from the living room and moving toward the stairs, Charlie came out from the kitchen.

She smiled when she saw her sister. "I'm surprised she lasted this long."

"Does this happen often?"

"No. But she had a full day in a few hours. That's exhausting and she ends up sleeping like a male lion."

"Look, Kyle's sister is here. She wants her jeans back."

"Okay."

"The jeans your sister is wearing. I'm not taking them off her."

"I thought you two were dating."

"Wait . . . what . . . I . . . huh . . . I don't . . . wait . . . *what*?"

Charlie laughed. "Calm down. I heard you guys talking when I was in the living room." She held out a plate for him filled with some of her freshly baked pastries. "Here. Take this. And I'll take this."

Reaching over, Charlie easily lifted her sister out of his arms and unceremoniously dumped her over her shoulder. The eldest MacKilligan sister might only be half She-wolf, but she'd definitely gotten that canine strength.

"Try these," she said, pointing at the pastries he held.

"I'm not really a honey bear . . ."

Her lips pursed in annoyance. "I know that. These are bamboo buns. You may hate them, though, because I kind of created the recipe from different things and borrowed some of your raw bamboo. And if you hate them, you can tell me. But I felt bad that you're here all the time and everything is so grizzly-centric. Pandas deserve treats too."

Yeah. He really liked Charlie. She was awesome.

"Thank you. That's really sweet."

"Enjoy," she told him before slapping her sister's ass—which didn't wake her—and hauling her up the stairs.

Once alone, Shen picked up one of the buns, sniffed, and took a little nibble; which gave him nothing. So he took a bigger bite and chewed. Before long his eyes were rolling to the back of his head and he was moaning. Charlie MacKilligan had managed to combine sweet bun yumminess with bamboo crunchiness.

See? She. Was. *Awesome.*

Charlie put her sister down on her bed and began to tug off the jeans.

"Wait," Stevie muttered. "I'm awake."

But she wasn't. Not really. She still managed to push herself up, though, and stand.

Charlie crouched in front of her and pulled the jeans down. Stevie attempted to help by lifting her legs, but she *kept* lifting her legs. Like she was marching with a band. It was ridiculous and made Charlie laugh.

"Do you think Shen likes me?" Stevie asked, still mostly asleep.

"I think he likes you a lot."

"Do you think he's too old for me?"

"Do you remember what I did to the professor I thought was too old for you?"

"That was mean," Stevie said.

"It was, but when it comes to sex, men only learn when you hurt them very badly. Besides," she added, finally tossing the jeans aside, "he got to keep his legs. Just had to wear a cast for a few . . . months."

"Still mean."

"But back to your original question, notice I haven't done something like that to Shen."

Stevie, wearing only a T-shirt, started to march her way over to the bedroom door. Charlie quickly caught her shoulders and turned her around.

"Let's get you changed for bed, sweetie."

"Okay."

Charlie went to the dresser and grabbed a pair of shorts and a little T-shirt. "Besides, regular guys your age just irritate the hell out of you."

"True."

Charlie turned around and discovered her baby sister dancing. Well . . . it was more like standing and bopping, her head going from side to side, her little hips wiggling. Stevie was listening to the music in her head. As powerful and real to Stevie as Charlie's car radio. It was her gift, music. And since she'd been here, in this big house in the middle of Queens, New York, Stevie had been moving back toward her first love.

Charlie didn't know if that meant Stevie would be going back into that world. A world that had been hard on her. Cruel, sometimes. So Charlie wasn't sure she wanted her baby sister to return to it. But, as always, Stevie's career was her own. Her choice. Her decision. Her risk. Charlie, as her mother had told her, was Stevie's protector. She was there to make sure her little sister was safe to do her work. Whether it was music or science.

Charlie only became involved beyond that when what Stevie was involved in could harm innocent people. But from an early age, Stevie understood how dangerous she could be and acted accordingly. She never wanted to hurt anyone. She just wanted to help people.

"Put these on," Charlie ordered with a smile.

Stevie tugged the shorts on and removed the T-shirt she'd gotten from Kyle's house earlier that day. Charlie didn't know if that belonged to Kyle's crazy sister, too, but it was best to get it now rather than having to wake Stevie up later. That dancer was clearly . . . intense. She wanted her jeans. Charlie could hear her barking orders about her jeans from the living room.

Was it really that hard just to buy a new pair of jeans?

"Now this," Charlie said, handing Stevie's T-shirt to her.

She pulled it on and sleepily smiled at her sister. "All set."

"You feel okay?"

"Waiting for me to die?" she asked.

"What? No! Of course not."

"I pretended to die at lunch."

"Did you scare poor Shen?"

"You know I hate when people watch me take my meds. It's too much pressure."

Charlie shook her head. "That poor guy. You're not going to be an easy girlfriend."

"But I've kind of made up my mind."

"Then there we go." Charlie kissed her sister's forehead. "Now go to bed. Get some sleep."

"Okeydokey!"

Charlie rolled her eyes because only her sister ever used that ridiculous term.

Stevie crawled onto the bed and when she reached the middle, she suddenly dropped; her face buried in the bedding.

Charlie picked up the jeans and T-shirt and walked to the door, opened it. That's where she found the two dogs. Berg's purebred Caucasian Shepherd Dog, Benny; and the rescue he'd adopted to keep Benny company, Artemis.

"You two waiting for me?" she asked, but the dogs ran past her and jumped on the bed to lie down on either side of Stevie, who was already snoring.

Knowing that the pair would be watching out for Stevie for a few hours relaxed Charlie completely, and she left the door partially open so the dogs could get in and out as needed.

Charlie reached the first floor and went toward the front of the house. When she stepped out on the porch, she held up the jeans.

"Here you go."

Kyle's sister stared at the jeans. "Do they still have pussy juice on them?"

Charlie, shocked, started to ask what the fuck she was talking about, but then she turned and looked at Max. When Max started laughing, Charlie simply went back inside and headed toward the laundry room.

Shen decided to get in some "sun time." That's what his family had always called it. Sitting outside in the sun, usually by water, and enjoying their bamboo. With family, it was a time to catch up with each other. When you were alone, it was time to just be.

He'd always enjoyed the "just be." It kept him calm. Happy. Unlike other shifter breeds, pandas preferred the quiet life. They preferred sitting around all day, reading or watching TV and eating their bamboo. Jobs were obtained and kept for survival, but there were few pandas that saw their jobs as the end all, be all of their lives. The only things that mattered to a true panda were bamboo and family.

"Aren't you uncomfortable like that?" a voice asked. And Shen could tell, merely from how superior that voice sounded, it was Kyle's sister. It had to be a Jean-Louis Parker prodigy. They all sounded like that except Toni, Coop, and Cherise. The three oldest. Whatever their parents did right with those first three, they didn't quite manage for the rest of the brood.

"If I were uncomfortable, I'd move," he replied.

"I see."

Hanging upside down from a tree limb, Shen stretched out his arm and grabbed one of the bamboo stalks from the pile beneath him. He unleashed his fangs and bit down on the stalk, breaking it into pieces. He picked one piece and went to work on it.

"How can you eat all that bamboo?"

"Why do you ask so many questions?"

"How do you learn without asking questions?"

"Except none of you ask questions because you're actually curious. You've already made up your mind. You're just putting your judgment in question form. It's irritating, in case no one has pointed that out to you."

"No. People have pointed it out to me. I just choose to ignore them."

"Why are you here?" Shen finally asked. "I was enjoying my day."

"Just killing time until my jeans are washed, and you didn't look like you were doing anything."

"Gee, thanks."

The back door of the house opened and Kyle yelled. "Your phone is ringing."

Before Shen could ask the idiot to bring him his phone—since he was hanging upside down from a tree—Charlie yelled from the kitchen, "I said to take the phone *to him*, you idiot!"

"I'm not his servant."

"Kyle!"

"All right, all right."

Kyle started across the yard and Shen's phone started ringing again. Shen recognized the ring. It was chosen specifically for his oldest sister. What he was hoping, though, was that Kyle wouldn't look at the caller ID because—

"Wait." Kyle stopped walking, gawking down at the phone. "Do you *know* Kiki Wen Li?"

Actually, her name was Ming Wen Li but, when she was four, she apparently informed their mother that everyone was to now call her "Kiki" as she would not answer to anything else. Their mother had thought it was a phase. It had not been a phase. Thirty-three years later . . . she was globally known as Kiki.

Now, of course, the question was whether he told Kyle the truth. Of course, lying would only put the kid off for so long. It was the modern age. If Shen lied, the kid just had to hit the Net to find out the truth. So why put off the inevitable?

"She's my sister."

Kyle dropped to his knees, eyes ridiculously wide. "Why didn't you ever tell me?"

"Why would I tell you that?"

"I thought you were just some useless, big-muscled wall to protect me from the plebes. But you know and are related to Kiki Wen Li. *The* Kiki Wen Li."

"What the hell's a plebe?"

Kyle sighed, shook his head. "Poor Kiki. She must be starving for real discourse if *you're* her family."

"Hey."

Kyle jumped up and ran to Shen's side. "You have to introduce us."

"Why would I ever do that? You just insulted me."

"With a word you don't even know," Kyle's sister interjected.

"I hope your jeans are *destroyed* in the wash."

"You need to introduce us," Kyle continued on. "Your sister will *want* to meet me."

"Why would she want to meet some kid?"

"Some kid? *Some kid?*"

"Now you're going to get it," Kyle's sister muttered.

"I am *not* some kid," Kyle ranted. "I am Kyle Jean-Louis Parker. The future of art. I *am* art. Entire buildings will be dedicated to my work, like shrines to a god. Never forget that."

What was really entertaining was that his sister was saying the words along with him. Exactly. So this was a standard speech apparently.

"I am not introducing you to my sister." She had enough leeches wanting something from her. Shen wasn't about to add some brat who thought he was the god of art.

"Then good luck finding your phone," Kyle snarled before turning and walking away.

It took seconds for Shen to drop from the tree, walk up behind the little brat, and pick him up by his throat. He turned Kyle around to face him and unleashed his fangs. Sure. He was a giant panda who mostly ate bamboo, but he was still a carnivore. Not only that but raw bamboo was hard as hell, making panda jaws—and the muscles that controlled them—one of the strongest among their order. Even stronger than the hyenas. Although his polar and grizzly brothers—not surprisingly—beat pandas in the bite strength competition.

But Kyle wasn't a hyena or a bear. He was a jackal. Tall and a little skinny. Stronger than almost any full-human but not in Shen's league, and they both knew it.

Shen removed the phone from Kyle's hand and, looking up at him, reminded the kid, "Don't fuck with me, little man. Stay away from my sister."

"Got it," Kyle squeezed out.

Satisfied with that, Shen dropped the kid and started back toward his tree. Kyle's sister cut in front of him. He thought she'd start yelling at him like Toni would, but no. She simply held out her hand.

"Hi. I'm Oriana."

He shook her hand. "Nice to meet you."

She glanced down at her younger brother picking himself up off the ground.

"I think," she said, "we're going to get along *great*."

It was late when Stevie woke up. She stumbled out of bed and made her way down the dark hallway to the bathroom. She peed, washed her hands, and stumbled back into bed. That's when she realized she wasn't alone.

She turned over and smiled into the dark corner near the window. "Hi."

"Hi."

"What are you doing here?"

Shen shrugged. "Just making sure you're okay."

"You don't have to stay. You must be bored sitting in the dark."

"I've got my phone. I only turned it off when you got up."

"Watching or reading?"

"Reading."

"Really? What?"

"Uh . . ." He turned his phone back on, the light illuminating his face. "*Their Life's Work: The Brotherhood of the 1970s Pittsburgh Steelers.*"

Stevie worked hard not to cringe. "Oh. Um . . . you do know there are other books to read than just . . . sports ones? Right?"

"Yeah." When she just continued to stare at him, he added, "My grandfather was a big Steelers fan. Loved Mean Joe Greene. Used to love showing me old footage of the best plays."

"Awww. That's sweet."

He shrugged again, turned off his phone, putting him back in darkness. But she was made up of two nocturnal animals. She could see him perfectly.

"Do you need anything?" he asked. "Water or whatever?"

"No. Thanks." She turned back over and snuggled under the sheet.

"If you get tired of the chair," Stevie suggested, "you can always get in here with me."

"Yeah . . . well . . ."

"Unless the dogs come back."

There was a long pause. "Excuse me?"

"The dogs. They were here earlier. They get first dibs. But you're welcome too."

"Wow. Thanks. That's big of you."

"No problem. Anytime."

"As long as I don't bother the *dogs*," she heard him mutter.

Stevie buried her face in her pillow, hiding her smile—and her laughter.

chapter EIGHT

Stevie woke up the next morning feeling better than she had in ages. The meds prescribed by her new doctor didn't make her feel worn down, but they also didn't make her feel confused or out of it.

The medications were a compound mix of chemicals and herbs that were based on Stevie's genetic makeup. Unlike her German doctors, her current doc knew exactly what she was and what that meant. Dr. Morgan was able to give her something made specifically for the human, badger, and cat within.

Bouncing out of bed, she hit the shower and was dressed and ready for action by the time Max came stumbling into the kitchen. Only her sister didn't come from her bedroom. She was coming from outside, her face and chest covered in more deep scratches and her leg viciously . . . chewed?

"What happened to you?" Stevie demanded, a jug of orange juice gripped in her hand.

Max paused in mid-limp, eyes blinking, before—after several seconds—she replied, "Nothin'. Why?"

"You been in a fight with that stray cat again?"

"She threw the first paw!" Max suddenly exploded.

Stevie held up her free hand. "I can't, with you. But Charlie's gonna freak out when she sees you."

Max stopped again, realizing Stevie was right. Their sister was going to freak out when she saw Max, and Stevie knew that Max did not want to hear it.

Max faced Stevie, looked her over. "What are you doing right now?"

"Shen and I are going into the city. To a gym. To work out," she finished when Max kept staring. "The doctor suggested it. More exercise."

"More? How about any?"

Stevie let out a frustrated breath and began to turn away.

"Wait ten minutes," Max asked. "I'll go with you."

"Why?"

Max started limping by, but abruptly stopped again. "What do you mean 'why'?"

"Why. Why do you want to come with us? Because you want to join a gym in Manhattan or because you want to make sure my meds are working?"

"What if I do want to make sure your meds are working? Isn't that *my* responsibility?"

Insulted, Stevie slammed the jug of juice onto the table. "First off, it's *not* your fucking responsibility."

"I—"

"And second, I'm going to a goddamn gym. Not a school for bears trained to startle."

"It's not just about your meds, idiot. We're still in danger."

"And I'm going with a trained security dude. I think I'll be okay."

Max limped close and Stevie covered her nose and mouth with her hand. She had to. It seemed the stray had sprayed Max in the chest.

"*Dude,*" she said between her fingers while trying to hold her breath. "The funk!"

"Look," Max went on, ignoring Stevie's struggle to breathe, "Shen likes you. Maybe too much to protect you the way you need to be."

"What are you talking about, and could you step back?"

"I have one job, boo. And it's to keep you alive. Because if something happens to you, Charlie loses it. And if Charlie loses it, no one is safe. Don't you get that?"

"But . . ."

Stevie shook her head, unable to take another second. She placed her hand against Max's face and pushed, sending her sister across the room and into the wall hard.

"Sorry," she said. "The funk. I just can't." She took a few steps back for even more distance before she went on. "That being said, I appreciate your protection, but it's a gym. I'm just looking for something I'll enjoy."

"And to spend some time with Shen?"

"Is that so wrong?" she barked.

Max rolled her eyes. "Then I'd better go. Because if I don't go, Charlie's gonna go. And if Charlie goes, you won't get anywhere with that panda."

Stevie had to admit Max was right. Annoying, but right.

"You'll bathe first?" she had to ask.

"If you insist—"

"I'm insisting."

"Fine. Don't leave without me."

Max finally made it out of the kitchen and Stevie was able to drink some damn orange juice. She stood by the open window—*ahhh, fresh air and funk free*—gazing out at the back-yard when she saw the stray cat that had probably sprayed her sister in the chest.

Stevie went outside and, with the cat watching, placed a bowl of water and an open can of tuna in front of the animal.

She smirked down at the feral beast. "You've gotta work on your aim, cutie. So next time you can nail her in the face." Stevie laughed, impressed with anyone or anything not afraid to tangle with Max MacKilligan.

She'd started back to the house when the Dunn triplets' two dogs came running around the corner. They did this most mornings, coming from the Dunn home across the street so that they could roll around in the grass, pee on every tree, and take enormous shits in the middle of their lawn because there was no way that two dogs with the combined weight of nearly three hundred pounds could take small shits.

Thankfully, one of the Dunn siblings always came over afterward to clean up because none of them wanted to hear Charlie screaming, "*Why do your mini horses keep shitting in our yard?*"

Normally, Stevie would leave the dogs to their own shit-making devices because who wanted to stand around watching dogs crap everywhere? But the cat . . . she'd almost forgotten about the cat. Worried the pair would go after the feral animal, Stevie rushed toward it, ready to scoop it in her arms to protect her . . . or him. She really didn't know which. But before she could reach the creature, the cat stood over the can of tuna, arched its back, and gave the craziest sounding hiss-snarl Stevie had ever heard.

Both dogs stopped and stared at the cat, but when they didn't do anything, the cat gave that hiss-snarl again and charged them. Like a tiny bull.

And the dogs ran! They disappeared around the house, the cat hot on their heels.

Stevie had just started to laugh at that cat chasing off two giant dogs when the back door swung open and Charlie ran out, screaming, "*Stevie don't!*" But when she spotted Stevie just standing there, Charlie stumbled to a stop . . . and simply stared.

When her sister didn't say anything, Stevie asked, "Stevie don't what?"

"Uhhh . . ."

One of the windows on the second floor flew open and a naked, wet Max launched herself out, legs and arms spread wide. And, as she fell, she yelled, "*I've got herrrr—ow!*"

The *ow* came when Max landed face-first on the lawn, body spread-eagled.

The best part of it all was when the cat returned to eat her tuna she made sure to walk across Max's back on her way to the can.

And Stevie would have laughed hard—if she wasn't so pissed off.

"You thought I shifted," she guessed.

Charlie winced before admitting, "We heard that weird noise you make just before you shift."

"What weird noise?"

"I don't know. Kind of a growling hiss or something. It's weird . . . but distinct."

"That was the cat."

"Right." Charlie nodded her head and adamantly added, "The cat inside you, which we *respect*."

"Not the cat inside me," Stevie bit out, her jaw tight with annoyance. "The cat." She pointed at the cat now enjoying the tuna by Stevie's leg.

Charlie gazed at the animal a few moments before suggesting, "You really shouldn't feed strays. Now we'll never get rid of her."

Stevie stepped in close to Charlie. "So I sound like a feral cat to you?"

"Only when you shift," she insisted.

"How does that make it better?"

"Uh, look, I just think—"

"So I've lost so *much* control, after all these years, that I would shift in the middle of our yard? That's what you are also saying?"

"You changed your meds," she said meekly.

"And yet," Stevie went on, "despite my grotesque shifter size—"

"No one said grotesque."

"—I still sound like a feral cat that weighs about eight pounds?"

The sisters stared at each other until they heard Max say, "I'm okay. Don't worry about me."

"We won't," Stevie and Charlie said together, then Stevie stormed back into the house, dropping into an empty chair at the kitchen table.

Kyle was on the other side, eating toast and sipping juice. Catty-corner was a still–waking up Shen who was in the middle of downing a big bowl of cereal, which normally wouldn't be something Stevie cared about except for the crunching. So much crunching.

"What kind of cereal is that?" she demanded when she couldn't take it anymore.

"Grape-Nuts," he muttered.

"Without any milk?"

Shen looked into his bowl . . . as if he wasn't sure. "No, there's milk."

"He added bamboo to his cereal. That's the noise you're hearing," Kyle explained.

"Well, it's annoying the fuck out of me."

Kyle's eyebrows went up but he knew better than to say anything. Instead, he focused on buttering more toast.

Shen, however, gazed deeply into her eyes . . . and continued to chew. Loudly.

Shen didn't know what Stevie MacKilligan expected. That he would stop eating? Bears never stopped eating. Because they were always hungry. It was even worse for giant pandas because bamboo wasn't nearly as filling as a good steak sandwich. But he didn't have nightlong dreams about sitting in a field of bamboo that went on as far as the eye could see and eating steak sandwiches.

And if there was one thing he would *not* let Stevie do, it was interrupt his bamboo-infused breakfast.

Thankfully, their staring contest didn't go on for too long because Charlie walked in through the back door. As soon as the door opened, Stevie's gaze moved to the far wall and she crossed her arms over her chest. Then she didn't move.

Charlie stopped behind Stevie, opened her mouth to say something . . . but nothing came out. She tried again, but still nothing.

Jaw locked in frustration, Charlie walked away; the front door slammed closed a minute or two later.

Just as that door closed, the back door opened again and a naked, filthy, and bloody Max walked in.

"No, don't mind me," she said to the back of Stevie's head. "I'm fine. Just great!"

"No one asked," Stevie shot back, still not turning around. "And we're leaving in five minutes!" she yelled after her sister had stomped out of the kitchen.

"More like fifteen," Shen tossed in before spooning more cereal and bamboo into his mouth. "What?" he asked when Stevie sneered at him. "I need to shower."

"Then could you pick up the speed? I'm not used to waiting for staff."

Head dipping lower over his now overly buttered toast, Kyle muttered, "Damn, Stevie."

Shen swallowed, looked Stevie in the eyes. "I'm merely staff now?" he asked. "I thought I was cute."

"You're getting less cute as the day goes on."

"Hey, don't take it out on me because your sisters have no faith in you and think you sound like a feral cat from their backyard."

Stevie slammed her hands on the table and Kyle suddenly bolted out of his chair and moved to the open window.

But all Stevie did was get up and storm out; Kyle let out a breath when she was gone.

"Are you trying to get us killed?" he asked in an almost hysterical whisper. "If she shifts, she could pop us in her mouth like an Altoid!"

"If she shifts, she'll crush us anyway, so stop your whining."

"You have no concept of how important I am to the universe, do you? Well, let me tell you—"

Stevie walked back into the kitchen and stood there for a moment. Shen waited for her to start yelling or something, but instead she asked them, "Did you see that? Was that awesome, or what?"

"Your insults?"

"No! I was really angry. Like livid. But look!" She spun around. "I have complete control of my anger. I was able to be angry without turning into a ball of rage that would tear this house down! Dudes! That's so huge!" She clapped her hands together. "Okay. Let's all be ready to go in fifteen minutes."

She turned toward the door but it swung open and Oriana walked in wearing the same clothes she'd had on the day before.

Stevie, startled, screamed and spun away and then . . . up. She latched onto the ceiling and gazed down at them.

"Holy shit," Oriana muttered. "That's amazing."

"Oh." Stevie let out a breath. "It's you."

Stevie dropped back down to the floor, retracted her claws, and smoothed down the front of her tank top.

"Sorry about that," she said to Oriana. "You startled me."

"No problem."

"What are you doing here?" Kyle asked his sister.

"I fell asleep on the couch watching TV and no one woke me so . . . here I am."

Kyle's eyes narrowed. "That's such bullshit."

"Excuse me?"

"What are you really doing here?"

"I just told you."

"Oriana, I've known you my entire life, unfortunately, and I've not known a day since I was born—and yes, I do remember that far back— when you didn't go to dance class first thing in the morning. I literally do not know a day. You always found time for, at the very least, a class. If not rehearsals for some production. So what are you really doing here?"

She briefly closed her eyes. "The director suggested I take a little . . . time for myself."

Kyle's head tipped to the side. "Because . . . ?"

"Because I may have attempted to dig Svetlana's eyes out of her fucking head. That's why."

Shen, not really caring about this conversation, was shoveling another spoonful of cereal into his mouth when both Stevie and Kyle began clapping. Applauding, actually. They were applauding.

"My sister popped her cherry!" Kyle announced and Shen nearly spit his cereal out on the table. "I'm so fucking proud!"

"What are you talking about?" Oriana asked and Shen had to agree with her. What the fuck were they talking about?

"You were always the goody-four-paws," Kyle explained. "You were cold and bitchy but you never lashed out. Not like that."

"Liberating, isn't it?" Stevie asked, sounding giddy.

"You've done it too?"

"Nearly took a fellow scientist's eye out with a pen. Didn't like his tone."

"When the great Leonardo di Mancini said my work was tepid at best, I bit him in the kneecap and punched his wife." Kyle grinned down at Shen. "I was eight at the time."

"Oh, when *I* was eight," Stevie joyfully reminisced, "I threw a hot bowl of mac and cheese at the conductor of the royal symphony. That boxed mac and cheese you get at the grocery store. Hit him right in the neck. Left welts."

"That's it," Shen announced, getting to his feet. "I'm going to go upstairs, take a quick shower, get dressed, and we'll go."

"You want to come with us?" Stevie asked Oriana.

"Where?"

"Sports Center. I need a . . . well . . . a sport. And hey!" she suddenly added, pointing at Oriana, "I need a friend too! We could"—she waved in Oriana's general direction—"try that out. Interested?"

"Do you want to be a dancer?"

"I have no dancing skills. So no. Do you want to be a great scientist?"

"No. But I do like engineering. It's like a hobby for me."

"Great. I can always use an engineer."

"This is the weirdest conversation I've ever been around," Shen announced. "I'm leaving."

"Forever?" Stevie asked and Shen could only stare at her. "No, I'm really asking," she pushed.

"Shower. Gym. Remember our plan?"

"Oh." She smiled. "Okay."

Worried that this would get too weird, Shen went upstairs to get his day started.

"What about him?" Stevie asked Oriana.

"Who?"

"Shen. Are you interested? Because I'm really interested but I'm not big on women fighting over a dude."

"The guy who just left?" Oriana frowned. "Doesn't he work *for* us?"

Kyle rested his chin on his sister's shoulder and smiled at Stevie. "Now do you see the family resemblance?"

Laughing, Stevie nodded. "Boy, do I ever."

Charlie sat on the front stoop of Berg's house, watching Stevie, Kyle, Shen, and Oriana get into Shen's dark blue SUV to head into Manhattan.

"She should be mad at me," Charlie said when Berg sat down behind her, his long, massive legs on either side of her, his hands resting on her shoulders. "I just panicked when I heard that noise."

"It's going to take time for you to let go. You've been doing this for . . . ever."

"Not just me . . . we."

Max ran out of the house, a small backpack slung over her shoulder. A few feet away from the SUV, she jumped at it, latching onto the passenger side. She pressed her face against the window and screamed.

Laughing, she dropped down and got into the backseat.

Charlie let out a sigh. "At least I never had to do this alone."

Berg pressed a kiss to her brow and said against her flesh, "Please don't worry."

"I'm working on it."

He chuckled. "Bacon?"

Charlie looked over at the platter on the stoop beside them. "An entire plate of bacon. Just a giant pile."

"I thought you loved bacon?"

"I live for bacon. I could eat bacon until the end of time. But I also like my arteries not being clogged. Because, right now, that's all I need. A heart attack or stroke on top of the bleeding ulcer everyone says I'm going to have because of my self-imposed stress."

Berg kissed the side of her forehead again, but she was smart enough to know he only did that to stop from laughing at her

"Your phone is vibrating," he pointed out.

"I know. I'm ignoring it."

"You've been ignoring it for two days."

"Because it's my aunt. I'm guessing she's calling about Great-Uncle Pete's funeral. A man none of us knew. Not only that, I don't feel like spying for those pricks."

"Totally understandable."

The phone stopped ringing . . . but started again almost immediately.

"But we both know she won't stop," Berg gently added.

"She will if I kill her. But then that would make any future family reunions awfully uncomfortable."

"More uncomfortable than they already have been?"

Charlie thought for a moment. "You know . . . that's a very good point."

chapter NINE

Stevie was happy to be back at the Sports Center. She loved it. The energy. The people.

Of course, the last time they'd been here it had been a bit of a whirlwind. There'd been so much excitement. Drama. Violence. And none of it had had anything to do with their father, which had been so refreshing! Because usually drama and violence had *everything* to do with their father.

They cut through what Kyle called "the boring part of the Center," where all the normal, everyday sports things happened with all the normal, everyday full-humans, and made their way to the backstairs that led down to the shifter-only part. That door was protected at all times by shifter security guards, but all you had to do to get through was pass the "smell test." Something that entertained Stevie to no end, having complete strangers sniff her neck to decide whether she was worthy of entrance.

She'd already researched the scent capabilities of a multitude of animals; now she just needed to compare that information to their shifter counterparts because she really wanted to understand the true differences between the "full-blood" animals and an electrician who could shift into a sloth bear. Sadly, though, she couldn't get anyone to agree to a few simple tests. Max especially became bitchy about it.

Of course, when people said no to Stevie, she didn't then take them hostage and test them anyway. Because that was wrong and everyone *knew* it. Even arrogant fucks.

Stevie pushed thoughts of her ex out of her mind and focused on what she hoped would be a good day.

Their small group went down the stairs and through another door that led them to the very busy shifter sports center. It was early in the day but it was also summer so all the pups and cubs were there with their protective parents for classes and play groups that allowed them to work off their excess energy without worrying about harming their playmates. Something that couldn't be guaranteed when the playmate was a full-human child.

Stevie was here to start some kind of exercise regime; she just wasn't sure what kind yet. Kyle said the Sports Center had a great gym built "just for them," so she was excited to see what kind of gym that was and what her options would be. Honestly, she was feeling so good at the moment, she was up for pretty much anything.

"So where do we start?" Kyle asked as Max split off from them and headed right for the Starbucks a few feet away.

"Breakfast?" Oriana asked.

"I think I'm supposed to eat after the exercise," Stevie reasoned.

"Excellent point."

"I just have to figure out what kind of exercise I should do."

"What kind do you like?" Oriana asked.

"Nothing. I hate all forms of exercise. All of them."

Oriana looked down at Stevie's legs, which were bare except for her shorts.

"Good God, woman, you have absolutely no muscle tone."

"I have it." Stevie pressed her finger against her thigh. "If you poke at it, you can feel it under the skin. Sort of."

Oriana shook her head and took hold of Stevie's shoulder. "Come on."

"Where?"

"I'm going to help you," Oriana said, her expression so sad. So earnest. "Because, really, girl. *Somebody* has to help you."

★   ★   ★

Max stood in the endless Starbucks line, waiting to get in her order. She was dying for a honey macchiato, which was like a caramel macchiato but way, *way* better.

Bored after standing in line for more than three seconds, she pulled out her phone and began reading her texts. She had one from Dutch Alexander. He'd been staying with them since Max and her sisters had moved into the house in Queens, but a few days before he'd suddenly departed, leaving nothing behind but a note stuck to the fridge: "Don't worry, Charlie. I'll be back. Love you! Smooches!"

The note had made Max and Stevie laugh, but Charlie had snatched it off the refrigerator and set it on fire because their sister was nothing if not dramatic and vengeful.

Charlie didn't hate Dutch as much as she liked to say she did, but one more fuckup and Max's best friend might find himself buried somewhere in the MacKilligan backyard.

Max was sure that Dutch had gone off on a job. Now she understood his crazy life. He worked with the ones who protected all shifters, which made sense. More than once, when they were growing up, that good-natured idiot had put himself between Max and harm's way. It was as if he couldn't help himself, even though he knew better than anyone that Max didn't need anyone's protection. But that was just his way. He did it for others too. Not just for Max.

All through high school everyone kept expecting Max and Dutch to hook up. Charlie used to live in fear of it. They were close. But it took an awful kiss at a homecoming game to prove what Max and Dutch had already known, deep down. They were close like siblings, but never like lovers. They knew too much about each other. Like the time Max had gotten drunk on vodka and python venom. She hadn't wanted Charlie to find out, so Dutch had taken her back to his family's house. There, in his bathroom, she'd evacuated the poison and nearly everything else in her system from nearly every orifice. She was too sick to stop herself and too embarrassed to talk about it. But she didn't have to talk about it. Dutch just cleaned up his bathroom and never mentioned it again.

But they both knew he'd also seen too much.

Just like she had when he'd ended up on the wrong side of seven football players because he'd been fucking around with the wrong girl.

Max had dragged a naked, sobbing Dutch back to the Pack house to recover. The linebackers had done a number on him, beating him within an inch of his life. Unfortunately, unlike the MacKilligan girls, Dutch was still going through puberty and had no control of his ability to shift. He could barely unleash his claws, much less turn into a vicious wolverine with a thought. To make matters worse, it had been Charlie who'd come to Dutch's rescue, beating the unholy crap out of the linebackers. Not because she liked or wanted to protect Dutch, but because she was *not* okay that seven seniors were beating up one sophomore.

But it hadn't been seeing Dutch at his worst that had permanently put him in the "love him like a brother!" category. It had been what he did afterward . . . he'd hooked up with the same girl again.

That was such a "dude thing" to do that to this day she really couldn't let it go. Because he hadn't done it for love, but for revenge. And Max didn't have time for that.

It didn't really matter, though. She needed loyal friends more than she needed another dick attached to some idiot man. She could get dick anywhere, but someone who always had your back? That was like gold.

Max was checking her phone for the fifteen-thousandth time—she was just so *bored* standing in this goddamn line!— when she noticed that everyone around her had gone silent. Her hackles went up and her claws itched to be released. But she kept control with an iron grip that Charlie had practically beaten into her. "If you just attack every time you feel in danger, you'll be in prison for the rest of your life," she used to say.

With her head still down, her gaze still focused on the phone, she sniffed the air; sorted the scents.

She recognized what was behind her. Recognized it well.

It was Dee-Ann Smith. A She-wolf of worldwide renown among shifters. Her entire Pack was world renowned, and not for good reasons. But Dee-Ann was known to be one of the worst. The "killer" of the family, which was saying a lot when the whole Pack was made up of "killers."

And this particular Smith hated Max. Despised her. Wanted her dead. Not that Max blamed Smith for feeling this way. It was sort of what she'd been aiming for when she'd snuck into Smith's Manhattan apartment and made herself comfortable with the female's young pup. She wanted Smith to know fear, to understand that Max "Kill It Again" MacKilligan was not the nice one in her family. Far from it.

Not that Max would have ever hurt that child. She wouldn't have. And not because of her sisters' moral leanings or because she knew she'd get into serious trouble if she crossed that particular line with the other shifters.

No, it was none of that. Max would never hurt a child because it was unfair. Kids were not a challenge. Even the scary ones, like hyena cubs who were born with fangs. And if there was no challenge, then what was the point?

So all kids—even the pain-in-the-ass ones—were never to be fucked with in the Max MacKilligan playbook. But that didn't stop Max from letting Dee-Ann Smith sweat, thinking that her kid *was* at risk if she fucked with Max's sisters.

The problem now, though, was Smith hated Max so much she could barely see straight. She went out of her way to let Max know that as soon as she could, she'd kill her. Even if she pissed off the wrong people in doing so.

That was why Max knew she had to show this woman exactly how dangerous a MacKilligan sister truly was. How much she risked.

"Dee-Ann?" she asked softly without lifting her head; without turning around.

Leaning so close Max could feel the canine's breath against the back of her neck, Smith replied low and soft, "Well, hey there, darlin'."

Girding her loins, Max moved.

"*Dee-Ann!*" she squealed, then spun around, throwing her arms around the woman's broad shoulders and hugging her close.

Smith went rigid and the Siberian tiger partner she had with her all the time—something Malone—stumbled back, eyes wide in shock.

"I'm so happy to see you! How long has it been?" Max stepped back and grabbed Smith's hands in her own. When Smith attempted to pull away, Max held on tight. "Look at you! Gurl . . . did you lose some weight? So pretty!"

"What the fuck are you—"

Max cut off Smith's next words by kissing her on the mouth. When she pulled back, the She-wolf was shaking with rage. Shaking. She wanted to wipe the very existence of Max MacKilligan from the entire universe. But she couldn't and they both knew it.

Keeping hold of one of Smith's hands, Max moved to the counter as the line seemed to have abruptly cleared away.

She swung Smith's arm like two girlfriends holding hands—which was making Smith nuts—and said to the barista, "Honey Macchiato with three extra shots of honey, please. And you, sweetie?" she asked Smith. When the wolf was too stunned or pissed to speak, Max pushed, "Do you want something? Bear claw? Croissant? Donut? Coffee?"

Smith only managed to shake her head.

Max pointed to the Siberian tiger. "You, hon?"

Tears poured down the cat's face, her arm around her stomach, her laughter silent only because she couldn't catch her breath. She waved a hand at Max, but that was all.

Max shrugged. "Okay," she said to the barista. "That's it."

She glanced at Smith, swung their clasped hands a little more widely so they resembled friendly toddlers. "New makeup regime?" she asked the face that had clearly never had makeup on; a seen-better-days Tennessee Titans baseball cap was pulled low to make that plain face appear even more terrifying. But despite that cap, Max could see those angry, yellow dog eyes glaring at her. "You have to tell me your secret, beautiful. You look awesome for fifty."

The wolf glare turned into wide eyes of horror and the Siberian tiger dropped to her knees, choking on her laughter so hard, Max was worried she'd have to get the feline an ambulance.

They stood around the treadmill, Kyle's older sister actually taking the time necessary to explain everything to Stevie. It was a nice gesture and Oriana was incredibly patient considering Stevie was a grown woman who should have known how to use a treadmill. It was especially entertaining when Stevie became so enraptured by the device that she started to take it apart *while* Oriana was talking, but Shen easily distracted her by pointing at the various options on the display.

"Press Feline," Oriana continued, "and that takes you down to the submenus where your options are Lion, Tiger, Leopard, Mountain lion, and Cheetah. But I wouldn't suggest the Cheetah setting unless you're *really* fast. Are you really fast?"

Stevie shrugged. "For short periods of time."

"Okay, so you press Tiger and then press here for location. Siberian landscape or Indian jungle."

Another shrug. "Uh . . . Siberian landscape?"

"Okay. We'll try that."

Once the machine started to go, Stevie jumped on and began running.

"You seem to know a lot about treadmills," Shen observed.

"When I was in high school I used to put in a few hours at a local shifter-only gym. They had the same kind of treadmills. Although these look top-of-the-line," she added, gesturing toward the machine . . . which was when they realized that Stevie was no longer running, but somehow had gotten her entire body tangled between the dashboard and the rails people used to balance themselves during their run.

"Geez!" Kyle ran over to Stevie. "What did you do?"

"I . . . have no . . . idea," she gasped out.

Kyle couldn't figure out what to grab to get her off the treadmill so Shen quickly stepped in. He gripped her under the arms and managed to untwist her and pull her off.

As he held her there, dangling in midair, bruises already starting to show on her calves and, somehow, her throat, Oriana nodded and offered, "Maybe we should find you an exercise *class* of some kind."

"I could try the step thing," Stevie suggested, pointing across the gym to a step machine.

"No," Shen, Kyle, and Oriana said as one.

"I agree with Oriana," Shen said. "You should stay away from the machines."

"I was just trying to see how it worked," Stevie clarified. "Then things went weird."

"Of course they did." Oriana reached over and patted Stevie's shoulder. "Of course they did."

Cella "Bare Knuckles" Malone had what many would consider a good life. She had a beautiful daughter. An irritating but loving family. And two jobs she loved. Coach of the New York Carnivores pro hockey team and recently promoted head of the "Wet Works" division of Katzenhaus, the protection agency of the Cat Nation. Both paid very well and they allowed her lots of freedom. Like continuing to work with the only canine she could truly tolerate for any length of time.

Many of her feline compatriots often asked her, "How can you put up with Dee-Ann Smith?" But that was just a narrow view. Because taking someone as laid-back and uncaring as the scariest Smith of all—next to Dee-Ann's father, Eggie—and finding something that actually irritated the living hell out of her was like catnip to this Siberian tigress.

Sure. She could be in Europe, working with the Parisian organization of Katzenhaus. But then she wouldn't be here, watching a snarling, angry She-wolf attempt to stare down a honey badger who was thoroughly enjoying her honey macchiato.

Malone had had staring contests with Smith more times than she cared to think about, but she'd always lost because at some point, she couldn't take it anymore, and she'd launch herself at the She-wolf and the fight would be on.

But the honey badger wasn't backing down. She wasn't freaking out. She wasn't even getting aggressive. She just kept sipping her drink and smiling.

The insane staring went on for so long that Cella was about to intercede—something she never did, because she wasn't stupid.

But before she could say, "Hey! Idiots!" Smith slammed her fist on the table.

Cella and the rest of the coffee shop inhabitants jumped. Although Cella was mostly shocked that Smith was the first to break.

The badger's eyes widened dramatically at Smith's sudden explosion . . . then again, so did her terrifying smile.

The badger placed her drink on the table and asked, "Something wrong . . . *ma'am?*"

Smith nearly had her hands around the badger's throat before Cella managed to pin them to the table, which forced Smith to sit back down.

"Call me 'ma'am' again . . ." Smith dared.

"Would you prefer 'spot'?"

Cella grabbed Smith around the waist and dragged her from the table she'd been crawling across so she could get to the badger grinning at her. Cella practically had to carry her outside, dumping her as soon as they were back in the middle of the lobby.

"You need to calm down," she told the red-faced She-wolf.

"That *woman*—"

"Is messing with your mind, and you are letting her, which hurts . . . because that's my job."

Smith pressed her fingers against her chest. "I don't think I've ever wanted to kill anyone as badly as I want to kill that woman."

Cella quickly realized that said a lot. Smith had tons of patience. She'd been known for it when she was a Marine. Able to wait for her prey for days, if not weeks. Yet this one, small woman was really getting under the She-wolf's skin. And Cella wasn't exactly sure why.

"Maybe I should talk to her alone," Cella suggested, and instead of being insulted, Smith just gave a short nod and turned away.

Smith exposing her back to a Siberian She-tiger? Something the wolf had been taught not to do since before she could walk. Eggie Smith had made sure of that.

Deciding it was best to get this over with as soon as they could, Cella headed back into Starbucks.

Stevie didn't appreciate how much laughter was going on between siblings who didn't get along. At least that's what Kyle had always told her. That he barely tolerated Oriana. "She's a genetic freak who's lucky I acknowledge her as a human being much less my sister," he had said to Stevie on more than a few occasions.

And yet here they were. Together. Shoulders touching. Laughing at her.

"It's not funny," she complained.

"Who gets punched by a yogi?" Oriana said around her laughter, tears pouring from her eyes.

"If he doesn't want his students to ask questions," she shot back, "then he shouldn't act like he's okay with it."

"He was fine with the first six questions," Kyle insisted, "but after that, you were just testing his will to live."

"And he didn't punch me," Stevie went on. "He accidentally slapped me with his elbow when he was turning away."

For some reason that seemed to only make them laugh harder, forcing them to lean against each other for support.

The locker room door opened and Shen returned with an ice pack. He pulled her hand away from her face, fingers gentle against hers. That gentleness was still there as he placed the ice pack against her eye and cheek. He positioned her hand so she could hold the ice pack in place and stepped back.

That's when he exploded into a fit of laughter and asked, *"How do you piss off a giant panda yogi? They're the* nicest *yogis!"*

Growling to herself, Stevie turned away from the *three* people who were now laughing at her and thought about all the ways she could bring this entire building down with nothing more than toilet paper, roach spray, and some raw almonds.

A bear-shaped bottle of honey was carefully placed in front of Max. It seemed the She-tiger had returned but not her pit bull friend.

"Thanks," Max said cheerfully. She loved the gift of honey

and, in her opinion, not enough people in the world gave that gift.

The She-tiger sat down across from Max and smiled. "Hi. I'm Cella Malone."

Max, sipping her drink, waved.

"So I guess you know why we're here."

Max placed her cup on the table and gazed at the She-tiger, making sure her smile stayed in place. But she didn't speak. She'd found over the years that smiling without speaking freaked people out. Effective, especially since she really had no plan to answer this chick's question.

At least not such a vague one. For all Max knew, this cat could be here for all sorts of reasons. What if Max guessed wrong? She could easily open up another can of snakes.

Yummmm. Snakes. Gosh, she hadn't had snakes in weeks. She could really go for some snake. Maybe a boa. Or a python, which was one of her favorites. Or perhaps she could risk it all and go for a black mamba. Eh. Probably not. Charlie would just get pissed again. She hated when Max played with her food and ended up briefly dying.

"Are you listening to me?" she heard the She-tiger snap.

She hated lying. "No." Max shrugged. "Sorry. I was thinking about snakes. I guess I'm hungrier than I thought."

The apology seemed to confuse the feline more than anything.

Max picked up the bottle of honey, twisted the top off, and poured half of it into what was left of her honey macchiato.

"Anyway," the woman continued, "we thought we'd have heard from you by now."

Max frowned. "Heard from me about what?"

The feline tilted her head the slightest bit. "Your aunts? Your cousin?"

"You'll need to be more specific than that. I have lots of aunts and a ton of—"

"Caterina and Celestina Guerra. Mairi MacKilligan."

"Oh! Right. Them."

That's what the feline was asking about. Nothing else. Good.

It wasn't that Max didn't think the shifter organizations that protected their kind wouldn't find out about what had happened with Stevie. She knew they absolutely would. But she was hoping to keep it under wraps at least until they could make sure that their baby sister was a little more . . . in control. Her shifted size freaked out everyone, but the real issue would be that she had little to no control over her shifting. That was what Max and Charlie were truly worried about.

Stevie was working on it, though. Hard. But, until the situation was managed properly, Max wanted these "agents" to be distracted from her little sister.

"Not much to hear, really," Max admitted about the three women it seemed everyone was looking for. "The twins haven't been seen since my cousin's wedding. And Mairi . . . don't know what to tell ya about Mairi."

"Do you know her?"

"No. I've only met a few of my Scottish relatives. Usually when my father fucks up something."

"A large group of them are heading this way from Scotland."

"Good for them."

"Maybe you could—"

"My sister already made this clear. We're not spying on them for you. So stop fucking asking. It's beginning to annoy me."

"What if the twins have made a deal with your uncles?"

"What if the moon didn't rise? What if detergent was actually dirt? What if aliens made you set yourself on fire?"

Eyes wide, the cat snapped, "What the fuck are you talking about?"

"Those two bitches stole the MacKilligans' money. A lot of it. But my uncles are criminals, so they had lots of money in different places, and they've been able to keep roofs over their heads and their businesses running."

"And your point? They could still make a deal with the twins if it means getting their money back."

Max had to smile. The cats and dogs . . . they never got it, did they? They went around snarling and snapping and hissing, but they never really got it.

"What? What are you smiling about?"

"The Guerras made my uncles look like idiots. They used some no-name hacker, I assume, to break in and take their money. The twins could come to them naked, on their knees, with twice the money in their hands, ready to give it all for absolutely nothing. And my uncles still wouldn't let it go. They don't forgive shit. They're MacKilligans *and* honey badgers. That means they're mean, vicious, cruel, and vengeful. Then again . . . so am I."

"Which means what?"

"It means no one needs to do anything. The twins will be coming for me."

"Why you?"

"Honestly? I couldn't tell them apart, so I fucked up the face of one of them and—"

"Stop," the cat ordered, holding up her hand. "Really?"

Max shrugged. "I like clarity."

"What about plastic surgery?"

"Won't help." She held up her hand, released her ridiculously long claws. They glinted in the florescent light of the coffee shop. "I went down to the bone."

Max retracted her claws. "So I wouldn't worry if I were you. They'll be coming for me. And then I'll deal with them. Until then . . . don't bother me anymore. Charlie finds out about my little arrangement with Hee-Haw and she'll waste *everybody*." She grinned. "My big sister is super protective."

"Trust me," Oriana said. "Team sports. That's what you should do. And playing accomplishes several different things."

Shen exchanged a glance with Stevie before they asked together, "Like what?"

"Exercise *and* friendship. From what I understand, people involved in team sports make friends."

"Is being in a ballet corps considered a team sport?" Stevie asked.

"It's a dog-fighting pit," she coldly explained. "Only the strong survive. You wouldn't last ten minutes." She glanced over at Shen. "Neither would you. But," she said, her demeanor abruptly changing back to casual friendliness, "we're not talking about ballet. We're talking about a team sport that would be perfect for you."

Stevie glanced down at the tiny shorts, cropped top, fishnet stockings, and quad skates she currently held in her hands. "Yeahhhh . . . I don't think this is it."

"You haven't even given it a try yet."

"Because I am positive it's not for me. I will never wear this shit. Ever." She motioned to the locker room. "I'll put it back."

Shen watched Stevie as she headed away from the banked derby track. From the opposite direction he saw two women heading toward them. And one of those women was Blayne Thorpe. The current captain of the New York roller derby team and the woman Stevie had batted around just the day before.

Blayne was deep in the middle of regaling her Asian companion with a story so she didn't see Stevie, and, thankfully, Stevie didn't notice her.

But then Blayne caught sight of a possible newbie trying to escape her future as a derby girl—most likely the way Blayne thought of it—and she reached out and caught Stevie's arm, sweetly asking, "Not leaving already, are—"

Startled, Stevie yanked her arm away and roared so loudly the chairs in the arena shook.

Blayne stumbled back until she hit the wall, eyes wide in panic. Her friend, a cutie tigon Shen sort of knew, immediately jumped in front of her, ready to protect Blayne.

But Stevie continued on, oblivious of the fear she was leaving in her wake.

"Hey! Look at that," Kyle said, smiling. "Her meds *are* working."

chapter *TEN*

Their first stop after roller derby was the minor league hockey team. Most of the players had dreams of moving up to the pro team, but Shen knew that there were a few who just played in the minor league for fun.

This hadn't been his suggestion. It was Oriana's and it seemed like a bad one since Stevie had just admitted she actually couldn't skate.

"What do you mean, you can't skate?" Oriana demanded. "Why didn't you tell us that when we were at the derby try-outs?"

"Two different types of skating."

"Can you do either?"

"No."

Oriana pushed a lock of hair off her face. "I'm so confused right now. Why did you agree to this?"

"Because I can learn to skate."

"Anyone can learn to skate."

"No. I mean, I can learn to skate faster than most people."

Oriana rolled her eyes. "Honey—"

"No," Stevie interrupted. "Really."

"And how do you do that?"

"Physics."

"Physics?"

"Yes. Physics. Once you understand physics, you can do pretty much *anything*."

"Really?" Oriana smirked. "So you can do what *I* can do?"

"Yes. But I'm lacking your musculature and body type; both of which would be necessary for me to do what you do for any length of time."

Kyle leaned forward and loudly whispered to his sister, "That's a really nice way of calling you a genetic freak."

Oriana unleashed her claws and nearly had them buried in her brother's face, but, to Shen's surprise and approval, Kyle jerked his head back out of clawing range.

"I also like my toes," Stevie suddenly announced . . . for no obvious reason.

"What?" Oriana asked.

"I like my toes. You can't be a dancer and have pretty toes. And from what Kyle has told me . . . you have some fucked-up hooves."

Shen cringed as the She-jackal's eyes narrowed into dangerous slits. But instead of trying to bury her claws into Stevie's face as she had her brother's, Oriana gestured to the ice they were standing on.

"Please," she said with a cold smile, "show us physics."

"Actually," Shen quickly cut in, "how about we take off the skates and find something else for you to do."

"No, no, no." Oriana glared at him before flashing that fake smile at Stevie. "Please, show us what physics does for you."

With a shrug, Stevie placed her left hand on Shen's shoulder for balance, bent her left leg at the knee, and rested her right foot on her left thigh. She leaned down, still holding onto Shen, and studied the bottom of her skate.

When she was finished doing that, she crouched down and pressed both her hands against the stadium ice.

She straightened, continued to study the ice for another minute. Then, without warning, she started skating.

At first, it was an awkward, wobbly performance that had Oriana grimacing along with Shen. She opened her mouth to call Stevie back, maybe afraid that Stevie would only hurt herself on those skates. But Oriana didn't get a word out before Stevie abruptly took off. Like an Olympic speed skater, she moved fast from one end of the rink to the other and back again until she reached their small group and slammed to a stop, a burst of ice hitting them all in the face.

"See?" Stevie said. "Physics! Isn't physics great?"

The sound of disgust Kyle made was definitive, but Stevie chose to ignore it. She faced Shen, smiling wide.

"So, what did you—"

"You here to try out for the team?" a male voice boomed behind Stevie.

Stevie jerked and her body twisted, flying into the air. But the stadium ceiling was much too high for her to reach, so she wrapped herself around Shen instead.

"You really have to stop doing this," Shen reminded her.

"Does this mean your meds are no longer working?" Oriana asked.

"If they weren't working," Stevie growled out, "I would be way worse by now."

"That's terrifying."

"Don't blame me," Stevie argued. "Look at the size of him!"

Novikov was more than a foot taller than Shen and nearly as wide. He was also a trained hockey player who enjoyed hurting his enemies on the ice. Even worse . . . Stevie had just tried to kill his wife, Blayne, the day before. An event that made Novikov more dangerous than he was normally.

Shen decided to end this before it got out of hand.

"Look, Novikov, I understand you're—"

The hybrid put his hand over Shen's face. Shen assumed it was to stop him from talking.

"You trying out for the team?" Novikov asked Stevie.

Stevie, who was hanging off Shen's left side, her legs wrapped around his waist, leaned forward.

"No," Stevie said firmly.

Novikov frowned and it was horrifying. How did anyone risk going up against this guy in a hockey game? "Why not?"

"Don't want to," Stevie snipped back.

Shen pulled away from Novikov hand and leaned close to Stevie, whispering, "How about *not* pissing off the psychotic whose wife you just tried to kill?"

"I was not trying to kill her," she whispered back. "I was playing with her."

"You two do know I can hear you . . . right?" Novikov asked.

"I don't want to play hockey," Stevie insisted.

"Why not?"

"It's boring."

Novikov's eyes widened and he moved back a bit on his skates as if he'd been struck. "It is *not* boring."

"It is to me. But, then again, I'm brilliant and it takes a lot to keep me interested. Especially in the kind of thing that *average* people enjoy. Of course . . . I doubt *you'd* understand."

Shen bit his tongue to prevent himself from laughing. He had to. The look on Novikov's face . . .

He was just so *devastated*.

Giving a low, vicious growl that rolled past them, Novikov skated off.

"The dogs make that noise sometimes," Stevie noted. "I wonder what it means."

"I can't believe you told him no."

"He was rude to you," she said. "He put his Gigantor hand over your face. Who does that?"

"Novikov," Shen and the siblings said together.

"Well, it's rude. Even for prodigies, there are rules. He needs to learn that."

Shen put his arm around Stevie's waist and hiked her up a little higher on his hip. "Look, I don't want you *not* to play simply to piss off Novikov."

"That's not what I'm doing. I don't want to play because I don't want to have to put all this crap on every time. All this padding. And my shirt is huge. It's like a dress."

"We thought this would be a good alternative," Oriana pointed out, "after your reaction to the derby outfit."

"I'm looking for a little . . ." Stevie glanced down at herself. "Something between those two options."

Kyle, who'd been pretty quiet this entire time, offered, "How about softball?"

★ ★ ★

Stevie snatched the softball out of the air with one hand, tossed away the bat she had in her other hand, and stalked over to Kyle and the others.

She held the ball under his nose. "You suggested a game that has a ball coming at my head at—" Stevie looked off and Kyle knew she was calculating something. "—seventy-three point five miles per hour? Does that really seem like a good thing to you?"

Kyle stared at his friend for a bit before replying, "I don't know what the right answer is here."

"Do you know how important my brain is?" Stevie asked. "Not just to the world but to the entire *universe*? Two years ago," she ranted on, "I stopped this entire planet from being sucked into a black hole. Do you think I could have done that if I had brain damage to my head from *this*?" She shoved the ball closer to his nose. "Well . . . *do you*?"

Shen scratched his big bear head. "Wait . . . we were almost sucked into a black hole?"

Kyle and Stevie ignored Shen, and Kyle asked, "So I'm guessing softball's out?"

Snarling, Stevie threw the ball down, hitting Kyle's foot in the process.

"Owwww! Viper!"

"How fucking soft is that, Kyle?" she barked, heading back to the locker room. *"How fucking soft is it?"*

"I should just go home," Stevie sighed once she was back in her shorts and T-shirt. It seemed she'd looked at all the team sports and none of them worked for her. They'd even stopped in at the football stadium, but she'd left three minutes later when she saw that most of the team was made up of gigantic bears who didn't seem as worried as Stevie about traumatic brain injury.

"I've got a suggestion for you," Shen said around the bamboo in his mouth.

"I think we should just end it," she replied. "It's . . . it's just too hard."

"One more," he said, taking her hand.

He walked off, pulling her behind him. Kyle and Oriana brought up the rear.

Together, they took the elevator down a few floors until they arrived at a floor that was completely dedicated to one arena. As they walked down the hall toward the main doors, Stevie examined the framed shirts they passed. Shirts with claw marks, blood stains, and last names.

"Are these . . . memorials?"

"Don't be silly," Shen said as he kept walking, continuing to pull her along. "Memorials for game deaths are in the basement."

Stevie tried to pull away at that point, but he kept walking, tossing over his shoulder, "Just kidding. Lighten up."

They arrived at the big double doors, one of which was already open. He pulled her inside and she quickly realized they were in a soccer stadium.

A group was playing but she doubted they were pro players. Not when she saw Kyle's oldest brother out in the middle of it all.

"Soccer?" she asked, looking up at Shen.

"Yes. Soccer. It's perfect for you. Short bursts of running, which is great for your tiger side. But still competitive, which is good for your child prodigy side. Your hands aren't at any major risk, and the ball is big and soft so your head is safe."

"Except that a kicked soccer ball can reach eighty miles per hour."

"Why do you even know that?" Oriana asked.

"That's true," Shen said, ignoring Oriana, "but you have a honey badger skull. A .38 wouldn't even get past the stone-like strength of your bone structure."

Deciding to ignore what could easily be seen as an insult, Stevie asked, "What made you think of this? For me, I mean."

"Soccer is a great sport. Takes skill, dexterity, and physics. Not only that . . . pandas love soccer!" he cheered, pointing to a group of sturdy-looking giant panda bears. One had hold of a soccer ball and the others were trying to take it from her.

While she giggled and laughed, the others rolled her around, taking turns trying to get the ball. It seemed like a waste of time and energy, but Stevie couldn't ignore the fact that they all seemed to be having a great time.

"Do you play soccer?"

"Used to. Played through high school on local shifter teams. Always had fun."

"Hey," Oriana cut in, "Kyle . . . is that our brother?"

"No way," Kyle snorted. "He'd never . . . oh, my God! That is him!"

The siblings looked at each other for a brief moment before they yelled out together, "*Coop!*"

The world-renowned pianist turned around, which was when he was hit in the back of the head with a soccer ball that had just been kicked at him.

He didn't move, but he looked annoyed, jaws clenching.

"Sor-ryyy!" someone called out before Coop jogged over to the stands.

"What are you guys doing here?" he asked.

"Shouldn't *we* be asking that?" Kyle wanted to know. "What else have you not told us? How much are you hiding from us? Are you even our brother?"

"You act like you found me in a drug den. It's soccer."

Kyle's lip curled in disgust and Oriana scrunched up her nose. She just looked confused. But Stevie didn't know why. A lot of great artists did things on the side to relax, which was exactly what Stevie was looking for. Something she could enjoy that had no real consequences.

Coop stared at his siblings for a few extra seconds before shaking his head, seemingly dismissing them, and faced Stevie and Shen.

"So why are you here?" he asked again.

"Stevie is looking for a way to work out her stress without using Blayne Thorpe as a cat toy."

Coop gave a little smile. "That's probably a good idea."

"So I was thinking," Shen went on, "soccer might be a good option for her."

Coop nodded. "We have a lot of the smaller cats on the team. Some jackals and foxes. Not a lot of tigers but that's because they like American football better. All that hitting and running bears down from behind." He gestured to the people still playing. "These guys aren't pro. Strictly for fun, exercise, and good times. We get to practice here in the afternoons before the pro players come in. Then we play the occasional weekend game every month or so with non-pro shifters from other boroughs, Philly and Jersey. It works out pretty well, even with my hell-on-earth schedule." He dipped his head down a little so that he could look Stevie in the eyes. "You want to try it? We're always looking for new players."

Stevie wasn't sure she wanted to do this, but she'd already failed at everything else. Might as well make it a clean sweep of failure.

"Okay."

"Great." Coop held his hand out so he could help her over the railing. "Let's get you geared up."

"Does it bother you that my very handsome brother is chatting up Stevie?"

Shen heard the question but didn't realize anyone was talking to him until he raised his head from staring at his phone and saw that Oriana was smiling at him.

"Huh?"

"Do I actually need to repeat the question?"

"I'm just surprised you asked me a question. Didn't you once call me 'the help'?"

"I probably did." She gestured toward the middle of the pitch, where Coop and Stevie continued to talk, "Everyone says how charming Cooper is. How friendly. Not like the rest of us at all."

"I don't know why you're telling me this."

"And they have a lot in common," she went on, studying her brother and Stevie for a few seconds. "Music and all that."

Shen looked over her head at her taller brother. "Why is she telling me this?"

"I think it's her attempt to find out if you have any interest in Stevie."

"Why?"

"I don't know. Maybe she hopes you don't so that she'll be able to tempt you with her raw and unappetizing sexuality."

Oriana glared at her brother. "I *loathe* you."

"Because of my brutal honesty or because you have no friends and are forced to hang out with us?"

Shen snorted. "Throwing stones from that glass house, aren't ya, kid?"

Insulted, Kyle looked around his sister. "What does that mean?"

"You don't have any friends either."

"I do too." He pointed at the pitch. "Her. Stevie. She likes me."

"I think she feels sorry for you. But what I mean is, you don't have any friends your own age."

"People my own age are beneath me. They consider stupid things fun. They don't understand life and art and true beauty."

"Plus, they keep hitting him," Oriana tossed in. "That's why my sister hired you."

"Maybe if you stopped saying they were beneath you," he pointed out to Kyle, "they wouldn't beat the crap out of you."

"I don't say it to them. I merely point out how inadequate—"

"Nope," Shen cut in. "Just nope."

"You don't even know what I'm going to say."

"Are you going to say that the school system lets down this nation's children?"

"No."

"Then stop talking."

"Don't blame him," Oriana said, looking at her own phone, and quickly typing a response to someone. "When Kyle was ten, he went through a very strange Ayn Rand period. It was *not* pretty. My father has been trying to pull him back from the edge ever since."

"Oh, please," Kyle huffed. "That phase only lasted six months. And at least I didn't go through that weird Russian literature phase like you. She wore black for a year and kept saying everyone's entire name when she talked to them or about them."

"You weren't even born yet," Oriana shot back.

"Mom told me all about it."

Shen knew that Kyle and Oriana were only four years apart . . .

"You went through a Russian literature phase when you were *four*?"

The siblings gazed at him.

"What age were you when you started reading Russian literature?" Oriana asked.

"That would be the age of never. I have *never* read Russian . . . anything. And, before you pity me, I am totally okay with that. Not having read Russian anything."

"So you're more into great Chinese literature?"

Shen shrugged. "I like Run Run Shaw movies."

"Run Run Shaw?"

"The Shaw Brothers. They made my favorite martial arts movies. From the seventies." The siblings stared at him but didn't say anything, so Shen added, "And I read the *Tao of Pooh*."

"When you were four?" Kyle asked.

"No, last year."

Oriana's head dipped low and she muttered, "Oh, *wow*."

Fed up, Shen informed the pair, "You do understand that most children don't read ancient philosophies when they're four. In fact . . . most *adults* don't read ancient philosophies. That's just your family. You are, to be quite blunt, a bunch of freaks. Good freaks," he added. "Talented freaks. But freaks nonetheless."

Oriana placed her hand on Shen's forearm and he had no idea why.

"I'm just concerned," she slowly explained to him, "that you won't be interesting enough for Stevie."

"Why would I need to be?"

"Because you're dating her."

Shen closed his eyes. "What is *happening?*"

"That's what Max told me last night."

"Your first mistake is you're talking to Max."

"Don't you want to date Stevie? Is it her lack of muscle tone?"

"Look, Stevie is really sweet, but she's . . . young."

"Oh, my God," Oriana whispered. "Are you really old? Like . . . are you ninety?"

Shen growled a little and looked off.

"I'm just kidding." Oriana pushed her shoulder against Shen's arm. "I know you're way younger than that. Like forty, right?"

"*I am not—*" Shen stopped when he realized he was yelling.

"What you need to understand about us—prodigies, I mean; at least the women—is that guys our age do not usually work out for us. They're usually stupid, grabby, and you have to forcefully tell them what no means. To the point where some permanent damage might be caused and their mother calls you a vile bitch beast. So, if you're a few years older than her, it's not a big deal. In fact, you could wisely use these early days when you're rolling around in the sheets to read a book . . . or two."

"I read books. I read!"

Oriana raised an eyebrow. "What are you reading right now?"

Shen cleared his throat. "A book about the Pittsburgh Steelers."

Her raised eyebrow turned down with the other one into a dramatic frown. "Is that about the steel industry in Pittsburgh?"

Kyle burst out laughing and Shen twisted his mouth so that he didn't follow suit.

"Something like that," Shen finally managed to get out.

Stevie, now in matching shorts and jersey and wearing black and white cleats, walked over to them. "What do you guys think? Do I look stupid?"

"Not at all," Oriana replied. "You just look weak . . . and very thin. Like you've been trapped on a boat at sea."

Shen pressed the palms of his hands against his eyes. "What is *wrong* with you?"

"Nothing. Why?"

He dropped his hands into his lap. "Why would you say that to her?"

"Because I'm being honest." Oriana looked at Stevie. "Do you not want me to be honest? I can be one of those girls who lies to you. I'm not good at it, but I can do it."

"No," Stevie said lightly. "I prefer honesty. I mean, I'd feel bad if I'd been working on my body for years . . . but I haven't. So, yeah, honesty's fine."

"Excellent. Now, I was also screening this one"—she motioned to Shen with a wave of her hand—"to be your boyfriend but I don't think that's going to work out."

"No," Stevie replied, gaze gliding over to his. "He's working out just fine."

Shen wanted to know *why* he wouldn't work out as a boyfriend, but he became immediately distracted by the fact that Stevie seemed to think he was already her boyfriend.

Seriously . . . what is happening?

"I'm not your boyfriend!"

Stevie's smile was small but very powerful. "Do you want to be?"

Shen's entire body became tight and he was having very dangerous thoughts at the moment. Extremely dangerous.

He decided to focus on something else . . . anything else

Shen turned to Oriana. "Why couldn't I be a boyfriend?"

"Not *a* boyfriend," Oriana clarified. "Stevie's boyfriend specifically. You could absolutely be"—she looked around the stadium, finally pointing at a long-legged cheetah, sitting on the barrier and reading a magazine—"*her* boyfriend."

"Why her?"

"Look at her. She's attractive. She's a cheetah, so I'm sure she's astounding in bed. Plus, she's reading *Vogue* magazine."

"So?"

"She's probably more your speed. Intellectually."

Kyle threw his head back, his laughter ringing out over the stadium.

Shen guessed, "You think I'm too stupid."

Stevie's eyes grew wide. "What? Why would you think that, Oriana?"

"Because I've never read Russian literature," Shen told her.

"What does that have to do with anything? My sisters have never read any literature ever, and if you think you're smarter than either of them," she said directly to Oriana, "you're only going to get your feelings hurt. Unless we're talking about Max. Then you'll just get hurt physically."

Oriana rolled her eyes. "I'm just trying to find you someone a little more up to your . . ." she glanced at Shen and back at Stevie before whispering, "level."

"I can hear you," Shen reminded her. "I'm sitting right next to you."

"As a fellow former child prodigy, all I have to say to you, Oriana Jean-Louis Parker," Stevie said as she reached across the barrier and grabbed Shen's hand, "is it's wrong to look down on and mock normal people. There's nothing wrong with average. With the every day. With the *common*."

Kyle, at that point, was down on the floor, on his back, laughing hysterically. Shen couldn't even be mad. He didn't blame him at all. But if either female noticed him, they didn't show it.

"It's average, everyday people," Stevie proudly continued, "with no special skills or the ability to change the world that make this country great."

Then with a good yank, she pulled Shen out of the seat and over the barrier so that she could drag him across the field to the team bench.

"I'm so sorry about that," she said when they were near the other players. "I hate when people are snobby like that."

Shen nodded. "Snobby people are the worst, right?"

"Oh, my God, Shen . . . I know!"

★ ★ ★

"Does Aunt Irene ever text you? She says the wild dogs are giving Mom a hard time about the house. Like I can do anything about it." Oriana waited for an answer from her brother, but when she didn't get one, she looked down at him and ordered, "Dude, get off the ground."

Wiping tears from his eyes, her brother climbed into the seat next to her and let out a breath. "That was great."

"What was?" she asked, texting back her mother's best friend.

"The way you tortured Shen, No wonder you are getting kicked out of your little dance troupe—"

"I wasn't kicked out. It's just a break."

"You're making giant pandas feel bad about themselves."

"That's not what I was—"

"I think I might be starting to like you. Wait. Like is too strong. Let's just say, I'm starting not to mind your existence on my planet."

"That's big of you, Kyle."

"I know."

Oriana rolled her eyes. She was used to her brother. "Just so we're clear . . . I wasn't questioning the panda just to be a dick."

"Really?"

"Yes. Really. I was trying to get your friend laid."

"Why?"

She shrugged. "Nothing better to do. And she looks like one of those . . . caring people. I knew she'd be all insulted for him."

"That's really sweet of you."

"I'm really sweet." She thought a moment, added, "When I've got nothing better to do."

"You know, it's funny," Kyle said, putting his long legs up on the rail in front of him, "I never have that little to do . . ."

"You don't have to do this if you don't want to."

Stevie shrugged. "I might as well. I'm out here. I'm wearing the outfit." She glanced at Shen. "Or are you saying that because you don't want to give me the ball?"

Shen pulled the ball tighter into his chest. "I wanna play with the ball."

She fought a smile and tried to sound stern. "Put the ball on the ground."

"The other pandas will play with me."

"Shen!" Then, despite herself, she laughed.

Stevie had to admit . . . she'd thought she'd be helping Shen deal with the psychological fallout of Oriana's bitchiness. But he didn't seem to care. Instead, he was trying to make her comfortable in this strange, new environment.

She knew this because it's what her sisters always did. Charlie by talking to her and Max by irritating the shit out of her so that she was distracted. Shen was using the "teasing" distraction. A type of distraction she'd never favored . . . until now.

"Can we get moving on this?" the team captain called out from the other end of the pitch. A cheetah who worked in software engineering. A field Stevie dabbled in herself when she was bored.

Shen placed the ball at her feet. "Now, remember," he said, stepping away from her. "This is just for fun. For relaxing. So no stress to succeed at all costs."

She shook her head. "You really have been around the Jean-Louis Parker kids way too much."

"You speak true words."

Stevie looked at the ball, the goal at the end of the field, the goalie standing in front of it, and then back at the ball.

Thirty-seven calculations—or twelve seconds—later, she took several steps forward and kicked the ball.

It skittered past the goalie and into the net.

There was a moment of silence, then everyone turned to look at her.

Stevie shrugged and explained, "Physics."

After ten minutes or so, Shen returned to the stands, again sitting with Oriana and Kyle. Together they watched Stevie MacKilligan tear her way around the pitch like she'd been born to it.

He wouldn't say she was necessarily pro level. That game moved way faster and was definitely deadlier. But for an occasional weekend team, she was too good, which everyone else seemed to love.

Shen's question, though, was how much did Stevie love it? *If* she loved it at all.

It was hard to tell. She was pretty expressionless out there when doing anything but focusing on the ball. And when she focused on the ball, she simply looked . . . confused.

Until she sent the ball careening into the net.

"Is that my sister?"

Shen had no idea how long Max had been sitting beside him, but he was proud that he didn't jump out of his skin and try to disembowel her.

"That's her," he said when he was confident he wouldn't yell at Max to never to do that again.

"Who knew she could do anything physical except run away?"

"I thought you guys taught her to run away."

"Charlie taught her that. You'd be amazed how many times someone has tried to snatch Stevie off the street. And not just because my father had sold her to Peruvian drug lords either."

Shen looked over at Kyle and he gave a short nod. *Don't ask,* he silently suggested.

But Shen had to know. "Your father sold his own daughter to drug lords?"

"Oh, he's done lots of things. Little tip . . . if Charlie is ever on your ass about something and you want her to stop, just bring up our dad. By the time she's finished telling those stories, she'll have completely forgotten whatever you fucked up."

"Good to know."

The practice-slash-tryout ended and a panting, sweaty Stevie walked over to them. And Shen still had no idea what she was thinking.

Although she'd definitely done this longer than anything else she'd tried that morning and, most important, not once had anyone "accidentally" wacked her in the face with their elbow.

"Hey," she said, standing on the other side of the barrier.

"Hey." Shen leaned over the metal railing. "Well?"

She nodded and said around her panting, "I loved it."

Shocked—he'd hoped for a "like," maybe an "it was okay," but "loved"?—Shen replied, "Really?"

"Yeah."

"You're not just saying that because I recommended it, are you?"

"Why would anybody do that?"

"To be nice?"

"I'm not really nice," she admitted. "But next to Max, I *seem* nice."

"It's true," Max added, her short pink hair now parted in the middle and each section pulled into two small ponytails. Different from when he'd first noticed her next to him a minute or so ago.

"Okay," Shen said. "What do you like about it?"

"Like about it?"

"Yeah. The exercise? The camaraderie? How cute you look in the jersey?"

"He's right," Max said, and when Shen looked at Stevie's sister again, her hair was now in a single, high pony tail, and she was fussing with the bangs. "You do look cute in that jersey."

Stevie looked down at her shirt, then glared at her sister. "Shut up. No one's talking to you."

"See?" Max pointed out. "She's not that nice."

Not in the mood to see yet *another* fight between the two, Shen pushed, "So? What do you like about it?"

"The physics."

Shen frowned. "Again with the physics?"

"*Always* with the physics." And now Stevie smiled. A big, wide grin that lit up her entire face. It lit up everything. Everything around her. It was like she suddenly glowed.

"Don't you see? It's all physics," she explained. "All equations and calculations that require me to solve them in seconds so that I can score or stop someone else from scoring. It's a constant, never-ending physics party! How could I not love it?"

"Couldn't you do all that with golf?" Max asked.

Stevie's wide smile abruptly ended and she glowered at her older sister. "Why don't you shut up?"

"Why don't you make me?" Max shot back, her hair now parted on the side, a few braids hanging . . .

"How do you keep changing your hair so fast?" he asked when Max stood next to him. But she never answered his question because she was too busy leaning over the railing and screaming at her baby sister while her baby sister yelled back.

That lasted nearly ten seconds before Stevie grabbed Max by her constantly changing hair and dragged her over the railing, the pair of them rolling across the turf, battering each other.

"Such a physical family," Oriana noted from her seat. "Jean-Louis Parkers don't fight like that."

"She's right," Kyle said. "Instead we attempt to exacerbate each other's personality disorders until mental health professionals are forced to intervene."

Suddenly Shen appreciated the "physical" approach to family resolutions.

chapter ELEVEN

They decided to eat in the Sports Center's food court. Of course, this particular food court was specifically geared toward shifters, forcing Stevie to rethink her decision on sushi when she found out that most of the beautifully designed food she was looking at was, in fact, made up of whale blubber and the meat of walrus, bearded seals, and—

"What the fuck is a narwhal?" Max had asked, staring up at the posted menu.

"Kind of the unicorn of the sea. I've just never heard it's edible."

"It is to polar bears," Shen had explained and, at that point, Stevie was done. Hearing "It's edible to polar bears" was simply too much for her at this moment in her life. And, in the end, they ended up getting normal, ground beef burgers. Except, of course, for the size of those burgers.

Stevie wasn't positive, but she thought the largest-sized burger was bigger than one of the Dunn triplets' heads. Even Shen didn't get the largest size. He got the "medium" instead and that looked like it could possibly choke an elephant.

Still, despite the weird food situation, it was a pleasant lunch. Max and Shen chatted about the derby team they'd briefly visited. Especially once Max found out that her cousin Livy Kowalski occasionally played on the Manhattan team, the Assault and Battery Park Babes. Max's sudden interest in a sport that she hadn't even known existed a few weeks ago had Stevie a little concerned, but she couldn't be bothered. What her sister did with her other relatives was low on Stevie's lists of things to worry about.

Stevie, however, spent her time discovering that Oriana wasn't nearly as dumb as her brother had accused her of being. In fact, they both had a love of robotics and artificial intelligence, and Oriana's hobby was advanced engineering.

"We should work on a project sometime," Oriana suggested, pushing her tray of empty paper plates away. "There's an engineering lab I'm allowed to use anytime I'm in the city."

"That sounds great, but I promised Charlie I wouldn't involve myself in AI anymore."

"Why?"

Stevie took a sip of her giant soda before admitting, "There was an incident."

"It was with the US Army," Max abruptly chimed in, turning toward Oriana, her grin wide. "In fact, it was a minor international *incident* that almost became a major international—"

"Hey!" Stevie barked. "Gag order. Remember?"

"I don't remember that."

"I don't know why. They put a gun to your head. Literally," Stevie reminded her sister. "Not to get you to sign, but because they felt threatened by you."

Max gazed off, eyes narrowing as she tried to remember. "Nope," she finally said. "You're going to have to be way more specific."

Shen, still working on his french fried bamboo sticks, gawked at Max and asked, "How many times have you had a gun to your head?"

"So many," Stevie and Max replied together.

Oriana's phone vibrated and she lifted it off the table, studying it. "What the fuck?" she growled.

"What?" Kyle asked.

"It's from Aunt Irene again. She says the wild dogs are pissed about the house and they are throwing us out. She said we should get over there to talk to them right now . . . and bring Dr. Stasiuk-MacKilligan." Oriana blinked. "Who?"

Stevie raised her hand a bit. "Uh . . . that's me."

"Oh. Oh! So that makes sense."

"Well, it's not gonna happen," Max cut in, shaking her head. "She could be setting you up to get murdered. She hates you."

"Irene Conridge does hate me," Stevie confirmed. "She probably *is* trying to kill me."

Laughing, Kyle disagreed. "I can say a lot about Aunt Irene, but I can assure you that she'd never do anything like . . ." He looked down at his hands and, after a few moments, finally admitted, "Yeah, she could be trying to kill you."

"We could just ask her?" Oriana suggested.

"Ask her if she's plotting to kill my sister? That really seems logical to you? That's stupid. What we *should* do is hack into her computer and find out if she's planning something. Like moving a large quantity of money into Swiss bank accounts. The hitmen I know keep their money in Swiss bank accounts."

"Hitmen?" Stevie asked. "That's so outdated. It's hit*people* now. Or assassin."

"Assassin is so snobby. That's like people who say 'wet works.'"

"I'm sorry," Shen finally cut in. "You *all* think Irene Conridge is planning to kill Stevie?"

"Of course not," Stevie felt the need to correct. "She'd never do it herself. She'd hire someone."

"Hence the use of *assassin*," Max interjected.

"Okay." Shen pushed back his chair, stood. "I am well aware that I am the most rational of this group. I've been informed of this by both Charlie and Toni. So, this is what we're going to do. We're going to go over there."

"So my sister can be shot from a rooftop like JFK?" Max demanded.

"That wouldn't happen," Shen replied. "Because that's stupid. Not only that, but I've found that if Irene Conridge does really hate you, she wants you to live a long time so she can use that time to make you miserable."

Kyle nodded. "He has a point."

"So, let's just go and talk to the wild dogs. Get that fixed, and then we can find out what Dr. Conridge wants. Although, why she wouldn't just ask Stevie over if she wanted to see her—"

"Because she knows that if she asked me over, I'd burn the house down with her in it."

"Let's just go," Shen said on a long sigh as he stepped away from the table and picked up his tray.

"Hey! Wait up!" a voice called out and Shen turned to see Coop running toward them. He liked Coop. A lot. He wasn't like the rest of the Jean-Louis Parkers. He was really friendly and didn't hold anyone's lack of Russian literature knowledge against them.

He was also tall, handsome, and one of those breeds that didn't look freakishly large when in their human form. He was also the one Berg called "music guy."

And Stevie used to be music girl. They understood each other on that prodigy level that Shen would never get.

So what did that all mean to Shen at the moment? That he suddenly hated Cooper Jean-Louis Parker. A lot.

"What do you want?" Shen asked. Or maybe he barked that at him. He probably barked.

Coop noticed, too, his eyes going a little wide, his head rearing back a bit in surprise. "Um . . . thought I'd catch a ride with you guys." He held up his phone. "Oriana said you were heading to the house to see the wild dogs." He grinned and Shen wanted to punch his lips off. "Well, you'll be happy to hear, I've got a way with the wild dogs. They really like me. So I'm sure I can help."

Unwilling to reply, Shen looked at Stevie. She was the one who wanted to go over there and try to reason with the canines.

Logically, he knew this. Yet he was still annoyed when she said, "Sure. Sounds great."

The group started off again, moving toward the elevator, and Coop moved up next to him.

"Everything okay, Shen?"

"Yeah. Why?"

"I don't know. You seem tense. I've never seen you tense. Even when you want to kick Kyle's ass, you never seem tense about it." He glanced at the back of his siblings' heads. "Is it the two of them together? They don't usually hang together, so I'm sure I can stop it. I can only imagine how obnoxious they can be as a working pair."

That's when it hit Shen. He was jealous of the handsome Coop. With his strong, chiseled jaw but without the round head that goes with being a giant panda. He was jealous of Coop because of Stevie. He saw the male as a threat to his interest in a female. There was a part of him at this very moment that wanted to challenge the piano player to a good old-fashioned animal fight. He wanted to take the male on to prove to Stevie MacKilligan he was worthy of her.

That he was a worthy mate. Good God! What was happening to him?

"Shen?"

"Huh?" He realized he hadn't answered Coop's question and now the man looked really worried. "Oh, it's nothing. Nothing. Just some stuff on my mind."

"Anything I can help with?"

Christ, he was being a friend. A good friend. And Shen wanted to tear his face off.

They stood in front of the bank of elevators, waiting for one of the doors to open. Shen placed his hand on Coop's shoulder.

"Thanks. But I'm cool. Just a long couple of days."

He chuckled. "I can imagine."

"Hey," Stevie said to Coop. "Did you hear Markinov was planning a concert in Romania? When did he crawl back out of the woodwork?"

"I can't believe anyone would ever work with him again. He's the absolute . . . ow. Ow! Ow! Ow!"

"Shen!"

Shen blinked, looked at Stevie. "What?"

"Let him go!"

Unsure what she was talking about, Shen looked at Coop

and quickly realized he'd gripped the man's shoulder so tightly with his hand that he'd brought the famous musician to his knees.

"Oh, shit!" Shen released him and quickly leaned down to help Coop up. "Sorry. Sorry about that. I . . . was thinking about something. Got lost in my thoughts."

The worst part of it all was Oriana. She stood behind everyone else, a smirk on her face, one eyebrow raised. And in that moment . . . Shen hated her too.

chapter TWELVE

They stood in front of the big wood door, all of them staring . . . and wincing.

"How many children do they have in there?" Stevie finally
asked. "It sounds like they're running an orphanage."

"I've never gotten the real count," Oriana admitted. "But
they do have a lot. From what I understand, that's normal for
wild dog packs."

"So is dragging their asses across the carpet," Max stated,
reaching around Shen and pushing the doorbell, "but that
doesn't make it right."

The front door opened and a pretty teenage girl with long
blond hair and big brown eyes gazed at them for several seconds.
Then she turned her head and yelled, "Ma! Jackals at the door!"

Surprised by the yell, Stevie took an instinctive step back
and moved into Shen.

"You okay?" he asked, his voice low, one hand pressed
against her lower back.

"That's a very loud child."

"I know," Kyle sighed. "And they're all like that."

Screaming children ran past the open doorway and another
set of screaming children ran the opposite way.

"Are you sure you want to do this?" Coop asked.

"It's my fault. I'll deal with it."

A blond woman appeared. She looked a lot like the teenager,
so Stevie didn't think she was going out on a limb guessing this
was the girl's mother.

"Why are annoying jackal pups here?" the woman asked, her Russian accent thick.

"Nothing better to do?" Oriana asked.

"We're here to steal your souls?" Kyle suggested with a smile.

With an eye roll, the woman began to close the door.

"No, no," Stevie said, putting her hand against the door before it could close all the way. "I need to see . . ."

"Jessica Ann Ward," Coop told her.

"Yes. Jessica Ann Ward. Wait . . ." Stevie looked back at Coop. "Why do I know that name?"

Coop shrugged. "I have no—"

"Oh! I remember!" Stevie smiled but then, she really *did* remember how she knew that name and she felt her smile fade. Along with her hopes. "Uh-oh."

"What?" Shen asked.

The Russian woman pointed a damning finger at Stevie. "I remember you." She spit on the ground near Stevie's feet and slammed the door shut.

Crinkling up her nose, mortified, Stevie faced her friends. "We should go."

"What did you do?" Oriana asked, laughing.

"It's kind of a long—"

The front door opened again and Jessica Ann Ward stood there, glaring at Stevie.

"You."

Stevie immediately raised her hands, palms out. "I can explain!"

"I'm calling the FBI!" Ward shot back.

She turned to march into the house, but Stevie followed, desperate for her to listen. "Please don't do that!"

"Fuck off!"

Ward continued down the hallway and Stevie stayed right behind her.

"If you'll just let me explain."

"There is nothing to explain. Nothing you can say that I want to hear."

Stevie followed Ward into the kitchen just as the wild dog picked up her phone from the long wood table where several other wild dogs were sitting on benches.

"I think I still have Agent Hall's number," she warned with a smirk.

"Please don't call him," Stevie begged, horrified. "If you would just give me a minute—"

"What did you do?"

Stevie winced, refusing to even look at her sister.

"I asked you a question, Stevie."

"Can we talk about this later?"

"No. We can talk about this right fucking now. What's going on?"

Finally, Stevie looked at her sister and instantly Max barked, *"This is Dad's fault, isn't it?"*

"Please stop screeching."

"I was not screeching. Now, what did that motherfucker get you into?"

"She stole my son's violin."

Max's head reared back a bit; a confused frown crossed her face. "A violin? Why?"

Stevie—and her sister knew this—could have any instrument she could ever want. All she had to do was ask and maybe perform for a dignitary or two with said instrument. So there was no reason in the world for her to steal a violin. Any violin. But there were some instruments that were worth their weight in gold and—

"It was a Stradivarius."

Stevie winced, watching her sister's confused frown turn into a glower of anger.

"That motherfucker!" Max exploded. *"I'll kill him! I'm going to kill him!"*

And Stevie did the only thing she could think of at that moment to stop her sister from doing something really stupid. She dove headfirst at her, dropping them both to the ground.

★ ★ ★

Nope. Shen never expected Stevie to tackle her own sister. And she hit Max hard too. Took her down like a linebacker sacking a quarterback.

It was such a surprising move that even the wild dogs were stunned into silence . . . and very little managed to silence wild dogs.

Shen reached for Stevie, but he couldn't get a solid grip because the two women kept moving. One on top, then the other. One punching her sister in the face, then the other punching the first in the stomach. It wasn't a cute "girl fight" either. Nor was it an attempt for either one to get control of the other.

This was an all-out brawl.

Max got to her feet. She had Stevie by the hair and she brought her up with her. Then she threw her across the room and into the stove. Pots and pans hit the floor. Thankfully, the oven and the burners were not being used.

Shen was shocked by the move. Although Max was crazy with everyone else, she never went too far with her baby sister. For her and Charlie it was always about protecting Stevie. But at this moment . . . it was like she was fighting a stranger.

Stevie snarled and rolled off the oven and dropped to the floor. When she straightened up, she bared her fangs at her sister and Kyle suddenly grabbed Shen's shoulder. Probably thinking Stevie was going to shift and wreck the entire wild dog house, but only after crushing everyone in the kitchen with her shifter weight.

But Stevie didn't shift. True, she bared her fangs and her eyes changed to a bright, *bright* gold. But then she charged across the room and threw herself at her sister.

Shen did his job first. He got Kyle and Oriana out of the way of the two flying women. He put them into the hallway.

"Run if you have to," he told them before wading back into the fight. He pushed Coop aside, not sure the musician could really wrangle two battling predators.

He reached for Max. Had her around the waist. But Stevie yanked her free without much effort and flipped her up and over, slamming Max's back against the big wood table. Most of the wild dogs made a run for it, except Jess and her second-in-charge Sabina. Not surprising. Jess was the Alpha female of the Kuznetsov Pack and was mated to the Alpha male of the New York Smith Pack. You didn't go into that life with a weak spirit.

Max reached up and grabbed Stevie's hair, pulling her head and shoulders forward. She raised her legs and wrapped them around her baby sister's neck. Then she flipped over, leaving her sister now on the table. And that's when Max sat down, pressing her butt against her sister's face. Not for some weird sexual reason either. She did it to suffocate her!

Growling, Max ground her butt against her sister while Stevie's arms swung wildly, legs kicking. She couldn't breathe and her sister knew it!

"*What the fuck is going on here?*" a low male voice bellowed.

Jess Ward's adopted son stood in the kitchen, a violin and bow hanging from one hand, and Coop standing behind him. The two were friends, so Coop had probably known where in the enormous house to find him. Thank God.

John DeSerio was an orphaned wolf that the wild dogs had taken in to their family when he was a teen. It had turned out he was also a brilliant violinist and his career had just started to take off under the tutelage of Kyle's mother, Jackie.

Yet no one answered him as Max continued to smother her sister.

Finally, John stormed over to the two women and reached for Max. She bared her fangs and her claws, let out a nasty hiss. John replied with a growl that had the hairs on the back of Shen's neck snapping to attention. John reached past the slashing claws and grabbed Max by the back of her neck with his one free hand, then yanked her off her sister.

Stevie instantly sat up, gasping for air, eyes wide in panic. Shen went to her side, stroked her back.

She glared at her sister and screamed, "*She farted on my face!*"

Jess's lip curled in disgust as she eyed the honey badger in her wild dog kitchen. "Ewww. That's just nasty!"

★   ★   ★

Stevie allowed Shen to lead her out into the wild dog's backyard. There were lots of pups out there, but they were mostly
silent. Staring at her. They appeared terrified.

She didn't blame them. She'd just been in a vicious fight
with her own sister. But they weren't around her for long—the
adults scurried them away in seconds.

Shen disappeared back into the house and Stevie looked
down at her hands. They were shaking and she hated that.

"You *do* make an entrance, Dr. MacKilligan."

Stevie slid her gaze a few feet away to Irene Conridge, who
was standing there, looking as haughty as ever.

"You did lure me here."

She shrugged. "I knew you'd come running to help."

"So this is all bullshit."

"No. The wild dogs are pissed. Whether you still want to
help, though, is up to you."

"Then what do you really want?"

Conridge walked to her side. She handed her a cell phone.
"Take this. You'll be able to contact me directly."

"Okay."

"And here's the information I have so far. I think you should
look at it. See if I missed anything."

"I doubt you did."

"Then see if there's anything in there that *I* would not notice. You and your sisters are much more on the . . . outskirts
of society than I am."

Stevie nodded and pulled off the gym pack strapped to her
shoulders so that Conridge could put the thick file inside, along
with the phone.

"Next time," Stevie said as the woman began to walk away,
"don't lure. Just text me if you need to see me. That'll concern
my sisters much less."

"Understood."

By the time Conridge disappeared around the corner of the
house, Shen returned from inside, a first aid kit in his hand.

He led her to a picnic table.

"Get up," he ordered.

She slid her ass onto the table and sat back until her legs hung over the edge.

He placed two fingers under her chin and lifted.

"What are you going to tell Charlie when she sees this black eye?"

"I . . . I don't want to talk about it."

"Uh-huh. Not even to tell me what your father did? How he got you into this?"

"It's my fault. I never should have believed him. I know he's a liar, a scumbag, a useless waste of space."

"And still your father."

She felt a tear slide down her cheek and she hated herself for the weakness. But Shen didn't say anything. He just wiped it with the tip of his finger before he began working on her cuts and bruises.

"I want my sister!"

Jess Ward Smith let her eyes roll back into her head before she looked over her shoulder at the honey badger that had invaded her home, and snapped, "Shut the fuck up!"

That's when she got hissed at by a mouthful of needlepoint fangs, which was just weird.

The last twenty-fours had been nothing but weird. The inside of the Pack's rental house had been nearly destroyed by what had been described to her as a giant tiger-striped honey badger . . . do those even exist? In nature?

And now the girl who had once betrayed her only son had arrived with the Jean-Louis Parker pups and her badger sister. If that was all, it would have been weird enough. But it got weirder! Jess had daughters. Too many daughters, some might say. And they fought *constantly*. But not like those two had fought. Like WWE wrestlers on primetime.

Now the betrayer was in Jess's backyard with a goddamn giant panda and the betrayer's sister was in her living room, screaming.

She had been doomed to this life, hadn't she? To never have a "normal" existence. And not because she was a shifter. Lots of shifters lived in the suburbs and had nice, normal lives. But Jess never had. Not once.

"We should call Dez," Sabina said next to her, speaking of the full-human head of the NYPD's shifter unit. "Let her take these bitches in for what they did."

"No." And, *of course*, that came from her son. "We're not doing anything."

"Do you remember what she did to you?" Jess demanded. "Do I need to remind you?"

"No, Mom. You don't need to remind me. And you need to let it go."

"You haven't figured me out yet? I don't let anything go. Ever. Ask your Aunt Sissy."

She looked down at her phone and quickly scanned her contacts, looking for the FBI agent's number until Johnny took the phone from her.

"Really?" she asked him.

He laughed. "Come on." He pointed at the crazed badger. "You too."

They started to walk and Johnny followed, looking back at Coop and his siblings. "Can you guys wait here?"

"But we're nosy," Coop replied.

"Stay."

"That doesn't work on us," Coop called out after them.

"It actually does," Johnny replied.

He was right too. It worked on the wild dogs all the time.

They went out into the backyard, the panda smoothing a small Band-Aid on the girl's cheek.

Johnny dragged Jess until they were right in front of the little con artist.

"Tell her," Johnny ordered the girl.

Those betraying eyes flickered over to the badger and back to Johnny. The girl shook her head, her lips tightly shut.

"Now what did you do?" the badger sister demanded, pushing past Johnny and slapping at the girl. Using her legs, the girl pushed her sister away, then began to slap back. The two of them no longer looked like well-trained wrestlers but Jess's twin daughters who had to be put in separate cribs when they got a little older because they kept getting into slap fights.

Johnny pushed them apart, making Jess wince. He had to protect his hands. Getting between a couple of predator siblings was never a good idea when your hands were priceless.

"Tell her what you did," Johnny insisted. "Now."

The betrayer rubbed her nose; her gaze focused on the panda's hand.

Still not looking at them, she began, "My father convinced me—and I stupidly believed—that he just wanted me to get your contact information so he could talk to your mother. He told me he wanted to sell her something. I assumed it was one of his stupid Ponzi schemes and I was sure she'd never fall for it. But he'd researched you. He knew you were a fan of my music and that your mother had a lot of money. I wanted to help and, at the same time, hoped I could steer him down a more logical path. Maybe help get him a straight job. But I didn't realize he'd lied to me until I got back to our hotel room and he was gone."

The sister threw up her arms, then placed her hands on top of her head. She began pacing in a circle, shaking her head and muttering to herself.

"Tell her what you did," Johnny said again.

"She just did," Jess replied. "If you believe her."

"Please, Miss MacKilligan," Johnny insisted, "tell my mother what you did."

The sister stopped pacing and her head slowly turned to focus on MacKilligan.

"I didn't know exactly what my father had done until I saw it on the news later that night. About how your Stradivarius was missing and there was this massive hunt for it throughout France. But I got out before then. Before the cops came. Because I knew when he left, he'd done something bad." She blew out a breath, finally looked at them. "I knew there wasn't much I could do to fix things, but I went ahead and sent a violin that had been gifted to me by a very generous royal who loved one of my operas."

Jess sucked her tongue against her teeth. "That piece of shit knockoff you sent us? I destroyed that fucking thing."

MacKilligan scrambled off the table and nearly dropped to her knees, eyes wide with panic; but Johnny caught her.

"No, no!" he said quickly. "The violin was *not* destroyed. Remember, Mom? You were about to destroy it when I wrestled it from your hands." He placed MacKilligan back on the table.

"I promise," he said to the little crook. "It's safe. Very, *very* safe."

"Wait a minute." The sister stepped forward, staring at MacKilligan. "Are you talking about *the* violin?"

"Can we talk about this later?" The thief practically begged.

"That was our security blanket. Jesus Christ! *What did you do?*"

"*I had to do something!*"

"Why? Because you allowed Dad to fuck you over? Yet again?"

MacKilligan didn't answer. She gazed at her sister. And her sister gazed back. Until the two women went at each other once more with fists and crazed screeching.

Unable to stand a moment more of this, Jess grabbed each woman by the hair and yanked them apart. Just like she did with her girls.

"*That is enough!*" she bellowed, separating them with a strong shove. "I honestly don't know what the hysterics are about. That piece of shit is not even a Stradivarius."

"That, Mom, is because it's a Guarneri."

Jess shrugged. "So? I've never heard of it."

"I know. That's why I didn't bother telling you. But Uncle Phil and I had it examined and priced by a specialist . . . and it's definitely a Guarneri."

"And?"

"And . . . it's worth about twenty-two million dollars."

Stunned by that response, all Jess could do was stare at her son. But MacKilligan nodded and noted, "So it's gone up then, since I had it."

"Yes," Johnny replied. "There was an auction a few years

back for a Guarneri, and it went for quite a lot. And the one you sent me is pristine, sooo . . ."

Finally able to speak, Jess asked MacKilligan, "You gave my son a twenty-two-million-dollar violin to make up for what your father did? Seriously?"

"Of course, she did," her sister snapped, livid. "Her and her high moral standards."

"*It was the right thing to do!*" MacKilligan screamed at her sister.

"*We can't live off your high moral bullshit!*"

"Enough with the yelling!" Jess barked. "I can't stand it." She pointed at her head. "Sensitive dog ears."

The sister shook her head. "I'm telling Charlie." She turned to walk away but her sister grabbed her hair and yanked her back. MacKilligan wrapped her legs around the sister's waist and began punching her in the face.

Johnny looked at the giant panda. "Are you not going to stop them?"

"They'll stop. Besides," he added with a straight face, "I'm dainty. Like a Fabergé egg."

"Fine. I'll do it myself."

"No," Jess said, pushing her son back. "You're not damaging your precious hands."

Then Jess did what she'd been avoiding this entire time. "Sabina."

Jess's best friend appeared and in just a moment she had the knives her husband had purchased for her years ago pressed against the throat of MacKilligan and the inside thigh of the sister.

Instantly, the siblings stopped fighting. They stopped moving. Which Jess found telling. These weren't spoiled brats who'd never been threatened before, who didn't realize they were in danger. They knew they were in danger and reacted instantly.

"Just a nick," Sabina said, her voice soft but her Russian accent thicker, "and you two bleed all over our nice lawn furniture. So you stop . . . or I will start cutting. Understand?"

MacKilligan pulled her hands away from her sister, her knuckles bloody from punching her sister's face. And her sister stepped away, her nose bloody and flatter.

"Thank you, Sabina."

Sabina winked at Jess. "You are welcome, my friend."

Jess moved closer to MacKilligan. "What your father did . . . is not on you. You know that, right?"

"Sure."

The sister rolled her eyes. "You are the *worst* liar."

"Shut up."

"Nick here . . . nick there," Sabina muttered and the siblings again stopped bickering.

"We can't keep that violin," Jess finally said. "I mean, when I thought it was a piece of shit, that's one thing." She reached out and grabbed Johnny's forearm. "And thank you for stopping me from destroying it that time." She cleared her throat. "Because that would have been awful."

Johnny smiled. "No problem."

"But now that I know what it's actually worth and what actually happened—"

"I can't take it back."

The sister threw up her hands in frustration but she didn't say anything. Smart. Sabina was dying to use her knives on actual human beings.

"As a collector, Stevie," Coop said from behind Johnny— how long had he been there?—"you could *donate* the violin to Johnny for his lifetime. As a collector, since you don't play yourself, it would be considered completely normal and no one would have to know anything but that."

Johnny suddenly shook his head. "I . . . I'm not ready to play a Guarneri."

MacKilligan suddenly made a scoffing sound and Jess thought she'd have to start punching bitches in the face, too, but then the hybrid said, "Of *course* you're ready."

"No, I'm not."

"I've heard you play," she said flatly, staring at Johnny like he was an idiot. "You're ready. And just so we're clear, I wouldn't say that if I didn't mean it. I don't care what my father may have stolen from you. When it comes to music, if you suck, I tell you that you suck. But when you're actually good, I tell you that too."

"It's true," her sister interjected. "She's a total bitch when it comes to her music or science. Anything else . . . she could give a shit."

"Yeah," Johnny said, "but a Guarneri . . ."

"You were playing a Stradivarius," MacKilligan reminded him.

"Well . . . I kinda had to. My mom bought it for me. But to get a donation of this kind and then to fuck it up."

"You won't." And MacKilligan said it so plainly, her gaze right on him, that Jess knew she meant it. She had no doubt in Johnny's talents. None. Something that meant way more to Jess than the four million she'd originally paid for the Stradivarius at auction.

"Just one thing, though," MacKilligan went on. "A favor. When you play the Met—"

"I'm not playing the Met."

"You will. And when you do, Vivaldi's Four Seasons." She smiled. "It's my absolute favorite and it will make you a household name. I know it's common and you hear it all the time in movies and commercials, but for violin . . . it never fails to make me feel. And I would absolutely love to hear you play that on a Guarneri. I mean, the power of your playing combined with the power of that violin . . . it completely outstrips the Stradivarius in intensity." She glanced at Jess. "No offense."

What was Jess supposed to say to that when the woman was donating a twenty-two-million-dollar violin to her only son? "None taken."

"About the jackal house . . . I don't want them to lose it."

Johnny DeSilvo's adoptive mom frowned. "Why would they lose the house?"

"Told ya," Max muttered. "Set up."

"Could you go away?" Stevie growled at her sister, completely fed up with her shit right now.

"But—"

"Go away!" she snapped, ready to start the punches again.

"Fine!"

Once her sister had stormed back into the house with everyone else, Stevie faced Jess Ward and put on her best audience smile. "Sorry about that."

"I have five daughters . . . I get it."

"Yeah, you probably do. Anyway, what happened at the house . . . my fault. I don't want the Jean-Louis Parkers held responsible for it."

"I get that, but our contractor says we're looking at six figures' worth of damage."

Six figures? *Holy shit.*

"O . . . okay. I can't pay that now, but I can get it. Just give me a little—"

"How about," she said, putting her arm around Stevie's shoulders and pulling her close, "we come up with another option."

Stevie glanced at the hand gripping her shoulder and back at the wild dog. "Is this a weird sexual request? Because I don't do that."

She stared at Stevie for a long time before asking, "The MacKilligan gals are a . . . unique group, aren't they?"

Finally, Stevie had to laugh. "You have *no* idea."

Shen waited on the stairs leading to the Pack house, his back against the railing, his legs stretched out in front of him.

"So when's your next match?" Shen asked Coop, who was opposite him and a step lower.

"Friday. I'm hoping Stevie will play."

"She probably will. She said she had a good time."

"Great." Coop glanced off, then said, "By the way, you have the night off. My mom wants Kyle home. Toni's coming over with Ricky Lee, which means his brothers and sister are going to be with them. And where there is Ronnie Lee Reed, there's Sissy Mae Smith and a good chunk of the Smith Pack."

Shen chuckled. "Sure you don't want me to take Kyle back with us?"

"If I have to suffer, so does that little shit. Besides, it's what my mom insists on calling 'Family Night.' No matter how many times we ask her not to call it that."

"Too pedestrian?"

"Basically." He smiled. "I'll drop him off tomorrow."

"Great."

The front door opened and the rest of their group walked out. Before Kyle could say anything, Coop grabbed him by his T-shirt and dragged him down the stairs and toward the house across the street.

"Oh, come on! Family Night again? Can't you talk Mom out of it?"

Oriana sighed. "I hate Family Night."

"What do you guys do on a family holiday like Thanksgiving?" Shen asked.

"When Cherise started describing Thanksgiving as a celebration of the massacre of an entire race of people and Kyle described Christmas as a ritual honoring a mass delusion . . . the family found other things to do during the holidays."

Shen nodded. "That sounds like a very good idea."

"But there's no fighting on Family Night." Oriana sighed again and started down the stairs. But she abruptly stopped, stood there for a moment, then turned around and came back up. She smiled at Stevie.

"I just wanted to say . . . I had a really nice time today."

"Yeah, me too. Are you as surprised as I am?"

"Yeah! I just didn't see that coming. Maybe we could do it again sometime?"

Stevie's grin was wide. "I'd like that."

"Yeah. Me too."

Max's lip curled. "Are you two going to start dating now?"

Stevie's fist came back so fast, Max didn't have time to duck, and her nose was slammed farther into her head.

"Owww! *You evil bitch!*"

Ignoring her sister, Stevie took Oriana's phone, which

seemed to be surgically attached to the ballerina's hand, and quickly typed in what Shen assumed was her phone number.

"Talk to you later," Stevie said, handing the phone back. "And sorry about getting Max's blood on the screen."

"No problem."

Oriana waved and made her way across the street.

Shen looked at the MacKilligan sisters. "You guys ready to—"

Before he could even finish his sentence, the pair began barking at each other.

"How could you commit to something so stupid?" Max demanded.

"Keep your voice down," Stevie snapped, quickly moving down the stairs. "And it's not like I had much choice. Did you want her to call the FBI on me? Besides, we need to keep her as sweet as possible here. Six figures to fix that house? Six figures?"

"What did you expect? It's New York. You're lucky it wasn't seven."

Shen followed the pair, remotely unlocking the SUV doors.

"Six or seven, we can't pay right now. But this gets us out of it."

"She will *never* agree to you doing this, you know."

Shen expected one of them to get in the front passenger seat, but they both got into the back. He was a little insulted. He wasn't their driver.

But he realized he had nothing to do with the decision once he got in the driver's side and saw that Stevie had pinned her sister to the seat and was screaming in her face, "One word to Charlie about that goddamn violin and I will *bury you!*"

Deciding he wasn't going to get into the middle of any of this, Shen started the SUV, turned on the radio to a rock station, and headed back to Queens.

chapter THIRTEEN

The arguing stopped once they were on the road and Shen had the foolish belief that the sisters would just spend the rest of the evening not speaking to each other. But once they were back at the MacKilligan house and before Shen could even settle on the couch and begin on a nice pile of bamboo stalks, they started again.

It got so bad—with the pair standing in the middle of the living room just screeching at each other—that Shen decided to spend his night off anywhere but here. He went to his room, threw a few things into a small duffel and texted his big sister.

Can I stay at your Long Island house tonight?

The Hamptons one? The Mill Neck one? The Old Westbury one?

Stop. Freeport is fine.

Yeah. Sure. Key under rock that looks like turtle. Everything OK?

Yeah. Just need a break. Thanks.

Anytime. Just don't bring whores to my hot tub.

Shen laughed.

I'll keep that in mind.

He picked up the small duffel and then a larger one that had a nice supply of bamboo. Just in case his sister's housekeeper hadn't kept her pantry stocked.

With everything in hand, he went down the stairs. He could hear the sisters going at it, still in the living room. Keeping his gaze on the floor, Shen moved into the room and got close to the couch, so he could slip by them and not be noticed. He'd just neared the door when Charlie bellowed from the kitchen, "*That is it!*"

Shen froze. He knew if he made a run for it, the three sisters could take him down. It was an instinctive response. Running made you prey. So he stood still and waited.

Charlie stormed into the living room, shoving her bickering sisters apart.

"I'm done with this bullshit!"

Stevie and Max started screaming at each other again; their faces close. But Charlie pushed them apart once more.

"Get out!" she ordered Max.

"Me? What did I do?"

"You exist!" Stevie barked.

"I want you out too," Charlie told Stevie.

"Me?" she gasped, abruptly sounding like the innocent "baby" sister. "But you love me."

Charlie ignored that and looked around the living room. She spotted Shen—he could *feel* those wolf eyes on him—and ordered, "Take her out of here, Shen."

Now he had to say it. "Me? Why me?"

"She's your girlfriend, isn't she?"

"No! She is not my—"

"She is now!" Charlie snapped and then she shoved her sister at Shen.

"*Hey!*" Now Stevie sounded like Stevie. Annoyed and petulant.

"Get out! Both of you!" She pointed at Stevie and then Max. "I want everybody out of this fucking house! I'm sick of this shit!"

"Fine!" Max yelled.

"*Fine!*" Stevie screamed.

Both sisters split off and Shen took his chance. He headed to the door, went outside, walked quickly to his SUV, got in, started it, and had nearly pulled away when the passenger door opened.

Stevie and her oversized backpack filled with her many, *many* notebooks nearly collided with his head before she settled into the passenger seat. She slammed the door, tossed the pack to the backseat, put on her seat belt, crossed her arms over her chest, and proceeded to pout.

"Look—" he began.

What?" she bellowed.

Shen briefly raised his hands, palms out. "Nothing."

She settled back into her seat and Shen pulled onto the road. After about twenty minutes, he began, "You know—"

"Do you mind not talking to me right now?" she snapped. "I'm not in the mood!"

"If I'm so annoying, I can take you back to your house."

Her head turned; her mouth dropped open in shock. "You would say that to *me*? I'm your girlfriend!"

"You're not my girlfriend!"

Stevie let out a disgusted sound. "Keep up that attitude, mister, and I won't be."

And Shen really didn't know what to make of that reply.

Stevie followed Shen into the house he said his sister owned. A five-bedroom, three-bath, two-story contemporary in Freeport, Long Island, overlooking the channel.

"I would live here," she told him once they were inside.

"It is nice."

"Hardwood floors? Cathedral ceilings in the living *and* dining room? Full, state-of-the-art kitchen with stainless steel everything?" she said, peeking into the kitchen next to the dining room. "This is a little more than nice."

"I guess."

She examined the living room furniture. "Your sister has very nice taste."

"She should," he muttered, dropping his duffel bags by the couch and walking to the large glass doors that looked out over the channel.

"What does that mean?"

"She's in the style business. It's her job to have good taste."

"The style business?" Stevie asked, immediately becoming annoyed. "God, you don't mean some idiot that promotes a tea that can help a person lose fifty pounds? Or shows twenty different ways to put on mascara?"

"I find those mascara tutorials very helpful."

Stevie was analyzing the ramifications of a tsunami slamming into this area, so it took a few seconds for that last comment to get inside her head.

"Wait . . . what?"

Shen chuckled. "My sister is editor-in-chief of a fashion magazine in Manhattan. She has her own fashion channel on cable. She hosts a fashion party each year that every celebrity wants to be invited to. People have tried to bribe me for thousands of dollars for tickets. So when I say style is her business, I mean—"

"Your sister is *Kiki* Li?"

Shen nodded. "That's her."

"*The* Kiki Li?"

"I have to admit, I didn't imagine *you* being a fan. You seem to have your own style."

"I'm going to take that as a compliment—"

"It was."

"—and just say that your sister's write-up of my opera *La Luna Destructo* put me on the map. Took my work out of rich-people-who-like classical category and into the movie-producers-and-ad-companies-calling-my-agent-everyday category." Stevie had to chuckle a little herself. "Actually, your sister is the reason I got out of music."

Shen jerked around to face her. "What?"

"What I mean is I didn't want to be a star. I didn't want to be famous. I just wanted to do my music. But once your sister noticed me . . . she practically made me a household name and I couldn't handle it. The pressure was too much—so I bailed."

Shen scratched his head. "I feel like I should apologize for her, or something."

"For what? Doing her job? She was just breaking out then anyway. It's not like she did it on purpose. She was still learning her power," Stevie teased. "And I was only ten. It was too much pressure already."

"I can't imagine doing any of that when I was ten."

"What did you do?"

"Run around screaming with my friends, falling from things . . . usually trees. And eating. I was constantly eating."

"Are you still close to your sister?"

"Sisters. And, of course. Why wouldn't I be?"

"Your sister's famous. That, sometimes, gets between siblings."

"Not ours. But we're pandas. None of that fame shit means anything to us." He glanced at her. "And it doesn't seem like your fame has gotten between you and your sisters."

"Well, these days, my fame is science-based. I mostly have geeky guys wearing T-shirts with Bill Gates as a Star Trek Borg coming up to me to challenge a recent paper I've just had published. And, honestly, my sisters and I didn't really have the luxury to cut each other loose. We don't have anyone else."

"Oh, come on. Don't sell yourself short. You have Kyle!"

Stevie glanced at Shen. He was gazing out over the channel again, but she could see the smirk on his face.

"You're an idiot," she said around her laughter.

"But we both know I'm right."

Shen paused the baseball game on his sister's giant screen TV in the living room and answered the front door.

"Mr. Li?" the young man asked.

"Yeah?"

"Hi. I'm from Chung Grocery. Ms. Li called in an order to be delivered."

"Oh, sure."

Shen stepped back, expecting a guy with one or two bags of groceries. He should have known better.

What traipsed into his sister's house was an entire crew of delivery people. About eight. And they each had to make several rounds. They didn't just bring in a fresh supply of high-end bamboo direct from Shaanxi, China, but bags of groceries, champagne, wine, and flowers in vases that were placed strategically around the home.

It was clear this was not the first time these people had performed such a function for his sister.

What confused Shen was why. He was here for one night, not a week. Not even a weekend. He texted her.

What is this?

Thought you could use a little glamour.

Since when?

When Shen didn't get an answer, he rolled his eyes and began typing.

Okay. What did Steinberg tell you?

Leonard Steinberg was his sister's neighbor. The old man had lived in his house for about thirty years and adored Kiki. Watched her house for her, kept her apprised of local gossip, and made sure that the place was locked down anytime there was a hurricane or bad storm. Kiki, in turn, had a handyman that helped out Steinberg whenever he needed it. He was on a fixed income, making Kiki's assistance really important. Shen was sure the old man had told his sister that Shen had not come here alone.

Now his sister had ideas. Kiki with ideas was never a good thing. Like Stevie, she was brilliant, though in a different way. She couldn't do math to save her life and science didn't really exist for her. She also couldn't draw, she was adamant that technology was out to get her, and she never read nonfiction anything unless it was a juicy gossip tell-all about celebrities. But when it came to fashion and art . . . Kiki had something not many people had. And she was positive she knew what was right and what was wrong; what was in and what was out. No one could tell her different, either. It made her an influential force to the world and an occasional pain in the ass to her baby brother.

All I'm going to say is . . . she sounds cute.

At that point, Shen just dialed his sister.

"What's wrong with you?" he demanded as soon as she picked up.

Kiki sighed. "I really should start having my assistant answer my cell phone. Suze, put my brother on the do-not-answer list, would you?" she called out.

"On it!" Suze replied.

"Look," he said, ignoring both women, "I just want to make it clear—"

"That you have a girlfriend and you didn't tell your sisters about her?"

"*She is not my girlfriend!*"

"Really? Because she told Steinberg she was your girlfriend."

"Oh my God! Seriously?"

"Shen . . . you're not going out with that girl who wanted you to meet her parents on the first date, are you?"

"No! She's a friend of my client. She needed to get out of her house for a little while. I was helping. But I'm starting to think she's delusional."

As Shen spoke, he glanced out the glass doors looking out over the channel. Stevie stood on the railing, facing the water.

"Oh, shit."

"What's wrong?"

"I'm afraid she thinks she can fly."

"Oh! Is she a bird shifter? Wait . . . do we even have bird shifters? I've heard rumors of crows. Although who'd want to shift into an angry black bird?"

Shen couldn't listen to his sister's rambling *and* deal with a delusional MacKilligan. Not at the same time.

"I'll call you back."

"What about eagles? Do we have any eag—"

Shen disconnected the call and pulled open the sliding door.

"Uh . . . Stevie?" He kept his voice calm. Rational. "Whatcha doin'?"

"Listening to music."

Except there was no music and she didn't have on earbuds.

"O . . . kay. Does the music talk to you?"

"Music always talks to me. And right now it's talking to me about flying over the ocean."

"Oh God . . . you do think you can fly."

She opened her eyes, looked at him. "No, I don't think I can fly." Then she added, "Go fuck off."

"I just want to make sure you're okay."

"I'm fine. Ballet," she said, closing her eyes again and facing the ocean and the wind coming off it.

"What about ballet?"

"Can't you see it?"

Shen didn't answer; he just closed the sliding door and looked at his phone again. He zipped through his contacts list and speed-dialed the number he needed.

"Yeah?" a voice said on the other end.

"I don't want you to worry, but I think your sister is having a nervous breakdown."

There was silence, a deep breath, then Charlie asked, "Okay. I'm not going to have an anxiety attack. Instead, I'm going to *calmly* ask you some questions and you're going to calmly respond. Can you do that for me?"

"Sure."

"Okay. What makes you think my sister is having a breakdown?"

"We're at my sister's Freeport house. By the water. She's standing on the railing. I'm afraid she thinks she can fly."

"Oh. Oh! My sister loves the water. She especially loves when the wind is coming off the water."

"Yeah. She's facing the wind."

"Okay. That's good."

"She also said she hears music. There is no music."

"My sister can hear music in her head. Like you listening to a radio. Hearing music when there is none, is totally normal for *her*."

"Then she suddenly said 'ballet.' For no obvious reason I could ascertain."

"That probably means she's writing a ballet in her head. The music for a ballet anyway. Most likely because of Oriana. She's probably inspired."

"I guess that makes sense."

"Just so you know, my sister isn't delusional."

"Manic?"

"No. She doesn't have huge highs. She has inspiration, which might make her seem manic, but it's just excitement over new ideas. Her depression can get bad, but she usually just crawls under her bed and cries for a while. Her anxiety is the thing you have to watch out for. She gets freaked out by—"

"Crowds?"

"Crowds of bears. Squirrels. She doesn't like hamsters. Crowds of people, however, are fine."

"Hamsters?"

"Anything that skitters. Oh, she doesn't like snakes either, which is weird . . . 'cause she's still half honey badger."

"Right."

"But you can tell when that anxiety is getting the best of her. You saw it the other day."

"She was shaking and naked in the cabinet because there were bears in her kitchen."

"Exactly. And that was when her meds had stopped working. It seems, though, that the new meds *are* working. And I'm going to have faith that they are working until I see definite evidence they're not. I'm not going to assume there is a problem. I'm not going to worry needlessly about problems that aren't there."

Shen frowned. He got the feeling she wasn't really talking to him as much as herself. "That's great to know, but I'm asking about Stevie."

"My sister is fine. It sounds like she's having a great time."

"So she won't try to fly away?"

"Not physically, no. But my sister does live in her head. So if she shuts you out for a few hours, don't take it personally. She's just creating something. Probably something amazing."

"Okay." Shen nodded. "I just wanted to make sure."

"It's so cute how protective you are of your new girlfriend."

"I'm hanging up now."

"You two would make such cute babies!"

Shen disconnected the call and shook his head, wondering—again—what the fuck was happening with his life.

"It's not my problem," he told himself. "It's not my problem. Her sister says she's fine. So I'm going to . . ."

During his speech, Shen glanced outside and immediately noticed that Stevie was no longer on the railing. Worried she had tried to fly, he went out on the deck and looked out on the water. But the wind shifted and he caught her scent . . . above him.

He looked up and saw her perched on the roof.

"What are you doing up there?"

She shrugged, lips briefly twisting before she admitted, "I chased a bird."

"Did you catch the bird?"

"Maybe."

"Did you eat the bird?"

"*No.* I still need my birds cooked, thank you very much. Perhaps with a light lemon-pepper seasoning. Or a wine sauce."

"Uh-huh. Was it a seagull?"

"Yeah."

"When you caught it, did it attack you?"

"It was really mean."

"Because you snatched it out of the sky."

"Then it shouldn't have flown over my head!"

Shen let out a sigh and went back into the house. He grabbed some of that high-end bamboo from Shaanxi, China, went to the couch, and continued watching the baseball game.

★   ★   ★

Stevie had nearly filled an entire blank music notebook with her latest work when Shen woke up. He'd fallen asleep in front of the TV, a stalk of half-eaten bamboo hanging out of his mouth, one leg slung over the back of the couch's headrest.

He hadn't snored the couple of hours he'd napped, which she was grateful for. And he'd left the baseball game on the TV, which for her was like a soothing white noise.

When he awoke, he sat up straight, the bamboo still in his mouth. He didn't remove it, though. He just began eating it again and looked around the room. When he saw her, he seemed relieved. Did he think she'd snuck out on him? Why would she do that? This place was awesome. The water. The mostly friendly neighbors. Except Mrs. Bartman down the way who'd told Stevie to "Get the fuck out of my yard, whore!" A reaction that seemed a little extreme, but Stevie didn't get mad. And the comment made the other nearby neighbors even friendlier because they all hated Mrs. Bartman.

"What time is it?"

"You're wearing a watch," she informed Shen.

"I am?"

"Since I've met you."

"Oh, yeah! Look at that. And, hey," he added, "it's a Breitling!"

Stevie finally looked up from her work. "You own a Breitling and you didn't know it? How is that possible?"

"My sister gets free shit all the time. If she doesn't want it, she gives it to me or Zhen."

"Lucky. All I ever get from Max is fistfights and from Charlie, concern."

"She's trying."

She again looked away from her work. "She's trying what?"

"To be better. About worrying over you."

"How do you know?"

"I called her earlier because I thought you were delusional and you were going to try and fly."

Stevie laughed. "That's so ridiculous!"

"I didn't know. I mean between you hanging out on the railing and the rumors you're spreading about us dating . . . sorry. I mean telling everyone you're my *girlfriend*."

"I am your girlfriend."

"You're not!"

"Since when?"

"Since forever!"

"Look—" Stevie turned in the chair, her arm on the back— "I know you think you have some say in this . . . but you don't. I've kind of made up my mind here."

"Meaning what . . . exactly?"

"That *I've* decided we're boyfriend and girlfriend."

"Because I'm cute?"

"That's a definite start. But come on. You have to admit we're perfect together."

"I don't have to admit that, because it's not true. At the very least, it's unknown. *And what is that noise?"*

She pointed toward the sliding glass doors. "Cats."

"Huh?" He got up and went to the doors to find that a large number of stray cats had congregated on the deck. "Why are there all these scraggly ass cats outside our house?"

Stevie laughed.

"What's so funny?"

"Our house."

He growled. "I meant," he bit out slowly, "my sister's house."

"Sure you did."

"Did you feed them?"

"No."

"You've been feeding that stray cat outside the Queens house."

"I might as well . . . she's not going anywhere. She's chosen us. As far as she's concerned, it's her house now. It doesn't matter what Max does . . . we're stuck with her. So we might as well feed her."

Stevie began doodling a dollar sign on the top of her music papers, but when Shen didn't say anything, she looked up. He was staring at her, his mouth open.

"What?" she asked.

"You. You're that stray cat."

"Pardon?"

"'She's not going anywhere. She's chosen us. As far as she's concerned, it's her house now.' *I'm* the house in this scenario. I'm your boyfriend now because you've *decided* I am."

"As long as we're clear."

"*We're not clear!*" he bellowed, but immediately pulled his anger back. "I understand that maybe you're at a point in your life where you're looking for someone to love. I'm just not that guy."

"Why?"

"I'm lazy. I have no real ambition. I just want to make enough money to have a relaxing home and an unlimited supply of bamboo. That's it. That's all I want from life. But you . . . you need someone ambitious. Someone who wants more from life."

"I've tried that. It never works out well. Oh! That reminds me." She stood. "We need to go out."

"We're having a conversation here."

"It'll have to wait. I have a date with Dr. Matt Wells."

"The hybrid *murderer*?"

"He's not murdering people, per se. He's experimenting on them, and when the experiments go bad and they die, he tosses their bodies out into the woods and sets them on fire."

Shen, his arms stretched out, hands palms up, just kept staring at her . . . with his mouth open.

"It's wrong," she volunteered. "Is that what you need me to say? Because it is wrong and I know it's wrong. It's not something I'd ever do. But I don't get emotional over it because he's a scientist, so I understand his thinking. It's wrong thinking, but I understand it."

"You do know you're a hybrid, don't you? Which means you're at risk."

"Chances are he's going after hybrids in the first place *because* of me. I've got to find out what's going on and, if I can, stop it."

Shen dropped his arms. "And what do you want me to do?"

"Pretend to be my security."

"I *am* your security."

She snorted. "I'd never actually hire you as my security."

"Why the hell not?"

"Because you're my boyfriend. Duh. You'd be too emotionally involved."

"But I'm not your boyfriend."

"Uh-huh," she dismissed him, because they were running late. "I'll go get changed."

Stevie walked over to Shen, walked around him, and headed toward the stairs that led to the bedrooms.

Shen was silent for a few seconds until he asked, "Woman . . . did you just *rub* up against my back?"

"Well," she chuckled, grabbing her pack, into which she'd shoved some going-out clothes, "I'm way too tall to wrap myself around your legs. And when I shift my tail can wrap around your entire body a few times . . . so I assumed unleashing that would just freak you out."

Without another word, she headed up the stairs, leaving Shen standing there, with his mouth open and the most adorably confused expression on his handsome face.

chapter FOURTEEN

S hen readjusted his gun holster under his light business jacket. He always had work clothes in his sister's many homes. More than once he'd had to help her out, keeping the leeches and losers off her back when she was trying to work an event.

So he had on his black jeans, black shoes, black designer T-shirt, and a black linen jacket to hide his weaponry.

"Your sister is so cool," Stevie said from upstairs. "She has all these designer shoes in different sizes."

"Don't wear those ridiculously high heels that she insists on wearing. I don't want to have to carry you from the car to the restaurant."

Shen heard Stevie bopping down the stairs, which surprised him. He'd mostly only seen her barefoot around the house, so he didn't think she could walk in high heels. Much less bop down the stairs.

But when he turned around, he found that Stevie wasn't wearing any of his sister's giant-heeled designer shoes but sneakers. Converse, specifically. Sparkly Converse. Plus jeans, a T-shirt that read, "Shut your piehole," and her hair in a messy ponytail.

"What are you wearing?" Shen had to ask, laughing.

Instead of being insulted, Stevie did a little spin on that bottom step. "You don't like?"

"I like, but I thought you were meeting this guy for drinks at that fancy restaurant in Old Westbury? That's a rich area."

"Right. He's trying to impress me. I don't care that he's trying to impress me. I want him to *know* I don't care."

"And you want me there . . . ?"

"You're my security. I need you to make sure he doesn't punch me in the mouth." She grinned. "Duh."

It was a five-star restaurant where she was meeting Wells. He'd said he happened to be out on the Island for an "important meeting" and had just enough time to get together for an after-meal drink.

Stevie was fine with that. She'd rather not sit through an entire dinner with him. And she'd rather meet him at a restaurant than a bar. Meetings in bars, in her mind, often gave guys the wrong idea. She didn't want Wells to know what she was up to, but she also didn't want him to think, even for a nanosecond, that he had a chance in whatever hell the world wanted to believe in that he could ever get back into her panties.

Shen opened the restaurant door and Stevie paused a moment to let go the little shudder she'd been holding inside.

"Are you okay?" Shen immediately asked.

"Oh, yeah. I'm fine."

"Are you sure? We don't have to do this," he said in a very low, quiet voice.

"You are so cute," she said, loving how he continued to kind of blush when she did.

"Get in the fucking restaurant so we can get this over with."

Giggling, she walked inside. It was a very nice, very elegant restaurant. She stood out among the wealthy diners, but she didn't care. Maybe they thought she was a CEO from some Silicon Valley start-up.

"May I help you?" the hostess asked, her snobby gaze giving Stevie the once-over.

"I'm here for Matt Wells. Name is Stevie MacKilligan."

"Yes. Dr. Wells is waiting for you."

The hostess started walking and Stevie fell in behind her. As they moved through the restaurant, she turned around to face Shen, now walking backward.

"Tomorrow morning, I have therapy. Can you take me?"

"Sure. I can pick up Kyle afterward."

"Great. But before you get Kyle," she remembered, "I need to go see Oriana at her rehearsal."

"Why?"

"Do I ask you questions?" she shot back.

"You ask *everyone* questions. Remember the yogi?"

"He was short-tempered and *rude*."

"Which yogis are known for."

Stevie bumped into something and realized it was the hostess, who'd stopped walking.

"Sorry." She moved around the annoyed woman and Wells pushed away from the table, stood.

He was tall. Nearly six-four. With golden blond hair and gold-green eyes. And a cat. Lion male, specifically, which had been part of the problem with their relationship. Some lions were fun and interesting. And some you wanted to shove in a furnace just so you could watch them scream about their burning hair as they were dying.

"Stevie," he said with that handsome smile.

"Matt."

"Matthew," he corrected. "I still prefer Matthew."

"Uh-huh," she said.

Stevie reached to pull out a chair, but Shen was already there, doing the job. She glanced back at him and saw that his whole disposition had changed. He'd gone from her adorable panda to the guy hired to play the Secret Service agent in a blockbuster summer movie.

He was even wearing his sunglasses. Sunglasses! At night! *Inside* the restaurant.

She bit the inside of her mouth so that she didn't laugh and took her seat. Then Shen stood behind her, his hands clasped in front of him, his gaze continually scanning the restaurant.

It was ridiculous and hilarious and she was loving every minute of his lunacy because she knew *exactly* how much it was annoying Wells. And completely relaxing her in the moment.

"It's so good to see you again, Matt," she lied.

"You, too. And it's still Matthew."

"Is it? Because you've always looked so much like a Matt to me."

A waitress came to their table and asked what Stevie would like to drink, but before Stevie could answer . . .

"She'll have an Old Fashioned."

Stevie felt her eyes beginning to narrow on Matt's stupid, *stupid* face. She'd always hated when he ordered for her, and he would order for her all the time. Part of it was to show how well he knew her, but it was also a form of control. And Stevie didn't like being controlled. It irritated the hell out of her.

"Actually," she told the waitress before the woman could walk away, "I'll have a beer. Anything you have on tap."

The waitress looked at Shen but he just shook his head.

"Your tastes have changed, I see," Wells told her.

"I've *never* liked Old Fashioneds, but you kept ordering them for me anyway . . . when I was eighteen."

Wells cleared his throat, then said, "So you're looking for work."

"No. I'm looking for a new home. CERN has been great, but I need something new. My old boss, though, has been calling me. The last message was a little hysterical. I hear you've got some great work going on at your lab. And awesome financial backing. That intrigues me."

"Really? You wouldn't mind working for me?"

"Why would I?"

"Well, the last time we met, you said you didn't want me anywhere near you."

"Noooo. What I said exactly was, I didn't want your hands or *penis* anywhere near me . . . ever again. And that still holds. But that was a social thing. Now, however, we're talking science, and you've always said you could separate the two."

"Of course I can. But I don't know what my labs would do with a theoretical physicist. As you know, my specialty is bio-engineering."

Stevie took her time, letting her smile slowly spread until

she couldn't stretch her face any more without ripping the skin. And she let that smile speak for itself.

Wells couldn't hide his sneer. "Oh, I see. You've studied bioengineering."

"Yes."

"And have your PhD?"

"Of course. Four years ago."

He looked down at his drink. An Old Fashioned. "And what brought you to that field?"

The truth was that one time Stevie forgot to eat and after fourteen hours of no food, she got what Charlie always called "the shakes." But before Stevie realized that's what was happening she decided she had Parkinson's. She'd freaked herself out so badly in the twenty seconds it took her to get to that point, she had a panic attack and had to go to the hospital because she couldn't breathe. She decided if she was going to cure her nonexistent Parkinson's—you know, in case she actually ever got it—she'd have to study bioengineering. So she did.

What she told Wells, though . . .

"I was bored."

Shen didn't know Stevie could be so mean. He knew she could be dangerous when startled. He knew she panicked easily. He knew she insisted on calling him "cute" and treating him like a giant stuffed panda bear before deciding they were boyfriend and girlfriend without his consent. He knew all those things about her. But he didn't know she could be mean.

And she was being *really* mean to this lion.

Which meant, to Shen anyway, that she truly hated the guy. Because she was nice to everyone else. Sweet Stevie. Known on the bear-only Queens street as "the nice one" among the MacKilligans.

Of course, this was Stevie he was talking about. She wasn't mean to Wells like her sisters would be. She was doing with words what her sisters would do with fists or the cutlery from a nearby table.

"I see you haven't changed much," Wells snapped, becoming more agitated the longer they talked.

"Was I supposed to change?"

"A little humility wouldn't hurt."

"In science? Are you high? You expect me to be humble when I deal with men like you all day, every day? Men who seem to make it their purpose in life to convince me I can't be good in science and math because I have tits and a pussy! My confidence is my armor. Against assholes like you."

"Speaking of assholes, how are your sisters?"

Shen winced behind his glasses. Going after Stevie's sisters . . . ? Probably not a good idea.

Stevie's spine straightened a bit and even without seeing her face, he could tell that a dangerous coldness had spread over her like a blanket.

"My sisters are great, thanks," she replied.

"Are they still following you around? Making sure their baby sister is safe? Making sure that no one else comes into your life who might get between you and them? Someone who might offer you a future."

"Like the future of living with a momma's boy who doesn't take a shit unless his mother tells him he can? Which, by the way, my sisters didn't point out to me. I pointed that fact out to *them*." Stevie folded her hands on the table. "Aren't you supposed to leave a pride at some point? So you don't end up having sex with your cousin? Unless that's your thing."

"Perhaps you should watch what you're saying to me."

"Or what?" Stevie pushed. "You'll call your mom and tell her that girls are being mean to you again?"

Wells slammed his hand down on the table, making the full-humans around them jump. But before the lion could say a word, Shen leaned around Stevie, placed one finger on the table, and calmly said to the male, "No, no. We won't be doing any of that."

Eyes that had suddenly turned bright gold looked at Shen, and Shen didn't like what he was seeing. Stevie had him so crazy the man didn't even have control of himself in the middle of a full-human restaurant. If he wanted to pull this bullshit with an ex, there was a Van Holtz Steakhouse a few doors down.

No longer feeling that Stevie was safe, he grabbed the back of her chair.

"I think it's time to go," he kindly but strongly suggested.

Stevie didn't argue with him, just let him pull her seat out. But before Stevie walked away, she stopped and turned back to Wells.

"How's your brother?" she asked.

Wells glared up at her, but he managed to force a smile. "He's doing great."

"Still a perpetual student?"

"He has his own lab now, thanks. His own lab, his own backers."

"Really?"

"Like I said . . . he's doing great."

"And I'm sure he did all that on his own without any help from you or your mother."

Shen gently pressed his hand against Stevie's back, trying to prompt her toward the door. And she did go, but not before mouthing at Wells, *Momma's boy.*

Well, that had gone poorly!

As Stevie and Shen waited for the valet to get the car, she couldn't help but silently beat herself up. She'd let Wells's idiocy get to her yet again. They used to have the same kind of vicious fights when they were dating. So bad that *Max* was the one who eventually took her aside and asked, "Is this really what you want?" She'd said it with no judgment, with no directive. She hadn't pushed Stevie to make a decision one way or another, but Stevie knew what her sister had been concerned about. Because what was going on between Stevie and Wells had seemed like the kind of relationship their dad always had. With dramatic fights and hateful statements and just being general dicks to each other.

Realizing that, Stevie had made the decision that the relationship had to end. Wells hadn't handled it well, though. Despite his need to constantly put Stevie down as a scientist, he loved bragging about her to other scientists. Because she was a prodigy, she was worthy of being with him. So her walking away had really pissed him off, and he clearly wasn't over it. Just as she wasn't over his cheap shots.

"Stevie, wait," Wells said, coming out of the restaurant.

As Wells moved in close, Shen automatically stepped in front of Stevie. He was just doing his job. Protection was what he did for a living. But the simple move set Wells off.

"Move," the lion male ordered Shen, towering over the panda.

"Sorry, no," Shen said. And Stevie loved how calm he was. He hadn't raised his voice once. Hadn't flexed his muscles. Hadn't flashed his fangs. He just kept his tone calm and even. As if they were in a concert hall.

"I said move!"

Shame Stevie didn't get that same calm behavior from Wells.

Instead, he moved in even closer, glowering down at poor Shen.

"I need you to step back, sir."

Wells brought his head down so that their faces almost touched. "Make me."

And in that same calm, cool manner, Shen opened his mouth . . . and bit down on Well's nose.

It looked like a little nip, but Stevie heard the hard "crunch," saw the quick snap of his powerful jaw. Stevie covered her mouth with her hands when Wells stumbled back, blood pouring down his face and into his mouth.

"*You insolent bastard!*" Wells bellowed.

Shen, still wearing those sunglasses, smiled, blood staining his teeth. "You did get a warning, sir. The rest is on you."

He walked to the SUV and opened the door for Stevie. "Ma'am?"

"Okay," Stevie said hurriedly. "Nice seeing you again, Matt. Tell your mom I said 'hi.'"

Stevie scrambled into the vehicle, letting Shen close the door behind her.

"Sir, are you all right?" one of the valets asked Wells, but Stevie wasn't too worried. No self-respecting lion male would ever have full-humans intervene in a common shifter fight. At the same time she wouldn't put it past him to unleash his fangs and claws and come after Shen.

Shen, however, didn't seem too concerned, taking his time to tip the valet, then standing by the open door of the driver's side so he could remove his sunglasses, put them on the dashboard; take off his jacket, fold it, place it in the backseat; slide into the SUV . . . adjust the rearview mirror and the seat; carefully check the side mirrors, and then, slowly, pull away from the restaurant.

Stevie had seen people deceased for several days move faster.

She looked out the back to see if Wells had attached himself to the SUV like a baboon attempting to flee one of those drive-through zoos, but after a few miles, she felt certain he'd decided not to make the situation worse.

Stevie turned around and got comfortable in her seat.

"You bit his nose," she finally said.

"If I had a rolled up magazine, I would have used that instead. I went with what was handy."

Stevie started to shake her head sternly, but the laughter spilled out first. And then it wouldn't stop.

"The look on his face!" she managed to get out, her arm around her stomach. "I've never seen him look like that before, and I've thrown things at his giant lion head."

"That particular expression you can only find on a startled lion male."

She wiped her eyes. "Conridge is going to be pissed. That did not go well. And I am *not* talking about your love bite."

"You don't just hate the man . . . you *hate* the man. It was an active thing."

"Why do you think I used to throw things at his giant head? Because he's an asshole. Personally, I think I was quite restrained."

"So now what?" Shen asked as he stopped at a red light.

"We follow the money. You don't get a fancy lab like that without some serious backers or the government involved."

The light changed but the SUV didn't move. Stevie leaned forward to see his face.

"Shen?" she asked softly.

"You don't think the government is—"

"No." She gave a little laugh. "No. If someone was testing shifters, just shifters, then maybe. Full-humans that know about our kind see us *all* as freaks. Maybe a challenge if they're hunters, but otherwise, we're just freaks to be destroyed. But to focus on hybrids—that's a specific sort of hatred. Like when full-blood wolves kill one in their pack because they're sick or something is wrong with them that we may not see but that they sense. I think that's what it's like for whoever is doing this."

"And I think you're giving animals that do that sort of thing way too much credit by assuming it's some kind of instinct. Even animals can be assholes."

Someone beeped their horn behind them and Shen pressed the gas.

"The question is," he went on, "whether *Wells* is doing all this stuff."

"I don't know. But I want to look into it. And I want to look into his brother too. The man has, like, four thousand degrees but he would never leave college. He seemed happy there. Now he's got a lab and backers."

"How are you going to check out either of them when you—"

"And you!"

"—have pissed Wells the fuck off?"

"I don't know yet, but I'll come up with something."

"Something that's actually logical . . . or at least your idea of something that's logical?

Stevie looked out the window, folded her arms over her chest, and muttered, "So not appreciating that sarcasm."

Charlie finished drying her baking pans and utensils and put them away in the cabinet near the stove. She folded up the towel and placed it on the sink rim. All the baked goods she'd created throughout the day were long gone. The bears had come in and wiped the table and counters clean of the last crumb.

She could hear Berg and his siblings talking in the living room while they watched TV. Based on the scorn in Britta's voice, it sounded like a reality show. For someone who always said how much she "detested" reality TV, she sure did watch a lot of it. She called it "hate watching," but Charlie didn't have enough time in the day to watch shit she hated just to mock it.

Unless it was a bad horror movie. Nothing entertained her more than watching a bad horror movie with her sisters. Actually, *any* horror movie. The MacKilligan sisters loved horror movies. Anything but torture porn, as Max called it. Two hours of watching people being hacked to pieces or pierced with things was too much for Charlie or her sisters. They preferred movies with demons or ghosts or witches. Anything supernatural.

Horror movies had always allowed them to get lost in fantasy rather than dealing with the reality of their daily lives. True, her mother would have preferred that her "pup-pups" spend their free time watching something with unicorns or girlfriends with traveling pants, but even she knew that sort of thing just bored her daughters.

Charlie pulled a cold beer out of the fridge, thinking that maybe it was time for an *Exorcist* marathon for her and her sisters. The first and the third were their favorites and the most terrifying. But the second and fourth ones—and there were *two* fourth ones—were the worst and most fun to mock.

Positive it was always a good time for *The Exorcist*, Charlie started toward the living room, but stopped when she heard something behind her. She turned, studied the kitchen. Didn't see anything out of place.

She sniffed the air, but Charlie was still learning how to sift out different scents and locate them. It was something that hadn't been taught to her when she was a kid. Her mother hadn't lived long enough, and when she moved in with her grandfather's Pack, she had more things to worry about with her two sisters than sniffing out the raccoon who kept destroying the shed behind the Pack house.

Frustrated, Charlie started walking and sniffing, trying to track something . . .

"Gotcha!" a voice barked behind her, hands grabbing her waist.

Charlie brought her elbow back, breaking the nose of whoever was behind her. She switched her beer to her other hand and with her free hand reached over her shoulder, grabbed a handful of hair, yanked the male body around in front of her. Then she kicked that body in the chest, sending it careening down the stairs toward the backdoor that led into the yard.

The door was snatched open and Max appeared, naked and covered in dead bees that had stung her when she'd attacked their hive.

Their gazes caught and Max frowned, looking down at the body at her feet.

"Dutch! What are you doing here?" Max asked.

Max's best friend glared at her, his hands covering his now bleeding nose. "Your sister attacked me!"

"You startled me!"

Max smirked at Charlie. "Right. That's why you broke his nose. But once you got him in front of you . . ."

Now Charlie smirked. "Then I was just beating the shit out of him."

Max laughed but Dutch didn't.

Tossing her beer to her sister—which Max easily caught—Charlie asked, "When Stevie gets back . . . *Exorcist* marathon?"

"*Exorcist* marathon!" Max cheered back. "I'm so in!"

"Excuse me!" Dutch complained. "What about me? Your sister attacked me!"

"But," Max said, pointing a finger at him, "she didn't *kill* you. And that makes you special and a little blessed."

Charlie nodded. "That's true."

★ ★ ★

Once Max put Dutch's nose back into place and put an ice pack on it, she asked, "So really . . . why are you here? I thought you were working."

"Still am."

Max sat down at the kitchen table across from her wolverine friend. The lights were still off but Dutch didn't seem to mind.

"What do you mean, you still are?" Max asked.

"Your Uncle Will. He's on his way to the States. Private charter."

"He's coming for the funeral."

"Yeah."

"So?"

"The Group wants to keep an eye on him."

"What does that have to do with you and me?"

"I'm here to make sure you and your sisters aren't secretly in contact with him. I'm spying on you."

"Oh." Max nodded. "Well then . . . good job!"

"You know, old friend, you're saying the right words, but that follow-up eye roll gives a vastly different message."

"You met with her?" Matt's brother demanded, stepping away from his desk. They shared the same home with their mother's Pride. Still. But it had been for the best. James didn't do well on his own. And local Prides didn't really have any interest in him. For a lion male he was too quiet, too obsessive, too . . . irritating to be tolerated by lion females who were not related to him. Of course, Matt could easily get into another Pride, but their mother had always said her two sons were "together forever." Then she'd remind Matt that he had to take care of James. "It's all on you. Never forget that."

And he didn't. How could he when he faced that weight on his shoulders every day he came home?

Matt poured himself a scotch. "Yes. I met with her."

"Why?"

"I thought we could work some things out. After all these years."

"And how did that go?"

Matt didn't answer, just drank his scotch.

"That woman can't be trusted and you know it."

Matt poured another scotch. "What does trust have to do with anything? I was just—"

"Bragging. You wanted to brag. To a woman who could probably not care less about you or what we've achieved."

We?

"Then why do you care we met?" he had to ask.

"She wants something from you. Don't you see that?"

"She doesn't want anything from me." And that's what had always bothered Matt about Stevie Stasiuk. Considering what a loser life she'd had growing up, it amazed him that she refused to ever ask him for anything. And when he gave her things, like jewelry or nice clothes, she never seemed interested. Maybe even bored. As if she were above all that.

And then her sisters. Good God, her sisters! He'd tried to be nice to them, but they'd made it clear they didn't like him. Thought he was too old for her. And they obviously didn't have thoughts that were higher than "flowers pretty. Day hot." They were cretins.

Stevie, though, he'd overlooked her genetic defects because her brain was so powerful, and he respected her for that. It wasn't enough, though. It was never enough.

He'd gone through most of their relationship never knowing what she'd wanted from him, but he did know that it had all blown up that morning when he'd been talking to her—he couldn't remember exactly what he was talking to her about, though—and one second she'd been sitting there, glaring at him, and the next he had a fork sticking out of his face.

Because that's where she'd shoved it!

He'd called the cops, of course. He was a shifter but he didn't really believe that logic many other shifters had of handling that sort of thing on their own. What else were cops for besides dealing with crazy women who suddenly attacked their boyfriends? But the cops didn't seem too interested and she didn't even get a night in jail. The whole thing appeared to be forgotten by everyone except Matt and his family.

Then he'd woken up one morning a few months after the breakup to find Max MacKilligan standing beside his bed.

"Drop these charges against Stevie, or I'll come back and cut your throat while you're sleeping." Then, for visual effect, she'd dragged her forefinger from one side of her neck to the other. While smiling.

Not needing a fight with the MacKilligans, he'd dropped the charges. Not because he was frightened, of course, but because it just made sense.

But his brother had never really let the whole thing go and was still angry Matt hadn't made sure she'd been charged and punished to the fullest extent of the law. James had always felt that Stevie was beneath his brother and didn't deserve any of the attention she'd always gotten.

"She's a freak," James had insisted then . . . and now. "And you continue to suck up to her."

"Let it go, James. It's over."

"Is it?" he asked. "Is it really?"

chapter FIFTEEN

Shen pulled the car into the attached garage at his sister's house and turned off the motor. All he could think about was getting on that great couch, watching some late-night TV, and eating some bamboo.

Ahhhh. Life was good.

"So," Shen said to Stevie, turning his head toward her, "want to go inside and—"

He stopped talking because he wasn't talking to Stevie's face. He was talking to her ass.

With her body between the two seats, she was leaning over so she could reach the back.

"What the hell are you doing?" Shen demanded. "Why am I talking to your ass?"

"I'm trying to get my backpack."

"You could have just gotten out of the car, opened the back-seat door, and pulled it out that way."

"You and your logic! This seemed like a good idea at the time. It's just the bag is stuck under the seat and . . . got it!"

She began to shimmy her ass back into the front, dragging her ridiculously oversized bag with her.

"Here—oooooh!" She cringed as her stupid bag sideswiped his head. "Oh, gosh, Shen. I'm so sorry."

"Why do you hate me?" he asked, rubbing his temple.

"I don't hate you!" she laughed. "It was an accident. Let me see your head."

"It's fine," he grumbled, reaching for the door. "Let's just go inside."

Shen got out of the car. He waited until Stevie had lugged her bag from the vehicle before engaging the locks and alarm, and then together they returned to the house. He put in the passcode to shut off the home's alarm. He secured the door, put on the alarm for the windows and doors but not for the inside of the house, so they could move around freely without accidentally bringing in the local cops.

Yawning and stretching, he tossed his jacket onto the nearest chair. Then he removed his holstered weapon, checked to make sure the safety was still on, and put it on the coffee table.

"You want some ice cream?" he asked. "I think the delivery guys brought flavors other than crunchy mango bamboo."

Not hearing a response, Shen looked over his shoulder, but Stevie wasn't behind him.

"Stevie?" he called out.

Thinking she'd already gone to bed—but wanting to check so he wouldn't worry—he started toward the stairs but stopped when something scrambled up his back.

Shen froze. "Stevie?"

He heard a purr and that's when she stretched herself over his shoulder; her legs resting against his back, her arms and torso free-hanging against his chest.

"What are you doing?"

"Throwing myself at you."

"Is that what this is?"

"I've found that for a woman to throw herself at a man, all she really has to do is get naked."

And that she was. Naked. Not a stitch on. Not even socks.

Sadly, Shen couldn't even argue with her logic. Naked was usually the best way to get a man's attention unless he had a specific kink.

"Stevie—" he began, but she'd started using her hands to knead a spot way too close to his groin and Shen jerked. A random, abrupt movement that sent Stevie head over ass off his back and onto the floor.

Before he could even reach to help her up, she was back on her feet.

"Sorry," he muttered. "You startled me."

Stevie pushed her hair off her face and shook off the embarrassment of falling flat on her ass in front of the guy she was so into. She'd admit that Shen was taking a lot more work than she was used to. Of course, most of the guys she'd been with were scientists who were more acquainted with their hand than a woman who was hot for them. Shen, however, was probably used to way hotter girls coming on to him. Rap artists and supermodels. The kind of girls Stevie didn't have a chance against except in a battle of intelligence.

But Stevie wasn't one to back down from a challenge. She knew what she wanted and she knew Shen liked her. So she'd give it one more shot.

"Look," she began, reaching back with one hand to brush something off her rear, "I like you." She brushed her butt again. "A lot. And if you're interested—*what is on my ass?*" she screeched, trying to look over her shoulder to see what was touching her.

Shen took hold of her upper arm and held her in place as he leaned over and removed whatever she'd picked up when she'd hit the floor.

He held it up for her. "Bamboo leaf."

"Oh."

"They're kind of all over the floor because of my eating. The cleaning staff will take care of it. But if you'd feel better, we can start cleaning tonight. Get all this stuff off the floor and—"

That was it. She didn't want to hear anything else about cleaning the floor, and she was tired of the mocking smirk on his face. She was going to take one more shot at this.

Stevie grabbed Shen's black T-shirt, twisted her hand in it, and yanked him down so that when she went up on her toes, she could reach his mouth.

She kissed him, hard, using her tongue to part his lips.

Now, if *this* didn't work, if he still showed no interest, then fine. She'd move on and forget about . . . forget about . . . something. What had she been thinking about? Because she really couldn't remember now that Shen was kissing her back.

Any doubts she'd had about his level of interest were washed away. Especially when he buried his hands in her hair and turned her head so he had better access to her mouth.

His tongue moved around hers; toying, teasing. Her body immediately responded. Her nipples getting hard. Her pussy getting wet. Just from one kiss.

The promise of that kiss alone had her lowering her hand to his crotch, her fingers searching out the zipper of his jeans. But he stopped her, pulled her hand away.

She was about to get angry. If he mentioned how young she was again, she was going to lose it!

"You threw yourself at me," he said, moving around her. "That means I make the rules."

"I've never heard that before."

He stood behind her now, both her wrists caught in one of his big hands.

Shen leaned down and moved her hair off her ear so he could press his mouth against it and whisper, "That's 'cause I just made it up."

She was fine with that, especially when his free hand slowly made its way down her stomach and slid between her thighs. He pressed two fingers inside her, moving them around, finding a spot deep inside that he pressed.

Stevie started to move against his hand, but he pulled out, gliding his fingers to her clit. He took his time circling, stroking, and brushing around and across.

Her knees went weak, but Shen's arm tightened so that she was trapped against him, unable to fall, his other hand still gripping her wrists.

As his fingers moved, his tongue did the same against her ear. Stroking the outside, teasing the inside.

Stevie pressed out her chest, but he ignored her breasts completely, which was making her nuts. She wanted his mouth on them. Or his hands. Something!

Sweat began to bead on her skin. And she could hear herself purring. Her hips were moving, trying to follow his fingers wherever they went as long as they kept stroking her clit or fucking her pussy. She didn't care.

Shen walked forward and she didn't even have to do anything. At this point, her feet weren't even on the floor; they were pressed against his lower legs, her toes rubbing against the denim.

Her entire body was rubbing against him.

She felt him going down.

"Bend your knees," he ordered gently and she did, assuming he was going to stop so he could get a blow job. She understood, though. She could feel his cock through his jeans and it was hard and ready. And, from what she'd felt . . . huge. She liked huge. Max had once called her a "size queen."

Stevie didn't know they were in front of one of the armchairs until Shen pushed her face down on the seat. He moved his hand away from her crotch, but only for a moment. A few seconds later, his fingers reentered her from behind, using the change in position to stroke her a little harder.

He released her wrists and brought his now-free hand back to the front of her pussy. He wet two fingers inside her and then dragged them back to her clit. He began circling and circling, while still taking her from behind.

Stevie pressed her cheek against the leather chair and let Shen work her body anyway he wanted to at the moment. Because it all felt amazing. Even though he wasn't touching her nipples, they were against the seat. Every time Shen pushed her forward, the grain of the leather rubbed against them, exciting her even more.

Then Shen licked his way up her spine and that first orgasm took her by complete surprise. She gasped hard, her legs shaking, her hips writhing.

She came, but it was quick. A shock to her system.

Shen didn't stop. He was too busy working her with his

hands and licking her back. She felt his fangs brush against her human skin, and that set off a second wave. Another orgasm about to crash down on her. About to take her over. She couldn't stop it. Even if she'd wanted to—and she didn't. Because Shen wouldn't stop. He just kept going and going until Stevie cried out into the leather cushion. Her hands reaching out and grabbing the arms of the chair, gripping them so tight she was sure she'd have to replace the whole thing. But it was the only thing grounding her, tethering her to this world as the second orgasm broke her down, left her panting and shaking.

Shen finally pulled his hands away, and she felt his absence when he moved.

She didn't even care. She should. She should call him back and return the favor, but at the moment she could only kneel in front of the chair, the rest of her limp against the cushion, and attempt to get her breath back.

She had no idea how long Shen was gone and, as she began to shake off the sex daze she'd been caught in, she wondered if he'd left her.

Her rational brain, which was buried deep at the moment, was trying to tell her that probably hadn't happened; but her irrational brain was just hoping they weren't done. And if he'd left . . . they would be.

Some time passed and Stevie placed her hands on the cushion so she could push herself up. She'd find out where he'd gone and deal with it.

But just as she'd levered her upper body off the couch, a hand wrapped around her ankle and yanked her down to the floor before she was unceremoniously flipped over.

Shen was kneeling in front of her. He was completely naked now except for the condom on his engorged cock and the scowl on his face.

To Stevie's own surprise, she wasn't frightened by that scowl. She recognized it. This was not anger or annoyance, it was focus. She'd seen similar expressions on her fellow scientists when they were trying to fix a problem.

With his hands gripping her waist, he yanked her close and

angled her hips up. He entered her without a word. And he was as big as she'd thought. He filled her completely and she briefly wondered, *Could he tickle my tonsils with that thing?*

More than willing to find out, Stevie slapped her hands on his shoulders, wrapped her legs around his waist, and left the rest up to him.

It was the wild panda in him. It was out of control. A fear he'd had as soon as he'd met Stevie for the first time in the Queens house living room.

The wild panda in him had wanted to grab her ankles, lift her off the floor, and have her suck his cock for an hour or so until he was completely drained. His wild panda side was like all wild pandas. Horny, demanding, and insatiable. That's why he kept that part of himself hidden except from other pandas. A full-human could never handle that. And most of the other shifter breeds just got freaked out. They, like everyone, expected giant pandas to be cute and docile. And, if Shen had grown up in a zoo, he probably would have been.

He hadn't grown up in a zoo, though. And Stevie MacKilligan had thrown herself at him. Naked and demanding. She'd even purred. Purred!

What was he supposed to do with purring other than fuck it? Fuck it hard. Fuck it long. Fuck it forever!

Then she made it worse. When he'd shoved his cock inside her without even the most basic, "You up for this?" she didn't start pulling away or telling him to wait or asking him to be nice. Nope. She'd just buried her fingers deep into his shoulders and growled at him. Growled.

Not able to stand another second of this, Shen stayed on his knees and took a tight—probably painful—hold of Stevie's hips. Holding her in place, he plowed into her, loving how her pussy gripped him. How it pulsated around him. And every time he entered her again, her grip tightened. Not on his shoulders, on his cock. Her pussy gripped his cock tight each time he pushed in, making Shen crazier than he already was.

He hadn't thought that was possible!

Did she know what she was doing to him? Did she care?

Too bad he couldn't be bothered to find out.

Then again, he wasn't really that worried. The harder he fucked her, the more she held onto him. She pulled her fingers away from his shoulders and moved her hands to his back. She gripped him tight again and he was just thankful that, unlike some cats, she didn't unleash her claws. He loved his spine and would hate for it to be split into pieces, even if it was during the best sex of his life.

And it really was the best sex. Not just because of the way Stevie's hips moved—she had this little swirl thing going on that was driving him insane—or the way her legs tightly held onto his hips or the hiss she let out every once in a while. All that was great, but it wasn't just that. It was her. It was all her.

Shen placed one hand flat against her back so he could keep her pressed against his chest as he turned on his knees away from the chair. It was in his way.

Still buried deep, he put Stevie on the floor, placed his hands on either side of her head, and raised himself up a bit. Then he just took her. He fucked her hard and long, loving every second of it. He placed his hands so she didn't slide across the hardwood floor, keeping her trapped by his body. But, again, she didn't seem to mind. Her hands gripped his sides and she raised her legs higher, spread them wider. Her back arched and he went deeper inside her.

He soon realized he had to come. But Stevie was nowhere near. Thinking she might need her clit stimulated to get there, he pulled one of her hands off his body. He brought the hand up and took her middle finger into his mouth, sucking it for a few seconds, getting it good and wet. Then he pushed her hand between their bodies, pressing the middle finger down on her clit. He couldn't tell her what to do. He wasn't a chatty guy when he was fucking. Thankfully, she understood without words, and began to massage her clit while he continued to brutally bulldoze into her.

The muscles gripping his cock began to tighten around him even more, and he knew she was close. He held on until her back arched and her legs shook. And as she beautifully came, he watched her. Watched her writhe and moan and desperately gasp right beneath him before he finally let himself go. Before he finally had what he wanted.

He threw back his head, suddenly realizing he was sweating and had sent droplets of that sweat across his sister's nice hardwood floor. But he didn't care.

He was too exhausted to care about anything.

He gave one last gasp and dropped on top of poor Stevie. Not even caring he was probably smothering her.

But he felt her wiggle her way out from under him and crawl onto his back. She stretched out, asleep seconds before he was. The last thing he remembered was her purring against his upper back and kneading her fingers against his shoulders.

chapter SIXTEEN

They sat on the floor, Shen's back against the base of the chair, Stevie on his lap.

She'd been heading to the couch when he'd gently steered her back to the floor. She got it, though. He didn't want her naked ass on his sister's furniture. Totally understandable.

Smiling, she snuggled in closer and closed her eyes. She started to drift off to sleep again until she heard the first crunch. Then another. Then another.

Opening her eyes, Stevie leaned back a bit. Shen held out the bamboo stalk he'd been eating.

"Want some?" he asked.

"You really don't get sick of that stuff?"

"Nope. I started teething on it when I was still a baby. I can't imagine my life without it."

"Okay." She snuggled back in. "You can keep eating."

So he did, holding stalks in one hand and cupping her shoulder with the other, keeping her tight against him.

What she never thought would be true, though, was that after a few minutes . . . the crunching was the most calming thing she'd ever heard. Because not only was it continuous, it was consistent . . . and soothing. So goddamn soothing. Because it never changed. He'd use his fangs to rip off part of the sheath of the stalk, then bite into the stalk . . . chew . . . chew . . . bite . . . chew . . . chew . . . rip off sheath.

It should have made her crazy. And she kept waiting for that to happen. Eventually, though, she simply fell asleep again.

*   *   *

From her spot on a hangar roof a good distance away, she saw that they had arrived. It was originally believed they would all arrive the day of the event, but then it was discovered they were already in the air and heading this way.

And now that they'd arrived, she could see that there were a lot of them. All male. All armed. Shorter than the Americans, but that didn't mean anything. For shifters, height and weight didn't always have much significance.

Dee-Ann continued taking pictures on the digital camera until the entire group disappeared inside the hangar closest to the landing strips.

When the last male was inside, she tucked the camera into her bag and quickly climbed over the hangar roof. Once she was back on the ground, she took off running, past the few workmen still around. As soon as she was across the street, she jumped into the waiting black sports car and closed the door behind her.

"Go."

Malone pulled away from the curb and onto the street. She careened around the slower moving vehicles and nearly ran down a late-shift worker.

Then, with a dramatic spin of tires and a turn that would make a lesser man vomit, they landed in a safe spot near closed businesses.

Malone turned off the headlights and looked over at Dee-Ann, grinning.

Dee-Ann knew that look. Kitty wanted a compliment so she gave her one.

"You drive like my daddy when he's had some of Uncle Buddy Ray's 'shine."

Not appreciating that, Malone contacted the other teams. They had every way out of this private airport covered so they could follow their prey. The plan was that the Group, Katzenhaus, and the BPC would not let these boys out of their sights while they were in this country.

But as the minutes ticked away and no one drove by . . .

Dee-Ann and Malone looked at each other, gazing directly into each other's eyes.

"Hey, Arnie?" Malone called out on her radio.

"Yo?"

"Check the hangar they went into."

"Yep," the bear replied.

And then they waited again, and still no vehicles came by.

"Cella?" Arnie called back.

"Yeah?"

"Uhhh. They're gone."

Malone let out a nasty growl. "Who the fuck missed them?" she demanded of the multiple teams listening in. "Who the fuck let them by?"

"Uh, Cella?"

"What, Arnie?"

"No one let them by."

"How do you know?"

"Because I'm looking at the hole."

Frowning, her head jerking back a little, Malone asked, "What?"

"I'm looking at the hole."

"What hole?"

"The hole they burrowed." When Malone said nothing, Arnie added, "They burrowed out of here. Literally. They burrowed."

Malone dropped back into the seat and said to Dee-Ann, "They *burrowed* out of the hangar and under the streets of New Jersey."

"Yeah," Dee-Ann replied. "I . . . I really don't know what to do with that."

"For once, my canine friend, we agree. Of course, this also means we have Scottish MacKilligans loose on the East Coast . . . and no idea where."

"Well," Dee-Ann said, lifting up her Tennessee Titans hat so she could scratch her scalp before pulling it back down, "If nothin' else . . . we know they'll be at that funeral. We just have to hope and pray they won't be burying any extra bodies."

She only napped for about twenty minutes but it was enough to make her energy explode like a three-year-old who had gotten into a bag of sugar.

But it got really weird when Shen, sitting on the floor with the couch at his back, looked away from the TV and realized that Stevie had perched herself on the tall bookshelf at the other side of the room.

When she realized she had his attention, she began to creep along the top on all fours until she reached the edge.

Shen shook his head. "Stevie, don't—"

But it was too late. She made a crazy leap from the bookcase toward him, but she landed stomach down on the coffee table. About five feet short of her mark.

"Almost!" she cheered, her face still in the table.

"Yes," Shen said, lifting her off the table. "Almost."

He pulled her down into his lap, her legs on either side of him.

"Are you tired?" she asked.

"Nope."

Stevie dug her hands into his hair, pushed it off his face, massaged his scalp. It felt amazing.

"Because I need to be fucked again," she said. "But I don't want to wear you out."

Shen couldn't help but laugh. "Yeahhhhhh, that's not gonna happen."

"It's not? Because I can be pretty demanding."

"And I'm a wild panda. All I need is a box of condoms and free time."

Stevie moved her hands from his scalp to his shoulders and leaned in close. "Then what are you waiting for?"

He pointed toward the TV. "*Storage Wars* is on right now."

Stevie's eyes opened wide and her lips parted.

"I'm kidding, I'm kidding," Shen said quickly, yanking her back onto his lap before she could get up and storm away.

"All right then."

"Besides, I can just record it."

She was halfway across the room before he caught up with her again, catching her in his arms and dumping her onto his shoulder. Her laughter entertained him just as much as having her naked body all to himself for the next few hours.

chapter SEVENTEEN

"Okay," Stevie said, turning in the chair so she could look right at Shen. "I have a suggestion."

Shen grinned but she rolled her eyes. "I'm not talking about sex."

"Oh." He shrugged. "Sorry."

"I never knew you could be such a horny monkey."

"Wild panda," he reminded her. "So what's your suggestion?"

"You might think it's crazy. It goes against *everything* I believe."

"Now I have to know."

She glanced at the receptionist who managed her therapist's office. Frowning a little, she leaned in and said, "I think we need to involve Max."

Shen shook his head. "Sisters are not my scene."

"That's not what I mean, perv."

"You started it," he murmured. Then he winked and she didn't know whether to punch him or put his cock in her mouth.

"Are you going to focus?" she asked.

"Well—"

"On the topic."

He chuckled. "Sorry. Bring Max into what?"

She leaned even closer. "Dealing with Wells."

"I thought you said if your sisters found out—"

"That's mostly Charlie. If Charlie finds out, she'll kill everybody. Probably even you. For not stopping me."

"Good to know. And a little terrifying."

"But Max—"

"Is an unhinged nut bag. Who I respect as your sister," he added when she glared. "But she is an unhinged nut bag. How do you know she won't flip out, too, because you're involved?"

"We give her a task."

She motioned him closer so she could whisper in his ear, "Breaking and entering."

"You sure that's a good idea?"

"She says she hasn't done it in a while but . . . I'm not sure I buy that. Anyway, it's like riding a bicycle. It's a skill you never truly lose. Only this time, instead of robbing people of their very expensive jewels, she'll be helping her kind."

"If you think it's a good idea . . ." He shrugged. "But you'd better protect me if Charlie finds out."

"I can try but . . . ya know. I may have to let you go."

"Thank you very much for that."

Stevie laughed but the sound got caught in her throat when her doctor's partner walked out to the front desk . . . with Charlie behind her.

"If you have any questions or experience any side effects," the woman told her sister, "just call. But there shouldn't be a problem."

"Thank you," Charlie said, taking an actual prescription from Dr. Lewis.

"Great. See you next week."

"Yeah." Charlie turned and that's when she saw Stevie. Their gazes locked and Stevie opened her mouth to tell her sister how proud she was of her, how excited she was that Charlie was taking her own mental health in her hands and managing it, how amazing her sister was, how she'd never loved her more. But before she could say any of that, Shen pressed his hand over her mouth. She tried to drag it off as Charlie looked down at the floor and began to quickly walk toward the elevator, but he wouldn't let go.

He dragged Stevie onto his lap and wrestled with her until the elevator doors closed.

"Are you two having fun?" Dr. Morgan asked, standing over them.

Stevie finally got Shen's hand off her mouth. "My sister was here!"

"Stevie, you of all people know that I can't discuss that with you or anyone."

"I know. I know." She jumped off Shen's lap and spun away from her doctor. "*But isn't it amazing!*"

Watching the ballet troupe on the big stage was interesting, but not as interesting as the woman sitting beside him in the theater.

"I don't think I've ever seen anyone so happy that someone was going to therapy."

"My sister's not nuts," Stevie replied, her eyes focused on the stage.

"Never said she was."

"You can't do what Charlie does and talk to the voices in your head or wear foil beanies to protect you from the alien rays."

"That is very specific."

"So I don't worry about my sister having an emotional breakdown. I worry she'll have a physical one. Stress can be very damaging to the body as well as the mind. Even to those of us with superior DNA. I don't want to wake up in twenty years with a sister who has heart problems and back problems and ulcers and any other number of things that can kill you. So, yeah. If someone needs therapy and medication, I'm all for it."

"Maybe she just went for medication."

"That's not okay. Medication should *never* be given without therapy." She suddenly looked at him. "And if you ever go to a doctor who tries to tell you otherwise . . . get another doctor."

"I'm a panda," he said and, when she frowned, "We're just happy."

"Well, lucky you."

A break was called on the stage and Stevie got up and started down the aisle. Shen grabbed her backpack and followed.

Oriana was standing next to the director. She was talking to him when the prima ballerina, Svetlana Romanov, cut in front of her as if she wasn't even there.

Shen, who had a high tolerance for other people's bullshit, thought even he would be annoyed if someone did that to him. That's when he noticed that Stevie had picked up her step.

She stopped when she reached the outside of the orchestra pit.

"Oriana!" she called out. "Hey!"

Oriana paused, taking her glare from the back of Svetlana's head long enough to spot Stevie. She blinked in surprise and came to the edge of the stage.

"What are you doing here?"

"Came to visit," Stevie replied. "Can I come up?"

Oriana appeared as confused as Shen felt, but she motioned to a set of stairs that Stevie could take.

When Stevie was on the stage, she threw her arms wide and loudly called out, "Oriana! Sweetness! It's so good to see you!"

It was so loud and annoying that the remaining dancers and the director all focused on her.

Stevie hugged Oriana for a little longer than was necessary. Poor Oriana widened her eyes at Shen over Stevie's shoulder, silently asking him what was going on. Like he knew!

When Stevie finally let Oriana go, she still held her hands. "I have such exciting news for you! I just have to . . . David?"

An older man, standing on the other side of the director looked up.

"David Connelly?" Stevie asked.

"Yes?"

Stevie released Oriana and placed her hands on her upper chest. "It's me. Stevie Stasiuk."

The man frowned, and then his eyes popped wide open. "Dear God! Stevie?"

She went across the stage and into the man's open arms. "I can't believe it! It's been ages!"

"Stevie, look at you. My God!" He stepped away, looking her over. "Last time I saw you, you were just a child. Now look at you." He dramatically kissed the backs of her hands, and Shen had to use his best "professional bodyguard face" to keep from rolling his eyes.

"What are you doing here?" Stevie asked.

"I'm the music director of the ballet." Still holding her hands, he tugged her a little closer. "And you? Why are you here?"

She motioned to Oriana with an elegant tip of her head. "We're very old friends."

They were?

"And I've been having a little bit of a rough time with my family."

Yeah. You could say that. If parts of your family trying to kill you is considered "a little bit of a rough time." Sure.

"So, Oriana insisted I come to New York to spend some time with her and . . . she's been such an inspiration."

The music director's head jerked a little. "Inspiration . . . in . . . in . . . music?"

Stevie glanced around a little and, leaning in, she loudly whispered, "I've been working on a little ballet for— Oh!"

The exclamation came when the director yanked Stevie so close that Shen was worried the man was going to kiss her, but no. That wasn't it.

"You've written a ballet?"

"Just the music part."

"Just . . ." He gave a harsh laugh. "Just the music part?"

"Uh-huh. You see, I've known Oriana for years."

Except she said you never remembered her name.

"And we've been playing around with some ideas. The things she can do as a dancer are just astounding and challenge me to come up with music that meets her talent head-on. Because, as you know, music should never take over the dance or outweigh it in any way. Just complement the beauty of what she and the other dancers can do."

"Oh, uh . . ." The music director's eyes snapped over to an older woman and man standing nearby. They both nodded toward Stevie, signaling the man to do something. Shen just

wasn't sure what. "Do you happen to have any of that music . . . uh . . . on you at the moment?"

"Ummmm . . ."

Uh-oh.

Stevie stretched out her arm toward Shen and wiggled her
fingers. He assumed she wanted her backpack. He brought it to
her, holding it in his arms as she opened the zipper.

"Let's see. Let's see." She glanced at Shen. "Oh. Sorry. Maestro David Connelly, this is Shen. My bodyguard. Say 'hello,'
Shen."

"Hello, Shen," he repeated back, letting them all believe he
was as dumb as they thought he was.

"Ahhh," Stevie said. "Here it is." She pulled out one of her
many notebooks; quickly flipped the pages. "Yes. This is it."

She turned, handed it to Connelly.

He grabbed it like a dying man offered a bottle of water. He
put on the glasses he had hanging around his neck and quickly
scanned the pages. From what Shen could tell, it was a music
notebook. He remembered those from his childhood days of
attempting to learn piano before his mother finally came in
during a practice session and closed the cover on the keyboard,
looked down at her only son, and said with as much kindness
as she could muster, "Let's just find something else for you to
do. *Anything* else for you to do."

"Do you . . . um . . . still have an agent for your music?"

"I haven't in years. Science has been my love for quite a
while now. Why do you ask?"

"Well, we might be interested in using this music and creating a ballet around it."

"Very interested," the older woman said. She stepped closer,
held out her hand. "Hi. I'm Ida. The ballet master."

"Ida Swan?" Stevie said, shaking the woman's hand. "*The*
Ida Swan? It's such an honor."

"And an honor to meet you. I remember seeing you conduct
once in Madrid."

"Oh, yes. I remember that. God, I was so young."

"But talented. Your music is wonderful. I was sorry to hear you'd walked away from composing."

"It was for my mental health." She suddenly reached out, her arm wrapping around Oriana's neck and yanking her close. "But Oriana and her beauty as a dancer just . . . brought me back. It's been revolutionary."

Ida smirked, her wise gaze sizing up these two women instantly. But she didn't call them out. Not when she had a chance to get a ballet written by the great Stevie Stasiuk-MacKilligan. At least that's what Shen was guessing. He watched players work all the time. Especially when he protected financial guys. This was a negotiation if he'd ever seen one. Even if the word was never actually used.

"Dear, Oriana," Ida said. "You've been keeping secrets."

Oriana nodded. "Stevie wanted to keep her time here quiet."

"About that agent . . ." the music director pushed with a gentle—but desperate—smile.

"You can use mine," Oriana suggested. "Dominique Gagnon."

"The cellist from Marseille?" Stevie guessed.

"No. The agent from Uniondale. Out on the Island. She has an office in Manhattan, though. She handles dancers and musicians."

Stevie grinned. "Perfect." She glanced at her phone. "Oh, I have to go."

"We'll get in touch with you," Ida promised.

"I look forward to it. Maybe dipping my toe back into this world through dance will change everything."

Stevie started to walk off, but stopped, turned, and gently attempted to remove the music notebook from Connelly's desperate grip.

"Can I just . . . can I . . . if I can just . . ."

She ignored his begging and yanked the notebook from him. She tucked it into her bag and zipped it closed.

"Ready?" she asked Shen.

"Yep."

Stevie took a few steps, and that's when Oriana's great enemy stepped in front of her. She was the stereotypical ballet dancer.

Long and lean, her hair in a perfect bun, not a strand out of place, her eyes big and easy to see from the back row of any theater. She was stunning, but obviously calculating. Hanging around his sister Kiki over the years, Shen had been introduced to lots of people like this woman. They had different livelihoods, were of different races, religions, but all had the same calculating gaze.

"Hello, Stevie. We met . . . very long time ago. I am Svetlana. Principal dancer here."

Stevie blankly gazed back at Svetlana and, with a calm, dead voice, replied, "I'm sorry. I don't know you."

Then she walked around the dancer who was used to people bowing at her feet and left the stage.

"'I'm sorry, I don't know you'?" Shen repeated to her as they sat in his SUV.

Stevie cringed. "Too much?"

He leaned forward a bit so he could see out her window. "I don't think so."

Stevie looked out the passenger window and saw Oriana running down the stairs. She'd taken off her toe shoes and put on an orange pair of Converse high-tops.

Rolling down the window, Stevie began, "I'm sorry, I shouldn't have—"

Oriana's hug cut off the rest of Stevie's sentence.

"So, I guess we're cool," she laughed.

Oriana pulled back. "You don't have to do this."

"Do what?"

"Get back in the game. I know you pulled out for a reason. And this is going to turn into a bidding war."

"Bidding war?" Stevie shook her head. "No."

"No what?"

"No bidding war. I'll give it to the company. They just have to make you the soloist."

Oriana stepped away, shaking her head. "No, no. You don't have . . . don't . . . why are you . . . what's happening?"

"I'm going to give your ballet company my music . . . for

free . . . but I keep the rights and they have to make you the soloist. And if they don't want to make you the soloist, I'll go to some other ballet company and give it to them as long as they make you the soloist. This isn't brain surgery."

"Why are you doing this for me?"

"Because we're friends." Stevie thought a moment. "Right? I mean . . . I thought we were friends. There was hugging. Right?"

"No. We're friends, but you don't have to give away a lot of money just for me."

"Dude, I can always make money. And as long as I keep the rights to my work . . ." Stevie shrugged, not really seeing the problem. "But you do know that all I can do is give it to you and the company. After that, what you do with it, is totally up to you. I can get you the shot at being a soloist but becoming a principal . . . In other words, don't fuck it up."

"There had to be a nicer way for you to say that," Shen said.

"Do you need me to be nicer?" Stevie asked her friend.

"If you're nicer, I'm going to assume you're up to some— wait. *Are* you up to something? You want something from me," Oriana accused. "What do you want from me? Why are you being so nice to me? Is this all a plot to destroy me?"

Stevie smirked at him. "See why I'm not nice?"

"Where have you been?" Kyle demanded, glaring down at Shen. "You should have been here hours ago!"

"Did you grow another inch?" Shen asked.

Kyle relaxed, smiled. "I think I did. Last night. Jackals have long legs."

Kyle's mother came up behind her son, his leather messenger bag in her hands. "Are you leaving, Kyle?"

"Well—"

"Oh, no. Do you have to go so soon?" She pushed the bag into his hands. "I will miss you, honey." She shoved him toward the door. "Remember Mommy loves you!"

She looked at Shen. "Why are you still standing here?"

"I'm waiting for Stevie. She went to talk to Dr. Conridge."

"Great," the mother of eleven muttered. Then she ordered, "Give me your car keys."

Shen handed them over and she chucked the keys to her son, hitting him in the face.

"Ow!"

"Why don't you go wait in the car, sweetie. Shen will be right out."

"He should actually wait in here for safe—"

"Shut. Up." She waved at Kyle. "Love you!"

"Long night?" Shen asked once Kyle had gone.

"I love him. I love him more than I can say. But I'm not sure I'd cry if he moved back to Europe. Or farther. Farther than Europe."

Stevie came down the stairs. "Hi, Maestro," she said to Kyle's mother.

"Hello, Stevie. Kyle's already in the car," she said, the smile on her face ridiculously forced.

Stevie put her hand on the She-jackal's shoulder. "He'll be fine with us, Jackie. I promise."

"Thank you." She let out a sigh and began to move away, but stopped. "Oh. Jess Ward wanted me to remind you about Thursday night?"

"Right. Yeah. Tell her we'll be there." But Stevie didn't sound eager about whatever Thursday night held for her.

"Okay. Have a good day, you two."

Shen held the door open for Stevie and, once he closed it behind them, he asked, "What was that about?"

"I had to make a deal with Jess Ward," she said, walking down the steps. "It was the only way I wouldn't have to pay for what I did to the living room."

"I thought that's what giving Johnny the violin was for."

"No. I let Max believe that. I sent Johnny that violin because I felt horrible for what my father did. I let him keep it because of guilt, but more because of a true fear of prison. Whether I realized it at the time or not, I was definitely my father's accomplice. And that rabid wild dog was not letting it go. By the time I got back to the States, the FBI was already interviewing my sisters and even my grandfather's Pack." She shook her head. "I did so much lying those weeks, I was positive I was going to federal prison forever. And that Jess Ward was going to be there to lock the door after me. But somehow, someway, Johnny must have calmed Ward down, because the Feds finally backed off."

"Then what kind of deal are you talking about?"

"I don't know. Something called Wild Dog Night. She was really vague . . . what are you laughing about?"

They'd reached the bottom of the brownstone steps and Shen was bent over at the waist, his laughter coming out so hard that it hurt his chest.

"What is so funny?" Stevie asked again.

"You didn't say yes, did you?" he barely got out.

"I had to. The contractor was talking a six-figure restoration of the ballroom. I couldn't afford that right now."

"You said you'd go?"

"Yeah."

"Just you?"

"I said I'd bring my sisters . . . *what is so funny?*"

Shen wiped the tears from his eyes, "You'll find out. I don't want to ruin it for you."

"You're being a very bad boyfriend right now. I just want you to know that."

"Still worth it," Shen admitted out loud after Stevie had already gotten in the car.

As they headed back to Queens, with Kyle in the backseat, Shen softly asked, "So what did Conridge say?"

"She didn't seem to like the idea of me involving Max. Something about her husband losing skin. But he's a wolf, so I don't know if she just meant shedding."

"So what are you going to do?"

"Not sure yet, but I've got to come up with something. We need to find out what's in Well's lab. Maybe even his apartment."

"Are you two having sex?" Kyle suddenly asked. He was

stretched out lengthwise in the backseat, his upper back resting on his messenger bag, phone in his hand.

"What?" Shen snapped.

"Yes!" Stevie cheered.

Shen wanted to press the palms of his hands against his eyes, but he couldn't take his gaze off the road.

"What are you doing?" Shen asked Stevie instead.

"What am I doing about what?"

"Why are you answering him?"

"What's the point of lying? He's not two." Stevie looked over her shoulder. "How did you know?"

"Because you two are acting very . . . wife-and-husband-like. Similar to my parents. Clearly your relationship has changed."

Stevie tapped Shen with the back of her hand. "We're husband-and-wife-like!"

Now he was worried. "You do know that we're not husband and wife . . . right?"

"Of course we're not." She reached for the radio, turned it on. "Yet."

Shen turned the radio back off. "Okay. I need to make this clear to you."

"Sure."

"What we have is just casual. Just friendly—"

"Fucking," Kyle tossed in from the backseat.

"Shut up or I'm going to make you stay with your family." He refocused on Stevie. "We just have a casual relationship. Right?"

"No, actually. Very wrong. Our love is grand and never ending."

"Never ending!" Kyle repeated.

"We will be together until *you* die."

"Until you die!" Kyle repeated.

"You know," Shen told the air, "I really have no one to blame but myself."

"But yourself!"

"*Shut up!*" Shen barked at the annoying jackal.

"It's okay," Stevie gently told him. "We'll be great together."

For a moment, Shen was soothed until he realized that Stevie was rubbing her head against his arm.

"Are you marking me with your scent again?"

"Is that a problem for you?" she asked.

"Well—"

Kyle's jackal head was suddenly in the seats between them, looking back and forth for a moment before he said, "It could have been worse. She could have unleashed her anal glands."

"Get thee back, Satan!" Shen barked.

"You know," Kyle remarked, "if I believed in the concept of a power higher than me, I'd be insulted right now. Lucky for you . . . I don't."

He relaxed back into his seat, again lengthwise, with one arm behind his head. Shen came to a red light and hit his brakes, sending the boy rolling off the seat and into the foot well between the rows.

"Ooopsie!" Shen called out.

chapter EIGHTEEN

Stevie walked into the house behind Kyle, who threw his bag onto the couch and his arms into the air, calling out, "I've returned home!"

"You're just visiting!" Charlie yelled from the kitchen. "Stevie?"

"Yeah?"

"I need to speak with you."

Stevie dropped her head forward and girded her loins. "She's going to be upset about earlier."

"Not necessarily," Shen replied. "Maybe she's found a whole new way of handling you and Max now that she's going to therapy too."

Stevie smiled. He really was the sweetest of all the bears. She kissed his cheek. "You're cute when you lie to me."

"It's a gift."

Stevie left Shen in the living room with Kyle, and as she entered the dining room, she met Max coming down the stairs. They stopped and glowered at each other for a few seconds before ramming into each other and putting themselves into mutual headlocks.

"If I have to go out there . . ." Charlie threatened from the kitchen.

Not wanting Charlie to come out to get them, but not wanting to release each other, they made their way into the kitchen still in headlocks.

Charlie had just put something in the oven and turned around, glaring when she saw them.

"What is wrong with you two?" Charlie asked. "I really want to know. Is it a mental issue or just general stupidity?"

When they began to ram each other's heads into the refrigerator, Charlie sighed out, "Yep. General stupidity."

Shen walked into the kitchen to get a soda out of the fridge but ended up catching Stevie before she could be flung into the dining room. She was lucky, though, because Charlie had only tossed her aside. She had Max by the hair and was shoving her into a chair.

Charlie pointed at an empty chair and ordered, "Put her there."

And Shen did what she ordered him to do because the look on Charlie's face suggested he shouldn't disagree with her at the moment.

He carried Stevie into the room and gently placed her in the chair across from Max, careful not to make any sudden moves. When he was done, he straightened up and looked at the sisters. When all they did was stare at him, Shen began to slowly back out of the room. Again, keeping his movements very nonthreatening.

He could get a soda from the store. Or he could just go thirsty. Whatever worked. As long as he got out of here with his life and sanity intact.

After Shen had left the room . . . and then the house—Stevie could hear the front door slam closed—Charlie asked, "Did you sleep with him last night?"

Stevie grinned. "I did. It was magnificent."

"Awww. He's so sweet."

"And God knows," Max sneered, "you needed to get laid— ow! What was that for?" she asked, rubbing the back of her head where Charlie had slapped it.

"Because we don't have time for you two to keep bickering. I talked to Aunt Bernice last night."

"Yeah, and?"

"They want us to come to the funeral."

Max frowned. "Who died?"

"Great-Uncle Pete. Remember?"

"Sorta."

"Why do we have to go?" Stevie wanted to know. She didn't want to go to a funeral unless she had to. And she didn't think she had to go to a funeral for a man she didn't even know.

"That's where it gets complicated."

Stevie and Max exchanged glances before looking back at Charlie.

"What's complicated?" Max asked. "It's a funeral."

"It's complicated because it's Uncle Will who wants us to attend."

Stevie shrank down in her chair. "Oh, man, he's gonna kill us all, isn't he?"

"Not necessarily."

Stevie sat up straight again. "What the fuck kind of response is that?"

Charlie rubbed her forehead with her thumb and admitted, "An honest one."

Shen checked his pockets again for his cell phone. When he didn't find it, he figured he'd left it inside. He looked back at the front door but muttered, "Eh. I can get it later."

He started down the front steps but stopped when a blue SUV pulled into the spot behind his vehicle. He grinned when Livy Kowalski stepped out of the passenger side and her mate— and Shen's business partner—got out of the driver's.

"Livy!" Shen exclaimed, walking up to her and giving her a big hug. He pulled back, grinned. "Love the hair."

It was their old joke but Shen loved it. Livy was a honey badger. Shen a panda. They both had evidence of both colors in their black and white hair. Unlike the MacKilligan sisters, they didn't bother dying their hair one color.

"You doing okay?" Livy asked.

"I'm fine. What are you guys doing here?"

"Orders from my mother," Livy complained. "The aunts have not been able to get in touch with Max. And her mother's been trying to contact her."

"Her mother? The one—"

"The one in a Belgian prison? Yeah."

Livy and Max were cousins, their families related on their mothers' side. The Yangs. A powerful honey badger clan from China known for their art thieving abilities. After Livy's mother hooked up with a Kowalski, she became one of the matriarchs of the Yangs. But Max's mother's connection with Freddy MacKilligan had done nothing for her. It was why she was still in prison. No one had tried to break her out.

"Is everything all right?"

"Doubtful. But no one's dead, if that's what you're asking."

Shen had always loved Livy's flat, uninterested tone. She could make, "You've won the lottery!" sound like the worst thing that could happen to anyone.

Vic Barinov now stood next to Shen, gazing at him in that weird grizzly-Siberian tiger way he had, and not saying anything until Shen finally asked, "What, Vic?"

"You're engaged?"

"What? *No!*"

"I heard you were engaged."

"Engaged to who?" Livy asked. "Oh, God . . . not Max. Tell me you're not engaged to—"

"No! I'm not engaged to anyone."

"But . . . ?"

"There is no but."

"Shen," Livy pushed. "What's going on?"

"Fine. I slept with Stevie."

"The little one?" Vic asked. "She's so tiny. Wasn't that just cruel?"

"*No.*"

"Really? Cause you're kind of wide. Like a wall."

"I am not like a—" Shen stopped, blew out a breath. "I can't have this conversation anymore."

"Because everybody else thinks you're too big for her too?"

"I'm not even addressing that bullshit. I mean, I'm not engaged to anyone. We're just hanging out. That's it."

"Really?" Livy asked, pulling away from him, her lip curled a little. "Because her scent is all over you."

"It's nothing. She just rubbed her scent on me when we were in the car."

"Aw, sweetie," Livy said, patting his shoulder. "You don't get it."

"Don't get what?"

"That tiny cat hybrid owns you now."

"She's right," Vic agreed. "That's what I mean every time I rub myself against Livy, but I don't say it out loud because she's a honey badger and I don't want to get hit in the face."

Livy nodded at Shen's questioning look. "That's exactly what I would do if he said it out loud."

"Are we going to go?" Stevie asked.

"*I'm* going to go," Max announced.

"And do what?" Charlie asked.

"Kill them all."

"No."

"You don't think I'd do it?"

"I think you think you're crazy enough to do it," Stevie explained. "But you're not."

"I could be."

"You're not."

"*We're* not," Charlie added. "People trying to actively kill us—strangers or family—we fight back. We always fight back and we lay waste. But we don't kill family for no reason."

"No, no," Stevie was quick to cut in. "We don't kill *anyone* for no reason."

Her sisters stared at her for what Stevie considered way too long until Charlie blinked and said, "Right. Right. We don't kill anyone for no reason. Exactly right."

Stevie swung her finger between her sisters. "It bothers me I had to clarify that for you two. Just so you understand the look of disappointment on my face."

Shen returned to the kitchen and as soon as he walked in, Charlie and Max let out an "Awwww."

"No," he said quickly. "No, no. We're not going to do any of that, thank you very much." He jerked his thumb over his shoulder. "Livy's here."

Stevie didn't know she had reflexes that anyone would call "fast," but she was up and over the table, taking her sister down to the ground before she could throw one of her blades across the room and into the only cousin on the Yang side of the family who would talk to her.

"*Really?*" Stevie demanded, still pinning her hysterically laughing sister to the floor.

Charlie, shaking her head, stepped close and snatched the blade from Livy's hand.

"She's family, dick-ass!"

Stevie couldn't help but scrunch up her face, and then she saw that Max had done that too.

"I think you meant *dumb*-ass," Max suggested.

"Probably. Let's just let it lie."

"Yeah, but why would you even come up with—"

"Let it lie!" Charlie tossed the blade onto the kitchen table. "What's up, Livy?"

Livy, completely unfazed by her cousin, said to Max, "Call your mother." She slapped a piece of paper on the table and walked out without another word.

"You haven't called your mother?" Charlie asked.

"Well, with all the shit that's been going on . . . and I forgot to give her my new number." She pushed at Stevie. "Get off me."

Unlike Stevie, Max adored her mother and had lawyers in Belgium working on appeals to get her out of prison. They kept in touch through letters, emails, and the occasional phone smuggled behind bars.

Stevie scrambled off her sister so Max could grab the piece of paper her cousin had left and quickly call her mother. Charlie was busy checking out whatever she'd put in the oven, so Stevie squeezed between Shen and the enormous hybrid blocking her kitchen door, biting back her squeal of panic at the mere sight of the man. She'd met him before, but she couldn't remember his name to save her life.

She charged through the dining room and living room and caught up with Livy on the porch.

"Hey!" she said, forcing a smile.

"Why are you looking at me like that?" Livy asked. "What are you doing with your face?"

"I'm trying to smile."

"Stop it."

"Can I talk to you for a moment?"

"I don't want to talk about the fact that Max came at me with a knife . . . again."

"This has nothing to do with Max."

"Oh." Livy shrugged. "Yeah, okay. What's up?"

Stevie took hold of Livy's arm and led her away from the house.

As they moved down the street together, Stevie said, "This may be a weird request—" And immediately Livy began to chuckle. "What's so funny?"

"If you knew my family, you'd know why that statement was funny."

Stevie stopped, glanced back at the house. They seemed to be alone. "I need you to break into a lab."

Livy didn't react. She just kept staring at her, waiting for her to finish.

"I think the scientist who runs it is up to some very bad things involving hybrids. I don't think he's doing those things there. In that lab. It's right in the heart of New York City, and that would be stupid. But I think we can find his second lab by going into his first."

More staring.

"I was never trained . . . to do that . . . sort of thing. I was going to ask Max, but if she tells Charlie . . ."

"Are you saying people are dying because of these very bad things being done?"

"Possibly. Yeah." And Stevie hated the way her voice cracked when she said that.

"Huh. Well, I don't really do that sort of work anymore."

"I know. I know. I've seen your photography. It's powerful. Which means you don't *need* to do this work anymore. It's just—"

"Let me finish. I don't do that sort of work anymore, but the man I love is a hybrid. And my idiot cousin's sisters are hybrids. And you two . . . I like. So, yeah. I'll do it."

Stevie threw her arms open, but Livy's hands immediately went up, blocking her.

"I don't really hug. I'm not a hugger."

"Right. Sorry. Forgot."

"So when do you need me to do this?"

"As soon as you can."

"What about you?"

Stevie grinned. "You want me to come? How excit—"

"*No.* I want you to have an alibi."

"Oh." She couldn't help but pout a little. "Fair enough." She thought a moment. "I've got to go to a funeral tomorrow morning."

"That might be a little too soon. I still need to research the place."

"Right, right. Well, tomorrow night I have to somehow drag my sisters to something called a Wild Dog Night with Jess Ward and her Pack."

Livy started laughing. Not a chuckle. A full-blown laugh that had Stevie greatly concerned.

"What?" she asked, becoming extremely worried. "What is so funny?"

The phone rang and Max pinned the cat she'd found lounging in her bed to the floor and used her free hand to answer.

"What?"

The cat slashed her claws across Max's arm, forcing her to release the animal. The little shit!

"Hey, baby."

Despite the pain, Max smiled because she recognized the gravelly voice that did not seem as if it should belong to a five-foot, one inch Chinese spitfire who could rob a man blind, punch his lights out, and steal his girlfriend all in the same day.

"Hey, Ma. Are you okay?"

Max had called her mother several times on the number her cousin had given her, but there had been no answer. Cell phones in prison, in any country, could come and go, so she hadn't left a message but had hoped her mother would manage to get her newest phone number. It seemed she had, but it was strange that her mother had gone to the trouble to track her down.

"I'm fine, baby. It's you I'm worried about."

"*Me?*" No one ever worried about Max.

"Devon's out, baby. He's out. And he wants his shit."

"What makes Devon think I have it?"

When her mother didn't reply, Max exploded, "*That mother-fucker!*" Max began pacing. "Why, Ma? Why? You could have had anybody. Any man. I would still be a Yang. I'd still be a honey badger. But you picked *him*."

"I've said it before and I'll say it again. Being with your father might have been a mistake, but you, my beautiful, beautiful girl never were. Ya understand?"

Max closed her eyes. "I understand."

"Good."

"And I miss you."

"I miss you, too, Ma. And if you hear from Devon again or if you hear from any of his hench-idiots . . . tell them the last person they should come at right now is me. There's a lot of shit going on here, and if they get in my way, I will make them regret it."

Renny Yang's brutal chuckle growled across their connection. "That's my girl."

"Always, Ma. Always."

chapter NINETEEN

It was the third *Exorcist* movie that upset the Dunn triplets the most. Shen sat next to them while they jumped and growled and sat curled in the corner of the couch, looking a little green. That had been Dag specifically.

Shen was worried that having three panicked grizzles this close would freak out Stevie, but she was sitting on the floor by Charlie's feet, eating popcorn and dark chocolate M&M's, and laughing. All three of the sisters were laughing hard, thoroughly enjoying the horror unfolding on the big-screen TV in front of them.

It became evident that they really loved horror movies. All of them. They cheered. They tried to scare each other. They especially loved to laugh. Not a typical laugh either. They each had their own versions of what they referred to as a "demonic laugh," and all of them were disturbing.

When the final film was over, Charlie asked, "What do you want to watch now?"

It was after midnight but none of them appeared tired. Still . . .

"What about *Suspiria*?" Stevie suggested.

"No," Shen immediately said.

"Why not?"

"My sisters made me watch that when I was ten. I'm not sitting through that shit again."

Max smirked. "Was it the maggots?"

"When that chick fell in the spiral wires?" Charlie asked.

Stevie crinkled up her nose. "The music?"

"What happened to the blind guy?" Max continued.

"All of it!" Shen barked.

"Can we just watch something *not* horrifying?" Berg begged.

"Like what?"

"*Anything,*" all the bears in the room said at the same time.

Charlie laughed. "Okay, okay. How about *John Wick*?"

"Yeahhhh!" the bears cheered. Happy for some regular ol' violence and revenge without the vomiting and head spin.

While Charlie went through her streaming collection to find the movie, the rest of them took bathroom breaks, got more junk food and drink, or simply stretched.

Kyle came back to the living room with a sandwich big enough to choke a rhino. The grizzlies saw it and quickly made their way into the kitchen to build their own sandwiches.

"Found your phone," Kyle said between bites, tossing the device onto the table.

"Where did I leave it?"

"Bathroom."

Shen swiped the phone off the table and sat on the floor, his back against the couch, to check his messages. A few from his sisters forwarding the latest ridiculous video or horrifying news story that always seemed to involve murder and Florida, but that was it.

Stevie came back into the room, but instead of returning to her spot by her sister, she came around the coffee table and sat down in front of Shen. He spread his legs so she could settle between them, and she rested her head against his shoulder so his jaw pressed against her temple.

What he really appreciated, though, was that no one said anything about it. No one even looked at them.

Then those behemoth dogs came in. The male went one way around the table, and the female came around the other. They sat down next to Shen and the male placed his massive head on Shen's left shoulder and the female on his right.

"Should I find this concerning?" he asked Stevie.

"They're just protective of me," she said. "And they haven't quite figured you out yet."

Shen looked over at the triplets sitting on the couch behind him. "Do you three have any control over these—"

"Nope," Berg replied.

"Out, you two," Charlie calmly ordered as she reached over and took half of the sandwich Berg offered her.

And with that, the dogs walked out of the living room and into the front room. The front door was closed, preventing the canines from returning to the Dunn house. Shen assumed they would sleep on the floor or one of the couches, which worked fine for him. Since he didn't appreciate being threatened by dogs. No matter their size.

The gun fight scene in the Russian-owned club was a couple of minutes away when Max again heard the scratch coming from upstairs. She rubbed a spot between her brows with her forefinger, allowing her to glance at her sisters without their noticing.

Worried that a raccoon or a squirrel had made its way into the house, Max got up.

"Where are you going?" Stevie asked, looking awfully comfortable cuddled up to her panda bear that way. And Shen didn't seem to mind, no matter how much he bitched. "Gun-fight at the club."

"I'll be back. And it's not like I haven't seen it ten thousand times."

Max stepped over Charlie's legs.

If a squirrel had made it into the house, she wanted to get rid of it before either of her sisters knew. Stevie was bad enough with her panic over all things that, according to her, "skittered." But Charlie was even worse. She hated, hated, *hated* vermin. And that's what she called them all. Whether rat, raccoon, squirrel, or possum, they were all vermin to her, and if she found any in her house, she flipped out. Calling a mere exterminator would not be good enough for the eldest MacKilligan sister. After the exterminator came the professional cleaners. The specialists that handle toxic cleanups. And, of course, getting rid of all the furniture because Charlie would worry that one of the "vermin" had left their "disgusting off-spring" somewhere.

Max wasn't about to go through all that if she could help it. So she'd track the little fucker down and get it out of the house without either of her sisters knowing.

Quietly heading up the stairs, Max occasionally paused to listen for more sounds. She inched closer and closer until she neared Stevie's room. That's when she began to worry it wasn't rodent vermin that was scratching away in the walls. But some-thing worse.

Dad vermin.

Growling softly, she made her way down the hall until she reached her sister's room. The door was partially open and she eased inside without touching it.

"Dad?" she called out softly. "Dad, are you in here?"

She sniffed the air, trying to locate his scent. Hoping this time he hadn't doused himself in cheap cologne like the last time she'd found him lurking in her baby sister's bedroom, try-ing to steal what wasn't his.

"If I have to track you down, you motherfucker, I will—"

The leather strap wrapped around her throat, tightening be-fore she could even react.

She reached back but her head was slammed hard into the solid metal bedpost, twice, and she was dragged to the ground.

That's when legs came over her shoulders, trapping her arms just as the leather strap was pulled tighter.

Smooth skin against her cheek and a soft voice with a lilting Scottish accent hissed out, "Hello, cousin. Our aunties send their best."

The gunfight on the TV was going strong when suddenly there was a moment of silence. The hero had just gone over the balcony and hit the floor, and around the same time Stevie heard a thud from upstairs. She looked over to where Max had been sitting earlier. She'd gone upstairs but she hadn't come back.

There was another thud and Stevie moved her gaze to Charlie. Their eyes locked for a split second. Then the dogs ran through and Charlie jumped up, following them. Stevie was right behind her.

"Hey!" she could hear the bears calling out behind them. "What's going on?"

But they didn't wait. They just ran. When Charlie hit the landing on the second floor, they heard growls and barks as the dogs tried to scratch their way past the bedroom door.

"Move!" Charlie ordered and the dogs ran back behind Stevie.

Charlie kicked the door in and Stevie stood on the other side of her sister.

Max was by the window seat, a leather strap around her throat. Their cousin Mairi was behind her, her muscular legs over Max's shoulders. She was leaning back, putting more pressure on the strap around Max's throat, while keeping Max's arms pinned.

"Hello, cousins!" Mairi called when she saw them.

Charlie's hands curled into fists and, growling from deep in her throat, she barked, "Stevie!"

Stevie charged past Charlie and into the bedroom. She launched herself from the dressing table, her feet hitting the wall and sending her over to the tall dresser. She bounced off that and up, attaching herself to the ceiling with her claws and running over to where her sister and Mairi were.

As she moved, so did Charlie, storming across the room with her own claws and fangs unleashed, slamming into the attacking honey badger and pinning her to the base of the window seat. Her claws fastened on either side of Mairi, her fangs snapping at her face.

Distracted, Mairi didn't realize Stevie had dropped down and slashed her claws against the leather straps.

Coughing and gasping, Max fell forward and into Stevie's

arms. Stevie dragged her sister away as the dogs viciously attacked their cousin, going at her as hard as Charlie was.

Once Stevie had Max a safe distance away, she started back
toward the fight, but she'd barely gotten a few feet when arms
went around her and pulled her to the ground just as she heard
Britta scream from the doorway, "*Gun!*"

Three shots rang out, followed by a surprised yelp. But not
from Stevie's sisters. Or the bears. Or even Kyle.

"No," Stevie gasped, pushing Shen's arms off her. "No, no,
no, no, no, no," she begged as she ran across the room, sliding
the last few feet on her knees until she stopped at Benny's side.
He was panting hard, blood coming from his side.

Slowly, Stevie looked up from the dog to the cold eyes of
her cousin.

A smile on her face, Mairi said, "Guess I missed."

As soon as Shen realized that the dog had been shot, he was
speeding across the room, trying to get to Stevie. But he was
too slow.

She shot up and dove at Mairi, the pair breaking through the
front window and out of the house.

He immediately turned and charged out of the room, down
the hall and the stairs. As he tore through the living room, he
heard Kyle yelling after him, "*What is going on?*"

He ignored the kid, assuming he could take care of himself,
and ran to the front door.

It was late, but the local bears loved to wander around the
neighborhood at night, in their bear forms, indulging in honey
and chasing nocturnal animals. The ones who weren't out,
who were sleeping soundly, would still hear those shots. And
they would all move, all be outside.

They would see everything.

Shen made it out of the house, down the stairs, and over the
fence that went around the yard.

Stevie was on top of the She-badger, her hands around her
throat, choking the hell out of her. But it wasn't doing any-

thing. This was a badger, and she was smiling. That's why they were both still alive and conscious after going out of a second-story window and tumbling to the ground.

As Shen neared her, he heard the weird cat sound Stevie made just before she shifted, and her head come up, her eyes a bright and angry gold.

"Stevie, no!" he called out, already feeling the local bears lumbering closer and closer. "Don't do it, baby! Don't do it!"

He knew what his words sounded like to the bears. Like he was telling her not to kill the badger. But he could give a shit about that badger. The badger was not his concern.

"Pull it back, baby. Pull it back."

Stevie's head turned and she looked directly at him, her fangs not fully out, but already past her bottom lip, her panting so harsh she was salivating. Abruptly, her gaze moved behind him, and he knew she could see the bears.

Bears needed to be slowly introduced to things. Especially things like two-ton, tiger-striped honey badgers. He did think they could accept Stevie's shifter form, but he knew they wouldn't react well if she suddenly shifted into that form and then ate her cousin.

That, they would never get over.

"Pull back, Stevie," he coaxed. "Please."

Stevie looked down at her still-smirking cousin. She suddenly released her right hand and lowered it so that Shen could no longer see it. He didn't know what she was doing until her hand came back up clutching a knife. She'd been wearing tiny shorts and a T-shirt that night, so he was sure the blade had been on the badger.

Raising the weapon over her head, Stevie brought it down in one brutal motion into the She-badger's chest.

"Oh, shit," Shen gasped when Stevie did it six more times, her grumbled roar turning into a pained—but human—scream.

On the seventh strike, she left the knife in the badger's chest and slowly got to her feet, stumbling back from sudden weakness.

Shen ran out and caught her in his arms, pulling her away from the body.

When he had her a few feet back, with a group of suddenly naked bears surrounding them—they'd all shifted back to their human forms because they knew their bear form upset Stevie so—the body suddenly jumped up, the blade still sticking out of the crazed bitch's chest.

The bears exploded in startled roars, a few returning to their animal forms.

The badger ran across the street and when she was on the other side, she turned around and screamed at Stevie, "You missed me heart, you dumb cunt!"

Stevie screamed in rage and tried to run after the badger, but Shen wouldn't let her go and a few of the older She-bears helped him by holding her arms.

When the badger had disappeared, Stevie let out a desperate gasp.

"Benny!" she screamed and pushed everyone away, returning to the house.

Mairi stopped when she was a few streets over and took the time to pull the knife out of her chest. It wasn't that the knife hadn't hit her heart so much as it hadn't hit anything *major* in her heart, like the aorta.

If she were not a shifter, she'd have to go to an emergency room and get emergency surgery. She definitely couldn't keep running or pull the knife from her chest. But she was blessed. Because she'd been born one of the toughest, hardiest shifters there was. And that crazy girl must have been a leftie.

It was nice how the good Lord looked out for her.

Her twin aunts would be disappointed she hadn't finished off cousin Max, but the message had been sent. Now she had some other things to do. And it wasn't like she'd be able to sneak back into this neighborhood again. Those bloody bears would be on the lookout for her from now on.

★ ★ ★

"You need to stop crying," Max growled at Stevie.

Max wasn't growling simply because she was pissed. She was growling because her throat was still recovering from someone trying to strangle her to death.

Stevie, however, didn't give a shit about that. "I'll cry if I want to!"

"Because it's your party?" Kyle asked and when they all gazed at him, he let out a sigh, and said, "Forget it."

Shen grabbed a box of tissues from the table beside him and held it out for Stevie to wipe her eyes and blow her nose. They'd been at the emergency vet's office for a couple of hours, but they still hadn't heard anything specific yet.

"Want me to get you some water or something?" he asked.

"Come on," Charlie said, standing up and stretching. "Let's get everybody some sodas from the machine."

She walked off and Shen followed her.

The vending machines were down the hall and around a corner near the bathrooms. Charlie began pulling singles out of her bag to purchase a few Cokes and a couple bottles of water.

Shen went to get the junk food.

As they both put in money, Charlie asked, "How did you do that?"

"How did I do what?"

"When Stevie was outside with Mairi. She was about to shift. But you pulled her back. How?"

"She was angry, not scared. And I figured it was worth a shot. I mean, she gets mad at Max all the time and manages to control herself. Her rage at her cousin was worse, of course, but that's where I was working from. Plus, she's been trying really hard to control her shifting since the event at the Jean-Louis Parker house, so I—"

Shen stopped talking when he realized that Charlie was standing right in front of him. And very close. Making him nervous.

"What?" he asked. "What did I do? What?"

Suddenly he was being hugged by Charlie MacKilligan. A woman who didn't really seem like she enjoyed hugging.

"Thank you," she whispered. "Thank you so much."

"No problem," he said, ignoring the weird feeling in his chest.

Charlie stepped away and Shen went back to pumping dollar bills into the machine and getting more junk food.

"So Stevie's trying to control her shifting again?" Charlie asked.

"Excuse me?"

She gave a little laugh. "Oh? Are we playing that game?"

"I don't think I understand—"

"Let me guess what she said to you. She wants to fuck with her DNA so she can never shift again. Never put anyone she loves in danger. And save the world from the horror that is her secret love of cat toys. Right?"

"What . . . no. That's crazy talk. Why are we even discussing this?"

"I was wondering why she hadn't said anything to Max about it. Now I see it's because she went to you first. What did you say to get her to stop? Because usually that sort of thing lasts for days. Lots of obsessing. And research."

Shen glanced down the hallway before admitting, "I told her I'd tell you."

"Perfect. Everybody uses me when she starts getting those self-destructive ideas and they want her to stop. It should bother me that I terrify her so much, but not if it helps."

With junk food and drinks in hand, they returned to the waiting room to find the veterinarian standing there, talking to Berg.

"What's going on?" Charlie demanded, putting all the sodas and water down on a nearby table.

"I was just telling Mr. Dunn," the vet said, "that Benny is going to be fine. The bullet hit a rib but didn't go past it. The rib did break, though. Thankfully nothing major was damaged and the rib didn't puncture the lung."

"How do you treat a broken rib on a dog?" Stevie asked.

"Wait for it to heal on its own. We've removed the bullet, cleaned and sutured the wound. Now we'll just need to watch the wound for a few days to make sure it doesn't become infected, and in a couple of weeks, we should X-ray the ribs again. Make sure they're healing properly. When you get him home, it's really about restricting his exercise and general movement. Just potty breaks. We'll give you pain meds, though. That will help. And antibiotics."

"Can we take him home tonight?"

"It's better if he stays here for a couple of days. That way we can drain the wound, if necessary, and keep an eye on him to make sure everything is healing properly."

"Okay." Charlie nodded. "Thank you, Doctor."

"No problem. Oh. Do you need a report for the police?"

They all became quiet, gazing at the doctor blankly before Max rolled her eyes and said, "That would be great, Doc. Thanks."

"It's so horrible what some people will do to animals," the full-human noted before motioning to one of the technicians. "Just unbelievable."

"Yeah," they all said in unison, which just sounded weird.

Stevie walked into her room. One or two of their nice neighbors had put a board over the broken window and removed the rug that had been stained by poor Benny's blood.

But the scent of gun powder and blood still lingered in the air.

Just thinking about poor Benny had her crying again, which made Max scream from her bedroom, "*Stop crying!* I was the one who almost died, ya know!"

Fed up with her sister ordering her around, Stevie started back toward the door, but Shen caught her just as she stepped into the hallway. He took hold of her hand and pulled her to his room. He drew her inside and closed the door.

Still crying but no longer in a mood to fight stupid Max and her stupid mean ways, Stevie just climbed onto Shen's bed, curled onto her side, and let herself cry as much as she wanted to.

An hour or so later, she woke up. Her eyes were swollen shut from all her tears but she wasn't alone. Shen, also fully dressed, was behind her, tucked in close. His arm was around her waist, his face buried against the back of her neck.

And asleep on her feet was Artemis. Stevie was relieved that all the snoring was coming from the dog and not the man.

Feeling safe and comfortable—despite Artemis's heavy head like a concrete weight on her poor feet—Stevie smiled a little bit before going back to sleep.

chapter TWENTY

Stevie looked up from her bowl of oatmeal and frowned. "What are you wearing?" she asked.

Max paused in the doorway. "What's wrong with it?"

"Everything."

Charlie rushed into the room, tugging on a pair of low-heeled black shoes. "Are you guys read—what are you wearing?"

"What's wrong with it?"

"It's red!" Stevie and Charlie said together.

"And a minidress," Stevie added. "You look like you're going to a club."

"Or hooking."

"I don't hook anymore."

Charlie slapped her purse down on the kitchen table. "That's *not* funny."

"I was just kidding," Max laughed. "You guys are so serious. You already called the vet to check on Benny. He's doing fine. The worst of my throat damage has healed, not that anyone asked about me."

"We were more worried about the dog," Stevie muttered.

"Thank you," her sister sneered. "I just don't see what the big deal is about this dress."

"It's a funeral!" Charlie barked.

"So?"

"You can't wear red to a funeral!"

"Even for people we don't like?"

"Yes! Even for people we don't like! It's tacky."

"But you plan to wear red to Dad's funeral."

Charlie threw up her hands. "That's different. Besides, you didn't even know Uncle Bob."

"Great-Uncle Pete," Stevie corrected.

"Whatever. Go and change," Charlie ordered Max. "Right now. We're running late."

Max walked out and Charlie sat down with a big mug of coffee.

"Are you okay?" Charlie asked Stevie.

"I stabbed her seven times in the chest."

"Sweetie, you were angry."

"As much as it pains me to say it, I don't really care that I stabbed her."

"Oh."

"She hurt our dog. She deserved what she got. What I do care about is that Mairi didn't die."

"What did you expect? You know you need to either shoot her in the back of the head or carve that heart right out of the bitch's chest. Otherwise, all you're doing is pissing off a badger."

"Think she'll be back?"

"No. She's not stupid. She knows all the bears on this block are on high alert. She won't risk it. But that doesn't mean those twin bitches won't have her try something else."

Stevie couldn't help but smile. "Is this where you give me the 'you have to be careful out there' speech?"

"Nah. You already know it by heart. And you may not have killed her, but she's well aware it wasn't from lack of trying. She won't want to go head-to-head again with you anytime soon."

Stevie shoveled another spoonful of oatmeal into her mouth as the Dunn triplets walked into the kitchen. All three had on dark blue suits, Berg and Dag wearing ties and Britta without one. Instead, she had on heels, which was pretty bold since they made her taller than her grizzly bear brothers.

Kyle pushed past the triplets and ran into the room, making his way onto Stevie's seat, and putting his arms around her shoulders.

"Please let me come today," he begged.

"What?"

"To the funeral. I promise I'll be good."

"Who *wants* to go to a funeral?" Charlie wanted to know.

"I do," he insisted. "I'm fascinated."

Charlie cringed. "With death?"

"Of course not," Kyle replied. "I've already decided I won't be dying, so why would I need to know about it?"

"He has a point," Berg laughed.

"I want to go to the church. To see the rituals."

"Didn't you once throw that Nazi quote at me about religion being the meth of the masses?"

Kyle rolled his eyes at Stevie, telegraphing how annoyed he was at having to deal with all these "normals" before replying to Charlie's question, "It's opium and it's not Nazi, it's Communist. A Karl Marx quote to be exact."

"Is that the guy from World War T—"

"That's *Stalin*," he barked before focusing on Stevie again. "I promise not to engage any of your relatives."

"It could be dangerous."

"Do you mean the cult-like activity and belief in a higher power?"

"No. My family. Badgers at funerals are unpredictable. In other words, I don't know what they'll do."

"I'll bring the burly servant."

Britta sneered at Kyle. "Do you mean Shen? Who is *not* your servant. He is the only thing standing between your ridiculous little ass and the bad guys."

"In other words he works for me? Like a *servant*?"

Britta took a step forward but Berg quickly put an apple in her mouth before she could start yelling, and Charlie called out, "Shen?"

"Yo?" he answered from the second floor.

"Mind coming to a funeral with us?"

"I was planning to. Figured we could lock the boy in your dark, moldy basement. For his safety."

Charlie grinned. "Ya gotta suit?"

"Already on it!"

"Great. We're leaving in ten."

"I'll be ready."

Max walked back into the kitchen. She was wearing black now. But it was still a minidress and it sparkled. Like the sun.

"Seriously?" Charlie snapped.

"What? It's black."

"She looks nice," Stevie felt the need to point out.

"Yeah. Like a high-priced hooker."

Max pointed at her. "But high-priced."

"Are you *trying* to get the attention of Creepy Roy?"

"Who's Creepy Roy?" Berg asked.

"He's the married father of four who has always thought that the possibility of birth defects shouldn't stop you from hitting on your own cousins."

Max's lip curled. "I forgot about Creepy Roy," she said softly.

"He'll definitely be there. He's probably hoping to get something from the will."

"And he will definitely misinterpret your outfit," Stevie added.

Max nodded. "Yeah. I'll go change."

She walked out again and Dag shook his head. "I don't think I've ever seen Max back away from anything."

"You've never met Creepy Roy."

Stevie pushed Kyle off her chair. "Are you planning to go to our great-uncle's funeral in sweatpants?"

"I'm an artist, so—"

"Just go. You've got five minutes to find a suit and make yourself presentable."

Kyle took off and Britta smiled.

"You handle him well, Stevie."

"I'm the only one he respects. And before you ask . . . he doesn't respect any of you." She motioned to her sister. "But he does fear Charlie."

Charlie shrugged. "That still works for me."

The funeral at the big Catholic church in Downtown Manhattan had already begun by the time their group arrived. Shen could hear the organ music. But people were still heading inside.

As they reached the stairs, a male voice from behind called out, "Wee little Charlie and her sisters."

The three sisters stopped and looked left. Shen saw a group of male honey badgers a few feet away.

"That's Will MacKilligan," Berg said quietly to Shen. "The sisters' uncle."

And the head of a crime syndicate, which was a problem since the MacKilligan sisters' father had stolen from him.

Black and white hair, cut short; untrusting dark brown eyes; and a sneer that was less than friendly. Will MacKilligan was staring at his nieces like he was meeting Al Capone to do a business deal. Like he felt that although he had to work with them, he didn't have to trust them.

Dunn and his siblings moved in behind the sisters and Shen pushed Kyle behind him. But the kid was a good three inches taller now, so he just watched the action over Shen's head, unable to keep his nose out of anything that appeared remotely interesting.

"If you see a gun," Shen warned him, "run for the church."

"Can't I just hide behind your giant, round, panda head?"

Shen briefly thought about tossing the kid into moving traffic, but Max suddenly jerked forward—for no apparent reason!—and then there were all these people reaching for their weapons. In front of a church . . . in the middle of Manhattan . . . in the middle of the day.

Before Shen could grab her, Stevie jumped between the two groups, arms outstretched.

"No, no, no, no, no!" she begged. "Please. Everybody. Just calm down. Charlie?" she prompted. "Max?"

Charlie gripped a Sig Sauer behind her back, finger on the trigger. Max had blades in both hands, her arms resting against her sides. Casual, but no one was fooled. Not by Max.

"Stevie," Charlie said through gritted teeth, "get your ass back over here."

"Not until everybody calms down." When no one moved . . .
"I'm getting very *angry*."

"*Da*," one of the male badgers warned.

"We're just here for a funeral," Will stated to Charlie while
he slowly moved his hand away from his gun.

The other male badgers followed suit, all standing down.

Sadly, Charlie and Max weren't in the mood to take the
same route.

Stevie faced her sisters. "Put them away." Neither sister
moved, but Charlie's gaze was still locked on the male badgers
while Max's was on Stevie. "Do what I tell you."

"Or what?" Max asked with a little laugh.

Stevie's mouth twisted to the side, her annoyance clear. "I'll
start coughing up hair balls *all over the place!*"

Now Charlie was staring at her baby sister. "You promised
you would never to do that again."

"Because it's disgusting," Max added.

"At least I don't go around threatening people with my anal
glands."

"At least that's normal. You know . . . for me. But you're not
a house cat."

Stevie's response was to lean over at the waist and start
hacking.

"Okay, okay!" Charlie held her hands up, revealing that she
no longer held her Sig Sauer. She'd tucked it back into the holster under her light black sweater.

"See?" Charlie asked. "Everybody's letting it go."

Stevie pointedly stared at Max, knowing the middle sister
hadn't let anything go.

Blades still gripped in her hand, Max asked, "What?"

"Put them away," Charlie said. "And I mean now."

Max flicked up her black skirt and returned the weapons to
the holsters strapped to her legs.

Stevie faced the male badgers. "Hello, Uncle Will."

"Little Stevie. It's good to see you again. Despite the circumstances."

As the older badger passed them, he touched his hand to his forehead like he was tipping a hat, and Max's response to that was to raise her middle finger.

Stevie slapped Max in the back of the head, which quickly led to a headlock that had Stevie squealing and Max telling her to, "Go to sleep. Just go to sleep."

Charlie grabbed hold of her sisters' hair and had just yanked them in opposite directions when a female voice came from the top of the church stairs. "Charlie MacKilligan. There's a pew for you and your sisters and your extremely large friends. Can't hold that space forever, though. So you better get in here."

"Coming, Aunt Bernice," Charlie called back, pushing her sisters to the stairs. "Inside!" she ordered her siblings.

With a snarl, Max went up the steps; Charlie and the Dunns followed right behind her. Stevie came over to stand by Shen and Kyle while she attempted to comb her blond hair into something a little less . . . attacked.

"You have the best family," Kyle said, laughing. But when Stevie didn't look at him, Shen knew she wasn't in the mood to joke about the MacKilligans.

"Go inside," he told the kid.

"Aren't you supposed to go with me? You know . . . my big protector?"

Annoyed, Shen snapped, "No one is after your ass. Get into the fucking church."

"Okay, okay."

Shen waited until Kyle disappeared inside before asking Stevie, "Are you all right?"

"I'm fine."

"You're lying, aren't you?"

She peeked up at him in that way she had. "Yeah. A little."

"Why? Because Max had you in that headlock?"

Stevie waved that away. "She always has me in a headlock. She used to choke me out, too, until I finally learned to get out of it."

"How did she manage not to kill you?" he asked, holding out his arm for her to take.

"Charlie," she replied, briefly resting her head on his shoulder. "The answer to any question like that, especially when it comes to me and Max, will always be Charlie."

Charlie had assumed that the pew her Aunt Bernice had told her about would be in the back somewhere. Hidden from the disgusted eyes of the rest of the MacKilligan family. But it wasn't in the back. It was the third pew from the front, which meant that they had to sit close to the main family. Something that confused Charlie.

"Stop it," Max whispered next to her.

Trying to get comfortable on the wooden pew, Charlie asked, "Stop what?"

"Scowling. You look like you're about to open fire."

Charlie let out a sigh, but she still had to ask, "Why do you think they have us so close?"

"To the dead body?" Max shrugged. "No idea. Maybe they're worried he'll come back to life and they hope he'll come after us first."

"That's stupid, Max," Charlie snapped. "If he comes back as a zombie, he's going to start on those toddlers in the front row. You know . . . young brains. *Much* tastier."

"Like an appetizer."

"Exactly. And if he's reborn, like, into some god, he won't be interested in us anyway."

Berg, who sat on the other side of Max, leaned forward and asked, "What are you two talking about?"

"Zombie attacks," they said in unison.

Berg's mouth opened as if he was about to respond, but then he shook his head and sat back again.

After a few minutes, Charlie glanced at her watch and wondered how long this service was going to be. She was already bored and they'd just arrived. And sadly she was not good at hiding her expressions. When she was bored, it showed on her face. When she was angry . . . same. Happy . . . same. It was a flaw that, thankfully, made many people trust her when she needed them to, but also revealed when she really disliked someone.

She simply couldn't hide it. She'd learned early in life that she would make a terrible con artist.

"Psssst. *Psssst.*"

Charlie studied the area, expecting to see a gas leak somewhere. But she quickly discovered that her cousin Kenzie MacKilligan was trying to get her attention from the front pew.

She frowned and mouthed, *What?*

Behind you, Kenzie mouthed back.

Charlie looked over her shoulder and she was positive her heart stopped.

With no regard to the priest who'd just begun the service, Charlie screamed out, "*Oh, my God!*"

Max was reaching under her jacket for the Glock she had holstered to the back of her black skirt but she froze and gawked too.

"What the fuck is he doing here?" she finally demanded in a furious whisper.

"I can't believe it." Charlie forced herself to face forward, ignoring the priest glaring at her from the pulpit. "He can't be that stupid," she chanted. "He can't be that stupid. He can't be that stupid."

"We both know he's that stupid," Max snarled.

And Max was right. They both knew he was *that* stupid.

Berg leaned forward so he could see Charlie's face. "What's going on?"

"*It's Dad,*" she spit out between clenched teeth, her anxiety spiking so high Charlie was sure she'd blow out a blood pressure machine.

"Oh . . . *no.*"

"What are we going to do?" Max asked, sounding shockingly panicked. "What are we going to do?"

Charlie heard a sharp gasp and realized that her baby sister had finally seen their father.

"Oh, shit."

"Exactly," Max muttered.

Now Stevie leaned forward and whispered, "What are we going to do?"

Freddy MacKilligan reached their pew and stopped. He gazed down at her, and Charlie wondered what he could possibly say at this moment to—

"Move."

Charlie blinked and felt Max tense next to her.

"What?" she had to ask.

"Move," he said again. As if she was supposed to follow his orders without comment.

Charlie took a moment to let that sink in before she reacted in the only way she could think of. She released her fangs and hissed at her father like he was a pushy lion male at an African watering hole.

"Oh, come on!" he snapped.

Max joined in, the pair hissing at him simultaneously.

"Just move," Freddy ordered, as if he had any real power when it came to his daughters. "I'm not leaving. So you might as well move the fuck over."

That's when Berg slowly got to his feet, facing Freddy MacKilligan, whose gaze moved up and up as Berg rose and rose.

Finally, when he was at his full height, Berg easily leaned over until he was eye to eye with Freddy.

The grizzly panted. Great puffs of air hit the older badger right in the face. Then he gave several short warning growls, and still Freddy was too hardheaded to simply walk away and find another seat.

That's when Berg's grizzly hump suddenly grew under his jacket, and he released a roar so loud that the church's stained glass vibrated.

"All right now. That's it!" the Irish priest snapped from the front of the church. "We'll have none of that grizzly shit in this holy house of my Lord. And you, badger, find a seat somewhere else." When Freddy didn't move, the tiger priest warned,

"Don't make me tear that puny head from your shoulders, my good lad. Because we both know I will, now don't we?"

"Ungrateful," Freddy snapped at his daughters. "Goddamn ungrateful!"

Charlie decided in that moment that it was in everyone's best interest if she just killed her father here and now. Sure. She'd go to prison for a few decades, but wouldn't having Freddy MacKilligan out of all their lives for good be worth that sacrifice?

Charlie thought so, which was why she unleashed her claws. But before she could gut the bastard in front of God and the MacKilligans, another badger rammed into Freddy from the side, wrapping big arms around his chest. Well . . . he was more part of the badger family than an actual badger. Because he was a wolverine.

"Freddy!" Dutch crowed. "I'm so happy to see you!"

Dutch lifted Freddy off the ground and while their father loudly protested, Dutch carried the idiot to the front pew with Aunt Bernice and her family.

"Well, we don't want him!" Bernice snapped.

"Aw, come on. Isn't it wonderful to see your brother? I'm sure you guys have missed him so much!"

Dutch dropped Freddy and pushed him into a spot that opened up when one of Bernice's daughters moved out of the way.

When Freddy started to stand up again, Dutch pushed him back down and warned, "Try and move from this spot, and I'll tear your arms off and eat them."

Dutch leaned forward and snapped his jaw shut, his strong wolverine teeth clacking together. Freddy's head jerked back to avoid contact.

But Freddy kept his seat after that, so Dutch nodded at the priest and said, "Sorry, Father," before returning to the sisters' pew and wiggling his way in by forcing Charlie to move over.

The priest continued with the service and Dutch whispered to Charlie, "Aren't you glad I'm here to bring joy into your life?"

Max barely caught Charlie's arm before she could ram her

still-unleashed claws into Dutch's belly, completely ending his presence in her life too.

Again, decades in prison might be totally worth *all* of it.

When Berg suddenly roared, Stevie grabbed Shen's hand and held on tight. He looked at her and saw that she was panting hard, staring at the hymn books tucked into the back of the pew in front of them.

Without really thinking about it, he released her hand and lifted her up, sliding over and placing her between himself and Kyle so she had a little distance from Berg.

"Just breathe," he said. "Everything's fine. Just breathe."

She nodded but she had her hands clasped together, twisting them hard.

It wasn't just Berg and his grizzly ways that were freaking Stevie out, though. It was everything. Her father. Her Uncle Will. Her cousin Mairi. Even the bruises that were still on her sister's neck had Stevie tense and panic prone. Knowing she wouldn't leave the church without her sisters, Shen instead grabbed her left hand and held it between both of his.

"You're doing great," he told her.

"What does that mean?"

"I have no idea."

That made her laugh a little and he immediately felt less concern. When Stevie was truly freaking out, she never laughed.

"Do you need me to do anything?" he asked.

"Eat something."

"Huh?"

"The noises from your stomach are starting to freak out my family . . . and honey badgers do *not* freak out, Shen. Eat something."

Shen looked around but didn't see what Stevie was talking about until his stomach grumbled again and the badgers in the two pews in front of them turned around to glare.

Shen reached into his inside jacket pocket and pulled out a pack. To a full-human it would look like a pack of cigarettes. But Shen didn't smoke.

He released Stevie's hand so he could take the cellophane off the pack, fold the foil at the top back, and tapped the bottom against his hand until one of the bamboo stalks popped up. He gripped the shortened stalk between his lips and pulled it out. Then, as the priest spoke in Latin, Shen took a bite . . . and the sound cracked around the church, echoing off the walls.

He tried to chew, but stopped at each cracking sound. He did it three or four times, cringing every time he made noise. Finally, an older, Scottish She-badger in the pew right in front of them looked at him over her shoulder and snarled, "Just eat the damn things, would ya? Anything's better than hearing that stomach of yours!"

Moving quickly, Shen ate several stalks, one after the other, until he knew he'd quieted his stomach at least for the next ten to twenty minutes.

"Thank you," Stevie whispered.

"You're welcome." He took her hand in his again.

Smiling, Stevie moved in closer to him and rested her head against his arm.

"You keep holding my hand," she whispered. "Are you doing that because you're still worried I'm going to freak out?"

"I was," he admitted. "But now I just like it."

The service seemed to go on forever, but Stevie didn't mind. Because she was holding Shen's hand and it was the nicest thing. His hand was warm and dry and soothing.

Using her free hand, she opened up the program to find out what was next. She was relieved to see they were on the last speaker of the day. After that, her great-uncle's sons and the older grandsons would carry his casket to the hearse.

Great-Uncle Pete's oldest son finished speaking and, as he was thanking everyone for coming, he casually asked if anyone wanted to say anything else about his father. A few people stood up and did add a little. Old friends who wanted to express how much they would miss Pete. One of his brothers letting Pete's adult sons and grandchildren know that he was there for them if any of them had a need for "some old man advice," which got a mood-breaking laugh. Then his eldest son let everyone know that after the burial, the family would be going to a pub in New Jersey for one last drink in honor of their father.

Thinking it was over, Stevie started to reach for the black leather backpack she'd pulled out just for the occasion. A Gucci bag that looked fancy and could still hold several of her notebooks and a wallet, but would hopefully not lead to anyone muttering, "I can't believe she brought a backpack. It's a funeral not a hike."

Before she could pick it up off the floor, though, she heard, "I have something to say."

Stevie froze. *No. No, no, no, no, nooooo.*

Sitting up straight, she watched in horror as her father stood.

Her father wanted to say something. He wanted to say something!

Oh, God.

She leaned forward to check on her sisters. Max already had her face buried in both her hands while Charlie was sitting so bone straight and absolutely still that Stevie was terrified what her eldest sister might do. Because when Charlie had you in her sights, there was no escaping. No avoiding. No making it out alive.

Freddy faced the shocked faces of his extended family, foolishly unconcerned that nearly everyone in the room hated him. He was the reason a good chunk of them were currently cash poor. And the fact that he hadn't even benefitted from that money only made them angrier. Because he was just so stupid. And yet . . . he was talking.

Freddy placed his hand over his heart and lowered his chin to his chest.

"What is happening?" Shen asked.

Stevie tapped Shen's arm and motioned him closer. He leaned down a bit and she brought her mouth close to his ear. "You and the Dunns need to be ready."

"To take down your father?"

"No. Charlie. She'll have no qualms about killing him in front of witnesses. I'm not too worried about the family, but the church people could be a problem."

Shen nodded and leaned over to whisper in Britta's ear, allowing Stevie to—unfortunately—listen to whatever ridiculous bullshit was coming out of her father's mouth.

Oh, and it was bullshit.

"It breaks my heart," he said, tears beginning to run down his cheeks, "that we've lost such a great man. The mighty Peter MacKilligan. Loyal. Amazing. Good to his family. Always so generous."

Stevie rolled her eyes. Her father was angling for money. From the people he'd stolen from.

Freddy took in a deep breath, wiped some of the wetness from his face. "But you know what made Pete MacKilligan truly wealthy? It wasn't his money. It wasn't houses and cars and property in the Caribbean. No. It was the legacy he left. The legacy of his sons. There is nothing greater in this world than for a man to have sons. Loyal, protective sons. Willing to do anything for their father and to carry on the family name. Sons are the most important thing in the world. Nothing else can compete."

It was then that Stevie heard bodies turning in the pews, felt the eyes on her and her sisters. Everyone was staring at them now, because they all knew . . . the idiot had forgotten he had daughters.

Daughters sitting in the same room where he was making this men's rights–like speech.

Embarrassed, mortified, and wishing she was back in Switzerland immersed in science and math and the future of the universe, Stevie looked up. She expected to see the rest of the family laughing at Freddy's pitiful daughters. But they weren't. They all felt bad for Stevie and her sisters. She could see it on their faces. Feel it in the room. For once, honey badgers felt pity.

"Does he remember you guys are in the room?" Shen asked her.

"Wow," Kyle said from her other side. "I thought telling my kindergarten teacher I was an only child and an orphan was bad . . . I was wrong."

Stevie sighed. "But you were in kindergarten, Kyle. Not a grown man."

"I still don't know what's happening," Shen muttered. "But I do want to call my dad and tell him I love him."

"And you should also thank him for not being an asshole."

"Oh, I will."

"Sons," her father went on . . . still oblivious, "give a man something that no *woman*—related or not—can ever give him. An empire."

"I guess all those royal daughters in the middle ages who married to solidify power were meaningless," Stevie said with a head shake.

"Pete was truly blessed to have as many sons as he did," Freddy went on, ignoring Bernice as she tried to stop him or, at the very least, remind him that he had daughters sitting in the room, "Because sons are so important. They're the most important thing a man can have in his life. Sons are *everything*. I know this because, unlike Uncle Pete, I was never blessed with sons. Imagine . . . going through life childless."

"Oh!" Stevie gasped in surprise, "he just forgot he had daughters . . . altogether. How nice for him."

Freddy stared at the sons and grandsons of Pete MacKilligan. The confused men and boys gawked back . . . their sisters, wives, and daughters beside them.

The silence went on for a very uncomfortable amount of time . . . until laughter rang out in the church. Hysterical, unstoppable laughter.

Stevie felt those eyes on her again but the family soon understood it wasn't her. The crazy one. Nope. It wasn't Stevie. It was Charlie.

Charlie was laughing so hard, she was the one crying now. She had her arms around her stomach and no matter how hard she tried, she couldn't stop. It got so bad, she finally stood and waved at the priest.

"Sorry . . ." she managed between the wheezing. "I have to . . . I have . . . go . . . bye!"

Now coughing, wheezing, *and* laughing, Charlie made the long walk down the aisle of the church to the exit.

"I'll . . . uh . . . I'll go with her," Max said before jumping up and running after her.

After the pair disappeared out the big double doors, Freddy shook his head in disgust and said, "Well . . . that was inappropriate."

That's when Stevie lost it too. She slapped her hand over her mouth to stop the laughter but it wasn't helping.

With tears filling her eyes, she stood and followed her sisters. Desperate to get out. Desperate to not be the one laughing at a funeral.

But come on! What else did anyone expect?

It amazed Max that sometimes her sisters—whom she knew so damn well—still managed to surprise her. She'd been thinking that, by now, she'd have to peel the remains of her father off the church altar, find an exit strategy from the country for Charlie, and calm down a hysterically crying Stevie.

But that didn't happen. Even after their father had insulted them and seemingly forgotten they existed, Charlie didn't go after him the way she had in the past for much lesser offenses.

Instead, Charlie and Stevie were leaning against a black Escalade, still laughing.

When the laughter didn't stop after a few minutes, but Max could tell that the funeral was coming to an end, she suggested, "Why don't we just go home? Or get something to eat."

"No way," Charlie said, straightening up; using the back of her hands to wipe her eyes. "We're going."

"Why?" Max had to ask because . . . seriously . . . *why?*

"Because, they should have to face what they've done."

"You mean not killing Dad at birth?"

"Yes. That's exactly what I mean."

Organ music played, heralding the beginning of the procession of the casket to the hearse, and Max quickly pulled her sisters away from the SUV and over to the stairs.

"Now stop laughing," she ordered.

In silence, the casket began down the steps and, once it was in front of them, Stevie snorted, and then all three of them were laughing so hard Max began to wheeze.

Then they were moving; someone had grabbed them by the backs of their necks and was yanking them over to one of the family limos. They were forced inside and the door shut. When Max was able to see through the tears in her eyes, it was their Aunt Bernice staring at them. Her daughter Kenzie sitting beside her, also trying hard not to laugh.

"You three," Bernice said. "Laughing at a funeral."

"Dad's fault," Charlie replied. "That was all Dad."

"Oh, I *know*," Bernice confirmed tiredly with a wave of her hand. "Your father—"

"Your brother," Max corrected, not willing to let anyone in that family dismiss the problem *they* had created.

"He was born a fuckup," Bernice went on. "My sister was right. We should have taken that little pillow that was in his crib and put it over his face and—"

"*Ma!*" Kenzie exploded in giggles, shaking her head at the same time. "I do not want to hear this!"

Bernice lifted a small door near her, revealing a row of liquor bottles. She grabbed the scotch and poured herself a splash in a crystal glass. "You can't say these girls wouldn't be better off if we'd done that."

"If you'd done that, they wouldn't be here."

"I'd be here," Stevie said, gazing out the window. "I was meant to be here. Genius like mine doesn't just come around every day."

Bernice shook her head. "The fact that your father would show his face here . . . with your Uncle Will in town."

"Why *is* he here?" Max asked.

"Not sure." Bernice swallowed her scotch in one gulp and began pouring another. She shrugged her big, honey badger shoulders. "Maybe he thinks he can get money."

"In what world . . . ?"

"He definitely wants money," Stevie said flatly and without doubt.

"He can't truly believe—" Charlie began.

"Wait." Bernice let out a bitter laugh. "When all the family members' accounts were hacked and their money stolen . . . no one touched Uncle Pete's or his sons."

"Do you think he's actually stupid enough—"

"Yes."

"—to think because he didn't steal from Uncle Pete—"

"Yes."

"—that Uncle Pete's sons will give him money?"

Bernice gazed at Charlie over her empty scotch glass. "Child, what part of *yes* are you not grasping?"

It took some time to find the limo that the sisters were in. They hadn't arrived in a limo and Shen didn't think they'd be going anywhere in one. The limos, he'd been told, were for "family only."

But, apparently, the MacKilligans were beginning to see Stevie, Charlie, and Max as family because they were in one of the limos with an aunt and a cousin.

Shen knocked on the window and the door opened.

Stevie leaned out. "Where's Kyle?"

Shen had thought the kid was right behind him. Sighing, he looked around. Not hard, because the honey badgers weren't very tall. But there were a lot of them at the moment.

The Dunns were still standing on the church stairs. "Hey!" he called out to them. "Do you see Kyle?"

Dag pointed. "With the coffin."

Shen briefly closed his eyes. "What is wrong with that boy?"

"He's simply fascinated by death and rituals," Stevie explained. "It's a phase many artists go through."

"Is it? Really?"

Kyle arrived before Shen could retrieve him. Britta's hand tight on his arm, she shoved him into the limo and followed him in.

"Do not be weird," she told Kyle as she settled into a space.

Shen entered the limo and was just sitting down when the Dunn brothers arrived. Berg started to step inside, but a foolish wolverine pushed past him and dove into the spot next to Max.

"Miss me?" he asked, grinning.

"Of course, my sweet love!"

"I didn't miss ya," Charlie coldly stated. "Liked it when you were gone."

"Damn, Charlie," Dutch laughed. "I don't even get props for manhandling your father for you? In front of a priest, no less."

"You've gotta give him points for that," Max insisted.

"No, she doesn't," Berg stated, settling into a spot next to Charlie. "She doesn't have to give him shit."

"Why?" Dutch asked. "Because *you* say so?"

The bear took his time turning his big bear head. When he finally faced Dutch, he let out one of his grizzly huffs, and the wolverine instinctively jerked back in his seat. He then turned red because he'd gone on instinct rather than the practical logic that Berg wasn't about to shift into a bear in the middle of this funeral limo and attack him.

But the look of fear on the wolverine's face was enough to have Charlie grinning like a little girl while Max laughed in her best friend's face.

"See why I love him?" Charlie asked, stroking Berg's arm.

The limo door closed and the procession began to move. Their driver was moments from pulling away from the curb when a knock startled them all. They looked to see Freddy waving at them through the window. He tried opening the door but it was locked. So he knocked again and pointed toward the door handle, urging his daughter to let him in.

"He must be kidding," Bernice said in awe.

Charlie and her father stared at each other for several long moments. Then, Charlie raised her fist and, after that, just her middle finger.

Snarling, baring his fangs, Freddy stepped back, raised his leg, and kicked at the door.

"Don't worry," Bernice said, shaking her head in disgust. "The limos are bulletproof. He can't get in."

Stevie frowned. "Well . . . maybe we should just let him—"

"*Stevie!*" her sisters barked.

Stevie shook her head. "Forget I said anything."

Their father continued to kick the door. Again and again, getting madder each time he did.

"Open the fucking door!" he yelled.

Charlie raised her other fist, then her middle finger. So now she had two middle fingers raised at her father.

The limo was beginning to pull out into traffic, and Freddy seemed to know he was running out of chances. When he took several giant steps back, Shen assumed he was going to throw everything he had at the limo in the hope of—

"Oh!" they all gasped as a semitruck sped by, going in the opposite direction.

Freddy hit the grill and went down, disappearing underneath the vehicle, which didn't even slow down.

Stevie spun around, her knees on the seat, her arms on the headrest.

"He's back up," she announced, and Shen almost laughed when he heard everyone else sadly sigh.

There was just so much disappointment in the collective sound.

"Yeah, he's fine," Stevie said, settling back into her seat.

"How is he fine?" Britta asked. "The man was hit by a semi."

"Dad's not very bright," Stevie admitted. "But he is resilient."

Gazing out the window, Charlie sounded on the verge of tears. "The motherfucker just won't *die.*"

chapter TWENTY-ONE

A fter she knocked, the door opened and Cella Malone threw
her arms around the priest who answered.

"Uncle Jimmy!"

"My sweet Cella. How are you?"

"I'm fine. Fine."

"Come in, come in," he said, stepping back.

Cella walked into the office. Uncle Jimmy wasn't the only
priest among the Malone clan, but he was the one based in
a Manhattan church and not one of the other boroughs or
Ireland. Jimmy had been running this church for nine years
and, thankfully, had never been called to the Vatican to face
disciplinary action. Unlike some of the other Malones who'd
made their lives in the Church, including a few aunts and cousins who had *literally* been sent to Siberia. A punishment that
would have destroyed other women, but Malones were Siberian tigers . . . they ended up battling Cossack polar bears so
that they could take over the towns around the nunnery. And,
in typical Malone fashion, once the aunts and cousins had control, they began to run some very successful scams and offered
brutal protection for the towns. Gangsters soon learned the
local nuns were not to be fucked with.

Uncle Jimmy, though, was "a good lad," according to his
mother, which meant he didn't like doing anything with his
church except help others and worship God. A life Cella
could never get into herself, but she understood how relaxing it must be *not* to have to deal with the family. She knew

for a fact that the Vatican was easier to deal with than the Malones.

"How did the funeral go?" she asked, sliding onto his desk so her feet dangled. She'd been sitting on Uncle Jimmy's desk like that since as long as she could remember, and not once had he slapped her off with his paw. Unfortunately, she couldn't say the same about a few of her other older cousins.

"A church full of honey badgers?" He shrugged. "It could have definitely gone worse."

"Do you have the video?"

"I just finished downloading." He pulled a USB drive out of his laptop, but when he faced Cella, he didn't hand it to her right away. "Now why do you need this again?"

"Nothing bad."

"Marcella *Malone*."

"It's not! We just need to see who was here. Scottish gang members were in your church, Uncle Jimmy. I'm here to ensure they don't do anything to upset things."

"I know what you do for a living," he reminded her. "And I don't like it."

"You and my daughter. But we both know that what I do is important. I don't, however, do it recklessly. My jobs mean too much to me to screw around with either of them."

He handed her the drive. "I don't know why you can't just coach. The team's doing great."

"I know," she replied, smiling. "Chances are we'll be going against the Swedes this year. You do know they're mostly descended from grizzly bear Vikings?"

"And you have the descendent of Genghis Khan as your power forward."

"Yes, I do." Cella couldn't help but smirk. "And Novikov can't wait to destroy them."

Uncle Jimmy's smile faded and he placed his hand on her shoulder while a frown pulled down his thick brows. "Will MacKilligan was here," he said. "Along with his sons."

Cella nodded. "We knew he was coming."

"The three girls were here too. The ones you wanted me to keep an eye out for."

"You're sure?"

"I didn't see any other African American or Chinese girls here. So I'm going out on a limb—"

"Got it. Got it," Cella said on a laugh. "That was definitely them."

Again serious, her uncle said, "I need you to be careful, Cella. Will MacKilligan . . . he's—"

"I know." Cella took her uncle's hand to reassure him. "But don't worry about me. I've got my backup."

Her kindly, God-loving uncle sneered dramatically. "You mean that *dog*?"

Cella giggled. "Uncle Jimmy, be nice. I am the godmother of that dog's child."

"I am aware of that and, speaking for the family, we're all disgusted by that fact."

Dee-Ann Smith planted herself on top of the mausoleum and took her time assembling the Israeli-made sniper rifle she'd brought with her.

She tightened the scope, loaded the weapon, and stretched out, stomach down, near the very edge of the building. Pressing her left eye against the scope, she searched for her target. He stood on one side of Pete MacKilligan's casket, his sons and the sons of his uncle beside and behind him. On the opposite side stood the rest of the American MacKilligans, including the three daughters of Freddy MacKilligan. And boy did those three little ladies stick out among this group.

They seemed out of place and *bored*.

Max yawned. Stevie stared at the dirt at her feet and made shapes in it with the tip of her shoe. Charlie blatantly focused on her phone.

"Smith? You there?" Malone's voice spoke in her ear.

"I'm here," she said softly.

"Do not shoot Will MacKilligan."

"I don't know what you're talking about."

"Don't lie to me, Marmaduke."

"You always get so moral after you've seen that priest uncle of yours."

"Now, now, Smith. Your Southern Baptist is showing."

"Look, I've got a clean shot. I'll be gone before they even know—"

"*No.* Just watch and report back. Think you can handle that?"

"Fine."

"Thank you. And the sisters are there, too, right?" Malone asked.

"Yep."

"Did they see you?"

"No. And I don't appreciate your tone."

"Just face it, Smith. You'll never be as good as me when it comes to being invisible."

"Please. With that big ass? That thing is like a neon sign." Dee-Ann continued to study the burial through the scope while the casket was slowly lowered into the grave, but she removed her finger from the trigger. Real shame, though. It was an easy shot.

But just as she was questioning Malone's decision to keep Will MacKilligan alive, the three MacKilligan sisters suddenly looked up at Dee-Ann. She knew she was too far away for them to see her.

And yet . . . all three of them were staring right at her, their heads angled the same way, tipped a little to the left, gazes narrowed.

They might not be able to *see* Dee-Ann, but they all knew she was here.

"Goddamn," she muttered.

"What is it?"

"I find these girls just . . . wrong, Malone. Real wrong."

"You're being paranoid. Again."

"If you say so . . ."

★ ★ ★

"Want me to kill her?" Max asked.

"Not yet," Charlie said, looking back at her phone.

"No," Stevie corrected. "She means *no*, do not kill her."

"That woman would kill you as soon as look at you," Max told her. "I've looked that bitch in the eyes. She is exactly what Gramps said all the Smiths are: a pack of rabid dogs. We're better off wiping her from the earth now rather than after she kills you."

Stevie took a step back. "*Me?* Why would she kill me? I'm lovely. You're the psycho."

"Thank you very much."

"I'm just being honest."

"She totally is," Charlie said on a chuckle.

Someone tapped Stevie on the hip and she looked over her shoulder at the elderly lady sitting in a folding chair in the black tent that had been set up beside the grave so the older MacKilligans would have a place to sit.

"Move so I can see," the woman ordered. "I want to make sure the old fuck gets buried."

"Not sure why you're here, Daphne," one of Uncle Pete's brothers complained. "Peter divorced you a long time ago."

"I'm still the only one that matters!" she yelled at Pete's younger and more recent wife, forcing the poor woman to start crying and rush away from the grave. She'd been a hysterical mess since Stevie had first seen her at the church.

"Can we just get through this?" Bernice barked.

The coffin was lowered into the grave, the rites nearly at the end. Immediate family would be throwing dirt on the coffin in the next few minutes. A step that Stevie never quite understood. Was it that "dust to dust" thing? Maybe she should research it. Then again, Stevie, Charlie, and Max had already decided that no matter when they died or how, they all wanted to be cremated. It was the only way they could ensure their father wouldn't sell their remains for easy cash.

"Oh, no," Stevie heard Kenzie gasp behind her.

Stevie looked to her left and saw her father stumbling toward them. Not because he was drunk but because he'd tripped on a headstone, knocking it over—and not caring.

"Oh, God." She turned away, wishing she'd stayed back in the limo with Shen, Kyle, and the Dunns. Kyle had wanted to come to the graveside portion of Pete's funeral, but Shen had insisted that he stay away from an open hole with a bunch of honey badgers encircling it. And Charlie had insisted the Dunns stay behind because, "You guys tend to lumber and when this is over, we'll be gettin' the fuck out of here."

Berg had not liked that at all, concerned about how "open" the location was, but when Charlie insisted on something, it was hard not to comply. It was something Max and Stevie already knew but Berg was still learning.

"You just left me," Freddy complained, speaking over the priest who'd replaced the older one from the earlier service. "I was hit by a truck and you didn't even stop to help!"

Charlie had to look away from their father because, Stevie knew, it was the only thing keeping her sister from beating him to death in front of witnesses.

"I'll take care of this," Dutch said, pushing past Charlie and Max, but Freddy threw his hand up.

"Back off, canine."

Stevie cringed, Max snorted, and Charlie started rubbing that spot on her forehead that told Stevie her sister was getting one of her migraines.

"Actually," Dutch corrected, "I'm a wolverine, which are not canines. We are not wolves. Wolverines are badgers." Dutch suddenly smirked and raised his arms as if he was pleading to the masses. "And are we all not badgers . . . together?" he solemnly intoned.

That made Max snort louder, her shoulders shaking. But Freddy tried to wave Dutch away.

"Do you mind? I'm talking to my useless daughters. Not you."

Stevie was used to her father's insensitivity. She'd grown up with it, but her uncles and aunts had never really seen how he

treated his own offspring . . . not until now. She fully understood that when both Bernice *and* Will cringed at his words.

"I thought you were childless," Charlie noted, not even
bothering to look away from her phone so she could properly
glare at him.

"Or do you prefer childfree?" Max asked.

"That was an accident," their father lied.

"I'm pretty sure it wasn't. But we get it. We like to forget
about you too."

"Look," he said, raising his hands, palms up. It was his
"placating" maneuver. "Let's discuss this later. At your house.
Right now we're here for Uncle . . . Uncle . . ."

"Pete," Stevie said.

"Right. Uncle Pete."

"*Our* house?" Charlie asked, finally looking away from her
phone with an incredulous expression.

"Well . . . I don't really have a place to stay right now and I
know if I come in *with* you guys, those bears won't be so bitchy
about me being there this time."

Max grinned. "You expect to stay at *our* house? Seriously?"

"I'm your father. It's the *least* you can do for me."

Stevie shook her head and sighed out softly, "Oh, Dad."

Max faced Charlie. "You all right with that?" she asked.
"Dad staying with us?"

Charlie's gaze cut over to their father's. She didn't say anything at first, but she also didn't reach for any of her weapons.
She still could, though.

After a time, Charlie finally suggested, "Let's just talk about
this later." She indicated a spot between her and Max. "Come
here, Dad. Let's just . . . get through this."

Grinning, Freddy practically danced over to the spot near
his daughters. Stevie knew what her father was thinking: that
the slightest act of kindness from his daughters meant he'd
get anything he wanted once he was in their house and could
charm them. There was just one problem . . . her father was
not nearly as charming as he believed himself to be.

Stevie looked across the open grave to see that Will and his sons continued to glower at Freddy, but so far none of them had attempted to climb over Pete's moving casket to wring the life from him. That alone was impressive.

"Sorry about that, Father Jones," Charlie prompted the priest who'd taken over for Father Malone. "You can go on."

The priest did, pausing briefly when Freddy landed face-first on Pete's coffin, pushed there by Charlie and Max as they stood behind him.

The priest even continued while most of the family laughed, including Will, and Freddy cursed violently trying to find a way out of the grave. No one helped. Not even Stevie.

She just couldn't. He was being a total ass today.

Dee-Ann chuckled, finding herself enjoying this funeral way more than her great-granddaddy's when a hungover Sissy Mae had thrown that punch at cousin Polly Mae, and all hell had broken loose right there in front of the minister who called them all "insolent whores!" which led directly to Sissy's momma slapping that minister right across the face. True, Janie Mae had called her daughter and Sissy's best friend Ronnie Lee "insolent whores" before, but it was a whole other thing coming from some man who wasn't kin.

"What are you giggling about?" Malone asked.

"Just enjoying the funeral."

"I'd call you a sick fuck, Smith, but the Malones are known for our amazing funerals. The whiskey flows, the brisket is tender—"

"Are there potatoes? Bet there are potatoes."

"Such a bigot, Smith."

Dee-Ann grinned until her ear twitched the slightest bit. Her wolf hearing had picked up a sound several hundred feet away. She tilted her head, sniffed.

"Malone?" she asked, moving her head slowly to look to her right.

"Yeah?"

"I'm seeing something that don't look right."

"We'll be there in a few."

★ ★ ★

Max sniffed the air again.

"Someone's here," she said to Charlie, keeping her voice low so that Stevie wouldn't hear.

With her middle finger raised toward their yelling father, still in that grave, Charlie softly replied, "When we start moving back to the cars . . . check it out."

"What are you two whispering about?" Stevie demanded. "What's going on? I know that you two are up to something— Dad, would you please *shut up!*"

"They're trying to bury me alive!" their father complained.

He was right. Will had given a few dollars to the men waiting to push the dirt back into the grave. They usually waited until the family left for that sort of thing, but everyone kind of wanted to see it happen now so Will pulled out a wad of cash to make it so.

But none of them were too worried—or too hopeful— because Freddy could burrow with the best of them.

"Is this your new medication?" Max asked, knowing the question would set her baby sister off. "Is this what's making you so paranoid?"

Stevie started slapping at her but Charlie quickly threw her arm around their baby sister's shoulders and steered her off toward Bernice and the limos waiting for them.

"There is nothing wrong with my medication, you ass!" Stevie yelled, struggling against Charlie's hold so she could get back to Max and slap her around. "You're lucky it's goddamn working!"

Thankfully Charlie had a good, firm hold on Stevie.

When they were far enough away, Max moved until she was behind one of the buildings and out of eyesight of anyone spying. She quickly slipped off her clothes, unleashed the claws on both her hands and feet, and began digging.

Shen was relieved to see the honey badgers coming back to the limos. The widow had already left, hysterically sobbing as she'd bypassed the family autos to grab the cab that had been waiting. Something told Shen she wasn't heading to the next stop at this event, the bar where they could all raise a drink in honor of Pete MacKilligan.

He knew someone running for her life when he saw it.

Arms angrily folded over her chest, blue eyes bright, Stevie practically threw herself against the limo he was leaning on.

"Everything okay?" he asked.

"My sister's an asshole."

"Come on," Charlie said, opening the back door. "Let's get to the bar. I need a drink."

"Where's Max?" Stevie asked.

"She'll meet us there."

Stevie grabbed Charlie's arm and yanked her hard, surprising not only Shen but even Charlie.

"Did you tell Max to kill Dad?" she demanded, not seeming to care that her voice was rather loud.

"Of course not!"

"Don't lie to me, Charlie MacKilligan!"

"I'm not! I didn't tell her to kill Dad. And she won't. She doesn't want to hear any shit from you." When her baby sister continued to glare, "I promise."

Stevie released Charlie and got into the limo, and Charlie followed. For the first time, Shen realized there were some lines that even Charlie MacKilligan would not cross.

He wondered, though, if Freddy even realized that the only reason he wasn't dead was because of Stevie.

From what Shen had seen of the man, he doubted it. Too bad. Because once Stevie stopped giving a shit whether her father lived or died, that would be it for him.

chapter TWENTY-TWO

Cella found Dee-Ann standing in a spot behind what looked like a shed.

She wasn't doing anything, though. Just standing there. Staring.

"What's going on?" she asked. The rest of their team standing behind Cella, all of them armed and ready.

"You know," Smith said, her gaze still locked on the forest, "I don't really know."

"Did you see someone or not?"

"Men. Military trained. About six of 'em. I thought they were going to make a move, but nope. They took some pics and headed out."

"Took pics of Will MacKilligan?"

Smith shook her head. "Don't think so."

"The three sisters?"

"Yep."

One of the team pointed at the ground. "What's that?"

Smith nodded. "That's when things got weird."

"How so?" Cella asked, enjoying how freaked out Smith was. The wolf was always so laid-back and calm that to see her confused and unable to hide it made the situation way more entertaining than it should be.

"The freaky little one."

"All of them are freaky and at least two of them are little."

"When I say the 'Chinese one,' y'all get upset!"

Reaching out, Cella caught hold of the neck of a South

China She-tiger's body armor, preventing her from launching herself at the She-wolf.

"Just say 'Max,'" Cella reminded Smith. "Since we do know their names."

"Fine. Max came here, got naked. I was over there waitin' on you all, so she didn't see me."

"She got naked and then what?" Cella asked.

"She burrowed away." Smith pointed.

"Into the forest?"

"Yep."

"After the truck?"

"I think so."

"Did you tag the truck?"

"Yep."

"Good." Cella looked at the rest of the team. "We were just going to track them unless they made a move. See where they went, but let's just get them now before—"

"I'm thinkin' it's too late for all that."

Cella faced Smith. "Why too late?"

Smith shrugged, again looked off into the woods. "We may do recon. Think things out. Arrange grand schemes. But that little honey badger . . . she ain't about to waste her time doin' all that."

They'd continued on their off-road route through the forest. The funeral was recon only. Because they couldn't just grab the girl. The client had made it clear. He wanted her alive and unharmed. So they needed to make a solid plan to ensure that happened.

It wouldn't be easy, though. She seemed to constantly be in the presence of others. And he recognized at least three of her "friends." They were a well-known protection team that worked for artists, actors, and politicians. The very large female once protected a dictator, and when she quit that job, he was assassinated by his enemies. So just grabbing the girl would be . . . challenging. But he was always up for a—

"*Fuck!*" the driver swore just before the SUV hit some kind of hole or pit, throwing him and his men forward. The front end landed in the pit and the back end flipped over.

It took a few seconds for him to figure out what had happened and get his men moving again.

"Out!" he ordered. "Everybody out!"

The doors on the passenger side were blocked by dirt so they had to go out the other way.

The men moved slowly, confused, some of them bleeding from head wounds. Once he got his team out, they climbed over the SUV to get out of the pit.

He studied the ground, staring at the SUV and the pit it was in. A pit that hadn't been there when they'd driven that way to get to the funeral.

"What the fuck . . . ?" he whispered.

"Sir?" his second in command called out. "Sir!"

He turned, saw what his injured and confused men were looking at.

She leaned against a tree, silently watching them. Her gaze examining but her expression weirdly blank. She didn't seem scared or concerned . . . just slightly curious.

"Why are you naked?" he asked, unable to help himself.

"You can't burrow in your clothes," she replied, laughing a little. He had no idea what that meant and he didn't want to know. She was a strange girl. Stranger than they'd all originally thought.

He'd been warned, though, to "watch out for her. She's not what she seems. Not if she's anything like her mother." A warning he wasn't about to dismiss.

He gestured to his men with a short nod of his head. Two split off and moved around the tree, but they took their time. Waiting for her to step away. To give them an opening.

"I know what you want," she said. "And you can't have her. I thought you guys would have figured that out by now."

"We can't have who?" he asked, oddly fascinated by all this. She was naked with a group of heavily armed men, but she didn't seem to care or even notice.

"You know who," she insisted.

"I honestly don't have any—"

"If you keep coming for her, I'll make you regret it. See, I'm trying to be nice here. For once."

"I have to say, I appreciate you trying to be nice. I really do. But it doesn't make a difference."

"It should."

"It doesn't. Because we're not here for anyone else . . . but you. In fact, you made this much easier for us. We thought we'd have to get you away from your protection. But here you are. All alone."

"Wait a minute," she said, finally stepping away from the tree, "you're here for . . . me?"

"Yes. We've been paid a lot of money to bring you in. And, if you play your cards right, we can make sure you're not harmed. But only if you don't do anything stupid."

She stopped walking, pressed her hand to her chest. "Me? You're sure it's *me* you want?"

Now he was getting a little annoyed.

"Yes. I'm sure."

"The Guerra twins sent you?"

"Who?"

She cringed, briefly closing her eyes. "Devon's paying you, isn't he?"

"Does it matter?"

"I guess not."

His men were behind her now, one of them pressing the barrel of his .45 to the back of her head. But he didn't have his finger on the trigger. Their target, however, didn't know this.

He stepped close to her. "You don't have to make this hard on yourself. Come with us; we'll get you some clothes and something to eat."

"Do you care what he's planning to do with me?"

"Sweetie, I've been hired to bring you in. That's it."

"So that's a no. Okay." She tried to pull away from the man behind her, but he held her arm and kept the gun on the back of her neck.

Devon had made it clear that they had to threaten the back

of her head. Not the front or the side. Must be the back. He had been very insistent.

"Are you going to move that gun off me?" she demanded.

"No."

"Fine." She crossed her arms over her chest. "You have no one to blame but yourselves."

Amused, he asked, "For what?"

She didn't respond. Just looked off. But he noticed his men. It started on their faces. Their noses twitching, their eyes watering. They began to gasp, hands going to their throats. A few coughed, the others just gagged.

When he looked at her again, she repeated, "No one but yourselves . . ."

The bar had no signage and was what Stevie would definitely call a "hole in the wall" that was buried deep in Jersey. Anyone who came to a bar like this didn't come here to see and be seen. They came here to hide from anything that could get back to the cops.

No wonder the MacKilligans came here for their after-funeral drinks. It was a very typical MacKilligan-type bar.

As soon as Stevie walked inside, she paused at the door, her eyes watering, her skin itching, and her nerves suddenly wildly alive.

She was going to panic. She was going to freak out. Because she scented bears. Grizzlies. Grizzlies she didn't know.

Stranger grizzlies would eat her! She knew it! They knew it! The world knew it! *Everyone* knew stranger grizzlies were going to use her bones like tooth—

"Want a beer?" Shen asked, placing his hand on her shoulder.

"I want a beer," Kyle said, coming in behind Shen.

"You can have a Shirley Temple and you'll enjoy it, *child*." Shen smiled down at her. "Or something stronger?" He leaned in and whispered, "You look like you need something stronger."

"There are bears here."

"You mean the triplets?"

"Of course I don't mean the triplets." She pointed across the bar toward the back. "I mean them."

"Those old bears?" he asked. "You're worried about old bears?"

"Old bears are just as dangerous—"

"Think they still have their teeth? Or do they just sit under beehives hoping honey drips into their open mouths?"

"They're going to kill us all. Most of us are honey badgers. Nearly everyone in this room has consumed large amounts of honey in the last few days. They're all like sacks of honey just waiting to be punctured."

"Uh-oh," Kyle said, gazing at her. "She's spiraling."

"I am *not* spiraling. I am stating the truth, and another thing—"

"Where's Max?" Shen asked and Stevie suddenly realized that he was right. Where *was* Max?

"You haven't seen her?" she asked.

"We left her at the graveyard . . . with your Dad."

She spun around, her gaze searching for Charlie. "I know they've killed him. I mean, *I* wanted to kill him. I just have restraint. Max has *no* restraint!"

Shen watched Stevie march through the mass of her relatives in order to find her oldest sister.

"You handled that masterfully," Kyle remarked beside him.

"What are you talking about?"

"What I've learned from living among canines—"

"You mean your family?"

"—is that the best way to get a wild animal off your back is to distract it. You tried one way with her and, when that didn't work, you went with another. Brilliant." The boy patted Shen's shoulder. "Look at you. Thinking through those issues."

"Is this why you never went to high school like normal kids?"

"Of course it is. Kindergarten was a nightmare of abuse. Like it was *my* fault they were still learning their ABCs while I was reading Chekov."

"Who?"

The kid cringed. "Good Lord," he muttered as he started off toward the bar. "She is really taking a step down with you, isn't she?"

"A minute ago I was brilliant."

"Where is Max?"

Charlie faced her sister. "I have no idea."

"Don't lie to me."

"I'm not lying. I don't know where she is." Charlie swept her arm in a half circle. "She is out in the wild. And I forgot to tag her."

"Amusing."

"She'll be here."

"When? And will Dad still be alive?"

Charlie blinked. "What does Dad have to do with anything?"

"We left him in a filled-in grave."

"And we both know he'll be fine."

"Not if you sent Max after him."

"I didn't send Max after him. I already told you that."

But her sister's pursed lips suggested she didn't believe Charlie, which Charlie found a little insulting.

"If I ever got to the point where I'd send Max to finish him off, I'd not only tell you about it, I'd have you locked in a secure room and stuffed into a titanium cage until it was over because we both know that you'd bring down the building to save that worthless motherfucker for no other reason than he put his *semen in our mothers!*"

As soon as Charlie started yelling, Stevie knew she'd made a mistake. Not because she'd caused her sister to yell. Charlie was kind of a yeller by nature. It was that although she had grasped how much their father's performance at the church and graveside had mortified and embarrassed her big sister, she had failed to see how much their father had managed to hurt Charlie . . . again. Even when you hated your father, you didn't actually want to *know* that he'd never cared. At all. That he'd only wanted sons and not the amazing daughters he'd been lucky enough to have.

Daughters that other people would have been proud to have.

Stevie glanced around, saw that everyone was watching them. Not wanting all these nosy badgers in their business, she grabbed her sister's hand and dragged her to the other side of the establishment, heading toward the hallway where the four old grizzlies were standing.

As she neared the bears, one pointed at her and began, "This area is off—"

"*Bears!*" she screamed, startling the four males and sending them off in different directions. Stevie didn't know why she'd screamed that, but it was the only way she could think of to alleviate her panic in that moment. She wanted a quiet place for her and her sister to talk without all their relatives listening. But that meant she had to get past the bears she'd been terrified of.

So she'd screamed. She'd screamed, "Bears!" And it had worked! Which was very nice. She'd have to try it again . . . at some point.

Stevie went down the hall and opened the first door she came to. And that's where she and Charlie froze, gazing at the two females across the room from them. One sat on a card table. She looked vaguely familiar but clearly not important enough for Stevie to make sure she remembered her down the line. But the other woman . . . the one standing by that card table . . .

That was the woman Stevie had accidentally mauled at the Jean-Louis Parker rental house.

Eyes wide, her prey . . . er . . . the poor *female* stared like she was afraid Stevie was going to come for her again. Not surprising, her fear, considering the damage Stevie had done to her.

Bruises covered her face and ran down her body. Easy to see since she wore a tank top and shorts. Anything exposed seemed to have a bruise or cut on it.

Stevie felt horrible. She'd never meant to hurt anyone that

way. And her cousin Mairi didn't count because she'd hurt their dog!

While Stevie and her victim stared at each other, her friend's confused gaze continued to bounce back and forth between them.

They were all silent for several very long seconds until Charlie said, "Hey! Aren't you the dumb-ass who hugged my sister?"

That's when Stevie yanked Charlie from the room, slamming the door behind them.

"*That's* the woman that kicked your ass?"

Blayne faced her best friend in the world. "You didn't see her, Gwenie! She was *huge!*"

"She's not a hundred pounds soaking wet. And honey badgers are like—"

"She's also half tiger."

"So am I. When I shift, I'm three hundred pounds. Pop-A-Cherry," she went on, using their one-time team captain's derby name, "is about a thousand pounds when she shifts—"

"I don't care. I'm telling you that girl was, like, a billion pounds."

Gwen smirked. "Just admit you were beaten up by a little girl."

"I was not!"

Stevie pushed her sister into an empty room, closed the door, and then locked it. She rested her head against the wood and tried not to cry.

"You didn't do anything wrong."

She faced Charlie. "Are you kidding? Did you see that poor woman?"

"Yeah, I saw her. And she shouldn't have grabbed you. Someone grabs me, I beat the shit out of them."

Stevie crossed her arms over her chest and began pacing the room. "This is why I should look into—"

"If this is about fucking with your DNA again . . . just forget it. I mean it."

"You can't tell me what to do. I'm an adult. And if I want to get—"

"Something that is unnatural and not fair to you?"

"Was it fair that I beat that woman to hell and back?"

"She shouldn't have touched you. It's not like you sneezed and accidentally shifted. And we'll get your panic disorder under control. I have faith."

"Wouldn't you at least like to stop worrying about *that* part of me?"

"That part of you is you. I want you the way you are. Gaining control of something is not the same as eliminating it forever."

"It's not like I'm getting anything surgically removed. I don't know why you're so against this—you don't shift."

"Right. But I was born this way. You were born your way. I'm not going to have you ashamed of what you are just because some little bitch decided to hug you. She's just lucky it was you and not Max."

"She did hug Max. She thought Max was Livy."

Charlie smirked. "And what did Max do?"

Stevie let out a sigh. "She . . . tried to kill her. But the woman's hockey player husband stopped her. At least that's what Max told me."

"Uh-huh. And you think you're worse than Max? You think you're worse than *me*?"

"It isn't about better or worse. It's about keeping people safe."

"Aw, sweetie," Charlie said, gently pressing the palm of her hand against Stevie's cheek. "No one is *ever* safe around a honey badger."

Cella stood in the middle of the Jersey forest. Her equipment told her that the vehicle Smith had tagged was here but she didn't see anything.

She could smell something, though. Something awful.

"What *is* that?" she finally asked when she couldn't stand it anymore, covering her nose and mouth with her hand.

"Someone unleashed their anal glands," a lion male informed her, a bandana wrapped around his nose and mouth. Not that she thought that would help cut down on the power of the smell.

"Anything that can smell like that should be destroyed at birth," a female snow leopard complained.

"I think I'm forced to agree." Cella spat, because the smell had settled in the back of her throat.

The lion male motioned to his least-favorite She-wolf.

Eyes now watering, Cella called out, "Hey, Smith."

"Yeah?"

"Where are they?"

The She-wolf faced the rest of the group and Cella was annoyed that whatever that smell was didn't seem to bother Smith at all.

"Well?" Cella pushed when Smith just stood there, staring at them with those "dead dog eyes" as Cella's mother called them.

Smith tapped her foot against the ground, and, Cella was embarrassed to admit, it took a bit for her to understand what the wolf was showing them.

That where she was tapping her foot . . . there was metal underneath.

Cella asked, "The SUV's . . . buried?"

Smith grinned, ignoring the fact that the snow leopard had suddenly passed out from the odor.

"I have to admit, as much as it galls me . . . I think those MacKilligan girls might be growin' on me. Because that's an inventive way to get rid of men trying to kill or kidnap ya."

At that point, Cella could barely see because her eyes were watering so badly and stung so much. Plus, she was having trouble breathing. At any moment, she might pass out like the snow leopard. But still . . . she had to say it.

"Smith . . . only a *dog* could tolerate someone who can make that smell."

Stevie and Charlie both raised their noses at the same time and sniffed the air.

"Oh, my God!" Stevie gasped, her hand covering her mouth and nose. "What the fuck?"

Choking, Charlie gasped out, "It's gotta be Max." She went to the back door of the room and pulled it open. Their sister stood outside. Naked, covered in dirt, and grinning, she waved at her sisters. But as soon as she tried to step into the room, Charlie held her free hand out—the other one was covering her nose and mouth—and motioned away with her forefinger.

"But—"

Charlie stomped her foot and gestured again.

"Fine!"

Max walked off and Charlie followed. Stevie debated about going after them, decided not to, then just as quickly changed her mind. She found her sisters behind the bar, which thankfully was surrounded by a high wood fence. Probably to keep the locals out of the bar owners' illegal business.

While Max stood in front of the fence, Charlie grabbed a nearby water hose. She turned it on, walked back over to where Max was, and, without hesitation, hit their sister with a blast of powerful water.

Charlie hosed Max down like she was a horse, taking her time, hitting every part of her until she was sure that Max was not just clean of all the dirt and grime but—more important—that she was also odor free.

But Stevie didn't feel confident water alone would do the job. She ran back into the building, knowing there had to be soap somewhere inside.

Lachlan "Lock" MacRyrie relaxed against the washing machine in his uncles' bar, popping honey-covered cashews into his mouth while his Uncle Duff bitched about the fact that "my bar has been taken over by weasels!"

"Didn't they pay for this?" Lock asked. "To use the bar for an after-funeral event?"

"I don't like 'em. And at the moment I don't like you."

"Thanks, Uncle Duff."

Uncle Hamish stepped inside. "How much longer are they going to be here?"

"You do know this event is to mourn a loved one . . . right?"

"Those people don't love anyone. And they're cleaning out our supply of honey-covered peanuts."

Lock mockingly gasped. "Not the peanuts!"

Duff slapped the plastic jar of cashews out of Lock's hand. "That was *not* mature."

A small, thin woman appeared in the doorway. She was looking down the hallway but when she turned to them she immediately screamed out, "*Bears!*"

Hamish jumped back, his hands raised like he was trying to ward her off.

"Bears! Bears! Bears!" she loudly chanted, running into the room, grabbing the liquid detergent off the cart next to the washing machine they used to clean the bar rags. Then, still chanting, "Bears! Bears! Bears!" she ran back out, squealing a final, "Thank you!" as she disappeared around the corner.

"What the fuck was that?" Duff demanded.

But, to be really honest, Lock had absolutely no idea.

Stevie returned to her sisters. "Got detergent!" She ran to Max's side, holding her breath, and dumped what was left in the half-filled bottle directly on her sister's head and shoulders.

"Scrub that shit in!" Charlie ordered.

"Is this Tide?"

"Probably," Stevie admitted, now standing by Charlie.

Max rubbed the household detergent on her body for a couple of minutes, then Charlie hit her with more water from the hose.

Stevie still didn't know what her sister had been up to, but she knew one thing for sure. Max hadn't gone near their father. Releasing her anal glands would work on almost everyone as a weapon except other badgers. Because Charlie and Stevie were hybrids, they found the smell gross and annoying, but it wouldn't knock them out. Or suffocate them.

Yet Stevie had to admit, at least to herself, she felt a little bad for whoever had forced Max to go this particular battle route. It was the height of unpleasantness.

Max walked over to Charlie and bared her neck. "Well?"

Grudgingly, their big sister leaned in and took a couple of whiffs. She nodded. "I think we got it all."

"Now can I go inside?"

Charlie waved her on before rolling her eyes at Stevie and following Max.

Once they were inside, with the door closed and bolted behind them, Charlie threw her arms wide and said to Max, "Should I even ask what happened to you?"

"What do you mean?"

"I expected you to meet us here in a taxi. Maybe a little blood on you, if you had no other options. But you come back smelling like you've been engaged in biochemical warfare and covered in so much dirt that I can only assume you've been burrowing."

"You could definitely say that things got a little . . . out of hand."

Max ended the statement with a shrug that had Charlie rolling her eyes and Stevie doing the only thing she could think of—laughing.

"So what do I have to do?"

Shen, who'd been keeping his focus on the cranky, hard-drinking honey badgers, rather than his client, now looked at Kyle.

"What do you have to do about what?"

"About getting you to hook me up with your sister, Kiki?"

"You are a child. Way too young for her. And she has a wife."

Kyle briefly closed his eyes. "Look, I know you commoners—"

"Seriously, dude?"

"—think everything is about sex. But that's not what I'm talking about here and you know it. Your sister has power. True power. She can open doors for me that will take my work far into the future. My genius needs to be seen and loved and talked about for thousands of generations to come. Your sister can make that happen."

"You *actually* believe the words you're saying, don't you?"

"Why wouldn't I?"

Shen had begun to tell the kid why he shouldn't believe anything he said when someone grabbed his hand and began dragging him away from the bar. He turned and saw that it was Blayne. Poor, battered Blayne.

She dragged him through the crowd and down a back hallway until they reached a room. She pushed him inside and he found Gwen O'Neill sitting on a table, grinning at him.

Gwen was a pretty half-Chinese, half-Irish tigon from Philadelphia. Shen had always found Gwen fascinating because she had been on the local shifter roller derby team for years, but her seriously long nails were goddamn immaculate! How did she keep her nails like that? They were real, too, not acrylic. He'd asked!

"Love the nails, Gwenie."

She held up both hands, wiggled her fingers; her nails red and white with swirls of blue glitter. "Thanks!"

"The color is in honor of . . ."

"We saw a Phillies game last week."

"Ahhh."

"Tell her," Blayne ordered. "Tell Gwenie the truth."

Shen frowned. "The truth about what?"

Blayne stepped into him, pointing one finger in his face. "You know what, panda. Tell her!"

Charlie heard a knock and opened the door. Her Aunt Bernice nodded at her. "You girls leaving soon?" she asked.

"Should we leave soon?" Charlie wanted to know. "Would they prefer we leave the back way? Or should we just burrow under the building so they don't have to see our faces?"

Bernice squinted in confusion. "What are you talking about?"

"They want us to leave, right? The family?"

"No. I just assumed you were leaving because you disappeared half an hour ago and we haven't seen you since. Plus, Creepy Roy is getting . . . creepy. And handsy."

"I'll handle it!" Max announced, running out in nothing but a bear-sized T-shirt they'd found in a metal cabinet filled with bar paraphernalia.

"Stevie, don't let her—"

"I'm on it!" Stevie said, running after Max.

"Anyway," Bernice said with a small shake of her head, "your Uncle Will wants to see you before you leave."

"To kill me?"

"Oh, no. If he wanted to kill you, he would just come in here and kill you. Besides, if he wants to kill anyone, it's your father."

"Why do you always call him my father when he's really your brother?"

"Are we going to have that discussion again? He's your problem now. I put in my time. Hard time. I got him through high school alive. My job is done."

Charlie nodded. "Fair enough."

"So come on," Bernice said with a jerk of her head.

Her aunt walked off and Charlie followed her, but she stopped outside the partially open door to one of the rooms. The room Charlie and Stevie had stumbled into earlier. This time, however, Shen was inside with the two women.

The tall black female—who, for some unknown reason was wearing skates—had her finger pointed in Shen's face while her Asian friend was smirking but quiet.

"Tell her, Shen. Tell her about the freakish size of that woman when she shifts!"

Charlie's head lowered, but her eyes remained locked on the two women.

"She was huge," Shen admitted, surprising Charlie. She'd thought he was more trustworthy than, say, Dutch. "Giant."

"Yes!" Stevie's chew toy chimed in. "Giant! She was giant."

"Like Godzilla."

"Yes! Well, wait . . . no," Stevie's chew toy corrected. "Not as big as Godzilla. But definitely big. Unusually, abnormally big. Right, Shen?"

"Right. Absolutely."

"Told ya, Gwenie!" she said, facing her friend.

But as soon as she turned her back on Shen, he raised both his hands, holding them a foot or two apart.

The one called Gwenie snorted a laugh and dropped her head. The chew toy spun around but Shen had already lowered his hands.

"What?" he asked when she glowered at him.

"Tell her the truth!"

"I did," Shen insisted. "She was giant. Like Godzilla."

"No! Not like Godzilla!"

"Like Mothra."

"So she had wings," Gwenie tossed in.

"Yes!" Shen quickly agreed. "She had wings! And two, tiny Malaysian women who sang her to life!"

"That is not what happened!" Chew Toy insisted.

He frowned. "It's not? Oh, wait. Were the women Filipino?"

"Shen!"

Charlie was no longer worried that her sister's true shifterself was being outed by some walking chew toy, and that's all she cared about. That her baby sister was safe. Even if it meant taking out those who didn't necessarily deserve it.

Relieved that she didn't have to make any murderous plans for her evening, Charlie went in search of her Uncle Will.

Will MacKilligan had just lit his cigarette when two of his younger boys—the meatier ones—dragged Will's half-brother from the street and into the alley beside the bear-owned pub.

"Where's me money, Freddy?" he asked right away, not wanting to spend anymore time than he had to with the man he called "The Idiot."

"I already told you I don't have it . . . anymore."

"That's not good enough. You'd better get it back for me. And you'd better do it soon."

"Or what?"

Two of Will's other sons began to work Freddy over. Blows

to the gut, kidneys, and spleen. Blows that wouldn't take a honey badger down, but would make him hurt.

Will waved his hand and his sons immediately stopped.

"I'll say it again. Get me money. Or I'll give your daughters exactly what they've always wanted . . . you dead."

"You know who has your money."

"You gave it to them!" Will barked back. "Those two slits are running around with me hundred million and you've got the nerve to show your face at Uncle Pete's funeral. It's like you wanna die."

"Because it's not my fault!"

Will growled and that's when his eldest son stepped in.

Dougie was the smartest of Will's boys. He knew well how to play the game but he was always smooth. Using the charm. Even with Freddy. He didn't explode at him the way Will wanted to. He just stepped in close, a cigarette between his middle and forefingers, his free hand stuffed in the jacket pocket of his Italian suit.

He leaned over, so he could look right into Freddy's eyes.

"We're not discussing this with you, *Uncle,*" Dougie said calmly. Always calm, that one. "We're telling you what you need to do. Or the New York coppers . . . they'll be finding pieces of you all up and down the Eastern seaboard. So if you wanna keep breathing, get us back our da's money. Understand . . . Uncle?"

The side door opened and Freddy's eldest girl stepped out. She looked right at her father, being held between two of Will's burly sons, blood and bruises on his face.

Freddy grinned when he saw her . . . until she turned away from him and faced Will.

"My sisters and I are about to leave, but Aunt Bernice said you wanted to talk to me?"

"Yeah, I do." He headed back inside, and Charlie followed, not even glancing again at her battered old man.

He led her into a room with a washer and a few grizzlies in it.

"Get out," Will ordered.

"Who the hell do you think you—"

Will bared his fangs and hissed while the grizzlies huffed at him and bared their fangs in return.

Charlie pressed her hand against Will's chest. "Excuse me, gentlemen," she said to the bears. "Could you give us just a few minutes? I have to speak with my uncle and we just need some place private. If that's okay."

"Well, since you've been so *nice*," one of the older bears replied, "we'll give you a few minutes alone."

"Thank you so much," she said with that charming smile.

The bears started to walk out, but the youngest stopped and said to Charlie, "There's a girl running around screaming, 'Bear!' every time she sees one of us. It's beginning to upset my uncles."

"Yeah, that's my baby sister. She's got a bear issue. But as soon I'm done here, we're out."

"Okay. Great."

"And I'm very sorry if she insulted anyone. She was just trying to manage her fear."

"No big deal," the grizzly insisted. "Really."

Charlie closed the door. "See what nice gets you?"

"But I prefer rude and violent."

"Why is your sister wet and wearing a T-shirt?"

Stevie shrugged at Shen's question. "It's complicated."

"In other words, I don't want to know?"

"Exactly."

Stevie rested her arms on the bar.

"Want a drink?" Shen asked her.

"No." She glanced around the bar and, making sure everyone was busy not noticing her, she leaned into Shen and whispered, "I have to figure out how to get my sisters to that damn wild dog thing."

"Is that really your only option here?"

"Do you have six figures lying around to loan us to repair the living room I damaged?"

"No."

"Then yes, that's my only option."

"What's your only option?" Max asked.

She was standing right by Stevie, but a few seconds before she'd been across the room.

"Nothing," Stevie lied with a smile.

Max leaned around her and said, "Shen, what's her only option?"

"You know what I'm *not* going to do?" Shen announced. "Get between sisters. I have two. I got between them once, and when I woke up from my coma, I decided I'd never do that again. With *any* sisters."

"You were in a coma?" Stevie asked.

"My mother said I was unconscious for less than thirty seconds, but it *felt* like a coma."

"Just tell me," Max pushed.

"No."

"Tell me."

"Never!" Stevie raised her hand, her forefinger pointed at the sky. "I will go to my grave never telling you anything!"

Max, always annoyed when Stevie became "stupidly dramatic," balled her hand into a fist and Stevie waited for the first blow, but her sister just stood there, gazing straight ahead; barely breathing.

"Max?" Stevie asked. "What's wrong?"

"Someone is touching my ass."

Stevie leaned around her sister and that's when she saw Creepy Roy on the other side of Max, his even creepier hand disappearing under her T-shirt.

"Hold my beer," Stevie ordered Shen.

"What are you going to—Stevie! *No!*"

"You want us to what?" Charlie asked her uncle.

"Was I unclear?"

"You want us to open a bar?"

"A MacKilligan bar."

"Oh, fuck you," Charlie tossed out, now pacing the room.

"That seems a bit rude."

"I know you're just being an asshole."

"How do you come to that?"

"Because you know we're not part of this family, but you're going to try to use us to launder your fucking gangster money. Fuck you and the Erin go bragh you rode in on!"

"That's *Irish,* ya little twat!"

"Do I *look* like I know the difference?"

Will took in a breath, gave himself a moment. Which surprised Charlie. From what she'd heard over the years, he wasn't one to curb his rage and hatred.

"I know the family hasn't exactly *endeared* itself to you and your sisters. And I mostly blame your father for that."

"So do I," she admitted.

"But this is an opportunity for us to bridge the gap between the Scots and the Yanks."

"Then use Bernice. She's got a lot of daughters."

"Thieves! Every last one of 'em."

"That is true."

"I can't trust them. But I know I can trust you and your sisters."

"To launder your money? Forget it. We're not risking going to prison for you."

"We don't need you to launder money. We've got that covered, thank you very much."

"Then what do you want us for?"

Will grinned. "Snakes."

"Snakes?"

Now he wiggled his eyebrows. "*Snakes.*"

Shen pulled hard, attempting to drag Stevie off Creepy Roy's back. But she wouldn't let him go. Gripping his shoulder with one hand, she just kept punching him in the back of the neck while Max continued to slam the man's forehead into the bar.

What annoyed Shen, though, was that no one was helping him. Berg and Dag wanted to, but they wouldn't get close to Stevie when she was like this. They didn't want to freak her out. Britta refused to because she'd seen what Roy had done, and the only thing that stopped her from breaking him in two was that Max and Stevie had gotten to him first.

But the honey badgers . . . they weren't doing anything. Nothing. Roy was family but not one of them stepped in to help. They weren't cheering either. Or reacting in any way that Shen would consider normal. Just staring. Like an entire group of sociopaths!

"Let him go!" he ordered, but Stevie ignored him.

There was one very good thing, though. Stevie was angry, but she wasn't panicking. Even though there was a group of grizzlies watching the drama from the corner of the bar. And if Stevie wasn't panicking, he wasn't worried she'd shift. And that was a good thing, right?

When he tried to heave Stevie off once again, he saw Charlie exit from the back hallway, her Uncle Will right beside her. They were talking—calmly, he was happy to notice—but as soon as she realized what was happening, Charlie walked away from her uncle and over to Shen.

"What's going on?"

"Creepy Roy here touched your sister inappropriately."

"Which one?" she asked, shockingly calm.

"Max. He says he was just joking, though," Shen added with a disgusted sigh. He hated guys like Roy. Always had.

Charlie gave a short nod. "Okay."

Shen was so surprised, he almost released Stevie. "Okay? That's all you have to say?"

"Uh-huh."

She stepped away, heading back toward her Uncle Will, and Shen wondered what her uncle had to say to her that was so important she would ignore what was going on right in front of her. But then she neared her uncle . . . and passed him, disappearing into the back hallway again.

A minute or two later, she returned. Walking confidently, casually, across the floor. When she stood directly behind Roy, she crouched down and Shen leaned over a bit to get a better look.

Charlie wrapped a cord she'd found somewhere around his ankles. His legs were spread apart, but she looped the cord in such a way that when she stood up and yanked, his legs shut tight. Then she wrenched him off the bar, snatching him away from Max's grip.

Roy's head slammed into the end of the bar and onto one of the stools.

Shen snatched Stevie off the badger's back before he hit the floor. Charlie spun around, placing the length of the cord over her shoulder.

"Max!" Charlie barked. "Door!"

Max ran across the bar top, jumped off, and quickly opened the front door.

"You know what really pisses me off?" Charlie asked as she dragged her yelling cousin behind her. "I mean, besides when assholes such as yourself believe they can put their hands on women without their consent." Roy unleashed his claws and jammed them into the wood flooring of the bar. It caused Charlie to pause, but with one strong tug, Roy was moving again, his claws leaving a deep trail across the floor.

"It's when some of you MacKilligans think," Charlie continued, "you can get away with bullshit when it comes to me and my sisters. You think that *I'll* let you get away with bullshit. After all these years, some of you still think that. Still believe that."

She reached the door and dropped the cord. Leaning down, she grabbed her cousin by the back of his jacket and lifted him off the ground. She jerked him around so he was in front of the door, but she spun his body so he faced her.

And that's when he punched her in the jaw.

The thing was, Shen didn't think Roy meant to do it. He'd been tossed around and his arm had just been . . . swinging. Unfortunately, it had swung at Charlie.

Even scarier . . . despite the fact that Roy had punched Stevie's sister really hard, snapping Charlie's head to the side, she didn't stumble, she didn't cry out, she didn't do anything but stand there a moment.

Berg and Dag jerked away from the wall they'd been leaning on, but their sister caught their arms, held them back. She knew better. Shen knew better.

Especially when Charlie slowly turned her head and looked at Roy. Just looked at him.

"Uh-oh," Stevie whispered. She was in Shen's arms and she seemed very happy to be there. Very relieved.

Eyes wide, mouth open, Roy brought his hands up, palms out, and begged, "I didn't mean to! I swear! I swear!"

But it was too late. Shen knew that even though Charlie's expression never changed. He was sure, in most instances, Charlie would have forgiven the punch. But she'd never forgive that he'd touched her sister's ass.

Charlie's head moved and Shen realized she was locating a sound. Listening for something. Her ears even twitched a bit. Then, her expression *still* not changing, she leaned back and, to his amazement, brought both her legs up in one, fluid movement, and rammed them forward into Roy's chest.

The badger flew out of the bar and into the Jersey street. A second later, Shen heard a truck horn blare and brakes being jammed as the driver tried to stop in time. But nope. He and everyone else in the bar could hear that truck hit Creepy Roy.

Grinning, Max sort of danced out the door, but returned quickly. "He's alive!" But then she added with a brutal laugh, "But he's fucked up." She looked at Charlie. "Unlike Dad, he didn't roll with it."

Stevie cringed. She'd hoped that a good beating from her and Max would be enough to keep Charlie out of it, but no. It hadn't. Instead, Roy had been thrown in front of a truck. And he hadn't rolled with it. One of the first things her sisters had taught her when they were growing up was how to "roll with it," when hit by a moving vehicle. A skill that had saved Stevie's life more than once.

And if Roy wasn't such a reprehensible creep, she'd feel bad for him. But she didn't. And she wouldn't. He simply wasn't worthy of her sympathy.

"You ready to go?" Shen asked.

"I am."

But Stevie still had to figure out how to get her sisters to the club where the wild dogs were going to be. They had a few hours, but she knew her siblings. Once they got back to the house in Queens and put on some comfortable clothes, they were in for the night. So she needed to come up with an idea and quick.

As she tried to think of something, Shen gently placed her on the ground, and a few of her younger cousins came in through the front door, carrying several boxes.

One of them jerked a thumb behind him. "What happened to Creepy Roy?"

"Don't worry about it," one of the uncles said. "Have you got it?"

"We sure do!"

They pried the top off one of the boxes and Stevie watched in horror as her cousins dumped a ball of snakes onto the floor. A hissing, rattling, undulating ball of snakes!

Screeching, Stevie jumped back into Shen's arms. But that didn't feel like enough, so she climbed up his body until she was basically wrapped around his head. Her legs hung over his shoulders, and her hands were over his eyes.

"So you're terrified of snakes too," Shen calmly noted.

"*They can swallow you whole!*"

"These aren't pythons or boas, sweetie," one of her aunts happily called out. She had a snake already wrapped around her arm, its fangs dug in deep on her hand. "These are just vipers and cobras."

Stevie shook her head. "*How does that knowledge help me in any way?*"

Shen had heard that honey badgers were big fans of live snakes, but he'd never thought they enjoyed them . . . like this.

They were all so happy. And eager. The bears weren't, though. Neither was Stevie.

Max, however . . .

"Yes!" Max cheered before attempting to dive into the loose snakes slithering across the floor. But Charlie caught her sister by the back of the neck and yanked her away.

"No," she said sternly.

"Oh, come on!" Max begged.

Charlie simply tossed her sister to the Dunns. Britta caught Max in her arms and was out the door before anyone else could say a word.

Dag followed right behind her. And it seemed as if Berg *wanted* to go, but he didn't want to leave Charlie. She made that easy, though, when she barked, "Berg, get out!"

The grizzly went out the door at the perfect time. Because a rattler suddenly reared up and bit into Charlie's leg.

"Oh, God," Shen cringed.

"Don't move," Stevie warned.

"Yeah, but Charlie—"

"Can take care of herself. Look to your left."

He did and saw a cobra slithering near. Trying not to scream like a girl, Shen moved his ass onto a barstool while Charlie reached down and unhitched the rattler from her leg. She then banged it again and again against one of the bar stools. When the snake was dead, she tossed it to one of her cousins, who bit the head off. Just like that. Bit it off and started chatting with one of her kin . . . while chewing.

Realizing he was more afraid of snakes then he knew, he asked Stevie, "How the fuck do we get out of here?"

"Bar top," she said, pointing. "Bar top!"

Shen scrambled from the stool to the bar top. On all fours, he rushed across the bar with Stevie still on his back. She'd moved so her arms were around his shoulders and her legs around his waist.

For once, he completely understood why Stevie was freaking out. Because that ridiculous hissing sound—multiple hissing, no less!—was making him panic too. He just wanted to get them both out of there. To someplace safe.

Once Shen reached the other end of the bar, he quickly climbed down and went out the front door.

On the street, he stopped long enough to rest his arm on a van and his head on his arm.

"Are you okay?" Stevie asked him.

"Yeah, I'm fine. I'm fine."

Her fingers pressed against the side of his neck. "Your increased heart rate suggests you're not fine."

"I guess I'm just not a snake person."

"I'm sorry."

"You didn't do anything."

"I know." She rested her chin on his shoulder, and pressed her cheek against his. "But I should have warned you that almost all honey badger events end with snakes. I just didn't think they'd bring them out this early. It's not even dark yet."

Charlie stepped out of the bar. There were snakebites on her legs, hands, and one on her face.

"Oh, my God!" Berg was at her side, sweeping her into his arms.

Charlie gazed at him. "What are you doing?"

"Rushing you to a hospital . . . ?"

"Why?"

He glanced at his siblings and Britta, who still had a firm grip on the back of Max's neck, gently pointed out, "Because you're covered in snake bites, sweetie."

"Oh, that. They'll heal." She patted the back of her hand against his chest and, frowning, Berg placed her back on the ground.

"So is everyone ready to go home now?" she asked.

"No!" Stevie barked, surprising them. "I mean . . . wouldn't it be fun to go shopping, get some clothes, then hang out in the city tonight? Maybe go to a club!"

"No," they all answered.

"Do it anyway," Stevie begged. "For me."

"I thought you'd want to head back to Queens," Charlie softly suggested, "and stop by the emergency vet. Check on Benny."

Stevie *did* want to go check on Benny. Especially because every time she called the animal hospital—which, she'd admit,

was often—the receptionists got more and more testy. "No,"
they'd say, "his status hasn't changed in the thirty minutes
since you last called."

She shook her head and lied, "Nope. Don't need to see
him—I'm sure he's fine."

"Okay, Stevie," Charlie said, "what did you do?"

"What? What are you talking about?"

"Who did you promise what? And why?"

Stevie placed her forehead on Shen's shoulder. "Well . . ."
she began. Then she just unloaded.

"You see, the damage I did to the Jean-Louis Parker house
was getting into the six figures, a sum none of us can pay at the
moment, except maybe Max, but only if she steals something
expensive, and I didn't want to be responsible for that, but the
wild dog queen or Alpha female, whatever, she said she was
considering taking the house away from Kyle's family, but that
didn't seem fair because it was my fault, but then she said she
wouldn't do that if I brought you guys to something they called
Wild Dog Night, which I'm afraid is just going to be a pit with
dogs fighting, but I figured if it turned out to be that scenario,
we could handle it at that time, so I said we'd be there, but ever
since I've been trying to come up with a way to tell you guys
but nothing ever really seemed to present itself, so now here
we are."

Shen wasn't surprised when Charlie, Max, and the bears just
gazed at Stevie, none of them saying a word. And they stayed
like that for more than a minute until the bar door opened and
Dutch walked out with Kyle hanging from his back—and yes,
Shen had completely forgotten about his client but that was not
his fault . . . snakes!

Dutch had a half-eaten rattler clutched in his hand and blood
covering his mouth and chin.

"So what's next?" he asked before taking another bite from
the rattler's corpse. "I'm up for anything."

chapter TWENTY-THREE

The leaders of the three shifter-only protection groups stared at each other for several long minutes. This was a very typical reaction for a wolf, a bear, and a cat when confronting each other out in the wild, and it was typical for three shifters of the same species to have the same reaction when confronting each other in a boardroom.

However, these stares weren't caused by the desire to rip out the throat of another predator or even someone really annoying. Instead, they were caused by a rare moment of confusion.

When no one else spoke up, Van finally asked for clarification from Dee-Ann and Cella.

"She *buried* a car? An actual car?"

"An SUV," Cella corrected.

"By herself?"

"Apparently."

"Dee-Ann?" Van asked his younger cousin's wife.

"I'm not sure what you want me to say."

"Have we dug it out yet?" Ric asked.

"We'll need wolves for that," Cella said.

Before Van could ask why, Dee-Ann put on what he could only call a "little girl voice"—which actually sounded like something out of a horror movie—and mocked, "The kitties got sick because of the bad smell."

"First off, bitch," Cella verbally slapped back, "three of my people passed out cold, two vomited until their stomachs practically burst, and one is still recovering at the hospital."

"From what was basically a fart."

"It was *not* a fart, hillbilly," Cella insisted. "She unloaded her anal sacks on those full-humans and between that and being buried in their SUV, I'm guessing getting them out would *not* be a rescue mission."

"Why don't you just admit that y'all kitty cats are weak?"

"Why don't you admit that you lick your ass so much, you don't even notice horrendous smells anymore?"

"Ladies!" Van cut in, "*Please.*"

"Were they sent by the twins?" Ric asked.

Both women shrugged.

"How long before you know one way or the other?"

"Not until we get them out of the ground, so we can find out who they are, where they came from, and what they were planning. But I'm not sure when any of that is going to be." Cella's entire face contorted in disgust. "It wasn't just a scent, you know. There was a . . . residue." Cella suddenly turned to look at Dee-Ann and said with great drama, "Rezzz-a-duuuuue."

Both women started laughing, leaning against each other.

When they saw Van and Ric just staring at them, they stopped.

"You know," Dee-Ann said, "I can round up some of my Pack and for a hundred bucks each, they'll dig it up. But it's a hundred bucks *each*. Don't try to cheat 'em. My daddy warned me about you Van Holtz boys."

Ric, gawking at Dee-Ann, threw his arms out wide. "Thank you very much . . . *wife*."

She smiled. Nodded. "Welcome, darlin'."

"Uncle Will wants you to do what?" Stevie asked her sister, sure she'd heard wrong.

"Open a bar so that the MacKilligans can use the basement to move illegal snakes around the coast for the benefit of paying honey badgers."

"But they had snakes at the bar," Kyle pointed out. "They didn't seem to have a problem getting those."

"They want to move the really dangerous ones. Tiger snakes, death adders, king cobras. Snakes like that."

Max clapped her hands together. "The black mamba?"

"If you eat another one of those goddamn snakes . . ." Charlie warned, a threatening finger pointing at her from across the restaurant table where they were having dinner.

"Are you sure they just don't want you to launder their money?" Berg asked, pushing his empty plate away.

"It doesn't matter. We're not doing it."

"We do need the money," Max reminded Charlie.

"We get tied up with Will, we're in it for life. I don't think that's something any of us want."

"Why are they being so nice to us?" Stevie wanted to know. "Our whole lives, they completely ignore us and now, all of a sudden, they're being friendly. It's weird."

"Did we ever find out who Dad worked with to get the information he rounded up?" Charlie took a sip of her coffee. "The man can barely deal with his phone. So I doubt he's become a hacker in his off time."

"I've had some old friends of mine in Germany look into it, but they don't have anything yet."

"Why Germany?"

"That's where my hacker friends are."

"Oh."

Max motioned to one of the waitresses and, when she arrived at the table, ordered a slice of chocolate cake.

"Which, to me," she said once the waitress had left, "totally proves Dad had nothing to do with it. He couldn't hide his tracks from a puppy."

"Maybe the family's being so nice because they're hoping we'll lead them to their money," Stevie suggested.

Charlie chuckled. "The sad thing is, even if we could, Dad's already lost all that money. You know if he'd come to our house tonight, he would be begging for cash because he's completely broke. Again."

More coffee was poured, a few desserts arrived, and they

relaxed until Berg glanced at his watch and said, "I think we'd better go."

Stevie put her head on the table, feeling nothing but shame.

"I'm so sorry about this, you guys," she told her sisters and friends.

"For what?" Max asked.

"For making you do this." She brought her head back up. "I'm always asking you guys for stuff."

Charlie and Max looked at each other, then back at her.

"What are you talking about?" Charlie asked. "You never ask us for anything."

"Yes, I do."

"No, you don't."

Stevie raised her eyebrows at Max, but she shook her head. "Nope. The only thing you've ever asked me for was to 'shut the fuck up.' And that was usually when you were working or on the phone. Other than that . . ."

"So, yeah," Charlie said, "to save us from paying money we don't have to repair a house that isn't ours, I think we can spend some time with a bunch of wild dogs."

Max agreed. "Besides, how bad could it be?"

Shen snorted next to Stevie and everyone looked at him, except Kyle, who suddenly found something interesting to stare at right outside the restaurant window.

"Dear God," Max whispered. "It's karaoke."

"With your choice of a full band or playback," Charlie noted.

Stevie shook her head. "Nope. Nope. Nope."

She turned to walk out but Charlie grabbed her around the waist and yanked her back.

"This is going to save us six figures," she reminded her sister.

"But," Stevie said, almost sobbing, pointing at the stage, "there's a lion male up there and he's caterwauling."

"True." Max lightly swung her fist. "But he's putting his *all* into it."

"We're staying," Charlie ordered. "And we're just going to

suck up the pain the way we *always* suck up the pain. But first I'm getting a drink."

Stevie spun around, sensing that Shen and Kyle were standing behind her.

"You knew, didn't you?" she demanded. "You both knew and you didn't warn me!"

The pair stared at her a moment before they both started laughing.

"Do you have any idea what torture this is for me?"

Kyle raised his hand. "I do!" He lowered his hand. "Sorry."

"Oh, my God!" she exploded. *"What is that cat singing?"*

"Pat Benatar's 'Shadows of the Night,'" Jess Ward said, stepping beside Stevie.

Stevie glared at the woman who'd just made the rest of her evening hell. "You didn't tell me Wild Dog Night involved karaoke."

"You didn't ask. Besides, I know you like music."

"Yes. Music. Not caterwauling." She pointed at the stage. *"That's* caterwauling!"

"Can I speak to you for a second?"

Before Stevie could say no and storm off, Ward had gripped her arm and yanked her into a backroom behind the bar.

Shen joined the rest of their group at a huge, half-circle booth, reserved just for them. It was between a similar booth on the left, filled with wild dogs, and another on the right, filled with a Pride of lions and other cats.

He sat down beside Kyle, taking the beer someone had put in front of the kid and drinking it down in several gulps.

"No alcohol," he told Kyle.

"I didn't ask for it."

"Look," Shen began, "I'm sorry."

Frowning, confused, Kyle shook his head a bit. "You said I can't legally drink."

"Not that. I left you alone earlier today in that crazy bar with snakes. Dutch had to get you out. I'll understand if you want to replace—"

"It's not like you had a choice. Stevie was wrapped around your head like a spider monkey. And I'm not surprised she was your first priority."

"She doesn't pay me. Your parents do."

"But you're in love with her." And the kid said it so . . . calmly! *Why was he so calm?*

"I am not. I'm—"

Kyle had already rolled his eyes and turned away to talk to Oriana. *Where had she come from?* Shen stopped talking, But then he noticed that Coop and their sister Cherise were also tucked into the booth and smiling at Shen. Like they knew something.

This whole wild dog "event" was turning into a nightmare.

"Okay," Ward said, standing in front of the closed door, "this is what we need from you."

"Need from me?"

"Take out the lions."

"No matter what you may have heard, my sisters do *not* kill on command."

"What? No! I want you and your sisters to go up against them."

"Like in a street fight? Because MacKilligans don't really do that either. Once Max starts stabbing and Charlie starts shooting, you'll have a bloodbath on your hands, and there's all that clean up afterward. Although Max probably knows a few places we can bury some bodies."

"No, no." Ward held up her hands, eyes wide. "Please stop talking." She briefly looked off, then said, "I don't mean attack them physically. I'm talking about taking them on with karaoke."

Stevie couldn't help but let her lip curl in disgust. "Why?"

Ward began to pace around what Stevie now realized was a storage room. "A few years ago, we started having monthly sing-offs. We provide the karaoke machine filled with several thousand songs, from as far back as the thirties up to today, or a live band if you prefer that. And it was all going great. Everyone was having a great time. Then the cats got involved," she sneered.

"You mean like the guy who was just butchering Pat Benatar?"

"No," she said with a dismissive wave of her hand. "That's Mitch. He was in my wedding. He has a pass. In other words, we've made him an honorary canine."

"But you know he can't sing, right?"

"You've got to let that go. It's Mitch—we love him!"

"So it's *other* cats you have a problem with?"

Stevie saw a bit of fang peek out from under Ward's lip before she hissed, "The Brunetti Pride."

"Okay. And your problem with them is . . . ?"

"They keep winning."

Stevie fought hard not to roll her eyes. "When you have competitions that happens. I used to win all the time too. And the other competitors hated me for it. That's a 'you' problem, though. Not a 'me' problem."

"You don't understand. The Brunettis are very wealthy, very bitchy, and very trifling. They pay top dollar for their costumes and choreographers."

Stevie snorted out a surprised laugh. "They use choreographers for *karaoke*?"

"One of those choreographers used to work with Madonna."

"Wait. I'm going to ask one more time, because I'm sure I'm mishearing this. They *hired* one of Madonna's choreographers to create an act so they could win a *karaoke* contest?"

"Yes."

"What do they win? A yacht?"

Ward walked across the room to a table. When she turned back to face Stevie, she held a cheap-looking trophy.

"Seriously?" she asked.

"Yes. True," Ward clarified, "this is for second place. But," she pointed out, "the first place trophy is only slightly taller."

Stevie clasped her hands together. "I understand that this means a lot to you. I really get that. Lions can be *very* irritating. But I create symphonies. I can master any instrument I hear played for more than ten minutes. *Any* instrument. And I've been able to do that since I was two. But singing is not one of my singular gifts."

"You sisters can back you up. They can cover for any imperfections in your voice."

"It's not about covering. I know this is going to sound *really* narcissistic, but I'm a musical genius. And although I've been out of the field for a long while, I still have my reputation. I don't want to ruin it in order to win a karaoke contest. You get that, right?"

"I do."

"That being said . . . I don't want to risk the Jean-Louis Parkers losing their rental house and—"

"No, no." Ward shook her head. "All I said you had to do was come here with your sisters. You did that." She slapped one hand against the other. "That whole thing is over as far as I'm concerned."

"It is?"

"Dogs do not blackmail. Cats do. We just look at you like this . . ."

Big brown eyes gazed at Stevie. Giant brown eyes. She immediately thought of poor Benny, still at the vet, recovering from that gunshot wound. He would look at her like that when he wanted her bacon.

"Okay, okay!" Stevie said, quickly glancing away. "Let me think about it."

Shen made his way to the bar, ordering another beer from the She-wolf server.

"Do you have any bamboo?" he asked now that he saw the place was run by shifters.

The server handed him his bottled beer. "Roasted, steamed, raw, or fried?"

"Fried, please."

As Shen waited for his food, he looked out over the dance floor. He didn't know if he was amused or disgusted by what wild dogs referred to as "dancing."

"You!"

Shen turned toward the voice barking at him.

"Oh. Hi, Blayne."

"Don't 'hi, Blayne' me. You lied to Gwenie. And she's here . . ." She glanced around. ". . . somewhere. And you're going to tell her the truth."

"I did lie. But I had to."

"You *had* to?"

"Yeah. Your running around telling the world that you were attacked by a two-ton badger does nothing but put our friend in danger. In danger from *us*."

"What are you talking about?"

"I'll put it to you in the form of a question: How welcoming have most shifters been to you and Gwenie? To Bo? I mean, if you take out his winning hockey ways. Have they loved you as you are, ready to accept you as one of their own? Or do they treat you like a freak?"

"I understand what you're saying—"

"Good."

"—but I wasn't telling everybody. I was telling Gwen. And both of us are hybrids."

"I know you guys are. Look, the way you and Gwenie have always protected each other? Dose that with steroids and some backwoods form of military training and you've got Stevie's sisters. And they would see you as a threat. And they extinguish any threat to their baby sister. Understand what I'm saying to you?"

"No."

"Seriously?"

Blayne began to giggle, her shoulders hunching over.

"*Blayne.*"

"I'm sorry," she replied, still laughing. "I just wanted to see your face. Totally worth it."

Standing on the edge of the dance floor, Stevie stared at the stage and listened to more caterwauling.

"How ya holding up?"

Surprised, she glanced at the woman standing next to her. "What are you doing here?"

Oriana shrugged. "Kyle told me the wild dogs had asked you to come here. I had a feeling they were up to something like this."

"Are you a regular at Wild Dog Nights?"

"No. Not a regular, but, more than once, our mother has insisted her older children attend these"—she sighed dramatically—"*events.* To suck up to her protégé's mother."

"It's good your mom wants to teach others. I don't."

Oriana laughed. "My mom would say you're still too young to care about passing on your skills to the next generation."

"Good. Then I don't feel so guilty."

"So what are you going to do?"

"I don't know," Stevie admitted. "I'm thinking I'm going to . . ."

Stevie, sensing she was being watched, stopped talking and began looking around the room to find all the exits and anything she could use as a weapon.

"Hi!"

The voice surprised Stevie and she jumped back into Oriana, who managed to keep both of them from falling on the floor.

When she was no longer leaning on a shockingly strong and steady Oriana, Stevie nodded at the five She-cats standing way too close to her.

"Hello."

"I'm Mary Marie Brunetti and these are my sisters."

Stevie wanted to say, "So?" but instead she just said, "Nice to meet you all."

"Are you the ringer?" Mary Marie asked.

"Pardon?"

"The wild dogs brought you in, right? To go up against us?"

"Well, I don't know about—"

"We are just *so* excited to hear you sing. Aren't we, girls?" Brunetti's sisters all clapped. "I looked up your name online—"

"How do you know my name?"

"—and you have quite the background. You're into that classical music, right? You should do, like, 'Ave Marie' or something. These guys would eat that up."

"Uh-huh."

"We cannot *wait* to hear what you'll sing. They even have a piano up there, and I'm sure they have someone who can play and accompany you. It will be *awesome*. Right, girls?"

"Right!" the She-lions said in unison.

Brunetti placed her hand on Stevie's forearm. Stevie gazed down at the excessively long painted nails touching her skin. "If you need anything, honey, you just let me know. We have extra costumes, makeup, a makeup artist. Whatever you need. Okay?"

"Sure."

"Okay. Talk to you later!"

Stevie watched the She-cats rush off in their ridiculously high heels.

"They seem nice," Shen said, stepping in beside her.

Both Stevie and Oriana gaped at him.

"Are you kidding?" Oriana demanded.

"What? They did seem nice. Very friendly."

"Yeah, Svetlana's 'nice' like that," she said with air quotes. "Like when she tells me, 'Darlink, you performed so wonderful tonight. I know that in few more years, you will be quite good.' Do you think that's a compliment too, Shen?"

"I would have but now I don't know."

"Don't be upset with him," Stevie graciously explained to her friend. "He's a panda and he's used to everyone being nice to him because he's so cute."

"I'm going back to sit with Kyle," Shen said. "That should tell you both exactly how I feel about this conversation."

He walked off and Oriana asked, "So what are you going to do?"

Coop rested his chin in his palm, his elbow on the booth table in front of him. In silence, he watched what was going on just a few feet away from him.

"What is happening?" he asked Cherise, motioning to the MacKilligan sisters.

The three women were standing between their booth and the booth holding the Brunetti Pride and their feline friends, which just seemed weird.

Cherise stopped sipping the fruity alcoholic drink she'd been indulging in, purchased simply because it was a bright "and festive!" red and had an umbrella in it. His sister did love umbrellas.

"I think they're trying to talk Stevie into getting up on stage."

"Yeah, I guess."

"What?"

"Well . . ." Cooper didn't really know how to explain it. Maybe it was the way Charlie insisted on stroking Stevie's hair. Something he'd never seen either MacKilligan sister do for the others. Or maybe it was the way Max kept saying, "We'll go with you. We wouldn't let you do this alone." Max was *never* nice to Stevie. Of course, Stevie wasn't nice to Max. A situation that Coop didn't question because that's how some siblings were. They'd rather fight than be nice to each other. It didn't break the bond they had as siblings.

But this all seemed *really* weird.

"Hiiiiiiii, Cooper."

Coop kept his cringe inside and forced a smile at the She-lion leaning over the two connected booths.

"Hi, Denise," he replied.

"You look very handsome tonight."

"Thanks." He knew she was waiting for a similar compliment from him, but he just pointed at his sister and said, "You remember Cherise."

"Oh. Yeah. Hi."

Cherise, again sucking up that brightly colored drink, waived her hand and smiled around her straw.

Denise's older sister, Mary Marie, forced her way in.

"Hi, Cooper," she said, leaning over a little more so he could see her cleavage. Something he didn't really want to see. To be honest, he saw cleavage all the time. Some enhanced. Some natural. But he saw it so much that it took a lot more than that to catch his interest. He wasn't some horny full-human male who would fuck anything that moved. He was a jackal looking for a future mate. He wanted something more than big tits and equally big nails. And although he didn't care if a woman he might like already had a kid or two of her own, he didn't like the fact that She-lions would have their kids with the lion males they kept around and then, when they felt they were done breeding, they'd start looking outside the Pride for males to have long-term relationships with. In other words, they didn't want to have "freaks"—as he'd heard the Brunetti Pack refer to Blayne and Gwen whenever the pair passed by the Pride at one of these events.

"Hi, Mary Marie." He returned his focus to the three MacKilligan sisters.

"You know them?" Mary Marie asked.

"Yes. They're friends of the family." Which was mostly true because anyone who could put up with Kyle for as long as the sisters had would always be considered family friends.

"Ahhh." She leaned down a little closer. "Word is Jess Ward brought them in to compete against us. Not sure what some fancy musical prodigy can do, though. Maybe sing an aria my grandmother would love?"

Smirking, Coop replied, "Physics."

"Huh?"

He didn't bother to explain as Stevie had made the decision to go up on the stage with her two sisters.

While they skimmed through the karaoke machine's offerings, Max's wolverine friend pushed his way between Coop and Cherise.

"Hey, all," he greeted the table. Then to Cherise, "My darling beauty." Cherise smiled and waved around that damn straw in her mouth. He then nodded at Coop. "Dude."

The wolverine caught sight of the Brunettis. Leaning across Coop, he took hold of Mary Marie's hand. "My lady."

"Hi ya."

"I'm Dutch Alexander. And you are?"

"Mary Marie Brunetti. This is my sister Denise."

"Lovely to meet you both," he said, kissing the back of Mary Marie's hand.

Denise tried to stick her hand out to get Dutch to kiss it, too, but an angry roar-and-snap from Mary Marie had her sister backing off.

"Oh, my God! Oh, my God!" one of Mary Marie's other sisters pointed out. "They're using the band and not the machine."

Delighted, Mary Marie clapped her hands together. "This is going to be *awesome*."

But Coop knew that when a She-lion said "awesome" she meant "ridiculously horrible." Especially when she saw the piano player join the rest of the band. To Mary Marie this meant "aria time," which would be a resounding failure at a wild dog event. Something the locals already knew.

Stevie stood at the front of the stage. Her sisters were on either side of her, each of them behind her own mic.

Looking shy and small, she lowered her head. But Coop watched her hands. She was a lefty but she used her right since that was the one the piano player could see.

She snapped out four beats with her fingers and the piano player began. He wasn't playing anything remotely new. It was definitely a "classic," but hardly classical. No, it was a one-time doo-wop hit that became a rockabilly hit when Wanda Jackson—the queen of rockabilly—came out with her own version of "Riot in Cell Block #9."

Wanda Jackson had always had one of those awesome, growly voices that belied her tiny size. A song that was perfect for Stevie MacKilligan and her sisters, Stevie's backup singers.

Gawking, mouth open, Mary Marie and her sisters couldn't take their eyes off the stage. Or the way the wild dog crowd not only cheered but stayed on the dance floor.

"I thought I heard she couldn't sing," Mary Marie demanded, looking at Coop.

"I told you. Physics."

"What does that mean?"

"Stevie always says that once you know how vocal chords

work and how the laws of physics affect them, you can get your voice to make almost any sound you want."

Dutch added, "She says she can't sing and she's right. Stevie *can't* sing. But she can imitate anyone who can."

"If you knew Wanda Jackson, who originated this version of this song, you'd see how much Stevie sounds like her. Right, Dutch?"

"Right, Coop."

But that wasn't all Stevie did. The kid had been on stage almost all of her life. Playing music herself or conducting entire orchestras of adults. And if there was one thing she had learned over all those years, it was stage presence.

And Stevie had stage presence in spades.

She owned that stage, singing *to* her audience. And her sisters weren't schlubs either. They didn't just back up their sister, they were right there with her, singing—and screaming, when the song called for it—and owning that stage. Plus, there were choreographed moves and some enjoyable sexiness to the whole thing.

When Stevie finished the last note, the entire room erupted into applause and a standing ovation. Something she was used to but the Brunetti Pride found endlessly upsetting.

But before the Pride could do anything, the crowd began to yell for more.

Stevie, grinning down at her audience, said, "Okay. One more. This is from Lillian Briggs. It's just called 'I.' Enjoy."

This song started with guitar rather than piano, and required Stevie to sing a lot faster, but she sounded just like Lillian Briggs. And again her sisters did a great job backing her up *and* dancing; the three moved to the edge of the stage as one unit to sing directly to the wild dog males who'd moved in close.

Leaning in to Dutch, Coop asked, "How did they manage to choreograph this in time for the show?"

"According to Max, after Stevie left her first career behind, she still needed to express herself musically—otherwise she'd get violent. So they used to go to private karaoke competitions."

"I thought she hated karaoke. That's what Jess just told me."

"She hates karaoke with talentless people. No offense," he added to Mary Marie, who hadn't been listening, so appeared a tad confused. "But the people Stevie played with at these earlier events were rock stars and well-known musicians. It was just their way of enjoying themselves without the pressure of fans. Just a bunch of ridiculously rich and talented people hanging out . . . singing karaoke. And, of course, her sisters had to go because Stevie was underage. The MacKilligan sisters didn't always win the competitions, but they always entertained."

The sisters finished and the crowd in the club completely lost their minds. But the ladies simply bowed and got off the stage.

Stevie walked through the still-applauding crowd to their booth and squeezed herself in.

At first, she didn't say anything. Just sat there, calmly.

Then she looked across the booth to the Brunettis, locked her gaze on a glowering Mary Marie . . . and smiled.

The fight started when Stevie wouldn't back down from the cats glaring at her.

Shen couldn't help but remember when he'd first met Stevie in the Queens house living room. His first impression was of a shy, sweet "girl." It took him a couple of weeks, but he finally figured out she was anything *but* that.

So when the threats and pushing started, he dashed over to the booth and grabbed Kyle, yanking him to safety near Blayne, Gwen, and their extremely large mates, Bo and Lock. A few seconds later, they were joined by Coop, Cherise, Oriana, and Johnny DeSerio, who'd only just arrived a few minutes before.

Jess stepped in to stop the fight before the club's wolf security was forced to intervene. The club employees were part of a wolf Pack that was more gang than Pack, even riding custom Harley-Davidsons like they were in their own versions of *Sons of Anarchy*. So Shen knew they were not wolves to fuck with. They wouldn't back down in the face of a little roaring and snarling between lions and honey badgers.

"Everyone calm down!" Jess yelled, waving her hands between the screaming factions.

"This is such bullshit!" Mary Marie Brunetti complained. "You brought in some ringer with a big musical background. This was supposed to be fun."

"You didn't seem to have a problem with my singing *before* I performed," Stevie reminded Mary Marie.

"Well, I have a problem with it now."

"'Well, I have a problem with it now' because you're better than me," Max mimicked in a high-pitched voice.

Mary Marie stepped up to Max. "You got something to say to me, bitch?"

"Yeah," Max replied. "You don't get away from my baby sister, I'm unloading my anal glands right here. I've done it once today," she added, "I will do it again!"

"Okay," Jess ordered, instantly stepping in. "There will be *no* anal gland *anything*. Here or anywhere."

Charlie gave a quick jerk of her head and Max stepped back.

"Now," Jess continued, focused on Mary Marie and her sisters, "the votes aren't in. But if the MacKilligans win, they will win fair and square. So you'll just have to suck it the fuck up."

"Or what?" Mary Marie sneered. "What are you and your *dogs* going to do?"

And, like that, the wild dogs went from dancing and drinking to surrounding the Brunetti Pride and yelling. So much yelling. And yipping. A lot of yipping. Because they were, after all, African wild dogs and that's what they did. Stuck together and barked *a lot*.

Until the lions backed off and walked away. Once they'd returned to their booth, the wild dogs returned to their good time, and thankfully, no anal glands were unloaded that night.

chapter TWENTY-FOUR

When the She-lions finally calmed down, they issued a challenge to the MacKilligans. Kind of a sing-off. Well . . . they issued a challenge to Stevie, specifically, which was fine with her. She was having a great time. It had been a while since she'd performed on a stage.

The Brunettis went up first, nailing a version of a Destiny's Child song that had the crowd pretty impressed.

Then it was Stevie's turn.

"What are you going to sing?" Coop had asked.

"Not sure yet. Maybe play something with the band."

He'd grinned. "Want to play with us?"

"Play with you?"

He shrugged. "We have a little band. Me and Cherise. We're mostly all here. Two of our regulars are touring in China right now, but we can still go on without them. And we all play instruments that we don't normally play. I'm on bass guitar. Johnny's on rhythm. Cherise plays drums."

"So she can hide behind them?"

"Yes. Wanna have some fun?"

"Can we win?" Because Stevie really wanted to make Mary Marie and her sisters suffer.

"We're all prodigies. Of *course* we can win."

So they'd gotten up on stage and Stevie, on lead guitar, played the song she called her "anthem." Jimi Hendrix's "Manic Depression." She could play the music on guitar just like Jimi Hendrix could. She could also play just like Jimmy Paige and

Carlos Santana. She'd had music agents trying to persuade her to put out an album with covers of great rock songs, but being able to mimic someone else's work didn't seem like a gift as much as just a skill she had. Her gift was in the music she composed. Because that was hers alone and it was unique.

Although to amuse herself when playing Hendrix, Stevie had even modulated her voice so she sounded like him, which freaked *everybody* out. The Pride actually tried to prove she'd been lip-synching. As if!

But Stevie didn't really care about the bitches complaining because she had found something more important. A group of people she could be in a band with. Musicians who wanted nothing to do with getting record deals or screaming fans. They didn't need to do any of that because they already *had* record deals and screaming fans. They were all world-renowned musicians who just liked to get together with friends and play instruments that had nothing to do with their livelihoods. Even better, Stevie fit in with them perfectly. Not just emotionally but musically. With barely a discussion between any of them, they jammed out Hendrix's music like they'd been playing together for years.

After they were done, Coop had taken her into a hallway past the stage. That's where he'd asked her if she'd liked to join the band full-time . . . ish. They met rarely because of their busy schedules, but when they did, they played whatever they wanted and everyone brought something for a potluck. On occasion, they would perform for an audience. Stevie wasn't sure about that until Coop promised it would just be the wild dogs for the occasional birthday party or celebration. And, of course, Wild Dog Night when they were bored.

It sounded perfect and just what she was looking for, so Stevie agreed. What shocked her, though, was that when Coop walked back out into the main club room, Shen was glaring at him.

"What are you doing?" she asked Shen.

"What? Nothing."

"Why are you glaring at Coop?"

"No reason. Why do you ask? Do you want a drink? I want a drink."

Stevie caught his arm and pulled him toward the hallway she'd just left.

"What's going on with you?" she asked.

"I told you. Nothing."

"Then why are you being so weird with Coop? I think he's starting to notice."

"Gee. I'm hurting Coop's feelings. What a tragedy."

"I thought you liked him."

"I do."

Stevie was so confused. Unless . . .

"Oh, my God, are you jealous?"

Shen didn't even want to hear that. "*No.*"

"You're jealous!" Stevie crowed.

"I am not!"

"It's okay. You can admit it."

"I admit nothing. And this conversation is over."

Shen started to walk away, but Stevie grabbed his arm again, yanked him back.

"I am not jealous!" he lied, and he knew he was lying. That was the worst part.

But Stevie just shook her head, her expression completely different. Instead of amused, she looked seriously concerned. "No, no." She pointed. "See that guy?"

Shen studied the man Stevie pointed out. He was by the second, smaller bar, hunched over a bit, his gaze roaming the crowd while he nursed a drink.

"Yeah. What about him?"

"That's Wells's brother."

Fucking great. "Any chance he's just good friends with wild dogs?"

"Who the hell likes wild dogs?"

Of course, when Stevie said that out loud, several of Jess Ward's Pack were walking by. They all stopped, stared at her.

Stevie cleared her throat. "No offense."

* ★ *

Max followed Dutch into the bathroom, standing behind him while he was at the urinal.

He finished, did a little shake, zipped up, and turned—

"*Jesus!*" he barked in surprise. "Don't sneak up on me."

"What did you find out?" she asked, trying not to laugh.

Dutch went to the sinks to wash his hands. "Devon is still in Europe."

"Is my mother safe?"

"Don't worry. I got money to people in the prison who'll watch out for her. Belgian bears. She couldn't be safer. There is one little problem, though."

"Which is?"

"What did you do to those guys?"

"You'll have to be way more specific."

"The ones you buried."

"They were going to kidnap me. What was I supposed to do?"

"I don't think it's that you killed them that has my bosses so concerned," he said, speaking of the Group, the organization he worked for as an agent. "It's that you unleashed your anal glands, suffocated them to death, then buried them and their truck in, like, five minutes."

"It was an SUV and it was more like ten minutes. Maybe even fifteen. But what was I supposed to do? Leave them lying there? Covered in my stink?"

"It's not just you, brain trust. It's *all* of you. The three of you are *freaking* them out. And the last thing you want is for them to unleash Dee-Ann Smith on you."

"The bitch who got her ass kicked by Charlie?"

"That was a close-in fight. She and Cella are not averse to long-distance attacks. If you get my meaning. What you and Charlie can do when you come face-to-face with your enemies, those two can do from a mile away in a high wind. Understand?"

Max nodded. "So you're saying I should kill them first."

"*No!*"

"Okay," she said, heading toward the bathroom door, working hard to keep her expression neutral. "I'll take care of it!"

"Get your ass back here, MacKilligan! You are not to kill anyone! What is wrong with you?"

Max stepped out of the bathroom and came face-to-face with Jess Ward.

The Pack leader looked at her and then at the bathroom door.

"Why were you in the men's room?" she asked.

"Because I won't be confined by gender constraints?"

"Do you even know what that means?"

"Not really."

Berg tracked Charlie down. She was in a balcony room that overlooked the dance floor. He wouldn't mind if she were simply leaning on the thick rail, but she was sitting on it, her legs dangling over the side.

Not wanting to startle her and send her hurtling to her death, he eased up behind her.

"Hey," he said softly.

"Hey." Her gaze continued to scan the entire bar.

"What's going on?"

"My sisters are up to something. Or not telling me something. But they're not doing something together. Instead they each have their own partners in crime."

"I thought you were going to allow your sisters to be adults," he reminded her.

"They're each up to something. Can't you see it?"

"I don't watch my own siblings as closely as you watch your sisters, so no. I don't see anything."

"Think Shen will talk to you?"

"No."

"I know I could get Max's shit out of Dutch, but it would take a lot of blood and pain." She glanced at him. "I know you wouldn't be okay with that."

"I'm glad we understand each other when it comes to my belief system on torture."

Berg watched Charlie for a few moments, wondering how to reach her.

"Have you ever thought," he carefully suggested, "that maybe your sisters won't tell you stuff because they're afraid of the way you'll react?"

"Yeah, sure."

"No. I don't mean with them. They both seem quite comfortable with the bizarre dynamic you three have. I'm talking about how you deal with others."

Charlie looked away from the club and directly at him. "What are you talking about?"

"In the few weeks we've known each other, you've threatened several people with death for even suggesting they get your sisters involved in anything you think is remotely dangerous. Not only that, but you beat the unholy hell out of Dutch just for getting Max a job offer. Threatened a Van Holtz with an actual flaying because he suggested Stevie might be able to help him with something . . . and those two examples are merely the most egregious. There are others."

"Your point?"

"It's simple. Maybe they don't tell you things because they're afraid you'll kill someone."

She frowned. "That's silly."

"Really? Because I didn't tell you when I felt one of your cousins trying to get my wallet out of my jacket at your great uncle's funeral. I was afraid more bodies would end up buried with Uncle Pete. So I just silently pulled his hand out of my pocket and crushed his fingers until he cried. But we both did it *quietly*. Because *you*, Charlie MacKilligan, are scarier than a grizzly bear. Especially to your sisters when it comes to the people they care about."

Charlie returned her gaze to the club. She didn't say anything and Berg just assumed she was pissed at him. But then she jumped off the balcony . . .

Berg made a crazy grab for her, but Charlie slipped through his fingers and landed on the ground hard, but unharmed.

"Wolf legs," he muttered, watching her walk away, ridiculously grateful for those long, muscular legs.

"Where is he?"

They'd pushed their way through the club crowd, but by the time Stevie and Shen had arrived at the back bar, Wells's brother was gone.

"We need to find him," Stevie said, backing away from Shen. "We need to find him now."

As Stevie moved, she heard Max behind her.

"I want Devon found," she was saying. "I want to know who those guys—"

They walked into each other, their backs colliding.

Stevie immediately faced her sister. Dutch was standing behind her. Stevie could tell they'd been conspiring.

"What are you doing?" she asked.

"What are *you* doing?" Max shot back.

"I know you're up to something."

"So are you."

Of course, Max was right, which meant it was best they just walk away from each other.

With a nod, Stevie moved away from her sister. But she'd barely gotten three feet away when a strong hand grabbed her by the back of her neck.

Max's eyes grew wide, her gaze directed behind Stevie. Max turned to go, but a hand reached out and grabbed her, too, yanking her close.

"Come with me," Charlie ordered, dragging Stevie and Max away from the dance floor.

Shen and Dutch watched the MacKilligan sisters disappear into the crowd, Charlie dragging the other two with an amazing amount of ease.

"Should we follow them?" Shen asked Dutch.

"No."

★   ★   ★

Charlie pushed her sisters into the room and closed the office door behind them.

Stevie immediately looked down at the floor. But Max . . .

"Oooh. A safe."

Charlie snapped her fingers in her middle sister's direction and pointed to a spot next to Stevie, right in front of a large wood desk.

Charlie began to pace in front of the pair. Back and forth. Back and forth. Until she came to an abrupt stop and pointed her finger at her sisters.

"Berg says you're scared of me."

Her sisters frowned, glanced at each other, frowned some more.

"Scared of you?" Stevie asked.

"Us?" Max asked.

"Well . . . he actually said that you were afraid of what I'd do to your friends."

"Oh," they both said, and then Stevie looked down at the floor and Max studied the safe.

"That's a top-of-the-line safe," Max said. "But, uh, I can break into it, like in thirty seconds."

Charlie put her hands on her hips. "Berg was right . . . wasn't he?"

No longer frowning, her younger sisters glanced at each other.

"We love how protective you are of us," Stevie began, her fingers twisting.

"We really do," Max insisted, sounding more sincere than Charlie had ever heard before.

"But you do . . . sometimes . . ."

"Just sometimes."

"Get a little . . . overwrought?"

"Overwrought?" Charlie repeated

"Like that time my tutor and I were having a philosophical discussion about Jean-Paul Sartre's *No Exit*."

"He was being rude."

"No. We were just discussing. But you didn't like his tone. So you hung him outside the window by his foot. Most philosophical discussions don't end with grown men sobbing and promising not to call the police if you just let them go."

"And that time you didn't like the football player I started dating—"

"He talked shit about his old girlfriend, which means he was going to talk shit about you."

"You're right," Max agreed. "You're absolutely right. Still, I don't think it was necessary for you to bind, gag, and shove him in the trunk of his car and leave him in the woods with a warning that if he put any part of himself near my pussy, you'd cut his throat and let the neighborhood dogs at him."

"Then," Stevie softly added, "there was that squirrel incident."

"He was rabid."

"*No.* He was just a squirrel."

"And what you did to Mr. Machenski's Rottweiler," Max tossed in.

"I just warned him off. He was scaring Stevie."

"He didn't scare me. He startled me," Stevie argued. "There's a difference."

"And you didn't just warn him off. You made that dog pee himself, and after that he didn't come out from behind his house ever again."

"So I'm a horrible person?"

"No!" Stevie quickly cut the distance between them and grabbed Charlie's hand. "You're a loving sister! You've protected us all these years."

"Do you actually think I'd be alive if it wasn't for you?" Max asked.

Charlie thought a moment, and replied, "Yeah, I do."

"Yeah," Stevie agreed. "You would have totally survived."

"Okay." Max raised her forefinger. "Let's try this . . . would I have survived *outside of prison,* if it weren't for you?"

"Oh, no."

"No, no. You wouldn't have."

Max nodded. "Exactly."

★   ★   ★

Stevie hugged her sister. "We love you, Charlie. You know that."

"I know." She stepped away, wiping her eyes. "Just wish you guys would tell me what's going on. I can't protect you if you don't tell me."

"Yeah," Max said, her hand caressing Charlie's cheek. "We're not falling for that, Charlie."

Stevie shook her head. "Not even a little. But the tears were a nice touch."

"Come on! Tell me!"

"No! You'll just go on a rampage."

"Tell me . . . or I'll start taking out people anyway."

"We'll tell you," Stevie said, pointing at her sister, "if you promise not to flip out."

"Fine. I promise."

Shen was wondering if he should go looking for Stevie when he saw Charlie tearing through the packed dance floor—a group of She-dogs were singing the Go-Go's "We Got the Beat" and it had set off a firestorm of bad dog dancing—and heading straight for him and Dutch.

He nudged Dutch with his elbow.

"You better run."

"What?"

Charlie shoved some wild dogs out of her way before raising her gun and aiming it at Dutch's head.

But then Max and Stevie were there, running up behind her. Stevie grabbed her eldest sister around the waist and Max put her hand over Charlie's weapon, removing the slide and disabling the weapon all in one motion before she tackled her sister from the front and carried her back through the dancing crowd.

Shen looked at the wolverine, who'd jumped into his arms at the sight of Charlie coming for him.

"Seriously?" Shen had to ask, still holding the man like the giant baby he clearly was.

"What do you want? I panicked."

★   ★   ★

Charlie had her arms crossed over her chest and she seethed while her sisters paced in front of her.

"You promised," Stevie reminded her.

"I lied."

"How do you expect us to tell you anything when you lie to us?" Max wanted to know.

"I should have killed Dutch the first time I met him."

"He was twelve!"

"Your point?"

"They're coming back," Shen warned and Dutch immediately got behind him. "I am not your human shield."

"You are at the moment. She likes you, hates me, and I'm relatively certain she wouldn't kill an innocent person just to get to me."

"That does *not* make me feel better."

The three women walked up to them and Stevie gestured at Dutch. "Go ahead," she pushed when Charlie just stood there.

Charlie took a deep breath before she exploded with unadulterated rage. "*You scumbag! I should have killed you when I had the chance! And you, Shen! I am so disappointed in you! You're supposed to be a protector and—*"

Shen didn't hear the rest of what Charlie had to say because her sisters each hooked an arm through one of Charlie's and carried her back to where they'd come from.

"That's it." Stevie marched up to Charlie. "You *will* be nice and you will apologize to Dutch and now Shen!"

"I will *not.*"

Charlie could be very obstinate so Stevie did something she only did with her sister when she was forced. Right now, she was forced . . .

"Aaaaaaah!" Stevie screamed in her sister's face.

"Do not—"

"Aaaaaaah!"

"Stevie, stop—"

"Aaaaaaah!"

"You better promise," Max warned. "Or she'll just keep it up."

"Aaaaaaah!"

"I will not apologize but—"

"Aaaaaaah!"

"—I will let it go!"

Stevie studied her sister. "You promise?"

"Yes."

"You're not lying again, are you? Because I will keep this up. All. Night. Long."

"Her energy is limitless when it comes to this," Max reminded Charlie.

"I know. I know. But I will tell you both that I'm very disappointed in you. You for not telling me that Devon is out," she said to Max. "And you for helping a woman you still refer to as 'that evil cunt.'"

"She *is* an evil cunt. But what's going on is more important than my never-ending hatred for Irene Conridge."

"PhD," Max tossed in.

"Shut up!"

"Hey, they're coming . . ." Shen looked around. "Are you hiding behind the bar?" he asked when he spotted the top of the wolverine's head.

"Do you blame me? That woman is a nut!"

"I thought wolverines were as tough as honey badgers."

"Oh, we are. But, unlike badgers, we're not crazy."

"Well . . ."

Charlie and her sisters stopped, and Charlie stepped a little closer.

"Shen, I have to say that I'm . . . disappointed that you did not come to me when you found out what Stevie was up to."

"I feel bad, too, but she is *so* persuasive."

"What did it for you?" Max flatly asked. "Her skinny-ass legs or her nonexistent tits?"

Max's head jerked back at the blow to her nose from Stevie's elbow while Charlie continued her chastising.

"And although I'm disappointed in everyone involved in this bullshit, I have promised my sisters that I will no longer threaten those who merely suggest they may want Max's or Stevie's help. So, Shen . . . I have forgiven you."

Shen gave a courtly bow. "Thank you, my lady."

"Suck up!" Dutch complained from behind the bar.

Charlie ran over to the bar and leaned over so she could yell at Dutch, "You, I am *never* forgiving! I will not kill you now. And as long as Max likes you, I won't. But let me tell you . . . when she gets tired of your ass, I am *so* wasting you!"

"Understood!" Dutch called out from his safe position.

Charlie stepped down and began to walk away, stopping when Dutch called out, "One thing . . ."

"What?"

"I'd like to do my thing on karaoke night. And I can't do it without you three," he finished in a singsong voice.

Shen didn't know what Dutch's "thing" was, but he was disturbed by the look Charlie had when she turned around.

"I am *not* singing backup for *you.*"

"But you already know the routine, and you're really good at it. The wild dogs will love it."

"I don't care what the wild dogs will love."

"Come on, Charlie," Max pushed, grinning. "It's gotta be all three of us."

"And," Stevie added, "it's a lovely way to make amends."

"'And it's a lovely way to make amends,'" Charlie mimicked in a brutal mockery of a little girl's voice.

Dutch, now leaning on the bar, smiled. "Is that a yes, Charlie of my heart?"

"What is happening?" Britta asked, standing between her brothers while Shen positioned himself near Berg. Coop and his siblings were right in front of them.

"I have no idea," Berg replied. "But it's . . . unique."

"It's an old eighties song," Coop explained. "From Kid Creole and the Coconuts."

"How do you know that?" Britta asked. "I've never heard of them."

"Encyclopedic knowledge of music. Stevie has it too."

"It's less the music, more the dance moves that I'm concerned about."

"They're just basically mirroring the video . . . which was taken from a movie. It's a whole thing."

"The wild dogs seem to love it."

"I could be wrong," Oriana noted, "but I'm pretty sure we can keep our rental house forever."

Coop laughed. "As long as we stay friends with the MacKilligan sisters."

The siblings suddenly fell silent and they all looked at their younger brother. Kyle gazed back, until he barked, "If Stevie hasn't gotten tired of me yet, I don't think you bitches have anything to worry about!"

Irene didn't realize how late it was until she heard the text arrive on her phone. That's when she noticed the time. She cringed just a little, knowing her husband would complain about her hours again.

But as she made her way down the hall of their New York home, he met her near the stairs, wearing nothing but sweatpants that exposed his perfect body . . . despite his age.

She held up her phone. "I heard from the brat. Her sister knows, but she says all is fine."

"Really?" her husband asked, holding up his phone. "Because I heard from the psychotic and according to her the next time she sees me, she's going to rip my face off."

"Well . . . at least we've gotten past the skinning."

chapter TWENTY-FIVE

They returned to the Queens house at three in the morning and everyone sort of went off and did their own thing.

Kyle walked into the living room, threw up his hands, and suddenly announced, "I must create!" Then left the house and went to the unattached garage out back.

Max shifted to a badger and trotted out of the house. Shen assumed she was going to raid some beehives. Until he heard a hiss and saw a cat run by the window, followed by Max.

"Leave that cat alone!" Stevie yelled, running through the house until Shen heard the back screen door slam open and closed.

When the screaming started in the backyard, Britta and Dag immediately walked out, heading back to their house, but Berg waited for Charlie.

"Tomorrow," she said to Shen, pointing her finger, "we have a meeting. All of us. Get all the details and information out on the table."

"Sounds good."

"*Still* disappointed in you."

"I know."

She stalked out, Berg silently following. Probably going to the triplets' house so she could complain about her sisters without worrying they'd hear her.

Shen scratched his head and sat on the couch. He unholstered his weapon, dropped the clip, cleared the chamber. It needed a cleaning, despite the fact he hadn't used it in a while—he hadn't made it to the range in several weeks, not since he'd taken on the job of protecting Kyle—but it was now three thirty in the morning and he was exhausted. All he wanted to do was go to bed and get some much needed sleep. Especially if he had to spend his morning listening to more of Charlie MacKilligan's chastising.

Putting the clip back and re-holstering his weapon, Shen was about to stand up when he decided that he could get some sleep just as easily on this couch. He'd slept on it before and it was pretty comfortable, having been built for grizzlies. But before he could stretch out, the back screen door opened and slammed shut again.

Stevie marched into the living room. The look on her face suggested she'd been unable to reason with her sister, but Shen didn't doubt the cat had gotten away. That was a wily cat and she was much faster than any badger.

"Where is everybody?" she asked.

"Charlie went with Berg to his house."

"Probably to complain about us so we wouldn't hear."

"Most likely."

"Are you hungry?"

"Always."

"I had Charlie order some fresh bamboo. I think it's in the kitchen."

"Awesome. Thanks."

"Yeah. Sure. I'm going up to take a shower."

Shen nodded and stretched out on the couch. He was so tired, he figured he could get the bamboo later.

He put his arm behind his head and let out a large breath, closing his eyes and relaxing into the cushions.

He was just falling asleep when he heard the shower in the second floor bathroom come on.

Shen opened his eyes, gazed up at the ceiling, and asked himself, "What am I doing?"

Stevie stepped into the shower and let the warmish water pour down on her. It had been a long day and she was just glad to be home, even if that meant spending ten minutes yelling at her sister for trying to take out that damn cat.

Pouring shampoo into her palm, she scrubbed her head, wanting to get the "club smell"—as she called it—out of her hair and body. The bathroom door opened and she called out, "Shen?"

"Yep."

"If you're still looking for the bamboo," she said, now rinsing the shampoo from her hair, "Charlie put it in my room for some reason."

Stevie stared at the six different types of bath foam her sisters had. Were so many necessary? Wasn't soap . . . soap?

"But I'm hungry now," she heard Shen say from right behind her.

Stevie glanced over her shoulder. He was in her shower, his naked shoulders taking up a lot of room.

Facing him, she asked, "Can I help you with something?"

"Hungry."

"Bamboo's in there," she said, pointing.

He moved in, making her back up until she was stopped by the wall behind her. His big hands slid around her waist, easily holding her.

Stevie slid her fingers across his forearms and up his biceps; Shen leaned down, his lips hovering over hers for a moment before he pressed his mouth against them. As soon as their lips touched, Stevie's entire body became hot, her nipples hardening, her pussy getting wet. She gripped his muscles, slid her tongue around his. She suddenly couldn't get enough of him. Wanted all of him. Their kiss intensified, each of them demanding, grasping.

Then Shen abruptly pulled away, and dropped to one knee in front of her. He lifted her right leg over his shoulder before he pressed his face against her pussy and began to lick her, deep and long.

He *was* hungry. She could feel it.

Stevie placed her hand behind his head, digging her fingers

into his wet hair, fighting the wetness of the tub beneath her feet, afraid she'd lose her footing and slip, and then he'd stop. She didn't want him to stop. She never wanted him to stop.

His tongue moved to her clit, circled it, flicked it, sucked it between his lips. She tightened her fingers in his hair, wanting him to take her over the edge, but he moved his tongue back to her pussy, slid it inside her, stroked her like it was his cock.

"I need to come," she begged. Because she really did. She needed it. Now. And she wasn't one for waiting.

And Shen didn't make her wait. He gripped her clit again between his lips and slid two fingers inside her. Then he just went to work, sucking and stroking her until Stevie felt crazed. Until she couldn't think straight. Until all knowledge left her head and nothing remained but need and want and more hunger.

She screamed out when the orgasm hit, but quickly shoved her free hand into her mouth. The last thing she needed was for local, night-wandering bears to come running to the house, thinking there was a problem. There was no problem.

Shen pulled away, dragged his fingers slowly out of her and, with water still pouring down on him, he smiled up at her.

"Better?" he asked.

"Much, but," she added, pushing him away, "fucking in a shower is never as easy as it looks in the movies." She reached around him and shut off the water, then threw open the shower door. "And I need you inside me now."

She was making him crazy.

Instead of that orgasm calming her down so they could casually play around in the shower, she was telling him what she needed—demanded!—and it was for him to fuck her. Not in some cute, romantic way either. Not the way she was dragging him from the bathroom and back to his bedroom. Both of them dripping wet, leaving a trail as they made their way across the hardwood floors.

Once they were in his bedroom, the door closed firmly behind them, she threw a condom at him before flopping onto his bed, her legs open.

He didn't argue. Didn't try to slow her down. Instead, he put the condom on as quick as he could, then reached out and grabbed her arm, yanking her off the bed. He spun her away from him and.bent her over his dresser, her body knocking over everything he had on the glossy wood top.

Shen slid his hand under her right knee and lifted it up, placing it on the dresser, before he entered her hard.

Stevie cried out, but there was a laugh there, too, along with a gasp of surprise.

He fucked her hard, one hand gripping her left hip, his other clutching her raised leg. To stop her head from hitting the mirror, she pressed her forearm against it, her rough gasps making Shen even more insane.

How was he supposed to be slow and playful when she made sure he couldn't think straight?

Shen pulled his cock out of her and flipped Stevie over, dropping her ass on top of his dresser before pushing his cock back inside her. She grinned at him, spreading her legs wider and resting her heels on the wood.

He gripped her ass tight, lifting it up so he could get a better angle. He pounded into her, staring down into her eyes. And she stared back. Not looking away. No shyness. No awkwardness.

"God, that feels good," she said, slapping her hands against his shoulders, digging her fingers into the muscles.

Shen broke out into a sweat despite the cold air from the AC hitting his still shower-wet body. He could feel it on his scalp, under his arms. He felt like he didn't have enough of her. He wanted more. He wanted all.

"Shit!" Stevie gasped. She closed her eyes and said, "Shit!" again. She came. And he watched while he continued to fuck her. Watched the way her entire body tensed and her back arched.

"Yessss," she hissed, her pussy clenching him so tight he nearly swallowed his tongue.

When her body finally relaxed, she opened her eyes, and gave him the sweetest smile while she panted from the exertion.

Shen picked her up off his dresser and took her to his bed. He went down first, his cock still buried inside her, stretching out beneath her.

She relaxed on top of him, her knees next to his hips. "What do you want?"

"Your turn. Fuck me. Get me off."

Her sweet smile turned positively devious as she tightened her pussy on his cock and began to rock her hips against him.

Shen reached up and cupped her breasts in his hands, circled her nipples with his thumbs.

"That feels good," she sighed out.

He couldn't even answer. Just grunted.

"When we're done here," she went on, gazing down at him, "we're going to need to get back in the shower. And while we're in there, I'm going to take your cock into my mouth and suck it so goddamn hard . . ."

Shen gritted his teeth and grabbed her hips, making her stop moving.

"You evil bitch," he panted out, working hard not to come yet. He didn't want to come yet. But she was playing with him. Teasing him.

Making him crazy! Again!

She laughed, tossing back her hair.

"And I'm holding you to that blow job," he warned her.

She leaned down, her breasts sliding along his chest as she moved her arms around his neck, and she pressed her mouth against his ear.

"You better. Because I'll be on my knees," she whispered. "Sucking you all the way down until you hit the back of my throat. I'm going to make you come so hard."

Then she bit his earlobe with her incisor and that was it,

Shen came. It was so intense, he worried he wouldn't be able to ever stop, his hips pounding into her, his fingers still holding her hips against his. When he groaned, she pressed her mouth over his, like she was taking the sound into her body.

And later, when they lay on his bed, panting and momentarily exhausted, Shen said the only thing he could think of . . . "Zing."

Stevie looked at him. "What?"

"Forget it." He pulled her close, resting her head on his chest. "It's too much to explain."

chapter TWENTY-SIX

N aked but clean, Stevie feverishly worked on her latest piece. Oriana's ballet. That's how she thought of it. Originally, she'd planned an opera and had been working on it when she and her sisters had first arrived in New York. But once she'd met Oriana and decided she wanted to help her, she'd changed the opera to a ballet.

And since she'd approached Oriana's troupe about the work, she'd been getting calls *constantly*. It was kind of funny, the way they were clamoring. Funny and a much-needed ego boost.

Writing her work out in her third music notebook, Stevie almost didn't notice that Shen was talking in his sleep again. She couldn't say whether he did that sort of thing often. She hadn't been with him that long, but the few times they had slept together, he had. Usually muttering something about bamboo. She continued to work at the end of the bed, not really bothering to listen to his sleep-induced ramblings about his food until she heard, "Come on, Stevie. Stop fooling around."

Shocked, she instantly looked up from her work.

"Give me the bamboo," he implored sleep-Stevie, making reality-Stevie roll her eyes that she'd bothered interrupting her work for—

"Of course I love you."

Stevie gawked at the panda in her bed, watching him sleep-eat bamboo he didn't have.

She might have briefly become catatonic. She wasn't sure.

Putting her notebook aside, Stevie stood and quickly pulled

on some shorts and a tank top. She tiptoed across the bedroom and went out, closing the door behind her.

When she got to the top of the stairs, she heard Charlie in the kitchen and, relieved, ran down the stairs to talk to her.

"Morning," Charlie muttered when she saw Stevie in the kitchen doorway. "I checked with the vet. Benny is doing great. We'll be able to bring him home soon. They sent pictures. They're on my phone. And I'm making cinnamon buns so I don't have to hear you bitch about how not everybody loves honey." When Stevie didn't say anything, she looked up from the dough she was kneading. "What's with you?"

Stevie pointed up; shook her head.

"I know we're close, but I have no idea what you're trying to tell me."

She stepped into the kitchen and whispered, "Shen just said he loved me. But he was asleep. He was also sleep-eating bamboo. So . . . that doesn't mean anything, right?"

Lips twisted to the side, her gaze focused on the ceiling, Charlie took a moment to reply. Making Stevie wait.

Finally, she said, "Welllll . . . he loves bamboo. And he mentioned you while dreaming about eating bamboo." Those brown eyes locked on Stevie. "I think it's love," she whispered.

"It can't be."

"Why does it bother you?" Charlie went back to kneading. "You're obviously crazy about him."

"I am not! I'm in total control of this relationship."

Charlie laughed. "You may have marked that panda with your scent, but you have *no* control over the relationship."

Stevie heard Shen coming down the stairs. She jumped onto the stool by the counter and attempted to look casual. He walked into the kitchen smiling.

"Morning," he greeted them and held up his duffel bag. "Thank you so much for the fresh bamboo, Charlie."

"No problem."

He glanced between Stevie and Charlie. "Is everything okay?"

"Yeah," Charlie said. "When I'm done with these cinnamon buns, we'll have a little meeting about next steps."

"Sounds good." He leaned over to Stevie and kissed her on the temple before walking out the back door.

"Just so you know," Charlie said once Shen was gone, "even when you're silent, you're as subtle as a brick to the head."

Stevie glared at her sister. "And what's *that* supposed to mean?"

Wearing loose gray sweats, a blue T-shirt, and no shoes, Shen checked the garage. Kyle was still working and by the looks of him hadn't had a break since he'd walked away from them the night before, which meant he would be impossible to deal with until he got some sleep.

Shen silently closed the side door and went to his favorite tree; the big one by the garage. Opening his duffel bag, he dumped the bamboo under it. He tossed the duffel bag aside and stuck one of the smaller stalks into his mouth.

Ridiculously happy at the moment, Shen climbed the tree until he found a sturdy limb. He sat on it, relaxing backward and letting his knees bend over the limb so he could comfortably hang there, his arms swinging back and forth, his fingers barely scraping the dirt below.

After a few minutes he started singing one of his favorite songs by Creedence Clearwater Revival, "Lookin' Out My Backdoor."

Why? Because he was in such a good mood and it was a great day!

Creedence Clearwater Revival was always for great days.

Stevie didn't realize someone was singing until the "doo, doo, doo"—*crunch*—"lookin' out my"—*crunch*—"backdoor" hit her. She put down her coffee and walked to the kitchen window. She bent over the small counter in front of it and opened the window.

Soon, Charlie was forcing her way into the small space so she could also look out the window toward the garage.

Together they watched Shen hang from a low limb, eating bamboo and, between bites, singing.

"I didn't know he had such a nice voice," Stevie informed her sister.

"You don't think it's weird we have a Chinese panda in our backyard singing a country song even though he was born and raised in Connecticut?"

Stevie shook her head. "No. Then again, you like polka music."

"It's *danceable*," Charlie snapped.

The back door opened, and once Charlie moved, Stevie leaned back inside to see Max come in naked, half her face swollen three times its size.

"*What the fuck, dude?*" Charlie asked, spotting Max at the same time.

Max said something, but it was hard to make out when half her mouth was so swollen.

"What?"

Max swallowed and carefully stated, "Cat . . . scratch. Cat . . . spray."

Charlie's entire body jerked and her face screwed up in confusion, but before she could ask yet again, "What?" Stevie interpreted for her.

"I think what Max is saying is that the stray cat she keeps fighting with scratched her face and uh . . ." Stevie cleared her throat to keep from laughing. "And then sprayed on it." She rubbed her nose. "She must be having an allergic reaction of some kind."

"Oh, sweetie." Charlie shook her head, her hand briefly over her mouth. "It's just a suggestion but . . . maybe stop fucking with that cat."

"*She started it,*" Max growled out, so angry that her words were relatively clear.

"How can you blame the cat?" Stevie asked, reaching into the freezer to get an ice pack for her sister's face. "It has no thumbs."

She turned and dropped the pack. Her sister's face, in the three seconds it had taken Stevie to get the ice pack, had doubled in size. Again.

"Okay," she said, trying to remain calm. "I think, at this point, we might be dealing with a combination of an allergic reaction and an infection."

Charlie, putting the buns into the oven, asked, "Why would you say—*dear god in heaven!*" She slammed the oven door closed and proceeded to tear through the kitchen drawers, desperately searching each one.

"Wha—" Max managed to ask.

"It's nothing," Stevie lied. "But I'm going to, uh, get my EpiPen."

Max mumbled something and Stevie replied, "I always keep several EpiPens on me. A lot of people I know have allergies, and you know how I like to be prepared," she finished before racing up the stairs to her bedroom. She grabbed her backpack and held it upside down over her bed. She shook it until everything fell out and dug around the pile until she found two of the pens.

Stevie ran back downstairs and returned to the kitchen as Charlie triumphantly held up a prescription bottle.

"Got it!"

"Wha's 'at?" Max mumbled, pointing at Charlie.

"Antibiotics," Stevie explained. "EpiPens," she said when Max pointed at the items clutched in Stevie's hand.

"You're having an allergic reaction," she went on. "We need to administer this and then get you to a hospital."

Since the entire right side of Max's face was now incredibly swollen—at this point, she didn't even look human, but more like a half-inflated balloon—she could only roll her left eye.

"No 'lergic 'tion. Fine."

"Sweetie, you are *not* fine."

"She's right," Charlie said, grabbing Max's arm. "We need to get you to the hospital now."

Max pulled away from Charlie's grip. "Fine. Show."

Stevie should have known better than to wait for her sister to "show" them how "fine" she was, but who in their right mind would *ever* think that someone would walk up to a wall and just slam the swollen side of their head against it?

Who would do that? Who?

Horrified, Stevie covered her mouth with her hands, the EpiPens still held tight. Charlie dropped the plastic bottle filled with antibiotics, her eyes wide.

"*Max!*" she screamed. "*What the fuck?*"

Max didn't answer at first, her back turned to them, her hands dug deep into her head. But then, finally, she faced them.

"See?" she asked, pointing at her deflated head. "I'm fine. Just needed to pop it like a balloon." She waved the EpiPens away. "So, I don't need that."

Stevie still pointed at her sister's face. "You do have some very angry red lines . . . *in* your face."

"*That's* the infection. I didn't say I don't have an infection." She watched Charlie pick up the prescription bottle. "Although why you have antibiotics just lying around the house, I don't know."

"You really don't know?" Stevie asked. "Even after ramming your head into the wall?"

"Don't be overdramatic."

"Wasn't being dramatic at all."

"How often do you have to do that?" Charlie asked, pouring out half the pills onto the table. Max would take half the pills now and the other half in about eight hours. None of that twice a day for seven to ten days stuff like with full-humans. Shifters had to attack any major health problems a lot quicker because their systems worked so fast.

"Take pills?" Max asked.

"No. Ram your head into the wall?"

"I don't know," she replied before taking several pills without even the assistance of water.

Stevie quickly grabbed a bottle of water from the fridge, opened it, and placed it in front of Max.

"Thanks. I guess, as often as I have to. Why do you ask?"

"Because I'm worried that if we X-rayed your brain, it would look like you've been playing for the NFL for the last forty years."

"I've got a badger skull." Max swallowed a few more pills.

"It can handle anything. It's the flesh around it that's weak and can't handle a little cat pee."

"That's right!" Stevie laughed. "This did all start with you arguing with a cat, didn't it?"

"She attacked me."

"Yes. Of course she did."

Stevie heard the front door open and close. She expected to see one of the Dunns entering their kitchen, but it wasn't any of the triplets. It was Kyle's older sister Oriana. She had on a tiny bikini, flip-flops, a giant straw hat, and a towel over her shoulder. She also carried a large tote bag with her that appeared to be filled with books.

"Hey, all," she said.

She stopped briefly in front of the refrigerator and reached in to grab a bottle of orange juice. "I'll be out by the pool, Stevie," she announced before walking back outside.

The sisters were silent for a long moment before Max asked, "Are we going to have to see her skinny ass strutting around here very often?"

"Hey!" Stevie reminded her. "That's my friend."

"Awwww," Max mocked. "Little Stevie has a friend."

Charlie returned to the kitchen table to make some quick breads she could pawn off on the local bears, thereby keeping the cinnamon buns for the rest of them. "At least I don't hate Stevie's friends . . . unlike your friends. Who I despise."

Stevie grinned. "Exactly."

"Shut up."

"You shut up."

"If you two are going to fight," Charlie warned, "do it in the living room. Not here. But before you two start grappling . . . Stevie, she smells like pee."

Max went to grab her, but Stevie made a crazed run for it out the back door.

Oriana walked into the garage, gaping at the work her brother was doing. He was working with marble and, even she had to admit, he was good. Maybe the best living sculptor in the world.

Not that she'd ever tell him that. Just like every time he was "forced" to watch her dance with the rest of their family, he asked when she'd last eaten.

Stepping away from his sculpture of a naked Bo Novikov—she could only hope her brother was just guessing at what a naked Bo looked like—Kyle put his hands together, as if he were praying, and stared at his work.

"So what do you think?" he asked and that's when Oriana realized he knew she was in the garage with him.

"It's okay, I guess."

He glanced at her over his shoulder, eyes like her own rolling. "You are just so jealous."

"I am hardly jealous of *you*. Mostly because I've managed not to walk into doors . . . unlike you."

"I always have a lot on my mind. Walking is a distraction," he dismissed with a wave. "What I'm asking is do you think this is good enough for Kiki Li?"

"Whom you'll never meet?" she asked, remembering Shen's reaction to Kyle demanding that the bodyguard arrange an introduction.

"Oh, I'm going to meet her today."

"Shen said he'd set that up?"

"Oh, no. He didn't say anything like that. So I stole his phone, cloned it, and when my piece was ready, about an hour ago, I texted her like I was him."

"You did what?"

Stevie heard the shower go on upstairs and returned to the kitchen now that Max was gone.

"Did you talk to Shen?" Charlie asked as soon as Stevie stepped into the room.

"No. Why would I talk to Shen?"

"Because you don't keep anything to yourself. I figured that's why you went outside."

"I went outside because Max was covered in pee."

"Just her face."

"Speaking of that . . . I should put some tuna out for the cat."

"You've gotta stop feeding that cat."

"She's chosen us," Stevie informed her sister. "Just suck it up."

Stevie had just pulled a can of tuna out from one of the overhead cabinets and was going to retrieve an opener when the doorbell rang. But before she could answer it, Charlie grabbed her arm, pulled her back.

"Stay behind me," she warned, her .380 gripped in her hand.

"Is that really nec—"

But her sister was already gone.

Stevie followed Charlie through the house and was behind her when she opened the door.

But Charlie took one look—and a sniff—and let out an annoyed sigh.

"I haven't made anything bamboo yet. And probably won't today."

She slammed the door in the faces of the two females who'd been standing on their porch.

"Damn greedy bears. I don't even recognize them."

But Stevie did recognize them, pushing her sister away and ordering her in a whisper, "Hide that damn gun! Now!"

Taking a breath, Stevie opened the door and smiled at the two scowling women.

"Kiki Li," she said. "It's so nice to finally meet you."

"Do I know you?"

"My work. I'm Stevie Stasiuk."

Kiki raised an eyebrow. "Holy shit. You've grown."

Stevie stepped back, waved her hand. "Why don't you both come in?"

Shen's sisters walked into the house. Kiki was wearing all black despite the heat outside. And the heels on her expensive-looking shoes had to be six inches high. How did she possibly walk in those things?

Zhen Li, the middle sister Stevie assumed, was dressed in oil-stained jeans and a T-shirt that had Firestone written across it. Plus big work boots that didn't seem to fit her small frame. The two sisters couldn't look more different style-wise.

Kiki seemed a little bit . . . angry, stepping up to Stevie and demanding, "We wanna see our brother." And she said it as if she thought Stevie would tell her no, which was just weird.

Stevie exchanged glances with Charlie and said, "He's right outside . . . eating bamboo."

The Li sisters walked out and Charlie asked, "Kyle did something . . . didn't he?"

Cringing, Stevie replied, "Yeahhhh, I think he—"

"*Kyle!*" they heard Shen suddenly bellow from outside.

And now both sisters were cringing.

"You pretended to be me?" Shen demanded, his hand on the back of Kyle's neck. He had Kyle bent backward and was leaning over him, glaring into his face.

"You wouldn't introduce me. I had to do something!"

"How did you even get my phone?"

"Telling you that will only upset you more."

"And you told my sister I was being held as a sex slave?"

"You should be more concerned she believed me. Or you, in this instance."

Shen popped his jaw and thought about bending the kid so far back that he broke his spine.

"Let him up, Shen." Kiki tapped Shen's shoulder. "Look at him. He's a little kid."

"I'm a prodigy," Kyle insisted, still bent over. "And I'd love to show you my work."

"I am not rewarding bad behavior."

"Shen," Kiki pushed. "Let him up."

Shen released Kyle. By now the MacKilligan sisters were outside, too, watching.

"Thank you," Kyle sneered at Shen before facing Kiki. "Some of my work is right in the garage."

"Kyle—" Shen began but the kid ignored him and escorted his sister into the MacKilligans' garage, which he'd made into a temporary art studio for his work.

Once they went inside, Shen turned to Zhen. Not even knowing Kyle, she cringed.

Oriana had her feet up on the small desk Kyle had in his studio, leaning back in the office chair, when the door opened and he walked in with an Asian woman who looked a lot like Shen. Maybe too much. Some features did not work on both men and women. But, despite that, Oriana liked the woman's style. Everything she wore was designer, including the Jimmy Choo shoes.

"My work is right over here," Kyle said, moving across the garage.

The woman stopped and studied Oriana.

"I know you," she said.

"Do you?"

"I've seen you dance. In Russia."

"Right. I danced with the Bolshoi a few years back."

"You did *Giselle*. It was very impressive. Especially for a dancer of your age at the time."

"Thank you."

"I'm Kiki Li. Shen's sister." Oriana liked that a woman who had made her own imprint on the world, whose very name carried power, added "Shen's sister" to her intro. She found that kind of cool.

"Oriana—"

"Jean-Louis Parker. I never forget the names of talented people."

"Yes, yes, she's great," Kyle said, coming back and taking Kiki's arm. He led her to his sculptures. He had a room full of small, medium, and large pieces. His older works were in storage somewhere. He wouldn't tell anyone where because he didn't want them to be stolen "by you commoners because you need money."

And while Oriana sat there, watching, Kiki went from piece to piece. She asked questions, had Kyle pull a few of the smaller ones forward. She took her time, didn't seem to mind the heat of the garage—there was no air-conditioning—and didn't rush.

After more than an hour, the pair ended up near the desk Oriana had been lounging at.

"Well?" Kyle asked, smiling. Eager.

"Your work is technically brilliant."

"Thank you."

"But soulless."

Oriana winced, looking up from the book she'd been reading on her phone.

"Soulless?" Kyle repeated, appearing stunned.

"I look at your work," Kiki said placidly, with no real emotion, "and I don't feel anything. There's no sorrow. No pain. No joy. Just . . . cold, soulless beauty." She shrugged. "You can sell all these pieces and make a fortune. If that what's you want. But if you want to be more than just a rich artist pumping out meaningless crap for the masses, you've got work to do. You need to find the soul of your art. Make me feel something, Kyle. I want to be able to say more than 'it's pretty.'"

She patted his shoulder. "Good luck."

Then she and her expensive Jimmy Choos walked out of the garage, and Kyle was left standing there, staring at the spot she'd occupied.

Oriana swung her legs off the desk and stood. She thought about just leaving. Most Jean-Louis Parkers were not good with raw emotions. She really wished her sister Toni was here. Or their dad. Even Coop. But they weren't here. It was just her and the younger brother she used to throw down the stairs of their house on the West Coast. At least until her mother told her she had to stop.

Then she thought about Svetlana and how that bitch had been critiquing Oriana's work "to help, darlink. Just to help." Although Oriana didn't think Kiki—unlike Svetlana—was being mean, attempting to make Kyle insecure. She was just being direct. But sometimes direct could really hurt.

She turned away from the door and walked over to her brother.

"You don't have to listen to her—"

"She's right," Kyle said, shocking her. She'd thought for sure he'd dismiss Kiki the way he'd dismissed all of his critics over the years. "She's right. I see it now."

Kyle looked at her with wounded eyes. "I don't want it to be just pretty, Oriana. I want my work to have meaning for the ages. I want it to live for centuries."

"Then find your soul. Make your art for the centuries."

He nodded, but she hated the way he stared at the floor. She could literally *feel* her brother's devastation. So she did what she'd never done before . . .

Oriana wrapped her arms around her brother's shoulders and hugged him hard. And she knew she'd done the right thing when he hugged her back, burying his face against the side of her neck.

"What did you say to him?" Shen asked his sister when she came out of the garage. The others had gone back into the house, but Shen and Stevie had waited outside.

"I told him the truth," Kiki admitted.

Shen rolled his eyes and groaned. That was exactly what he'd been afraid of.

"What?" his sister asked.

"He's seventeen. He's a baby!"

"He's a prodigy and he didn't want me to mollycoddle him. So I didn't. I gave him the unvarnished truth so he could turn from 'some artist' into '*the* artist.' I was doing what I do. That's why he brought me here."

"What if you killed his spirit?" Shen wanted to know.

"If a true and honest critique that has nothing to do with personality kills his spirit . . . he was never meant to be an artist. But you," she added, pointing at Shen, "know I'm right. I can see it on your face."

"He's good."

"But he could be great. I want great. Anybody can be good. Now I'm going inside. I'd like something to drink. Why don't you come with me?" she asked Stevie.

"I'll be right in," Stevie promised.

She nodded and left them.

"You okay?" Stevie asked Shen when they were alone.

"I knew this would happen. My sister is—"

"Direct."

"That's the nice way of putting it."

"It's the only way. If I thought she was just being a destructive twat, you know I'd say something."

Shen smiled. "Yes. I know now that you'd say something."

She looked over at the garage. "Maybe I should talk to Kyle, though."

"Oriana's in there with him."

That made Stevie feel better. No matter how much the Jean-Louis Parkers bickered among themselves, Stevie knew they still protected each other when necessary. Not the way Charlie and Max did, but with the same determination. Just less bloodshed.

Stevie went up on her toes, kissed Shen's cheek.

"What's that for?" he asked, his cheeks turning a touch red.

"Because all this time you weren't being a dick . . . just protecting Kyle from your sister."

"He's a kid. I had to do *something*."

chapter TWENTY-SEVEN

Kiki didn't consider herself a hard ass. She was direct, yes, but not a hard ass. In her opinion, hard asses were people who said mean things simply to be mean. They seemed to get a kick out of breaking people down and, if they felt like it after, building them back up. Kiki, however, just told people the honest truth if they asked.

The kid had asked.

Besides, why would she go out of her way to hurt him? She didn't care that he'd used her brother's phone to lure her here. People had done weirder and unhealthier things to get her attention. To get her to mention them in her magazine, online, or on TV. Even if the mention was bad, they wanted it, because it would get them publicity. To be truthful—and when was she not?—she'd known it wasn't her brother texting her. "Trapped" as a sex slave? Her brother would never say he was trapped in that situation.

Kyle Jean-Louis Parker, though . . . he had true potential. He had a future. She could see it. Of course, it didn't hurt he was gorgeous, even as a slightly pimply seventeen-year-old. He had that shoulder-length hair the color of his jackal fur—people probably assumed he dyed it to look like that but Kiki knew better—those golden eyes, and those sharp, angled cheekbones. Even better, he had those long legs that gave him a good height, but he wasn't freakishly tall or buff like the grizzlies and polar bears, who often had to live in their own enclaves so full-humans didn't question why so many very large men and women had an unhealthy love of honey. But Kyle was a good-looking jackal whose entire family easily slipped into the full-human world without seeming strange or different. Except for their inherent talent.

And Kiki *had* seen Kyle's sister dance at the Bolshoi a few years back. Oriana hadn't even been an adult yet, but what Kiki had seen had blown her away. The beautiful lines, the delicate skill, all combined with the muscles and strength of an animal that could drag a much larger gazelle back to its den to feed the rest of its family.

But unlike Kyle, Oriana put her entire self out on that stage. Her skill alone would make her a great dancer but what made her brilliant was what she gave to the audience. What she revealed through a look, a move. She exposed everything while fully clothed. That was something that couldn't be taught. Couldn't be learned.

Kyle had to find that soulfulness and put it in his work the way his sister did. Then the kid would have a chance.

Of course, Kiki could have left after she'd blown the kid's world up; she and Zhen could have headed back to the safety of Manhattan for some drinks and an expensive lunch at the latest hot spot downtown. But she wanted to get to know, at least a little, this woman who'd caught her baby brother's eye.

Kiki didn't care that Stevie Stasiuk was a hybrid. That she was part cat, part badger. She didn't care that she was, at least physically, one of the whitest white girls she'd met in a long time with that pale skin and dyed, dark blond hair. All she cared about was that this one-time prodigy wasn't an asshole to Shen. When people were as brilliant as she knew Stevie to be, they could be huge assholes because they felt they were better than everyone else. And Stevie was a genius on two fronts: science *and* music. She could slide from one to the other like an eel in water.

In fact, Kiki had already heard rumors that Stevie might have written a brilliant ballet, and New York was already sitting up and taking notice, people ready to spend a fortune on tickets just to hear Stasiuk's music one more time.

And yet . . . this woman who could have anything she wanted, live anywhere she wanted, *do* anything she wanted, was in a relatively small, old-ish kitchen with a seemingly new oven and refrigerator, bickering with her sisters. One black. The other Chinese. The three of them didn't look remotely alike, but Stevie had introduced them as her sisters, so who was Kiki to question?

The middle sister, Max, appeared freshly showered, still towel-drying her hair. The eldest sister, Charlie, was covered in flour and, at some point, she dropped a pile of what she called "bamboo buns" on the table and gestured to them.

Zhen immediately grabbed one, taking a bite and crossing her eyes in delight at the taste. Then she elbowed Kiki. A grizzly was hanging outside the kitchen window, sniffing the air.

"Hey, Charlie," the grizzly greeted her. "Thought I smelled—"

Charlie closed the window in the grizzly's face.

"Not cool, MacKilligan!" the bear barked, but Charlie didn't seem too disturbed by it.

The back screen door opened and Shen came in. He looked right at Kiki.

"Good job. You destroyed another artist."

"Don't be so overdramatic."

"Kyle will be fine," Stevie said, handing each of the pandas in the room a big stalk of Chinese bamboo. "I'll make sure of it."

"Are you his mentor?" Kiki asked.

"I wouldn't say that. I don't know anything about sculpting. Instead I'm more his . . . pre-psychologist. We're both sure he'll need one in a few years, so I'm prepping him for that. Speaking of which . . ." She glanced at her watch and dug into the backpack next to her chair. After a few seconds, she pulled out a bottle of prescription pills.

Stevie shook a pill into her palm and Charlie smoothly placed a bottle of water in front of her younger sister. Max took the pill bottle from Stevie, put the cap back on, and returned it to Stevie's backpack. Then, for some reason, Max slapped the back of her sister's head *while* she was taking her pill, which led to a little bit of choking . . . followed by yelling.

"If I choke and die, it'll be your fault!"

"I would never be so lucky!"

The doorbell rang and Max calmly stated, "I'll get it."

Zhen grabbed another bamboo bun. "So . . . you're on medication?" she asked Stevie.

Kiki winced and their brother barked, "Zhen!"

Their sister didn't say much, but when Zhen finally did talk . . . oy.

"What are you doing?" Kiki softly asked her through clenched teeth.

"She's dating our brother," Zhen replied, softly and also through clenched teeth. "What if she's a nut?"

"It's rude."

"This from a woman who just destroyed some kid's will to live."

"It is *not* the same thing."

"You do know we can hear you, right?" Charlie asked.

Stevie held up her hand. "It's okay. Really." She smiled at Zhen. "I have a panic disorder and bouts of depression. But I manage both with medication and therapy."

"It's really none of our business," Kiki said.

"Like hell it's not," Zhen snapped.

"Like hell it is," Charlie growled.

"Charlie," Stevie said, quickly raising her hand at her sister. "You promised. Just last night."

"Zhen," Shen said, "maybe you and Kiki should just head out."

"You're throwing me out because I'm worried about you?"

"I'm throwing you out because you're being rude."

"Uh, guys . . . ?"

Max stood in the kitchen doorway, a weird smile on her face.

"What?" Charlie asked.

Max stepped to the side and Niles Van Holtz and Ulrich Van Holtz moved into the kitchen.

Kiki knew both men. She'd written more than once about the Van Holtz Steakhouse chain. But why they were in the MacKilligan house, Kiki had no idea.

"Oh, come on!" Charlie shouted. "Now I'm just being tested!"

Stevie jumped from her seat and faced her sister. "You promised."

"But—"

"You promised!"

"You never said they'd be standing in my kitchen!"

"Aaaaaaah!" the former prodigy screamed.

"Do not start that ag—"

"Aaaaaaah!"

"I can't believe you're do—"

"Aaaaaaah!"

"*Fine!*"

Shen let out a relieved breath. His sisters probably hadn't noticed, but Charlie had a holstered .380 semiautomatic attached to the back of her jean shorts; the flour-covered red T-shirt that reached past her waist hid it from sight.

But once Stevie screamed a little into her sister's annoyed face, Charlie released the butt of her weapon and dropped both her arms to her sides.

He hadn't been worried that Charlie would harm his sisters. He knew she wouldn't—although Zhen was clearly testing the hybrid's patience—but take out two Van Holtz males standing in her kitchen? Yeah. That she might do, which would look awful in front of his sisters.

Oh! And it would be wrong, too. Definitely wrong.

Shen was thinking it was about time to get his sisters out of here when he noticed that the room had fallen ominously silent.

Stevie stepped close to the wolves, and both her sisters looked tense. Ready. Of course, those two were always ready.

Placing her hand on Ric Van Holtz's forearm, Stevie asked, "What's happened?"

He swallowed. Glanced at his cousin. "They took my friends," he said, his voice tight. "They're both hybrids. Blayne and Gwenie."

"I just saw Blayne last night," Shen said. "She was at Wild Dog Night."

"They both were."

"So was Matt Wells's brother." Stevie looked at her sisters. "He was there last night. It has to be him."

"You don't know it's him," Max cautioned.

"James is *not* social. Going to a wild dog karaoke night would be one of the seven hells for him. Trust me on this. I knew when I saw him something was going on. And then he was gone before I could reach him. It was him."

"They also grabbed her mate, Bo Novikov," Ric added. "He had a scrimmage game last night and he went missing right after."

"What about their kids?" Shen asked.

"They're at my house. Dee-Ann and Cella Malone are watching them. And the Malone family is protecting the building."

"Well, *they're* safe," Max muttered with no sarcasm. And she was right.

"We need your help," the elder Van Holtz said. "We can't wait—"

"Stop talking." Charlie, her back to all of them, held up her hand to silence everyone, and Stevie's cringe was so intense, Shen felt her pain. They might have to go it alone on this without Charlie and Max. And he would go, just as he knew Stevie would. No matter what her sisters said. She was ready to move right this moment to help those who needed it.

"Look," Van Holtz began, "I know we've had some issues, but—"

Charlie shook one forefinger. Then she faced them and Shen realized she was already on her phone.

"Livy. It's Charlie. We need to move. Now. Yeah. Stevie told me. Yeah. Do you know a bear bar in Jersey?" She shook her head. "Not gay bears. Bear-bears. Yes. That one. Meet us there in the hour."

She disconnected that call and started calling someone else. "Max. Text Berg for me. Tell him we're moving out in ten minutes. Uncle Will. Hi. It's Charlie. When are you guys going back home? Good. I need a few of your boys. Tonight. Great. We're meeting at the bar we went to after the funeral. Go there now. Make sure the snakes are all gone, please. Eat them. I don't care. I just don't want any there when we arrive."

With another call disconnected, she pointed at Stevie. "They're going to assume it was you when they discover the lab break-in so you need an alibi."

"I'm not going into hiding and I'm not staying here."

"No. If you go into hiding, they'll know we know and they'll move everything. It's better you're out and about. Let everybody see you. Like it's a regular thing."

Stevie pulled her phone out. "I got an invitation to something for tonight . . ." She put in what appeared to be a ten-digit code and quickly scanned her email. "Here. I've been invited to a soccer game at the Sports Center. I can go to that."

"They invited you because you're on the team," Max reminded Stevie. "Remember?"

"Oh. Yeah. I do now. Okay. I can do that."

"Perfect. Shen, I need you to work with Livy. She asked for you specifically."

"We've worked together before."

"I'm going to have her hit Wells Pride's home. Max and I will take the lab. I'll have the MacKilligans secure the outside."

"I can do the lab on my own," Max protested.

"And not kill everyone?" Charlie asked, not even looking at her sister. When Max did not answer, "Yeah, exactly. I'm going with you."

"The Wells brothers still live with their mother's Pride." Stevie scratched her forehead. "If you send Livy in there—"

"We need to get the family all out."

"How?"

"I can do that."

Shen looked down at Kiki. "You can do what?"

"You're talking about the Wells Pride, right? Jennifer Wells? And her scientist sons? She's always hitting me up for financial backing for her sons' work. If she thinks she can meet some connections . . ." She smiled at Shen. "I can do it. Trust me."

"Are you sure you want to get involved in this?" Stevie asked.

"Are innocent people being hurt?"

"Yes."

"Then I'm in."

"Great." Charlie focused on her phone while walking toward the living room. "I have to get changed." She stopped by Ric, looked up at him. "We'll do our best to get your friends back."

"Thank you."

A brisk nod and Charlie was walking again, barking over her shoulder, "Max! Stevie! Let's move out!"

Max immediately followed, motioning to the Van Holtz males to follow her back to the front door, but Stevie stopped right outside the kitchen, looked over her shoulder at Shen.

"I love you, too," she said sweetly, giving him a warm smile. Then she was gone.

Stunned, Shen simply stood there. Staring at where she'd just been.

"That sounded like she was responding to something," Kiki noted.

"Yeah. It did, didn't it?"

Zhen, rubbing her nose, asked, "Do you not remember saying anything to her?"

"I . . . don't." Shen pressed his palms to his eyes. "She is driving me *crazy!*"

"Good crazy? Or bad crazy?"

Shen shrugged. "A little of both . . . ?"

chapter TWENTY-EIGHT

Stevie, sitting on the bench, glanced at her watch again. She kept trying not to. She kept trying to focus on the game. But how could she? With everything that was going on at the moment?

Kiki had turned out to be as good as her word. She'd invited the Wells Pride to some art thing in the Village and they had cleared out of their Park Avenue apartment, even leaving their youngest offspring with an adolescent She-lion. Thankfully, she'd taken the kids out for dinner, giving Livy at least an hour to get information from the computers.

Stevie checked her cell phone again, but still no word from her sisters. A few of her cousins and Uncle Will were at the bar when they'd arrived, but she didn't trust them. Not fully. Especially because none of this had anything to do with the MacKilligans, which meant they would be helping others out of the kindness of their hearts. That was not Uncle Will's thing.

She heard a roar and realized it was the crowd. It was a surprisingly large one for a friendly amateur game. They didn't really sell tickets so much as ask for donations. But if you just wanted to wander in for free, you could do that too.

"Stevie?"

Coop was standing in front of her. "Hi, Coop. What's up?"

"You ready to go in?"

"Um . . . okay." She put her phone down on the bench, automatically turning off the screen. "Where do you want me?" she asked, standing.

"You wanna play forward?"

"Yeah, sure."

"There is just one thing, though. On the other team . . ."

"Yeah?"

He pointed and Stevie studied the players on the field.

"What about them?"

"You don't recognize them?"

"Should I?"

"You just stole the wild dog karaoke trophy from them."

"Oh, no."

"Oh, yes," Coop laughed.

"I just can't get away from the *lions* today."

"Pardon?"

"It's nothing."

"You don't have to play if you don't want."

She waved him off. "It's all right."

Maybe playing would distract her from all her worries.

Livy fell out of the overhead vent and landed face-first on the floor.

"Ow," she moaned.

"You all right?" she heard Shen ask in her ear.

"I'm fine."

Shen and Livy's mate Vic were in the communications truck. Sadly, this was not the first time they'd done something like this. Where she'd broken in someplace and Shen and Vic helped from outside. She wasn't a thief, though. She prided herself on that. She'd merely been born into a family of thieves. On both sides! And she had the skills. But she was *not* a thief herself.

Of course, the last time she'd been in a situation like this, she'd found her father's still-shifted body. He'd been stuffed and was displayed in a rich woman's home. That had been traumatic. Not so much because her father was dead—she'd already thought he was dead—but because her mother had buried someone and told everyone it was Livy's father.

Turned out that had been a lie. Even worse, to this day, Livy had no idea who was buried in that grave, and her mother wasn't talking.

That was the past, though. Right now she had bigger issues. She'd been shocked when she'd found out that people she knew had been taken, and now time was a factor. They needed information and they needed it quickly.

Ignoring the pain in her face, Livy got to her feet and cracked her neck.

"I'm in," she told Shen and Vic. Then she got to work.

With the help of their cousins—more than just a few had agreed to come with them from the bear bar in Jersey, Will shockingly giving his blessing—they had been able to get inside Wells's lab. There were security guards but the cousins set up a drunken fistfight in the front of the building as a distraction and using the heating vent to get around, they easily bypassed the labs with people working late.

They located Wells's office and snuck inside. They didn't bother with the computer on his desk, knowing he'd keep anything really important on his own laptop at home. Instead, Max picked the locks and they searched his physical files. They kept silent and moved fast, taking whatever they thought could help.

When Max found papers that seemed to be a grant proposal for Wells's brother, she stuffed the file in Charlie's bag and they scrambled back into the heating vent.

By the time they made it back outside, they could hear the sirens of New York's finest responding to the destruction of the glass front of the lab building by the cousins. One of them spotted Charlie and Max, and he grinned a mouthful of blood, motioning for them to meet up with the Dunn triplets around the corner seconds before a fist jammed into his face.

Charlie gave her kin a thumb's up—the first time she'd ever given one of them that—and ran, making sure Max was right behind her.

As they neared the armored van, the side door opened to reveal Britta crouching inside, motioning them forward. Berg outside the van; Dag driving.

Pushing her sister in front of her, Charlie scrambled into the van. She'd just moved to the far side when her cousins came tearing around the corner and dove headfirst into the vehicle. They knocked Max down, forced Charlie into the corner, kicked Dag in the back of the head, and one of them managed to ask Britta out while dripping blood on the van floor and climbing over his brother's chest.

"All right then," Berg sighed as he stepped into the van and closed the door, "glad we're all safe."

The ball rammed into Stevie's head. Again.

Now she was sure those lion bitches were purposely kicking soccer balls at her.

Coop jogged over to her. "Okay. At this point, I think we should just . . . let you take a break."

"Clearly they have not let the lost karaoke trophy go." Stevie wiped blood from her nose.

"Yeah. It's no longer a game. Just assault." He picked up the ball. "But hey, we have a game next week. The opposition is all pandas. They're from Chinatown. They mostly grab the ball and run, but . . . they're extremely nice and lots of fun."

"I am not backing away from them or anyone." Stevie yanked the ball away. "I'm so over this shit."

Stevie went around Coop and dropped the ball. She stopped thinking about all the stuff going on outside the game. All the danger her sisters and friends were in. She temporarily blocked it and let her mind do what it did best. Analyze.

When she was done, she readjusted her body, moved her feet a bit, then kicked the ball. It spun across the field, hitting the farthest column, ricocheting into another column, which sent it slamming into another, slicing past the goal and ramming into the side of Mary Marie Brunetti's head. The power of the hit knocked Mary Marie into one of her sisters, sending both women to the ground.

"Wow," Coop sighed out in awe. "It picked up speed."

Stevie began to explain how she'd calculated the potential

velocity, but she saw the blank expression on Coop's face and just ended with, "Physics. It's the best."

Shen dropped Livy and Vic off at their vehicle and headed to the Sports Center. They'd already given the copied drives to Irene Conridge, who had been waiting for them. She had someone at the ready to hack into those things and he hadn't wanted to lose a minute getting the information into Conridge's hands. Now he just wanted to get back to Stevie. He knew she was safe, but he still didn't feel right without her in his sight, which was ridiculous. He was just being pathetic and needy at this point.

Even though there were no big games going on, he still had a hell of a time finding a parking space. When he finally did, he was parked on the roof, which meant it would take him ages to get down to the lower levels where all the shifter activities took place.

He got on the elevator with a full-human family, watching as the numbers moved slowly from one to the other in reverse order.

Shen blew out a breath, tapped his foot, and continued to watch the numbers. At least he did until he felt a small hand grab his T-shirt.

He slowly looked down at the toddler. His father had just realized he was touching a stranger.

"Oh. Sorry."

The child held out his stuffed giant panda toy at Shen and said, "Pan-daaa."

"Yes. Panda," the mother replied, which had Shen confused for a second until she grabbed the stuffed panda from her son and wiggled it in front of him. "Pan-*da*."

"No!" the child snapped, angry, pointing at Shen. "Pandaaaaaa!" He reached for Shen, trying to wiggle out of his father's arms.

"What is with you?" his father asked, becoming as frustrated as his son.

"No, sweetie," his mother corrected, pointing at Shen. "Man." She held up the stuffed toy again. "Pan-da. Panda."

The elevator doors finally opened and, with a nod and a smile at the family, Shen stepped out. That's when the kid started screaming, because his real-life panda was walking away.

Shen never knew what it was, but kids under the age of four seemed to know a panda shifter as soon as they saw one. When it came to the other predators, kids that age usually just started crying or trying to move away from them to the safety of their parents. But they *always* knew the pandas and they always wanted to cuddle them.

Shen reached the private entrance to the floors that were for shifters only, passing the fox and jaguar security guards who kept the full-humans out. One sniff and they pulled the door open for Shen so he could go inside.

He saw Dag standing in line at Starbucks. He hurried over, tapped his shoulder. "All cool?"

"Yeah. Charlie and Max are in room twenty-B. It's one of the offices. They're going through the paperwork they grabbed. Hoping to find a property address."

"Okay. I'll go get Stevie."

Dag nodded. "Want a coffee?"

"I'll get one later."

Shen left Starbucks and went over to the elevator, which he took down to the floor where the soccer field was located. As he stepped out, he could see crowds coming through the main doors. It looked like the game was over. He went on his toes to look over the big cats and bears. He spotted Stevie arguing with a couple of the Brunettis.

"Don't tell me they play soccer," he muttered to himself.

Shen, trying to push his way past unhelpful bears and bitchy cats, raised his arm. "Stevie!"

She looked up, went on her toes. Their eyes caught and she smiled. Waved. She walked away from the Brunettis and a fast-talking Coop, who thankfully blocked the She-lions from following her with his long jackal body.

Shen headed toward her, trying to keep eye contact, but

it seemed a lot of people had come to the game tonight and Stevie kept dipping in and out of his . . .

He stopped. Looked over his shoulder, then back to where he'd last seen Stevie.

Moving forward, now pushing past the bigger breeds, he ran to the last spot he'd seen her, but there was no sign.

"Coop!" he called out. "Where's Stevie?"

The jackal turned away from the Brunettis and took a quick look around. "She was just here. I saw her."

"Stairs! Where are the stairs?"

Coop pointed. "Emergency exit that way."

Shen ran, slamming into the doors and taking the steps two at a time, heading up.

He reached the first floor. The two guards who protected these doors from unknowing full-humans and made sure all the shifters got out safely if there was an emergency were out cold, blood seeping from wounds on their heads.

Shen jumped over them and raced out the door and onto the city street.

"Stevie!" he called out. "*Stevie!*"

But she was already gone.

Irene continued to pace around the room. The one person she knew who could do this level of illegal hacking—at least the one person she knew who'd nearly served hard federal time for this level of illegal hacking—continued to work.

"How are we doing?" she finally asked.

"I just started. Back off."

She glared at her one-time PhD student, Miki Kendrick. Although Miki now did a lot of work for the government to stop the sort of hacking she was currently performing, she was willing to return to her old ways. Not for money, but for friends. Thankfully—and surprisingly to many—Irene was one of those friends. Of course, they were two full-human geniuses married to wolves. It was logical that they'd end up friends.

A knock and the door opened. Van stuck his head in.

Irene frowned, tried not to panic. "They didn't find—"

"No, no. But we have another problem. They got Stevie."
He stepped into the room, studying Miki. "How much time?"

Miki shook her head. "I'm shocked Stevie's little device
could actually make workable copies from those hard drives.
The problem is that they have thirty-five-digit passwords and
layers on top of layers of encryption." She looked at Irene.
"You didn't tell me they were *this* paranoid."

"We need to do *something*, Miki," Van insisted. "We do not
have time to—"

"I'm doing my best but these aren't house husbands hiding their porn or their latest girlfriends. These are incredibly
brilliant scientists who know how to set up a system and keep
people out of it. And you pressuring me with your annoying
wolf barking is not helping."

"I'm not barking. Trust me, you'll know when I'm barking!"

"Stop. Stop," Irene ordered, her mind analyzing the current
situation. "You are forgetting something."

"What?"

"Stevie MacKilligan's sisters."

"I have *not* forgotten about them. They're under the watch-
ful eyes and ready chains of a full tactical unit. All my best
people except Cella and Dee-Ann."

"You misunderstand me." Irene raised her forefinger. "I
don't want you to hold them back. I want you to unleash them."

"Have you lost your mind? You love my skin!" he reminded her.

She waved that forefinger. "No, no. They're not thinking
about you anymore. They'll track their sister down quicker
than we will hacking into these drives." She pointed at Miki.
"But I still need you to get in and find their research."

Van blinked. "Why?"

"He or they took her because they think they're ready to use
this . . . project, for lack of a better word, on her. Otherwise,
they wouldn't bother. I need to know what's in those files so I
can . . . counteract, I guess, whatever they do to her."

"They *don't* want to just kill her," Van said, giving a little
shudder.

"No. They're going to use her as their pièce de résistance. The proof that their experimentation and murders were worth it. But I'd prefer not to let it get that far. And if we let Stevie's sisters go . . ."

Van pulled out his cell phone, speed-dialing his team as he walked out of the room.

"Are you sure about this?" Miki asked. "I've heard about Stevie MacKilligan from my friends at CERN. I *especially* heard about her sisters. They will leave a trail of bodies behind in their search for her."

Irene shrugged. "Then the Wells Pride would be wise to give them the information they're looking for."

"What if they don't have it to give?"

"Then their night will be very, very sad."

chapter TWENTY-NINE

Her head throbbing, Stevie forced herself to sit up. It wasn't until the extreme nausea passed that she realized someone was touching her shoulder.

Stevie jerked but Blayne immediately threw up her hands, palms out. "It's me! It's me! Please don't eat me!"

Chuckling a little, Stevie said, "It's okay. I just didn't know it was you." She pressed her hand to her head. "What the fuck did they give me anyway?"

"A bat to the back of the head."

That came from Gwen. She was on the other side of the room, sitting on the floor. She had her knees raised, one arm resting across them.

"Bats?" That was new.

"Yeah," Blayne said. "It's all very tacky."

Her eyesight becoming clear, Stevie gazed at the bright silver bracelets on Blayne and Gwen's wrists. And then her own. Except they didn't look decorative.

"What are—"

Blayne held up her wrists. "We were told that these are titanium. If we try to shift, the titanium will cut into our flesh and eventually . . . there go our paws."

"Oh, my God," Stevie said, disgusted; she was appalled anyone would go this far, but especially a fellow shifter.

"Where's Bo?" Stevie asked.

"Next door. They didn't want to put us in the same

titanium-lined room because they didn't want us to think about making more—and I'm quoting here—'freak babies.'"

"Stop, stop." Stevie couldn't hear any more. Instead, she struggled to her feet with Blayne's help.

Once she stood, Stevie waited another minute for a new wave of nausea to settle down. Although she didn't appreciate getting banged in the back of the head, she understood why it had been done. Because with hybrids it was impossible to know what amount of knock-out drug to administer. Too little and you had a struggling and angry freak of nature ripping apart your van. Too much and you ended up dropping hybrid bodies on the side of the road and lost out on any experimentation you may have wanted to try.

Stevie pointed at the giant TV on one of the bright-steel walls. Or was that titanium, too? "What's that for? Cartoons?"

"We don't know," Gwen replied. "It hasn't been on since we got here."

Stevie let her gaze roam around the room, looking for any weakness. Anything she could exploit.

The hermetically sealed doors opened and James Wells walked in. He wore a suit and tie under his long white lab coat. Four guards were with him. All of them heavily armed shifters in gray body armor.

Staring at Stevie, James pointed at Gwen. The men grabbed her, yanking her off the floor. Blayne was on them in seconds, fighting to protect her friend. One of the guards threw her to the ground, aimed a nonlethal but pain-inducing weapon at her.

Stevie stepped between them and focused on James.

"So it's not *really* ready," she said to him. She would only speak to him. The guards were following his orders, whether for money or out of loyalty, she didn't know. She didn't care.

"What?"

"That's why I'm here, isn't it? So you can show me how what you're working on is fabulous and ready to change me forever. But it's not ready. That's why you're starting with them."

"You think I'm like my brother? You think you can manipulate me with a few words and—"

"If your great experiment works . . . show me."

Big hands grabbed Stevie and pulled her out of the room.

Shen wasn't surprised when one of the Group's tactical units surrounded them, keeping them trapped in room 20B. He wasn't surprised when the Dunn triplets began to growl and huff in warning. He wasn't even surprised when the MacKilligan cousins who were still hanging out with Charlie and Max for some reason, didn't leave or cause any problems. It was as if they were just waiting to see what would happen next.

Oh, he also wasn't surprised when Max came within inches of snapping off an agent's face. Inches. But that seemed pretty expected by nearly everyone in the room except for the guy who nearly lost his face.

But what did surprise Shen was that Charlie wasn't saying anything. Or doing anything. She wouldn't talk to Berg. She wouldn't talk to Shen! To tell him he didn't need to worry. Where the fuck was soothing-Charlie? Why wasn't she trying to make him feel better?

Instead, she was just sitting . . . and staring. And everyone in the room knew that was not good.

But then one of the agents got a call and, suddenly, all of them left. Just walked out. Without a word. And that's when Charlie moved. Went out the door, Max right behind her.

"This is going to be bad," Britta noted, but the triplets followed. The cousins followed. And so did Shen. Because he needed Stevie back. Safe and all of her just like she was. If that meant doing things he wouldn't be proud of, he was ready.

They got back into the armored van that was waiting for them right outside the Sports Center, but this time Max drove and Charlie sat in the passenger's seat. No one spoke. No one moved. They all just waited.

After they drove for a little while, Max double-parked the van in front of a Park Avenue apartment building.

Shen knew where they were. And Britta had been right. This was going to be bad.

Matt sat in his Pride's living room, listening to his mother roar at him—she was using words, but all Matt could hear was angry roaring—about how stupid he was. How he didn't think of others. How he was an embarrassment to the family. To the Pride. Why couldn't he just be normal?

But how was he supposed to know that the person he'd been talking to about the awfulness of the artwork was the actual artist? How was he responsible for that? And how was he supposed to know that the artist was the one with the family trust fund that gave huge amounts of grant money to important medical and science research.

How was he supposed to know? And why wouldn't his mother stop roaring at him?

Finally, he couldn't take it anymore and stood.

"Where do you think you're going?" his mother demanded, following him.

"I'm going to my room! And you're not allowed to come with me!"

He'd just entered the hallway—his aunts, sisters, and cousins laughing at him as they liked to do—when the front door was kicked open.

The very secure, thick, metal door on a secure apartment in a building with a twenty-four-hour doorman. Where the fuck was the doorman?

He watched Charlie MacKilligan storm into his home; her smaller, psychotic sister right beside her. Then there were bears and a panda. *That* panda! But when the group of honey badgers charged in, hissing and running at the She-lions, forcing them away from Matt, he knew he was in real trouble.

He tried to stand his ground and be brave. He was six four, two hundred and sixty pounds of muscle and a lion! But then that hybrid's hand wrapped around his throat and she pinned him to the wall.

"Hi, Matt," Charlie said softly, Max grinning behind her.

* * *

They wanted to strap her down onto some table but Stevie shook her head.

"Not necessary. Just do it."

Stevie knew that Charlie would lose her mind about this. That she was sacrificing herself. But it just seemed right, didn't it? For years, she'd been talking about fucking with her genes so she could stop shifting. Her sister had forbidden it each time, but she knew it would save a lot of people. Did she want to do this now? No. She'd wanted to try it on her own terms, with her own work. But she wasn't going to let her prey . . . er . . . Blayne—and her friend go through this. No way. And the thing was, she knew she just had to delay Wells. Because her sisters would come. They would come for her and the others, and no matter what James did to her, it wouldn't matter because the others would be safe.

Stevie sat at a table and one of James's assistants pulled her left arm out and prepared it for injection.

James sat down catty-corner from her, smiled.

"Is all this because I dumped your brother?" she asked.

"I know why you broke it off with him. He's an idiot. You had no choice really."

"Then what is it? Because you seem a little obsessed."

"I saw you once," he said, gazing at her. She could see the fanatical light in his eyes.

"Saw me?"

"Change. Into that thing."

It felt like her heart dropped, but she didn't let those feelings show on her face.

"It wasn't normal. It wasn't right."

"I don't know about right or wrong," she said, feeling a needle slip into her skin but refusing to react to the pain, "but it's definitely not normal. But Blayne and Gwen are normal. Blayne's a wolf-dog. Gwen's a tigon. Both are found in nature."

"Those things *aren't* found in nature. They're found in foreign zoos. And Novikov? You going to tell me he's found in nature?"

"Yeah, I can't really say that about him."

"You, all of you, are a danger to our society. But instead of wiping you out as some would like to do, I've created something that will allow you to become more like us."

"But not too much like you," she said with a teasing smirk, pointing her finger.

"Think about it. You'll be able to keep that brilliant mind of yours but you'll no longer be ashamed of what you are. Won't that be a relief?"

A week ago she would have said yes, but now . . .

"So how long does this process take?" she asked.

"Well, for your safety and the safety of my guards and assistants, we'll put you back in your room for the changing process. But you'll be able to watch what happens to your DNA on the monitor we have set up in there. Exciting, right?"

Stevie forced a smile. "Absolutely."

"Where's your brother?" Charlie asked again.

"I don't know!"

"Where's his lab?"

"I don't know what you're talking about!"

"You're lying."

"Unlike you, I don't obsessively watch where my brother goes and what he does. And he won't tell me anything because he thinks I'm going to steal his precious research. Like I give a shit."

"Hey!" a young, nonrelated male lion barked from the doorway. Berg and Dag started to move, ready to challenge him, but Britta knew her brothers would just get in the way. She grabbed their arms, held them back.

What the fuck is going on? the male roared.

Her eyes still locked on Wells, Charlie softly said, "Max."

The blade was out of Max's hand, across the hall, and buried in the male lion's chest before he could move. He fell back into another male lion's arms.

"Don't pull it out," Max warned the second male. "He'll bleed out and that'll be the end of him. You may want to carry him to an emergency room, hon."

"Go," one of the She-lions urged, and the males were gone as fast they'd come in.

"I don't think he's lying," Max said about Wells.

"You sure?" Charlie asked, leaning in, staring intently into his face.

"Yeah. I'm sure."

"The thing is . . . based on what Stevie has told us, your brother is not going to do anything on his own. Because, like you, he's a momma's boy."

Slowly, Charlie's head turned, her cold—suddenly gold—wolf gaze locking on the head of the Pride. Jennifer Wells.

"Mommy," Charlie said, her voice low, "where's your boy?"

"Go to hell."

Charlie's body spun away from Wells and she faced the She-lion, her .380 now in her hand, aimed at the older woman. She stalked across the hall toward the lioness, the gun raised. The other females attempted to attack, but the MacKilligan cousins got in the way, fighting the women and mostly getting their asses kicked. But they were all honey badgers, so they just kept fighting, seemingly tireless, keeping the females at bay.

Charlie pressed the barrel of the gun against the She-lion's head.

"Where's his lab?"

But she wouldn't reply. She just smirked. It was like she was daring Charlie to kill her.

"You know me," Charlie said. "You know what I'll do."

"Then do it. Pull the trigger."

Charlie shrugged. "Okay." She pointed the weapon back at Matt Wells and shot him in the leg.

Roaring, the lion male dropped to the ground, his hands wrapped around the bleeding wound.

"Now," Charlie explained, "you're gonna lose a son tonight. The question is . . . do you wanna lose two? Because what you need to understand about me, lady, is that I. Don't. Give. A. Fuck. I will wipe out every last one of these bitches and leave you the last cat standing, and won't lose a bit of sleep. So think carefully before you answer me."

"Jersey," the She-lion spit out. "His lab is in Jersey."

Charlie walked away, saying softly over her shoulder, "Max."

Max charged at the lioness, launched herself into the air, and caged her in by putting her legs and arms on the wall behind the She-lion, claws dug into the marble keeping her aloft. Then Max, sounding awfully perky, asked, "Can I have the address please? Or the coordinates. Whichever."

"Is it weird," Blayne asked, "to be able to look inside yourself?"

"Nah. But I am curious how he's able to do this. He must have injected me with something other than just the genetic material."

The three of them sat on the floor, staring up at the giant monitor. They were into the second hour, waiting for the injection to start to work. To change her.

To make Stevie "normal."

"Hey," Gwen pointed out. "Something's happening."

She was right. On the monitor, something was definitely happening.

"That's your DNA?" she asked.

"Yes. My *shifter* DNA."

"And that's . . ."

"What Wells created. It's remaking my DNA now."

"Do you feel anything?" Blayne leaned in. "Are you in pain?"

"No. It's supposed to be a relatively painless process."

"That's something, I guess."

Once the process was completed, Stevie could *see* that her DNA was now that of a normal—

Gwen reared back. "What the fuck was that?"

Stevie wasn't really sure. "I . . . I don't know. I've never seen that before."

The replaced DNA had suddenly been attacked by . . . something and just like that, her original DNA had returned.

"Is that *supposed* to happen?"

"I doubt it."

"Wait . . . it's starting again."

Gwen was right. The process repeated itself, ripping apart her shifter DNA and replacing it with—

"Oh, shit!" all three of them exclaimed.

"Your shifter DNA *ate* that shit." Blayne grinned. "That was awesome!"

"No, it wasn't." Stevie looked at the two women on either side of her. "He's not going to like this."

"What do you think he's going to do?"

"Nothing good."

Gwen stood. "We need to get out of here."

"There's only one air vent," Stevie pointed out. "It's very small and very high. The walls are either lined or made out of titanium. Or a combination of steel and titanium. We are fucked."

Blayne stared at Stevie. "Are you having trouble breathing?"

"No. I'm fine."

"Are you lying?"

"Probably."

"Oh, shit."

"No, no. I'm okay. I'm okay." She took in a deep breath, let it out. "I'm okay."

"What are you two talking about?" Gwen asked.

"She panic-shifts," Blayne explained

"So?"

"We do *not* have that much room in here."

Gwen crouched in front of Stevie. "Look, I don't know you, sweetie. But all this is for *you*. To keep the rest of us imprisoned, they just had to put us behind iron bars. That's why when one of us goes to prison, we usually stay in prison."

"I don't understand what you're trying to say."

"Why did they build this for you? What do they think they're stopping? And I'd also like to point out that they thought their little DNA thing would shut you down. But that didn't work either."

Stevie gazed at the woman with the ridiculously long fingernails.

Scrambling to her feet, Stevie faced the wall and unleashed the claws on her right hand, which didn't affect the width of her wrist, didn't cause her any problems with the titanium cuff she had on.

She pulled her arm back.

"Are you sure about this?" Blayne asked.

"Nope," she replied. Not wanting to see her claws mangled and destroyed, Stevie closed her eyes tight and swung her arm forward with all her strength.

"Holy shit," she heard Gwen whisper and Stevie opened one eye, then the other.

Her claws had torn a giant gash through the titanium-steel walls.

Carefully, slowly, Stevie pulled her claws out of the wall and examined them. Her hand was shaking but her claws were undamaged. Thick and strong and lethal.

She looked down at her wrists, studied the titanium bands.

"Stevie?" Blayne said softly. "They're coming."

Blayne was right. Stevie could feel the vibrations through the floor.

She faced the women. "I'm about to do something," she informed them, "that is probably very, *very* stupid. But I think we've run out of options. So . . . yeahhhh . . . I'm sorry in advance."

"If we survive this, Gwenie," Blayne said to her best friend, "I'm going to tell you very loudly, *I told you so!*"

chapter THIRTY

The trucks and SUVs pulled to a stop in front of the single-story building.

From the outside, it looked like a small office building with reinforced doors and state-of-the-art surveillance equipment. But that was only because the real doings were going on in the floors underneath the ground. The floor on top was just the entrance, and it was heavily guarded, according to the Wells Pride, who eventually told them everything just to get the crazy MacKilligans out of their house.

Like the Group members, Shen and the Dunns were dressed in black body armor. Shen had his weapon unholstered and a round in the chamber as he stepped out of the SUV and walked around to the front where he met up with the Dunns and Dutch Alexander. The MacKilligan cousins had wanted to come, but their uncle had ordered them back to their hotel. Probably a good idea. This was more a job for professionals, not guys who just enjoyed terrorizing cats.

The sun was barely coming up when Ric Van Holtz, who was leading this raid, stepped in front of his people.

"Everybody knows what they need to do. Stay calm. Move fast. Don't forget we've got at least four civilians in there. Maybe more. So be careful."

Charlie, dressed just in jeans, a blue T-shirt, and sneakers—not looking tactical at all—had a gun in each hand, and the back pockets of her jeans were stuffed with fully loaded clips. She listened silently to Ric's unusually gruff speech. Her expression was blank until Max stepped in beside her. The smaller MacKilligan also had on jeans, a black T-shirt, and thick work boots.

They looked at each other and something passed between the siblings. It felt like an entire conversation in one glance.

Max went back to the SUV they'd driven up in and while Ric ensured that his team knew the details of the plan to breach the building, Shen watched the sisters.

A minute later, Max returned. She stepped in front of Charlie and placed a small rocket launcher on her shoulder. One shot and the blast took down the door . . . and blew out a good chunk of the building's front as well.

Everyone except Shen and the Dunns ducked, because they hadn't been expecting the MacKilligan sisters to let Ric and the Group lead anything.

Glancing over her shoulder, Charlie said, "Wait here. We'll let you know when it's clear."

Then they were gone, Max briefly stopping to toss her rocket launcher at Dag before pulling out blades, one in each hand.

Ric stared at the half-destroyed building. "What just happened?" he asked no one in particular.

"It's best just to wait until they're done," Berg explained. "Trust me on this."

Gwen had a giant furry ass pressing her into the titanium wall. She was afraid she might die from suffocation, but she couldn't be angry. That furry, striped ass had so far protected her and Blayne from Tasers, tear gas, and beanbag rounds. When the nonlethal didn't even give Stevie MacKilligan an itch, they moved to lethal. That's when the furry ass protected Gwen and Blayne from gunshots.

Of course, the gunshots were what made two-ton Stevie really angry. Roaring so loud the walls shook, she lashed out with her front paw, sending a group of guards flying out of the room.

It turned out the titanium bands didn't cut into Stevie's flesh. When she shifted, they just broke off and fell to the floor.

The rest of the guards ran out, closing the doors behind them.

Gwen assumed Stevie would tear the door open, but instead, she stomped to the wall and began to climb it, and not by digging her claws in. She just climbed it. Like a goddamn lizard.

"Holy shit," Gwen gasped.

"*Told you!*" Blayne said, yet again.

They watched Stevie easily move up the wall until she reached the extremely small air vent. She nosed the grate a few times, then used her claws to yank it out. The thick metal clattered to the floor and she poked her nose in. With a little push, she got her head in, too, but there was no way her body would . . .

"Holy shit!"

"I told you!"

Stevie managed to get all two tons of herself into the vent, her giant shoulders slipping in after her head; the rest of her body following. Gwen worried the hybrid would get stuck, but they could hear her claws and fur moving against the metal above them.

They waited in silence, their gazes locked on the ceiling until the doors were thrown open again. The armed guards had returned with weapons that could take down an elephant. But when they stepped inside, they froze and looked at Gwen and Blayne.

"Where is she?" the woman in front demanded.

Smiling a little, Gwen raised her hand and pointed her forefinger to a spot . . . behind them.

She saw the color drain from the woman's face before the guards all turned at once. But it was too late. Stevie had eased her gigantic body out of the tiny air vent on the other side of the door, lowered herself to the floor without a sound, and had attacked without hesitation.

Blood splattered across the room, hitting Gwen and Blayne in the face. Then they had to duck the spitout body parts, boots, and weapons.

Guards arrived from the hallway behind Stevie. Gwen didn't

think Stevie saw them and was about to call out a warning, but Stevie's long, tiger-like tail lashed out. It wasn't a tiger-like tail functionally. Nor was it like a honey badger's. Because it cut through the three men charging toward her. Cut right through them, splitting all three in half like they'd been hit with a giant sword.

The tail was also whip-fast and prehensile, picking up guards and tossing them around the room like toys.

Finally, Gwen had to say it, "I'll never doubt you again, Blayne."

"Yes, you will."

"You're right. I will."

All hell was breaking loose on the third floor lab, but he didn't have time to check it out. Instead, he was running toward the explosion and gunshots coming from the ground-level floor.

He stopped, silently ordering his men to stand by with a raised fist. He peered around the corner and saw the fight taking place in the hallway. There were two women. One had guns. The other knives. While the taller one shot her way down the hallway, nailing guard after guard with shots to the head; the other, smaller woman slashed and stabbed her way around. She moved fast, swinging herself onto guards' backs and cutting their throats or stabbing them in the top of the head.

One guard grabbed her off another's back, and she turned lightning fast, slamming him into the wall and ramming one of her knives under his chin and into his head. She stared into his eyes, smirked, before letting him slip to the floor and yanking her weapon out.

"Down!" the taller woman called out, and she fired, killing another guard about to attack the smaller one.

He looked at his team, made a motion with his hand to ready for attack. His group had automatic weapons so they were just going to sweep the entire area with gunfire until everyone in that hallway was down. Unfortunate about any of his fellow guards, but he didn't have time to play nice. Not when something had gone very wrong downstairs. They didn't have time to play games with little girls.

With a nod, his team started around the corner but the roar that made the glass in the office doors shake and then shatter, and the screams from below made everyone who wasn't already dead stop.

The building began to shake more but not from roaring. From something else. It took him a second but he realized it was running. Like a herd of animals, coming right for them.

He turned back the way he'd come just as the stair door crashed down. The first thing that came running out had tusks. Behind it were a cat and a canine. But the thing bringing up the rear . . .

"*Run!*" he screamed, trying to get his people to move, to use another exit, but before he could take a step, the blade slid across his throat and he saw that smile flash by him as he dropped to his knees, his hands wrapping around his neck, trying to stop the bleeding.

But he only managed to give himself enough time to feel the paws slam into his back, push him into the ground, and crush his bones to dust.

Ric wasn't exactly okay with the massacre that was going on inside that building, but he wasn't going to complain either. He just wanted his friends back. Then he felt the earth move beneath his feet. Like an earthquake. And he heard the roaring.

Shen stepped past him, staring into the building. Then he yelled, "Run!" And everyone scattered. No formation. No pulling back in an orderly line. Nothing. Nope. Like the true predators they all were, they thought only of themselves and made a crazed run for it.

That's what predators did when they came across a bigger predator. It was always your best bet.

When Ric felt he was far enough away, he stopped and looked back.

Bo Novikov came out of the damaged building first. He was

in his shifted form, but once he was outside, he turned back to human, grabbed the still-shifted Blayne and Gwen around their waists, and ran. Then the front of the building was destroyed even more as something galloped from it.

He watched at least two tons of beast tear out into the open. Tiger striped but built like a honey badger, it wasn't alone. It had James Wells caught between its fangs.

He was screaming, begging, trying to fight. But Stevie MacKilligan, in her shifted form, dove over the trucks and SUVs and went on a sort of romp around the property, shaking Wells, tossing him up in the air and catching him again. Then she dropped him to the ground. He tried to drag himself away, but she just batted him around with her front paws. Stopped once to scratch her ear with her back leg, which gave Wells a chance to get to his feet and run.

That's when Stevie pounced. Literally. She just watched him running for a few seconds and then up she went, crashing onto him with her front paws.

He stopped screaming then.

She batted his limp body around a few more times, but when he didn't respond, she picked him up between her teeth, walked over to the front of the now-totaled building, and laid him out.

It seemed a strange move until blood-covered Charlie and Max walked out. Unlike everyone else, the sight off their sister hadn't sent them fleeing, so they'd continued their original mission and "cleared" the building.

Now, standing outside among the debris, they gazed down at what was left of James Wells.

Finally, Charlie looked up at her sister and grinned. "Breakfast?"

chapter THIRTY-ONE

I t was the silence. Such intense silence.

Stevie looked away from her sisters and saw that the agents who'd come here today to rescue her and the others were gawking at her. Some with wide eyes. Others with unleashed fangs and claws. They were disgusted, appalled, and absolutely terrified.

Stevie lowered her head, began to back away. But her sisters had moved in front of her, Charlie's forefingers tightening on the triggers of her guns. Max stood next to her, her blood-covered hands working the handles of her knives because, Stevie knew, they were sticky and Max hated a sticky grip when she was in a fight.

Stevie didn't want this, though. She didn't want her sisters destroying those who'd risked everything protecting all of them because they were a little bit . . . overwhelmed by her.

She'd shift. That would help. She'd shift to human and everyone would calm down.

"Is there a problem?" Blayne Thorpe asked, walking through the group of agents, with Gwen by her side. "I'm not sure why you're looking at *my* friend that way, but I have to say that I don't appreciate it."

"You're okay with this?" a jaguar asked, arms folded over his chest. "I mean . . . look at her."

"Look at her? I do look at her. And you know what I see?"

"The woman who saved our lives?" Gwen asked. "Please say the woman who saved our lives."

"Of course that's what I see. But I also see the mighty tiger badger! Ruler of *all* badgers!"

"Oh, God," Gwen glanced up at Stevie. "I'm so sorry."

"What's happening?" Charlie asked.

"Look, Blayne," the jaguar said, "I get that you feel beholden to this woman—"

"Tiger badger," Blayne corrected.

"But, I think we can all agree"—he looked around at the other agents—"that whatever she is, she's just . . . she's just . . ."

"She's just what?" Blayne demanded. "My husband would really like to know."

The cat glanced over his shoulder, where Bo Novikov was standing behind him, back in his shifted form, while the other agents had silently moved out of the way of the one-ton animal. When she'd first seen him, Stevie had been fascinated by the two big fangs that hung down far past his massive jaw. Like a saber-toothed cat. Yeah. That's exactly what he reminded her of. A saber-toothed cat of yore!

"Well?" Blayne pushed. "Bo's waiting."

The cat shook his head while trying to inch around Bo. Especially when he started huffing.

"You know what?" The jaguar cleared his throat. "I think we are all"—he began to walk backward, away from Bo—"wonderful and interesting in our own ways. And it doesn't matter if you're normal . . . like me. Or have freakishly sized tusks."

"Those are fangs!" Blayne snapped.

"Or are disturbingly large and yet weirdly house cat–like. None of that matters because we're all one important thing. We're human." Stevie glanced at her sisters and all three of them rolled their eyes in disgust. "You. Me." He looked over at Stevie. "It."

"Hey!" Charlie snapped.

"We're all human. And isn't that what we need to remember when we talk about . . . Oh, my *God!* Would you stop it with that!"

The group of trained agents faced the sound that had been

getting louder and louder as the giant panda in human form walked closer, munching on a bamboo stalk.

"What?" Shen asked, calmly gazing back at the others. "I was hungry."

"Do you have to make so much noise?" the cat demanded.

In response, Shen bit down on the stalk, and the crunch echoed out in the fresh morning air.

The bears began heading back to the SUVs first. "I can't with that goddamn noise," one of them complained. "I just can't!"

"Don't you want some?" Shen called after them. "I have more in the car! They're directly from China," he finished in a singsong voice.

When no one responded, and everyone simply packed up to go, Shen went back to eating, but he grinned at Stevie around his bamboo, winking at her.

Stevie finally shifted back to human while Charlie held out shorts and a T-shirt for her. But before she put them on, she saw Shen coming toward her. She ran to him, jumped into his arms.

Holding her, he asked, "Are you okay?"

"My DNA eats other DNA for lunch. So I am great! Emotionally *and* genetically."

"I don't know what any of that means," he admitted.

"I know. But trust me . . . it's astounding."

He pressed his forehead against hers. "I'm just glad you're okay."

"Me too."

They stayed like that for several wonderful minutes. Just holding each other, eyes closed; Shen's hands under her bare ass, her arms around his massive shoulders. She'd never felt safer. Not simply physically safe. But fully understanding that she could be all she was with this man without doubt or fear.

"You two gonna do it?" Max asked, standing right by them and being typically annoying.

"Go. *Away*," Stevie snarled at her sister, refusing to move from her lovely position in Shen's arms.

Thankfully, Max did as Stevie asked, but, sadly, it seemed no one wanted to leave her alone with Shen.

"Sorry to bother you two," Ric Van Holtz said. "But I was just wondering, Stevie, if, um . . . the lab there"—he jerked his thumb toward her former prison—"is it still mostly intact or was the equipment destroyed?"

"Why would I destroy equipment?" she asked, still refusing to move from where she was.

"Huh. And do you know what all that equipment does?"

"Of *course* I know what the equipment does."

"Huh. Interesting."

"Is it?" Stevie snapped, beyond fed up at this point.

"You know what?" Charlie said, coming over and placing Stevie's clothes on her shoulder. "We're going to go now. My sister has had a long twenty-four hours and she needs her rest."

"Right. Of course." It looked as if Van Holtz took the hint, appearing to start to walk away. But then he stopped and again pointed at the lab, "You see, I'm just wondering—"

Max stepped in front of the wolf. "My sister needs her rest," Max reiterated, her eyes wide and dazed. "And I need to get the blood off my hands." She shoved her blood-drenched hands close to Van Holtz's pretty face. "Blood off my *haaaaaaannnnnnnddddddsssss!*" she ended on a hysterical screech.

"Okay, then," Van Holtz said, moving away from an openly sobbing Max, who was still holding her hands out and waving them at him. "I'll see you guys back in the city. Okay? Great!"

The wolf sprinted back to the waiting SUV and when he'd driven off, Max faced them. Before any of them could speak, she burst into hysterical laughter.

To Stevie's surprise, it was Berg who asked the question they were all thinking. "What is *wrong* with you?"

Still laughing, Max said, "He just wouldn't *leave.*"

"So you terrify him?" And now Berg was laughing. His brother and sister joining in.

Max shrugged, heading toward their vehicle. "It worked, didn't it?"

Finally alone, Shen said to Stevie, "I know I don't say this enough but . . . you have the *best* family."

Now Stevie laughed. "I know, *right?*"

Stevie fell asleep on their way back to Queens and didn't wake up even when everyone got out of the SUV and headed inside. So Shen carried her upstairs and took her to his room. But he was quite annoyed when he went inside and discovered that one of the bear neighbors had picked up Benny from the emergency vet and had placed the dog in the bed.

With a big bandage around his middle and a small set of stairs leading up to the mattress—so the dog wouldn't have to jump down or up, Shen guessed—the bastard looked quite at home. When the big dog saw Stevie, his giant tail began to hit the bed.

"Benny!" she said, although Shen wasn't sure she was actually awake. Her eyes weren't even open. But she stretched out her arm and Shen knew she wanted to touch the dog. Unable to deny her anything, he laid her out on the bed beside Benny, who'd risked his life for the three sisters.

Stevie moved in close, her hand settling on the dog's ridiculously thick neck.

Shen turned to walk out, but Stevie's "Don't go," stopped him.

"Sure there's enough room for me?" he teased.

"Get your ass over here," she ordered, still looking like she was asleep despite their conversation.

Shen placed his gun on the side table and slipped in behind Stevie. He put his arm around her waist and buried his nose in the back of her neck.

"Better?" he asked.

"Perfect," she purred. Then she started snoring and Shen grinned. Because Stevie was right.

It was perfect.

chapter THIRTY-TWO

Shen joined the cheers of the wild dogs when Stevie stepped up to the mic in the small downtown club. She'd gotten a call earlier in the day asking if she'd like to play with "The Band" as they referred to themselves since the former prodigies/current geniuses refused to actually give themselves a proper name. "Too much like we're really a band rather than just a group of like-minded geniuses," Stevie had remarked when Shen mentioned it.

It turned out just to be a last-minute Kuznetsov Pack get-together that evening because some wild dog friends from Germany had shown up and they all wanted to celebrate as only wild dogs could: by badly singing along to great music performed by musical geniuses.

"We got a request," Stevie said. "From the lovely ladies at the bar there." Shen glanced over. The women didn't look or smell like shifters, but he had no idea who they were. It was unusual for full-humans no one knew to attend a wild dog party, but there was something about the group that no one wanted to challenge either. So, they just left them alone and that seemed to work for everyone. Besides, wild dogs didn't really have the kind of parties that involved the unleashing of claws or fangs.

"So get ready, Zeppelin fans," Stevie continued, "it's time for a little 'Immigrant Song!'" she yelled out. The music started and everyone cheered, many others head-banged, and Stevie sang in her best Robert Plant voice while she was Jimmy Paige on her guitar.

It was great.

An hour later, The Band took a break and Stevie came over to Shen, jumping onto his back as she liked to do. She was so petite, though, he barely felt her.

Arms around his neck, legs around his waist, Stevie kissed his cheek.

"You were amazing," he told her, placing her beer in her hand.

"Thank you."

"Why didn't your sisters come?"

"Max had plans and Charlie was, to quote her, 'not in the mood to be around labradoodles.'"

"Ouch."

Stevie laughed. "Yeah. I know. That's my bitchy sis."

"Not bitchy. Direct. I enjoy that in a woman that I don't want to kill me. There's no confusion about what crosses her boundaries."

Stevie loved that Shen didn't mind walking around a bar with her attached to his back. Not many men were comfortable with that sort of thing, but he seemed to enjoy it.

As they made the rounds, Stevie spotted Kyle. She hadn't seen him in days. Since she'd dealt with James Wells. A problem that had quietly gone away. Thankfully. But she had to admit, she wasn't surprised when Conridge called her and asked if she wanted to go back to the lab. To see what he had there. Shen had to go with her because Max had freaked out so badly about how Conridge was "going to wipe you from the world!"

Not really. Instead, they barely spoke to each other, too busy going through Wells's notebooks and computer files.

Although the damage to the walls and windows still remained, the bodies and blood had been removed. Something Stevie greatly appreciated. It allowed her to focus on the work while Shen sat in an office chair, eating bamboo, and turning in circles. The man really didn't need much to be entertained.

She patted Shen's shoulder and pointed at the ground. He let her down and she went to Kyle, sitting across from him at his small table.

"How's it going?" she asked him.

Oriana, who'd been walking over to the table with a big smile and a vodka tonic in her hand, stopped when she heard Stevie's question. When Kyle's only response was to sigh—deeply—her eyes crossed and she found another table to sit at.

Stevie knew she could talk to her friend later. Or even to-morrow. They'd been working on the ballet together and were spending several hours a day on it. But right now, Stevie had to check on her neediest friend.

"Are you really just going to sit here and feel sorry for your-self," Stevie asked, "or are you going to get back to work?"

Kyle rested his cheek against the table. "What's the point? So I can just prolong my failure?"

"Or you could create something new."

He sighed again and Stevie ran out of patience just like that. She expected this from other artists. Regular, everyday artists. But not Kyle. Never Kyle.

So she did what she had to in order to help her pathetic, whiny, needy friend.

"It's okay," she said. "I understand. Besides, with Denny . . ."

She let the nickname of Kyle's younger brother Dennis hang out there.

And, as she expected, he took the bait.

Kyle raised his head, stared at Stevie. "What about Denny?"

"Nothing. Forget it. Forget I said anything."

"Said anything about what?"

"Well . . . I heard that there's been some interest from your old school in Italy."

"What?"

"You know. The one you were thrown out of a few years—"

"I know which one you're talking about. What interest?"

"In Denny's hyperrealistic paintings. That street view of Paris that he did from memory . . . *everyone* is talking about it. It's garnered a lot of interest."

"Interest?"

"Yes. Interest." She reached across the table, placed her hand on his forearm. "So I don't want you to worry about anything. The Jean-Louis Parker name *will* be known for art. Because of Dennis."

Kyle sat up straight. "I have to go."

And he did, leaving Stevie there until Oriana walked over.

"That was brilliant," she said, taking Kyle's seat.

"You heard us?"

She pointed at her head. "Jackal ears. And you were . . ." She began to laugh. "I'm surprised his fucking head didn't explode."

"I'm not about to let your brother fuck up his career because of Kiki Li. Despite the fact that I *really* like her."

"Kyle will be fine," Oriana said with a dismissive wave. "But were you serious about Denny?"

"Oh, yeah. I heard from a friend of a friend of a maestro who had been at an auction that included one of Denny's pieces, and he bought it for eight hundred and fifty thousand dollars."

Oriana's mouth dropped open. "Holy shit . . . he's *that* good?"

"Yeah. He's that good."

"But he never speaks. For years we all thought he had been born mute. Then one day he just started talking in very short, very quiet sentences. He wanted a grilled cheese sandwich."

"Because a grilled cheese sandwich is the best sandwich. Even then he was showing his genius."

"Come to bed, woman!" Miki Kendrick heard Irene Conridge's wolf husband yell from their bedroom.

"He's persistent," Miki chuckled, continuing to print pages from the Wells brothers' files she'd finally hacked into. The more pages she discovered, the more fascinated Irene became. Miki had no idea what her friend was discovering and she really didn't want to know. That kind of science was not her thing. She liked computers. She liked how they worked. Plus she didn't have to worry about putting a few elements together and creating a virus that would turn everyone into zombies. Win-win.

Of course, Miki hadn't planned on being in New York this long. Her mate and his Pack lived on the West Coast, but Irene had called and the job sounded so interesting, she'd come. Besides, according to Miki's daughter, "You need to go. You're getting on my nerves."

Brat.

Miki found some new files buried beneath more encryption than she'd thought possible, but when she looked up to tell Irene, she saw the woman's cold gaze fixed on a spot behind her.

Miki, who'd grown up in a rough part of eastern Texas, surrounded by wolves and bikers who could shift into wolves, had the blade she'd purchased when she'd arrived in New York out of its holster and pressed against the neck of the Asian woman standing behind her.

And the Asian woman had her blade pressed against Miki's neck.

She smiled. "Nice, for a full-human."

"Can I help you with something?" Miki asked, figuring if the woman had wanted her dead, she'd have slashed her throat by now.

"As a matter of fact, you can."

"What are you doing here?" Irene asked. Then she snapped, "Both of you put your weapons away before I get terse."

Gazing into each other's eyes, Miki and the woman lowered their blades.

"Miki Kendrick, this is Max MacKilligan."

"One of the sisters. I've heard about you guys."

"And you're the hacker."

Miki slid her knife back into the holster. "I prefer computer expert. For legal reasons, of course."

"I need your help."

"With what?"

"I need you to track a few things down."

"Like?" Irene asked. "Because she's working for me right now."

"Hey, bitches," Miki said, her gaze bouncing between both women, "I don't belong to either of ya. Now what do ya want?" she asked Max.

"My twin aunts sent my cunt of a cousin to come to my house and kill me while my sisters were downstairs with their boyfriends."

"Wow."

"Yeah. I'm on the trail of my cousin, and I'll find her. But my aunts also stole money from my family by using my father. Now, he is an idiot. I don't think he can even send email. But he used a hacker and I want to know who it was so we can track down the stolen money. Or, at the very least, just get the fucking money back. And I'm guessing you're the one who can find it."

"I can. But what do I get out of it?"

"A feeling of accomplishment?"

"Bitch, please. I get nearly a thousand bucks an hour *minimum* to do that sort of shit. You'll have to come at me with something better than that."

Max shrugged. "A few days ago I went into an underground lab and wiped out a whole lot of fellow shifters because they kidnapped my baby sister. Now, my older sister was with me and she did the same thing. For *her*, it was something she had to do to protect the family. She didn't enjoy it, but she did it. She's like a . . . Marine. Doing what she needs to do to protect the homeland. I, however, enjoyed every second of what I did. Because they crossed us and went after my baby sister, who is ridiculously nice and didn't deserve any of that. So, if nothing else, for those on the outside looking in, I am *wonderfully* entertaining."

Miki looked over at Irene and she nodded her head. "It's true," Irene admitted. "That did happen."

"Well, then," Miki said, throwing up her hands. "I'm in."

★ ★ ★

The MacKilligans got on their private plane and Will settled into his seat. His time in the States hadn't been as bad as he'd thought it would be. And the boys were still talking about how good a time they'd all had taking the piss out of an entire Pride. So everyone was happy.

Although he didn't really understand why Mairi and the twins had done all this. Kill Uncle Pete, he meant. They'd wanted to lure him and his boys to the States, but for what? The only one who'd gotten hit was Max, nearly strangled to death in her own house.

But Mairi could have done that at any time, and the same message would have gotten to the rest of the family. So then . . . what was the point?

The whole thing bothered Will but not enough to distract him from the bigger issue. His fucking money! Where the fuck was his money?

Dougie sat in the seat across from Will. "You all right, Da?"

"Pissed. Very pissed."

Frowning, Dougie leaned down. "What's this?" he asked, pulling a briefcase out from under his seat. "Did you put this here?"

"No. What is it?"

Dougie opened it up and his breath caught, his gaze lifting to Will's.

"Fu—"

She was telling the pilot of a private plane to get in line for takeoff when the entire building shook.

Screaming, she dropped to the floor, arms over her head. Some of her coworkers hit the floor around her. Some dove under desks. Glass from the windows exploded around them and she just tried to hold on. Tried not to panic.

Finally, in what felt like hours but was really only seconds, everything calmed down. The building no longer shook. The sound of glass falling all around them stopped.

Carefully, she stood and looked out the now glass-free window at the airstrip. The private plane owned by the Scottish men was now nothing more than bent and twisted metal that was still burning. Around what was left of the plane were bodies. And, from what she knew, all of them were family. An entire family wiped out in one second.

"Call nine-one—" She froze, leaned closer to what was left of her windows.

"What is it?" one of her coworkers asked.

But she didn't know how to answer. She didn't know what she was seeing.

Shen found Stevie sitting on the stage, her legs dangling over the edge. The Band had done one more hour-long set. This time of Jimi Hendrix and Beatles favorites. The whole thing was a success and he sensed that he'd be spending way more time around wild dogs.

With the other bandmates packing up behind her and the bar starting to clear out for the night, the regular lights came on and Shen noticed that Stevie was frowning.

He sat down next to her. "I saw Kyle running out of here. Everything okay?"

"Yeah. I just told him his baby brother was his competition and the kid was going to outdo him if he didn't get off his ass and stop feeling sorry for himself. But I said it much nicer."

"Then what's wrong? You look upset."

"No. This isn't my upset face. This is my thinking face, which I've been told is a little scary."

"What are you thinking about?"

"I got a call from Van Holtz earlier today. They are confiscating—his word—the underground lab James Wells was using. They're going to take it over and they want me to run it."

"To do what?"

"Not sure yet. I know they want me and Conridge to keep looking into what Wells was up to. In case he was doing anything besides fucking with the DNA of hybrids. But after that . . . I don't know. And I'm not sure they know."

"Then you might be able to make of it what you will."

"Yeah. Or it's their way of keeping a close tab on me."

"It's probably partly that too."

"Yeah. But if I take the job, my old boss won't be happy. He just emailed me again this morning."

"Do you want to go back to CERN?"

"I don't really know." She looked at him. "Do you want to live in Switzerland?"

Shocked by the question, Shen said, "I, uh, don't really know."

"Do you like Switzerland?"

"Um . . . I like Toblerone."

"Toblerone?"

"The Swiss candy."

"Yes. I know what Toblerone is."

"Other than that, though . . ." He cleared his throat. "So, are you expecting me to move with you?"

"Why wouldn't you?" She was silent for a minute, then added, "Speaking of which . . . You haven't said 'I love you' again, since that first time."

"It's funny you mention that . . . I don't remember saying 'I love you' to you at all."

"Well, you said it in your sleep."

"Ohhhhh. Oh, I see." He nodded, relieved. "So you're not completely insane."

"Not about that." She frowned again. "Wait . . . you do love me, right?"

"Sadly . . . yes."

"Why sadly?"

"Because it's against my better judgment, and it's not like you gave me an option."

She grinned. "I really didn't. But I'm a girl who knows what she wants."

"Clearly." He took her hand in his. "But I really do love you, Stevie."

She rested her head on his shoulder. "I love you too."

"Isn't it nice when *everyone* is awake when those words are spoken?"

"Eh."

Shen chuckled, kissed her forehead.

When they received enough glares from the staff cleaning up, Shen jumped down from the stage and reached up, grabbing Stevie around the waist and carefully placing her on the floor. He again took her hand in his and together they slowly walked out of the building.

As they made their way down to the street one block over so they could catch a cab, Shen asked, "You know what's really great about all this?"

"What?"

"That with you and this family, I will never be bored."

"That's very true. Of course, that's really a blessing and a curse."

Shen grinned. "Yeah. Just like you."

EPILOGUE

Charlie was stretched out on the couch with Berg. He was behind her, his big legs on either side of her hips.

They'd been relaxing the last few hours, watching old episodes of *The Twilight Zone*. One of her favorite shows because of how advanced it was on all sorts of political issues, considering the time it had been created.

But she was ready to go to bed. Berg had already dropped off a few times before jerking awake again a few seconds later. He was trying to stay awake for her because she couldn't sleep. She just didn't know why.

Then she heard something and sat up.

"What?" Berg said, snapping awake again. "What's wrong?"

"I think we have rats."

"Rats? In this neighborhood? Between your sister and that cat, I doubt it."

But Charlie heard noises in the . . . she turned her head trying to locate . . .

Kitchen!

Charlie scrambled off the couch and charged through the house, coming to an abrupt halt right outside her favorite room.

"What the fuck?" she demanded of the badgers in her kitchen.

"Oi, niece," Will said in greeting, his mouth filled with what appeared to be a sandwich he'd put together himself. "Where ya hidin' the honey? This needs honey."

It was all of them. All the Scots who'd come to the states for

Great-Uncle Pete's funeral. And they were in her kitchen. Eating her food. Making themselves at home.

"What's going on?"

"They blew up our plane," Dougie explained, going through her cabinets, probably trying to find honey.

She looked over her kin, finally noticed all the burn damage to their faces and hands and expensive clothes.

"Were you standing next to it when it blew?"

"On it," Will said.

She glanced at Berg, who was standing behind her, his confused frown deep. And Charlie was guessing she had the same expression.

"You were on the plane? *On* it?"

"Yeah," Will shrugged. "Well, *in* the plane. And the bomb was right next to me and Dougie when it blew."

"But how are you all alive? In my kitchen. Eating my food."

"Luck?" Will suggested.

"Oh, my God." Charlie faced Berg. "There is *literally* no way to kill a MacKilligan male, which means my father is going to live forever."

"Awww now, sweet Charlie," her uncle said, attempting to soothe. "You've gotta have faith, lass. I'm sure that someone will kill the bastard. And then we can all have a party. Wouldn't that be nice?"

"Not really." Charlie gave a small, defeated shrug. "But I'll take it."